OF

THROKAR

THE SUNDERED TREE: BOOK ONE

MARNIY JONES

FIRE*PAPER*STONE

FirePaperStone.com

Cover: Marniy Jones
Stock photo: "Alanna" by Jessica Truscott (http://faestock.deviantart.com)
Author photo: Francis Zera by Zera Photography

Title font: Carta Marina by Insigne
Interior font: Garamond

Published in Portland, OR by FIRE*PAPER*STONE Books.
www.firepaperstone.com

Printed in USA

Names: Jones, Marniy.
Title: The seal of Throkar / Marniy Jones.
Description: Portland, OR : FirePaperStone, 2016. | Series: The sundered tree, bk. 1.
Identifiers: LCCN 2016935370 | ISBN 978-0-9973815-0-4 (pbk.) | ISBN 978-0-9973815-1-1 (Kindle) | ISBN 978-0-9973815-1-1 (EPUB) | ISBN 978-0-9973815-1-1 (PDF)
Subjects: LCSH: Magic--Fiction. | Gods--Fiction. | Avatars (Religion)--Fiction. | Imaginary places--Fiction. | Fantasy fiction, American. | BISAC: FICTION / Fantasy / General. | FICTION / Fantasy / Epic. | GSAFD: Fantasy fiction. | Epic fiction.
Classification: LCC PS3610.O6272 S43 2016 (print) | LCC PS3610.O6272 (ebook) | DDC 813/.6--dc23.

For all the strong female characters in my life,
especially my mother.

THE SEAL
OF
THROKAR

CHAPTER ONE

FOUR CORPSES DANGLED FROM the branches of a dead oak. Blood still dripped from their fingertips, hair, and feet. Steam still rose from the bodies of their protectors, tumbled together beneath them like storm-driven wheat. Quin swallowed hard and glanced at Sarael.

The Avatar of Healing hunched miserably at the edge of the clearing, mud clutching at the hem of her plain gown, face ashen. She usually appeared to be a few years older than Quin, no more than thirty, but now her wide, horror-filled eyes reminded Quin of a young girl who had lost everything.

Quin unpinned the wool cloak from her brigandine and swung it around the other woman's shoulders. "We can't stay—"

"Cut them down. Please. Just ... get them down."

"We'll come back. After we find the others, and those cultists move on." Quin scanned the forest. Branches drooped with water, and the patter of heavy drops landing on the thick pad of fallen leaves could easily mask the footsteps of an enemy. She tightened the grip on her sword hilt and took Sarael's hand, pulling her toward the game trail that provided the only access in or out. Any other direction would require hacking at brambles with a blade.

A bird erupted from the underbrush, bellowing a challenge to the sky and shaking a torrent of water loose. Something startled the creature into flight. Quin stepped in front of Sarael, sword drawn. She heard nothing but blood and rain and the pounding of her heartbeat in her ears. "Let's go."

Down the path, another cascade of water accompanied a curse. "It was right around here we left 'em." The voice was faint.

Quin hitched her breath. Tree cultists. If she and Sarael ran, the sound of their passage would alert everyone to their presence. No choice but to hide. The oak had split and soured years before and sported no leafy canopy that might conceal them. The wide trunk might hide them, but only if their pursuers were blind or fools. How many were there? Could Quin fight?

Sarael's eyes widened. "Go! I'll ... I'll try to stop them."

"*I'm* supposed to protect *you*." Quin's gaze returned to the pile of bodies, and she paused.

Sarael paled further. "May blessed Yhellania forgive us."

Quin huffed. "She likes you. You'll be fine." She pulled the reluctant woman over to the tree and pushed her down between the corpses of the soldiers and the blackened trunk. "You have to admit, they'd never think to find you there." She covered Sarael's dress and pale hair with the cloak and shifted the body of a scarlet-clad man over her hips and legs. Quin tried to smile, but bile rose in the back of her throat. She resisted the urge to scrub her hands clean. Liquid dripped on them from above. Hot and cold.

A lighter voice laughed. "Dalanar is quick to send us out in this weather. I notice he ain't so quick to join in."

Quin jerked upright and turned toward the path. Dalanar was here? Had he been at the village that betrayed the slaughtered Servant-priests to the cultists? Had it been *him* who betrayed them?

"Keep your damned tongue civil," the first voice growled,

"if you don't want it burnt to ash. Sorcerers don't have a sense of humor."

"I warn't joking." The lighter voice sounded baffled. "He's on our side, anyway."

The growling man grunted. "Maybe."

"Quinthian," Sarael's tone held ice. "I order you to hide."

"But...." Dalanar was tucked up warm and cozy at some inn not three miles from her. This was probably the closest Quin had ever been to the rotting sorcerer, and she had no way to get to him.

"Now."

Quin clenched her teeth and wiggled into the morbid pile, her skin shuddering away from contact. These were her friends, companions, and peers. That they passed into the realm of death shouldn't change anything. She gulped down nausea. The proscription against touching the dead was too strong. She couldn't do this. A scream built inside her chest.

"Hush, child." Sarael's fingers brushed Quin's arm. "Hush."

Warmth and comfort flooded through Quin like sinking into a hot bath on a frosty day, making her sleepy. She shouldn't be tired. They might have to fight for their lives at any moment. She tried to pull away but failed.

"This will only work if they don't burn the bodies," Quin whispered.

"Tree cultists never burn Yhellani bodies."

FIVE PEOPLE DRESSED IN oilskin cloaks and hoods sauntered into the clearing. Rain had blurred the ash-drawn tree symbols cultists used to identify themselves; only smudges remained on their foreheads. Too many for Quin to take on alone. She might beat two. Possibly, hold off three—long enough for Sarael to escape. Not five.

Where were the other members of Sarael's party? The guardsworn and the Servant-priests? Had they survived the ambush that forced Quin and Sarael into the forest? Misfortune or divine will led them to the site of this massacre. There had been no sign of their companions. Quin's stomach clenched. They couldn't be dead. Barrand would never allow that to happen. She smiled grimly at the thought of his reaction to her method of hiding Sarael. Quin would gladly endure his lecture on the respect due an avatar as long as he was safe. As long as they all came through this alive.

"Doesn't look like any of them've been here." The light-voiced man threw back his hood to reveal an unlined face and thinning hair.

A cultist with a jutting black beard kicked one of the bodies to Quin's right. "They always come for their dead meat." The gruff-voiced man. He called over his shoulder to the others, "We wait." He pointed at the young man. "Go to the end of the trail and hide. Whistle if you see anyone coming."

"Aww, Cass—"

"Quit whining. It's your turn."

The young man shuffled down the trace muttering to himself.

Four. Could Quin kill them before the boy returned? She'd have the advantage of surprise.

Two of the hooded figures began swinging the suspended bodies back and forth, setting them spinning like obscene children's toys.

"Fine bunch of crab apples." A female cultist brayed with laughter.

Hanged Servants had been nicknamed *crab apples* for the color they turned when their pain had ended and they were allowed to begin dying. It had been an abundant year for the terrible harvest. Quin's cheeks burned and fury grayed out the edges of her vision. The two cultists stood so close to where she hid, the hems of their cloaks brushed her boots. They would die. She would send them to meet their foul god in person.

One of them poked the smallest of the Servants in the thigh with a sword. In life, the woman had been a quietly competent healer, with a knack for dice that left a number of guardsworn penniless. Quin blinked away tears.

Sarael made a dangerous sound low in her throat. Her grip on Quin's arm hardened. *Oh, no. Not now.* Quin grabbed for the avatar, but the woman shifted out of reach. Sarael wasn't in control any longer. The goddess was coming.

The sword tip ripped the Servant's robe open. "We shoulda left them naked. Yhellania likes that sort of thing."

Sarael erupted from her hiding spot with an animalistic roar, eyes blazing with white fire.

Quin had only seconds to act. She heaved aside the sheltering bodies and leapt to her feet, shoving three feet of steel between the ribs of the cultist closest to her. Without pausing, she swung around and decapitated the second.

The goddess glowered out through Sarael's eyes, incandescent with wrath. Her body straightened, the unassuming woman taking on the bearing of an empress. Yhellania's divine presence thrust everyone down, grinding them into the wet earth with heads bowed and air forced from their lungs. "*Who has done this to my children?*" The avatar's hair swirled around her, blown by eddies of power.

Quin turned her head to one side to avoid a puddle, but mud oozed into her ear. She sucked in a breath and hoped the goddess relaxed her hold before she passed out. "These ... cultists, Great Lady."

The cultists whimpered somewhere nearby.

The air crackled and hissed. "*Where is Barrand? Why are you not in Csiz Luan?*"

The pressure eased enough for Quin to breathe. "We were separated by an ambush. Dalanar knew we were coming, and—"

The goddess scanned the dead. The glow from her eyes cast deep shadows into the woodland beyond. "*This does not look like Dalanar's work.*"

"It's Dalanar who locates your Servants. Dalanar who passes the information on to the cultists. If we stop him, we can slow or prevent these massacres." Quin managed to sound calm. This was her last hope of getting permission to kill the sorcerer; Sarael and Barrand had already forbidden it. If she convinced Yhellania, who could object?

Yhellania peered down at Quin, the goddess's regard pressing like a mountain against her spine.

"*Slay them, Quinthian. We shall discuss your hatred of Dalanar another time.*"

"He's so close! We—"

"*Now.*"

The pressure lifted. Quin leapt up, the sudden weightlessness giving her energy. She drew the dagger from the sheath at her lower back and raised her sword. Would the one on the right throw her ax before the bearded man charged?

The cultists remained motionless.

Quin paused. They were to fight as the goddess demanded. Were they surrendering?

It took several moments to realize that they remained trapped by Yhellania's presence.

"But they can't move."

"*Are you defying my command?*"

"No, I...." The cultists deserved to die, probably more gruesome and painful deaths than Quin could deliver, but to simply kill them when they had no chance to defend themselves? It wasn't right.

Quin shook her head. She was being a hypocrite. The cultists she had slain moments before had no chance to defend themselves, either. That hadn't been a fair fight. This was ... different.

How could the goddess of healing ask this of her? How could she disobey?

Reluctantly, Quin moved toward the bearded cultist. Cass? The man's eyes were wide with terror. He had shown no mercy to the Servants still swinging from their makeshift gallows. She gripped the hilt tighter, attempting to muster her resolve. Quin had never executed an incapacitated enemy. A prisoner. She was a soldier, not a headsman. The cultist stared at her with helpless resignation.

"*You disappoint me, Quinthian. Kill them. Now.*" The words held divine compulsion.

Quin's resistance evaporated.

With two strokes of her blades, the cultists lay dead, their blood dripping into the soil to mix with that of their innocent victims. Quin retched when Yhellania's command faded. She fell to her hands and knees, weapons discarded by her side.

"*These sights cause Sarael great pain. See to her.*" The goddess gestured at the corpses of the Servants and the soldiers beside them. In a flare of light, they disappeared, leaving only sparks rising to the leaden sky.

The crushing presence of Yhellania vanished, and the glow faded. Sarael alone occupied the space vacated by the goddess. Quin rose with a curse. She wiped her face on the last dry spot on her shirt and attempted to tuck a tendril of dark hair back into a braid.

Her brigandine was covered with mud. She swiped at it, but

only succeeded in smearing the muck around. It would take weeks to scrape the filth from the leather plates. Her conscience might never come clean.

CHAPTER TWO

A TRILLING WHISTLE FROM SOMEWHERE at the end of the trail cut off with a sharp cry, then silence. Seconds later, Barrand and the other guardsworn burst into the clearing, weapons drawn and teeth bared for violence. They stared around wildly for a moment before Barrand straightened and sheathed his sword, panting with reaction.

He strode over to Sarael. "Are you all right? Are you injured?" Graying red hair lay plastered against the guardsworn commander's scalp, and water funneled into the creases of his sunburnt face. Barrand mopped at his eyes with the sleeve of his coarse brown tunic and returned to inspecting the avatar. The blood on her clothing elicited a deep frown and a disapproving glance at Quin.

Sarael nodded gravely, but a small dimple appeared on her cheek.

Quin's shoulders relaxed, and she took her first full breath since she and Sarael had been separated from the others. The avatar no longer depended on her for protection.

The top of Sarael's head only reached Barrand's shoulder, and he ducked down to listen as she spoke to him in a low voice. Although the commander hovered solicitously, he never stopped watching for danger.

A cluster of Servants peaked into the grove, leading their horses and the pack mule loaded with herbs and medicine. When they saw the area was free of conflict, smiles of relief broke out.

Several of them rushed to till the soil where the goddess had appeared, reverently sprinkling the damp earth with handfuls of seeds. Quin doubted anything would grow in the blood-cursed ground under the tree. Perhaps it would be a miracle.

At last, Barrand turned to Quin. "What happened?"

"Sarael and I escaped down a game trail when the cultists attacked. We tried to circle away from the fight, until we stumbled on this." The signs of the horror that had taken place were obvious to anyone who had seen them before: singed ropes, deep furrows in the dirt, blood droplets on sheltered leaves.

"A group of them returned, and we hid. Yhellania decided not to wait for you to arrive." Quin paused. She didn't want to tell him about killing those prisoners. It felt raw and dirty. Something shameful, even if it had been a command. "How did you find us?"

Barrand snorted. "I can tell when Yhellania manifests from miles away. Sarael told me what you did. I'm disappointed, but I suppose you're predictable."

Quin looked down, unable to meet his eyes. What did that mean?

Sarael frowned at Quin, a flush of pink rising into her cheeks. "How dare you try to go around me with Yhellania? I do not give you permission to pursue Dalanar. You are my handmaiden, and you belong with me." No trace of the goddess remained.

Quin exhaled. They were talking about the rotting sorcerer. She lifted her chin and didn't bother to act repentant. She was a terrible liar. "I am also your personal guard, and I will protect you. If I could find a way to kill him *and* his master, I could sleep at night. We *all* could."

Barrand crossed his arms over his barrel-chest. "The most important thing right now is getting Sarael to Csiz Luan. No one is running off to get killed while I'm in charge."

"They said he's close. In the last village—"

"Then we'll stay as far out of his way as we can. Someone murdered an avatar. I don't know how, but I will not let Sarael be next. We keep together."

"Conthal might be with him."

"By the godless void, then we stay even farther from the both of them." Barrand glared at Quin. "Go away." He pointed. "Find my lieutenant, get everyone mounted and moving. I don't want to remain in this wretched place any longer."

THE ROLLING HILLS OF the region provided ideal farmland. Dark, rich soil covered fields filled with young plants beginning their growth in earnest. Clumps of patchy forest shielded home-steads and villages from the dusty road leading south to the King-dom of Dacten and the main trade routes.

When the sun eventually broke through the oppressive layer of clouds, it burned away the shadows that had fallen over Quin's mood. It didn't undo the effects of the two cold, sleepless nights spent in the deep woods after the ambush, but it helped. The far-ther they got from the massacre, the more she relaxed.

The Servants finally felt safe enough to insist upon stopping to tend one of the countless shrines that dotted the countryside. The chest-high wall of crumbling stone was the oldest Quin had ever seen. It held deep niches dedicated to each of the four gods. Leaves and blown debris mixed with dried herbs and woven sun circlets inside Yhellania's space. One of the priests swept it out, while the others collected flowers and constructed a new wreath from the long grass beside the road. As the goddess of healing and fertility, Yhellania was beloved by farmers.

Quin examined the other shrines. The God of Art's alcove had been painted again and again until the pigment was caked on inches thick. Worshipful visitors added to the collage until it was a bright clash of color and design. A placard inlaid with the Goddess of War's dagger and scales was bolted in the next hollow. A few coppers and tiny bags of spices were piled inside by passing merchants seeking blessings for their endeavors. With a petition for the strength to slay Dalanar, Quin tossed in a tarnished coin. It clinked against the metal and settled beneath the blade. A good omen.

Some gifted carpenter built a wooden door for the God of Knowledge's niche, the tree the cultists venerated painted on the front. The shelter protected a precious collection of books that formed a small library. Only a prosperous community could afford such luxury.

One end of the wall had been chipped away in antiquity. The edge was uneven, and showed signs of tool marks, even after years of weathering. Why would anyone risk defacing a shrine? Rocks grew like weeds in the fields; they couldn't have needed the extra stone for construction.

Hoof beats drew her attention. Barrand cantered back from a nearby farm with a grim expression. Her commander wouldn't meet her eyes, and Quin knew what he was going to say.

Barrand reined his mare in beside the avatar. "They passed by several days ago."

"I told you they would come this way." Quin muttered a prayer for rot to bury itself in Dalanar's genitals. The Servants cast her disapproving glances. "If we headed straight here, we might have caught them."

Barrand shifted in his saddle, and the leather creaked in protest. He sighed and surveyed the land across the border. Jagged peaks watched over the neat orchards and olive groves from the east and west. In the valley between mountain ranges, smoke from small settlements curled above the trees.

Barrand spoke again, his gruff voice unusually gentle, "Waiting is hard, I understand. And what he did was unspeakable, but Sarael comes first." He rubbed the knots where his nose had been broken and re-broken. "Don't waste your life hating him."

Quin opened her mouth to object. He cut her off.

"This is too personal for you." Barrand studied her face. "Let it go."

"She was murdered."

"So were those Servants. So were countless others."

Quin wanted justice for the dead. Retribution. Was that so hard to understand?

"You don't act like any handmaiden I've ever heard of." Barrand snorted. "You're supposed to delight Sarael with your wit and charm. Provide cheer and sagacious advice. Not stomp around, plotting against avatars and their pet sorcerers."

She grimaced. *Unsuitable* would be the kindest way to describe Quin's service. But after Dalanar destroyed a town to kill her mother, she was the only remaining heir. Sarael had been adamant that Quin assume the role. The avatar wasn't always practical.

Barrand cleared his throat. "Think they're heading back to Utur?"

"They'll probably take the Road." The words tasted like ash. *They* traveled freely, while the Servants were forced into hiding.

"You know the area. What's the safest town between here and Csiz Luan?"

Quin sifted through her mental maps. They needed a place

13

sympathetic to Yhellani and large enough to provide anonymity. "Crador, if we're willing to travel after dark. It might be full of drunken mercenaries, but they'll take care of us."

Barrand shrugged and signaled for the group to proceed. "Start now and we'll sleep in real beds tonight."

Quin frowned west toward the disappearing chance of confronting her enemy.

CHAPTER THREE

QUIN LED THEM INTO Crador before midnight, although they lost their way more than once in the darkness. A few dogs ran out to bark at them as they passed the hushed fieldstone cottages on the outskirts of town. Smoke hung in the chilly air and swirled around their shoulders. The stench of refuse strewn in the gutters and alleyways crept out at each intersection to assault their noses. Quin started out of her doze when the horses' hooves clattered on the cobbled streets of the city proper.

"Well, Quin, where do we go?" Haze and dim light blurred Barrand's outline.

She pondered for a moment, trying to place their location. Quin had only visited the town twice, briefly. "There should be an inn ahead."

"You're not sure?" Father Jol's voice pierced the mist like an arrow.

The weasel-faced priest was still annoyed that Quin hadn't taken the vows of service. His lack of authority over her made him peevish. More peevish. She snorted. "No, Jol. I'm not. If you can do better, lead on."

Sarael touched her arm. "Please continue, Quinthian."

The first inn they encountered stood defiantly in the middle of the road, forcing travelers to either side to pass by the impos-ing building. It was not the place Quin expected to find, but she shrugged inwardly. Anything was better than sleeping on the rain-soaked ground again. Jol never needed to know of her mistake.

The only disadvantage to the site was the boisterous taverns that surrounded it. Alcohol and entertainment were the lifeblood of the town. To judge by the numbers of staggering off-duty Ravendi mercenaries crowding the street, Crador thrived.

Jol regarded her with a curled lip. "I see why your memory is hazy."

Quin ignored him. He was probably right, though. She had done her part to enrich the local economy.

Barrand handed his reins to one of the guardsworn. "This is good enough, if they have room."

"I'm not sure any place will. We may need to split up," Quin said.

A Servant groaned. "I just want a bed."

"Where's your commitment to a life of deprivation?" Bar-rand sounded far too cheerful. Indistinct grumbles greeted his comment.

Sarael patted the exhausted priest on the shoulder, and a tiny spark passed between them. The man straightened, shoulders relaxing. He smiled and bowed his head to the avatar.

THE INN COULD HAVE been any in a hundred towns Quin had visited. The door from the street opened into a central chamber that stretched the full height of the two-story building. Hot breez-es laden with tempting spices washed over her from the kitchen on the right, fighting against the pungent scent of wine and stale beer from the bar on the left. Two simple staircases ran up the rear wall to sleeping chambers; between them hung the quartered shield representing the gods. Although a few tables and chairs lined the walls, most of the floor space was dominated by a sunken seating area that ringed a bonfire.

The smell of juniper smoke and saffron brought back memories of Quin's service with the corps. She smiled fondly at a group of cadets who eyed her fighting braids, and nodded politely as they stumbled past and out into the street in search of excitement. Those had been good times.

More rosy-cheeked soldiers lounged on the pillows and thick carpets that covered the broad ledge running along the inside of the pit. Several spice traders idled among them, their rich robes clashing with the scarlet uniforms.

The innkeeper pushed his way over, but stopped when he caught sight of the Servants. The white edges of their rough-woven smocks glowed in the firelight. He looked anxiously around the room, and paled, his coppery skin turning sallow. "I don't want any trouble. Get them out."

"Are tree cultists in town?" Quin scanned the crowd, fingering her sword hilt. Who was he searching for?

The innkeeper shook his head and gestured to the street.

Quin and Barrand exchanged a glance, and he ushered the group out.

"Have there been attacks on Yhellani?" Quin stared pointedly at the shield, then back at the man. It was reprehensible to appeal to the gods for protection, and turn away the priests of Yhellania.

He pursed his lips. "No Servants. Too risky." The man's tension eased slightly when the door closed behind Barrand. "You'd best go with them."

"Why?" Overt prejudice against Yhellani was rare in larger towns, and surprising to find close to the fortress of Csiz Luan. The ties between the Ravendi and the Servants were strong. Maybe he thought they'd be too poor to cover the charges? "We have money."

The man's gaze flickered toward the staircases before he leaned closer. "I can recommend another place. But no room for Yhellani." He jerked his head towards a beefy bouncer leaning against the bar.

Quin raised her hands in defeat. It was too late at night to start a fight. "Fine. I'll go." She hoped he remembered this the next time he needed healing. The Yhellani would. "Where is this other place?"

QUIN, I DON'T LIKE this," Barrand said when they reconvened in a sheltered corner of the street. "That was more than simple bigotry. The man was scared—*of* the Servants or *for* them."

"Maybe those cultists came through here first. Stirred up trouble."

"He didn't warn us to leave town. Sending us to another place doesn't sound like he's concerned now."

"He seemed confident we'd find rooms ... I don't know. We can move on."

Barrand surveyed their tired faces and relented. "Wouldn't be any safer thrashing around in the woods with those Throkari sorcerers close by."

THE INNKEEPER'S RECOMMENDATION LAY hidden on a pleasant street away from the tavern district. The inn was clean and quiet, despite being named The Gilded Rat.

As soon as the proprietor showed them to their bunkroom, Sarael collapsed in the rickety chair. The Servants and soldiers threw their packs down and sprawled on the cots with relieved sighs. A few of them fell asleep without bothering to spread out their bedrolls.

Quin sat on a bed near the door. Something about the exchange with the first innkeeper still bothered her. He had been scared. Nervous. He kept looking at that staircase. Who was up there that he didn't want them to meet? Not tree cultists. Throkari priests?

"I'm going out," Quin said. "I'll try to find out what's been happening. There must be rumors."

Barrand rumbled his approval. "Glad you volunteered before I had to order you out into the cold. I'd order you to do it just the same, but I'd feel guilty." He sobered. "You know the place better than us. Just, be careful."

Quin nodded and pulled her cloak closed again. The bed looked inviting, if thinly padded. She tucked her pack under the frame, and unrolled the bundle of blankets she used on the road. Hopefully, there wouldn't be too many bedbugs.

Sarael motioned Quin closer. As she did every night, the avatar pressed her fingertips against Quin's temples, and shut her eyes. A sensation of affection and security eased into Quin like a sip of mulled wine. The barrier the avatar had set in her mind was strengthened and refreshed. A necessary precaution when being persecuted by sorcerers capable of performing the geis. It was Quin's favorite time of day. To be reassured of the goddess' protection, and enjoy Sarael's closeness, however fleeting.

Jol sniffed. "Try not to get so inebriated you forget your purpose."

Quin shrugged at the annoying weasel. "No promises."

THE TAVERN WAS NEARLY empty when Quin returned. A sleepy scullion swept around the feet of the last few patrons lingering over a dice game at a low table.

Quin stood near the serving counter until the proprietor emerged from the kitchens. If there was one thing she had learned from Barrand, it was that tact was almost always a waste of time. "What are you hiding?"

"What are you doing back here?" The innkeeper took her elbow and pulled her towards the door. "Hurry," he whispered.

A creak on the floor above caught her attention. A tall man of about forty, wrapped in a thick coat, paused at the landing. His face was lean, almost gaunt, emphasizing sharp cheekbones and deep-set eyes. His alabaster skin was touched with sun, and ink-dark hair swept back from his forehead. A spark of desire fluttered low in her belly. It had been a long time since the goddess stirred inside her. Quin smiled. Maybe he would join in her devotions and help wash away the stain of death that clung to her.

The man, who had been surveying the room, turned to them. He inclined his head like a lord deigning to notice unimportant servants. Quin bristled at the arrogance of the gesture. Yhellania wanted her to pair with this ass? Was he intended as a punishment or a reward? The man stared at her for a moment before starting down the stairs.

"My lord," the innkeeper wheezed. "How may I serve?"

Recognition cut through Quin's sleep-deprived haze, and her throat squeezed shut. She understood the proprietor's fear. Although she'd never seen him in person, he had been described a hundred different ways. Drawings that did little to capture the intensity of his presence had been posted at the Chapterhouse. Dalanar.

The innkeeper squeaked and slid away, but Quin stood transfixed, her insides icy. This was the murderer she wanted to destroy since she was barely older than a child. Everything slowed; even sounds became muted. Wood creaked as the sorcerer descended. The man beside her moaned softly. The rhythmic rasp of a water pump came from the kitchen.

By the time Dalanar reached the bottom of the stairs, Quin couldn't draw air. He moved like a predator. Unhurried. Implacable. Terrifying. Heat radiated from him, through his clothes. He burned with casting Fever. Magic turned his body into a kiln capable of scorching any who touched him. He stopped before her, and she looked into his eyes. They held no emotion, no curiosity. Reflecting her image like shattered obsidian, revealing nothing.

I am about to die. He will geis me and force Sarael's location from my mind. As he did to my mother.

The sorcerer shook his head as if clearing it and walked to the door. The smell of fog and chill night air seeped in as it closed behind him.

This was her chance to kill Dalanar. After years of searching, Quin needed only to follow him into the darkness and cut him down. But ... if she lost, it would put Sarael at risk. The avatar had to be warned. Quin's sense of duty warred with her desire for revenge. So close.

If she killed him, Sarael would no longer be in so much danger. No more children would be orphaned. No more nightmares of her mother burnt and broken at Dalanar's hands.

Quin clasped her sword hilt and walked towards the entrance.

"Don't do it," the innkeeper whispered.

She jerked her head at him and opened the door.

CHAPTER FOUR

THE STREET WAS EMPTY. Good. No witnesses. No one to get hurt or involved. Quin wanted to do this on her own. She drew her sword; the comforting solidity of the hilt focused her mind. Her shaking hands stilled. *I'm coming for you, abomination.*

The scrape of a boot heel echoed in an alleyway to her right, towards the back of the inn. Quin followed the sound, alert for ambushes. Dalanar had tortured Yhellani. Murdered Servants. Leveled a city. There were conflicting rumors about his other abilities. Did he know she pursued him? Could he sense her with his ungodly powers? Could he feel her hatred?

When the alley met a cross street, she crouched and peeked around the corner. No light from the main thoroughfare penetrated this far. One direction was completely black. A dead end. She turned left, stumbling on unseen refuse. Her eyes were acclimating, but couldn't yet pierce the darkness.

The side street rambled through the city, turning abruptly to enter a poorer district. At each intersection, a flicker of motion, a shadow cast by a lamp led her on. The air reeked with his malevolent presence. Of course, he had likely already eluded her. She was no tracker, but Quin wasn't ready to give up.

Sagging buildings, four and five levels high, lined the narrow street. The mortar between the bricks and stone had crumbled, and litter gathered around their cracked foundations. Two taller tenements huddled against the burnt out husk of a third. Black soot smeared their sides, but they had been spared real damage. Quin wrinkled her nose at the acrid odor.

A blinding light flared from the gap between buildings. Quin threw up a hand to shield her eyes. Something large and hot wrapped around her throat and hauled her into the alley. The action was swift; even her battle-trained reflexes had no time to respond. Quin's attacker slipped an arm across her hips and pressed her head down to his chest before she reacted. *A feint,* she cursed. *The rotting sorcerer feinted me.*

"I didn't catch your name," Dalanar murmured in her ear.

Quin elbowed him in the side and twisted away. The sorcerer wheezed, but kept his grip. She jabbed the sword over her shoulder. He grabbed her wrist, and sent a numbing shock up her arm. She growled when the weapon fell from her limp fingers. Quin kicked and threw herself against his hold on her waist. He jolted her again. She slumped forward, unable to control the muscles along her spine.

Dalanar pulled her upright and drew her into the geis position. "What is your name?"

Quin didn't answer. She could still move her left arm. She might be able to reach the knife sheathed at her lower back without him noticing.

The sorcerer's body burned with the heat of a forge, and sweat trickled down her temple.

"You know who I am, what I can do to you, and you resist a simple question?"

"Rot in darkness, abomination." Her palm brushed the dagger. She let her feet slide out, away from him, giving her more space between their bodies.

Dalanar swept his hand up until his fingers pressed against her temple. She clenched her teeth in anticipation.

"So, you *are* Yhellani. Where is Sarael? Tell me, and you will live."

"I'll tell your corpse." Quin drew her weapon and tried to shove it backward up under his ribs. The sound of the blade clearing the sheath gave her away. He twisted aside. The knife caught his coat and tore cloth, but left him unharmed. It clattered to the ground and he kicked it down the alley.

The sorcerer set his thumb along her jaw and began the spell.

Quin's body expanded and contracted in horrifying pain. The searing brand of his presence dug at her consciousness. Quin refused to scream as he searched for a way in. Sarael's block squatted in her mind like an iron gate, protecting her from the sorcerer's fire. Quin forced her hatred of him up to reinforce the barricade. He slithered across her senses as he probed for weaknesses.

The pain in her head stopped and Quin collapsed. Dalanar supported her with one arm. Her skin stung, scalding from his touch.

"Breaking Sarael's barrier will break your mind. Tell me where she is."

It took tremendous effort to speak. "No."

"Why are you in Crador? Did you follow us?"

Quin understood few of his words. Follow Dalanar here? They must have. She wanted to find him. "Came ... to kill ... you."

"I see." He sounded amused.

Dalanar pulled her upright. His hand traced a path up her face until his thumb touched her cheekbone and he started the spell again.

He pounded at the door in her mind. It weakened and began to crumble. Pieces of Sarael's power, her love, and strength slid away into the darkness. Quin used her fury to make her own barrier stronger. The torment stopped.

He shifted her to one shoulder and removed the arm from across her chest to wipe the sweat from his face. His breath and skin steamed, wreathing them in mist. She gulped in cool air. Quin sagged against him, still unable to support herself. Her back twitched from the earlier spell, but her legs were strong.

Dalanar wrapped his arm around her again. Quin kicked him in the shin with the sharp edge of her boot heel and her remaining strength. He released her with a curse. She fell hard. Her cheek slammed into the pavement, and the air was knocked out of her chest. She could only wait until he collected her again.

For a moment, he remained motionless. Gravel crunched as he walked around to stand in her field of vision. With her head wrenched sideways, her view was limited to his shoes. Dalanar knelt beside Quin and rolled her over. Flesh sizzled at his touch. The smell of decay mingled with burnt skin and the copper tang of her blood.

"Where is Sarael?" He could have been inquiring about the weather. "What are the Yhellani plotting?"

She didn't reply.

Dalanar lifted her into position again and commenced the next phase. She no longer possessed words; she reacted with primitive emotion. Her hate for him solidified into an opaque black shield. She used her hands to nail it to the walls of her mind. There was no way in or out. Her barrier held.

Dalanar's hand pinned her against a wall at the shoulder. "Who are you?"

The deep shadows gave him the appearance of a nightmare. He stretched out a finger to touch her chin. Quin spat, and watched in fascination as the liquid seared and cracked his skin. He jerked back.

The sound of people running and shouting as they searched the area made him glance at the alley entrance. The sorcerer glared at her for a moment before he rose and walked away. She was gratified he limped.

TIME STRETCHED ON. VOICES rang out around Quin, grating against her raw nerves. Dalanar would return. He would geis her again and never stop, until even her hatred crumbled into nothingness. Her body throbbed. Blisters tore and wept as she rolled over into a slimy puddle.

At last, a figure appeared at the entrance to the alley. A woman gasped and called to others. Silence. Quin didn't know whether she passed out or her memory failed, but in a rush of sensation, people and light surrounded her.

Barrand dropped to his knees. "Quin? Say something." His voice cracked.

The commander spread out his long cloak and gently rolled her onto it. Quin's body erupted in pain. A weak whimper escaped her. She sounded witless.

"Blessed Lady, he broke her mind!"

The avatar's clean, mossy scent washed away the stench, and Quin relaxed. Sarael would know what to do.

"He only completed the geis three times. She is still with us." The avatar took Quin's hand. "Take her to the inn. I can't treat her in the street."

Barrand pulled at Sarael's arm. "You must go! Dalanar knows where you are."

"She kept him from reading her thoughts. He doesn't

know. Hurry, she's in pain."

"But he ... three times?"

"Four? I'm not sure." Sarael motioned for the guardsworn to pick up the corners of the cloak. Quin moaned when they lifted her off the ground.

A FLOORBOARD SQUEAKED AS Sarael wrung out a cloth in the wash basin beside her handmaiden's bed. Quinthian lay on a thick pile of blankets in a private room of the Gilded Rat. Sarael had dosed the woman with poppy oil to ease the pain, and her quiet whimpers and weak thrashing had finally stilled.

Sarael wiped the hair from Quin's gray face and dabbed at dirt and tiny rocks embedded in the scrapes. The sturdy brown clothes she wore were dark with sweat, blood, and other, unrecognizable stains. Sarael sliced away the cloth.

Quin's body was ravaged with burns. In places where the sorcerer concentrated his touch, moist welts had spread across the skin. Muscle and bone showed through pitted wounds on ribcage and cheek. A huge blister in the shape of Dalanar's hand covered one shoulder and collarbone. Her back was scalded a vicious crimson.

Barrand placed a trembling hand on Sarael's chair. He drew in several long breaths and steadied. "Heal her, Sarael. Don't let her suffer any longer." Tears gathered in the big man's eyes.

"I'll do what I can." Sarael patted his arm. "Find Jol and have him make a balm for the lesser burns. I'll require a lot. You may need to help him."

Barrand jerked his head and stumbled from the room, yelling for the priest.

When it was quiet, Sarael whispered the prayer that summoned her magic. Her aura swelled with cool brilliance. She pulled in the power and focused it on her fingertips. The handprint needed to be dealt with first. Dalanar's energy pulsed inside it, fighting the healing. The blister melted at her touch, but his magic was strong enough that the skin didn't mend completely. When she lifted her glowing hands, an imprint of shiny scar tissue marked the shoulder.

Sarael panted and loosened her focus. Yhellania's blessing swirled into its proper channel, encircling her like a river. She tucked her hair behind her ears and wiped perspiration from her forehead.

Images of Quin as a small child overlaid the figure of the woman on the bed. Light brown curls and aqua eyes, toddling after Sarael on chubby legs; following everywhere, watching solemnly. Sarael had been furious when the girl was apprenticed to the Avatar of War. No handmaiden should have been educated by the avatar of another religion, let alone a bombastic peacock like Gardanath. But Sarael allowed her to go. This was as much her fault as Quin's mother's. If the girl hadn't been trained to fight, she wouldn't have been so quick to follow the sorcerer. Sarael sighed. Even as a child, Quin hated injustice. She refused to remain passive while people suffered. Certainly not the attitude of a proper Servant; Yhellani faithful endured.

Sarael began again. This time, the burns faded with her touch. She mended the deep and blistered wounds before the light gave out. She'd be helpless until her power regenerated, but her handmaiden was worth the risk.

Barrand returned with a bowl of salve. His shoulders relaxed when he saw that the worst of the damage was repaired. His face clouded when he noticed the scar on the woman's shoulder. "I've seen his handprint glowing on walls, but never anything like that. What was he doing?"

Sarael examined the mark again. "I don't know."

"Did he ground his magic on her?"

"Dangerous, but possible, I suppose." Sarael shook her head. "To shove energy through a living creature takes incredible power. Dalanar has never been foolish or wasteful. I don't understand the message he's sending us. Why would he bother?" She dipped her fingers in the lotion and rubbed it on the handmaiden's arm.

"I have a bad feeling about this."

She nodded. Not many Yhellani survived capturing the attention of the Throkari sorcerer. It could be deadly for them all.

CHAPTER FIVE

ONTHAL SETTLED GRACEFULLY INTO a chair. "I ordered more wood be brought up, and tea."

Dalanar tightened his lips to prevent his teeth from chattering, and inclined his head at the avatar. Several braziers had been provided to assist the hearth in heating the room. They did little to dispel his chill or the shadows beyond the circle of firelight.

A frown creased Conthal's forehead. "What did you do? You're the worst I've seen you. Is that a gash on your lip?"

Dalanar dabbed the side of his mouth with a cloth soaked in boiling water. It stung his Fevered skin as if it had been dipped in a glacial lake. His jaw ached with the need to chatter. He dropped the bloody rag on the table and winced as icy air touched his abrasion.

Conthal regarded him unsympathetically, and turned away with an irritated grunt. The avatar of Throkar smoothed his short dark hair into place with his palm. He still appeared to be in his thirties, with boyish features and piercing slate eyes. He hadn't changed since Dalanar was a child. Now, Dalanar looked the older of the two.

"Another assassination attempt tonight. A Yhellani zealot." Dalanar drank more of the boiling water. It felt painfully cold on his superheated tongue, but it helped to bring down his temperature.

He wasn't sure when he'd last run this hot with power. The woman had been covered with blisters from their contact, but Sarael would doubtless attend to her. He grimaced and wrapped a bandage over the liquid burn she had given him. There was no healing grace in Throkar's service.

Who *was* she? Vaguely familiar, yet he couldn't place her face. Those eyes: aqua green. The Yhellani would've been attractive enough, he supposed, if she wasn't snarling at him. Younger than he, mid-twenties or a little older. Skin the dusky tan of a finely-bound book. Hair braided in the Ravendi military style, yet a trusted guardsworn.

What had she said about coming to kill him? That didn't make her any easier to identify. He'd lost count of his potential assassins years before. But how did she find him, much less resist his geis? Clearly, the woman was involved in one of Sarael's plots. To merit such elaborate protection from his spell must mean that she worked against the Throkari. He might have made a mistake in not taking her prisoner.

His thoughts kept returning to her eyes. Aqua green. Running with tears. Full of fear and pain, but brave. Stupidly stubborn. A meeting fifteen years ago. *Great Lord.* Dalanar dropped his cup. It shattered and lay steaming on the floorboards.

"I believe the Handmaiden of Yhellania was tonight's assailant," Dalanar said, pouring tea into another mug and taking a long gulp. Once he made the connection, the woman's resemblance to her mother was unmistakable. They embodied the blend of ethnicities that occurred at major crossroads ... or among the less cowardly Yhellani.

"Who is Sarael's lackey now? Iyana?"

31

Dalanar stiffened. The avatar knew very well it wasn't. "Iyana is dead. Her daughter. Q ... something."

"Quinthian." Conthal raised an elegant eyebrow. "Sarael always travels with her handmaiden, does she not?"

"Not always." Fifteen years ago. Ash and death. Cries of suffering. Dalanar shook away the memory.

Conthal stared at him, unmoving, jaw clenched.

The back of Dalanar's neck prickled. He needed to proceed with caution. The avatar had been edgy for days; the wrong word might set off his temper. "She could be visiting Gardanath for personal reasons." Truly, he knew almost nothing about the woman, except that she had been fostered in Gardanath's household and trained as a Ravendi mercenary, for the gods-knew-what reason. To become a weapon against the Throkari? To assassinate him? He wasn't impressed with her attempt.

Conthal rapped his ring against the table. "With Morgir's avatar murdered, would Sarael allow her handmaiden to take a pleasure trip? You *happened* to run into her on the streets of Crador?" Unhealthy patches of red bloomed on his pale cheeks. "No. Sarael is here. Preparing a trap. Or ... she hopes to find Astabar first. To use him against us. I will stop her, even if we have to rip this revolting city apart, down to the last maggot-infested soldier and sewer rat."

Now Dalanar was relieved he hadn't taken the woman prisoner. With Conthal's mood so volatile, the avatar might have destroyed her before they obtained anything useful. They certainly didn't need another decade of famine as Sarael dithered around, deciding on a replacement handmaiden.

"Conthal!" Dalanar snapped, trying to startle the man from his fit. "This is Gardanath's city. These are *his* soldiers and sewer rats. If we damage them, we're going to earn a cold reception when we reach Csiz Luan requesting asylum."

Conthal stilled.

"We have no confirmation Sarael is here. I couldn't enter the woman's mind."

That caught Conthal's interest. "Handmaidens don't resist your geis. Tell me." The avatar studied him as if Dalanar were a recalcitrant apprentice instead of his closest adviser.

Dalanar recounted the incident, downplaying the answers the woman gave to his questions. Conthal didn't need to hear she came to Crador specifically to kill him. He would mention it when the avatar was less likely to dismantle the city searching for Yhellani conspirators.

"Sarael's block broke after the second attempt, but she constructed her own? Fascinating. You left her alive?"

Hopefully. One couldn't always predict how people would react to the geis ... or the burns. "I tried a new spell on her. A mark."

"And?"

"It will alert me if she's involved in any endeavors hostile toward us." *Assuming she lives.*

Conthal drummed his fingers pensively. "Can it gain me access to Sarael?"

Dalanar considered ways the link might be useful beyond reading the woman's intentions. He should be able to locate her, if he were in close enough proximity. Truthfully, he'd never used the spell before and couldn't even be certain it worked. Dalanar rubbed the back of his neck. "I don't know."

The avatar sighed. "Find a way."

"Won't killing Sarael cause another famine? We can't afford that happening again. Not so soon."

"Bah. Sarael's feeble mind and sentimentality render her incapable of making an actual decision. Yhellania has no such weakness. If Sarael dies, a new avatar would be selected within hours."

"It's Yhellania you despise, why—"

"Enough, Dalanar! I will not debate this with you again. Sarael is an affront to everything Throkar represents."

Dalanar gritted his teeth and splashed more water into his cup. If Conthal wanted Sarael dead, Dalanar would do whatever was required to achieve that goal, even though it was wasted effort. He owed the man too much. "I'll find a way."

"Get me close to her. I'll figure out the most *fitting* means to destroy her." Conthal gave Dalanar a rare smile of approval and began to cough. "Now pour me some tea."

CHAPTER SIX

BARRAND ENTERED THE ATTIC room where Sarael sat with Quin and his lieutenant, Thera. He set the ewer of cool water on a side table and eyed the woman on the bed. The handmaiden's nastiest burns were healed, but strange dark marks lingered under her skin, shifting and causing pain. Cuts that should have closed at Sarael's touch were infected like deep wounds instead of simple scrapes. Not even the avatar could explain the reaction.

Sarael prodded the edge of the scar gently. "I'm still not able to penetrate his spell. It appears to be a link between you, but I don't know what kind."

"Three feet of steel in his guts would break it, if I ever get the chance." Quin's words came out as a croak. She looked up at Barrand. "Are they gone?"

Barrand rubbed the bridge of his nose, trying to pinch away another headache brought on by worry and lack of sleep. "According to that innkeeper, they slept late and ate dry toast with boiling water for breakfast. Then they mounted their scaly Nags and strolled out of the city going west. No attempt to hide or search for us."

"I don't like it," Thera said. "They must know Sarael is here. Why didn't Dalanar geis the whole town until he found her?"

She squinted in the afternoon light that shone into the room, turning her tawny skin a radiant gold.

Sarael traced a finger through the ring of water left by the pitcher. "Maybe they're afraid, too."

Thera snorted. "What could scare them?"

"Avatar Laniof *was* murdered."

Sarael rarely spoke up in conversations related to her safety. As flattering as it was to be so trusted by his patron, Barrand wanted her to be involved, to show that she understood the risks. At times, she didn't seem to be part of their world...probably a side-effect of her near-immortality. It was the *near* part of her exceptionally long life that concerned Barrand.

"You think they're heading to Csiz Luan, and not Utur?" he asked.

Sarael nodded.

Barrand slumped against the door frame and sighed. "That would explain why they didn't break any of Gardanath's things, and kept to themselves."

Quin grumbled in protest.

"Mostly," he amended.

"They didn't bother sneaking out of town today. That doesn't sound fearful to me." Thera slid one of her daggers in and out of its sheath with an irritating snap.

"Showing off," Quin said.

Rotting sorcerers. Who knew why they did anything? Barrand wished them all into the godless void, and good riddance. "Well, that brings me to the next problem. When can Quin travel?"

Sarael touched the handmaiden's forehead. "Not for some time. The infection is bound to worsen and I'm already using all my energy to maintain her. His power is fighting me."

"No!" Quin said. "You can't remain here, waiting for them to come back to hurt you. For all we know, they killed Laniof and you're next. Leave me or take me with you, I'll understand. But please don't stay."

"You'll die if we move you. You'll suffer *before* you die if I leave you. These options are unacceptable." Sarael turned to Barrand. "Think of something."

"Riding is out?"

She tsked at him.

"What about a wagon?"

Sarael considered. "If driven slowly over good roads ... possibly."

"What good roads? There's nothing but wide dirt paths between Crador and Csiz. A wagon would attract more than cultists, and bandits are better armed." The effort of speaking obviously exhausted her; Quin laid her head back on the pillow with a wheeze.

"You rest. I have an idea." Barrand patted Sarael's hand with a confident smile. "Thera, step outside with me. I'll send someone else to sit with them."

"I won't have Sarael's death on my conscience, Barrand," Quin said weakly.

"Don't worry, dear," Sarael murmured as the door closed. "If I die, you're sure to die, too. Now, drink more water."

THE WOOD SQUEALED UNDER Barrand's heavy steps as he and Thera descended to the common room. At his sharp nod, a pair of brown-clad guardsworn slipped up the stairs to take the lieutenant's place. They weren't missed from the throng of scarlet tunics and tan work smocks seated at the trestle tables.

The Gilded Rat's meal hall was popular among Gardanath's Ravendi mercenaries. Hot food at low prices lured them away from the tavern district like starving whelps to their mother's teat. Barrand didn't trust being surrounded by so many people, but he hoped the mercenaries would help if an attack came. He shrugged and turned to his lieutenant.

Thera regarded him with one black eyebrow raised. "You don't have a plan."

"I may have exaggerated." He pulled up a chair beside a Ravendi soldier. The man bobbed his head at them before turning back to his meal.

Barrand lowered his voice and hoped the general noise would cover their conversation. "It's too risky to stay here."

"Quin's right, though. There's no better way to announce our presence than to travel with a wagon. We must be able to run or hide."

"Quin's out of her mind with fever, and I'm tired of behaving like rabbits," Barrand growled.

"We all become prey when one of us has been savaged by a hawk."

The soldier beside Barrand turned toward them. "You talking about Quinthian, 'Nath's ward?"

"What's it to you?" Thera sat up straighter and shifted her sword belt.

The man eased back. "Don't mean nothing. I trained with Quin. We did our first posting in Byzurion together, and well ... she's the Handmaiden. If she needs help, I was just...." He shrugged and returned to his food.

Another man, in the scarlet and gold of the Ravendi elite guard, leaned around from the next table. "Do you mean Kalin's fiancée?"

"No, you fool, Quin didn't accept." A lush brunette in the same red uniform rolled her eyes at him.

The man frowned. "She didn't? Don't they have babies?"

"Which one was Quin?" A muscular woman with close-cropped gray hair looked puzzled.

"Are they still together?" someone asked.

"Yeah, but she travels with Sarael and the Servants."

Their gazes lingered over the brown of Barrand's plain tunic and unremarkable sword.

Barrand bellowed with laughter and slapped the first soldier on the back. "Don't you Ravendi have anything better to do than gossip about each other?" They joined in sheepishly. At last, he wiped his eyes. "Quin *could* use your help. I have a plan, if you care to listen."

SARAEL PUSHED INTO THE bunk room and stalked to the window overlooking the street. She pointed mutely at the crowd gathered to gawk at the Ravendi volunteers below. Barrand took her hand, and held it between his palms.

"It will be all right, Sarael. I promise." He squeezed, then let go and turned to his saddlebags. "My Lady, I am tired of hiding in bushes and wearing sack cloth. I am guardsworn to the Avatar of the Goddess Yhellania. I, and my soldiers, are going to dress like it. For once." He held up his white tabard, edged in a rich brown ermine, emblazoned with sun and wheat.

In the intervening years since he stuffed it in his pack, the fabric had aged, rusted, and darkened. Barrand's shoulders slumped, and he smiled ruefully at Sarael. "Much like me. Not as bright and hopeful as I once was." He touched the silver that frosted his temples. Hadn't he just been a boy joining her service yesterday? With all those youthful ideals and an unbroken nose?

The avatar gazed at him for a long moment. She took the tabard from him and gathered it to her chest, closing her eyes. The warm glow of sunlight reflecting off a field of wheat poured from her, and the smell of summer, hot and languid and sweet, rolled over him like a childhood memory.

When the spell faded, she stood, breathing heavily, eyes closed, with the tiniest hint of a dimple showing on her cheek. He wondered if anyone else ever noticed. A trace of the innocent village girl she had been, centuries ago, when Yhellania pulled her out of her own world and threw her into one filled with horror and violence.

Sarael handed him the tabard. It was brilliantly clean ... better than new. Barrand slid it on and tightened the lacing at the sides. Belting on his formal sword made him feel complete. Laughter bubbled up inside him, and he almost winked at the avatar. He stifled the impulse.

Barrand threw his saddlebags over his shoulder and offered her his arm. Sarael's gown, too, was blinding white. He resisted an urge to grab a cloak to cover her. She must also hate having to hide from the sun like a thief. For once, he could give her a few days to walk freely. "Let me show you what I've done."

The street below had the air of a village fair. He needed to get things moving before they fell apart.

CHAPTER SEVEN

WHEN WORD WENT OUT that Sarael's handmaiden, an ex-Ravendi soldier, was injured and required safe passage to Csiz Luan, there was an outpouring of volunteers.

Thera regarded Barrand with a skeptical expression. "Sixty-two mostly drunk, at-will mercenaries, who agreed to cut short their leave to escort one of their own, vowing to defend her against attack from two powerful sorcerers. For free. We'd better be well on the way before they sober up, commander."

He surveyed the chaos. "I'm not sure this is what Yhellania meant when she asked me to protect her children."

Barrand handed Sarael up into the covered wagon where Quin rested. Although they had to buy the cart, a merchant, grateful for past healing, donated a bed.

"This is a bad idea, commander." Quin's voice quavered, but carried up to the driver's bench.

"Don't let these fine Ravendi hear you say that. You wouldn't want Kalin to find out you don't trust the elite guard."

"Kalin is here?"

She sounded so hopeful; Barrand hated to disappoint her. "No, Quin. Kalin will meet you in Csiz Luan. Just hang on until then."

The young guardsworn didn't reply, and he assumed she had fallen asleep again.

Mercenary corps tradition dictated that the designated head and intermediary for any group was the ranking officer. Major Actas, the gray-haired woman from the inn, moved in and organized the volunteers: archers, infantry, armored elite guard, and engineers.

"I've sent engineers ahead to repair the roads on our route. They groused a bit about their talents being wasted filling ruts, but we need a smooth ride for the girl."

"Can we trust engineers?" Thera asked. "They all studied at the University of Dacten, and it's known to have close ties with our enemies."

Actas' face wrinkled up with her broad smile. "That may be true of sorcerers, but engineers are a peculiar lot. We might find them building ballistae in the bushes, or arguing over the best way to fill a hole. I doubt they'll run off to warn Conthal or sabotage a bridge."

Thera looked unconvinced.

BARRAND WAS ALWAYS PROUD of his guardsworn, but he felt a special stirring of satisfaction to see them in their white tabards, riding beside their radiant avatar, as they approached the gates of Csiz Luan. The drumbeat sound of water rushing through the limestone passages under the city gave the occasion a martial air.

Sarael unbound her hair and left it flowing down her back. A crown of white flowers, woven by one of the Servants, perched slightly askew atop her head. She was the embodiment of innocence and light. The only thing that could make that moment better would be Quin riding at the avatar's side as befitted the handmaiden. Barrand doubted he would ever see that particular sight again.

Progress had been agonizingly slow, but despite Thera's doubts, the Ravendi volunteers were attentive and disciplined. Since bumps caused Quin pain, they did everything possible to prepare the road.

None of the Servant's remedies or Sarael's gifts did more than sustain the handmaiden. She remained feverish and barely conscious most of the time, and suffered nightmarish visions whenever she slept. More than once, her screams startled horses into bolting. Barrand hoped being in a familiar place, around people Quin loved, would ease her passage through the Mysteries and into Yhellania's arms.

The Ravendi let up a cheer at the sight of the city's scarlet pennants rising above the trees. However, when the procession cleared the forest, they found troops arrayed in front of the gates to meet them. Gardanath, Avatar of the Goddess Ravendis, waited at their head.

Of the four avatars, Gardanath looked worthiest to consort with gods. Armored in red-enameled plate mail, he was a colossus astride his ebony warhorse. He hadn't bothered to wear the helmet slung over his saddle-bow, and sunlight gleamed off his shaven scalp. He watched them, face impassive as he scratched the silvery stubble of his beard.

Both sides quieted and stopped, leaving a hundred paces between them. Barrand didn't remember the last time any of the avatars met. He wasn't sure of the protocol, especially with the added complication of the peace accords within the city. Had they already violated some unwritten rule?

"Have the Yhellani finally decided to invade, Sarael?" Gardanath's booming voice mocked. "Using my own troops? That's cold."

Sarael flashed a small smile and urged her horse forward. Barrand began to follow, but she waved him away.

The hooves of Sarael's mount clicked as they passed inside the vast, inlaid ring of stone surrounding the fortress-city.

"Gardanath, beloved of the mighty Ravendis, my Servants and I seek refuge."

"You are granted refuge, my sister. Your people are welcome. They, and you, shall find peace within these walls." His words were solemn and had the air of binding, but his eyes twinkled with suppressed mirth. "You just may not like your housemates."

With a flash of gray and a shout, an engineer darted from the crowd with a crossbow aimed at Sarael. The mercenary fired and ran toward the forest on the opposite side of the gate.

Crimson blossomed on Sarael's back and she half-turned with the impact. Barrand let out a cry and spurred his horse forward. He swept up as she was about to slide from her saddle and grabbed her, halting her fall. A single bolt couldn't kill Sarael, but her pain was no less real.

The Crador Ravendi flowed around them like flood water, shielding Sarael and the Servants with their bodies.

The Yhellani Guardsworn turned and surged after the assassin. Gardanath was faster. On his massive warhorse, he was on the archer in a few lunges. The avatar seized her by the hair at the scruff of her neck and squeezed. She jerked and went limp. The mounted man dragged her to the gates.

"Who are you to break my peace?" Gardanath snarled.

"For the Tree of Knowledge...." She gulped.

Gardanath roared and threw the engineer to the ground. The sound of bones cracking, and a howl of pain rose from the crumpled pile.

"Throkari zealot. Where the fuck is Conthal? I will have restitu—" The big man went rigid, and red fire blazed from his eyes. Ravendis leered out at the gathered soldiers and laughed.

Everyone but Sarael bowed, the presence of the divine pressing down on them in a cruel wave. The war goddess dismounted and stalked to the cringing assassin with a sway that was both alien and aggressively feminine.

The captive debased herself before the goddess' pounding gaze. "The Tree ... Great Lady! Yhellania destroyed it and—"

"*You violated the truce, worm. My sworn truce. Do you know what the penalty is for that?*"

"N-n-n no," the woman burbled.

Ravendis bent down, and peered into the engineer's face. "*Neither do I, because nobody has ever broken it.*" She paused. "*Let's make something up.*" She drew Gardanath's sword and plunged it straight down into the prisoner's chest.

Where there had been a woman, now was nothing but a wail of soul-destroying agony and a fine pink mist of tissue and blood that coated everyone around the goddess.

The world moved again. Gardanath inhaled with a gasp and coughed out the bloody fog as the goddess left him. Someone threw up.

Over her objections, Barrand pulled Sarael into his lap. Their pristine clothes were streaked black and red with gore.

"Let them pass!" Gardanath bellowed, between fits of coughing and spitting to clear the blood from his mouth. He swung up on his own horse, and followed the Servants through the gates, signaling to have the engineers rounded up for questioning.

CHAPTER EIGHT

NAMED AFTER AN ANCIENT city in a language Gardanath alone remembered, the fortress of Luan was Ravendis' triumph and the result of many lifetimes' worth of her avatar's planning and labor. It served as both a military base and the hub of a trade empire along the Great East-West Road from Lyratrum to Utur. Rising above a lucrative bend in the Afris River, it offered moorage to fishing boats and ocean-worthy sailing ships under the city itself. Engineers and geomancers had augmented its limestone caverns to provide warehousing and canals for transporting goods. A monarchy technically ruled Dacten. Gardanath paid his taxes as a loyal subject, but ignored any laws he found inconvenient.

Dalanar liked Csiz Luan. It was flawlessly maintained and orderly to the point of obsession. The dictates on cleanliness were enacted when Eulesis became second-in-command ... a distinct improvement since his last visit. He resolved to compliment her on the achievement.

The staff of the manor stayed out of his way while he wandered the gardens, which suited him. As Conthal said, the weak should defer to the strong.

Dalanar hadn't needed to draw power in over three days, and the Fever had receded. He wore his cassock unbuttoned over a wool shirt and pants, and anticipated real food at dinner. His mouth watered. The casting diet of desiccated bread and meat grew tiresome, even dusted with a variety of expensive spices. Dalanar tended to lose too much weight if the fast went on for long.

A commotion in the entryway drew his attention, and he could hear Gardanath's furious, booming voice, even from the rear of the house. Who would confront the avatar in his own home? Dalanar strode through the halls; his fingers tingled in anticipation of casting.

He drew up at the sight of white-garbed Yhellani, covered in shocking amounts of blood spatter, huddled in the atrium. Soldiers in Ravendi and Yhellani uniforms milled around in the sunlit courtyard beyond. When Gardanath's voice rang out again, Dalanar started for the door, but a pale hand on his arm held him back.

"Wait. This should be good." Conthal appeared far too pleased not to be involved.

Someone threw open the double doors and the captain of the Yhellani Guardsworn entered, carrying Sarael. She acted more irritated than injured, but when the man turned toward the other guest wing, a dark stain of blood was visible on her gown.

"Alas," Conthal said.

As Dalanar was about to return to the garden and reflections on dinner, a quiet sob caught his attention.

Gardanath stalked in, covered in gore, cradling the handmaiden in a mass of blankets. The woman was obviously unaware of her surroundings. She whimpered and fought with the big man.

"What happened?" Dalanar demanded.

Conthal gave him a wintry smile. "Why don't we welcome our new neighbors and find out?"

They followed the avatar into a suite of rooms decorated in muted pink and green. Several lavishly appointed bedrooms opened off a main gathering area, which featured sofas and a small evening room. The furniture had been built of pale ash wood, and the carpeting was a dark pine color, lending the chamber the appearance of a forest bower. Far different from the polished mahogany and rich sapphire of the Throkari chambers.

Gardanath pushed through the first door and lay his burden down on the massive bed. The redheaded guardsworn carrying Sarael followed.

"Barrand, I can walk. I'm fine," Sarael said.

"My Lady, you've lost a lot of blood—"

"Which I've no doubt already regained."

The captain frowned, but set her on a chair beside the handmaiden.

Gardanath examined the ashen-faced woman curled in an untidy heap on the bed. "What have you done to my Quinny?" The big man turned glacial eyes on Dalanar and Conthal when they entered. The humor that normally sparkled there dampened. "You," he said to Conthal, "will not cause any more trouble today."

"My Lord?" the slender avatar asked innocently.

Sarael's head snapped up and she stood, glaring at them.

"I wanted to take a moment to introduce myself to your newest guests." Conthal approached the Yhellani avatar, regarding her like one of the unappealing specimens he kept in jars. "In all this time, we've never met in person."

Sarael's eyes narrowed and she pressed her back against Barrand. The guardsworn was having difficulty keeping his sword sheathed. As Conthal moved closer, Dalanar wasn't sure which impulse would win.

Gardanath saw it too. His expression suggested that he

didn't want to clean more blood and debris from the cracks in his armor.

"May I express what a ... pleasure ... it is, dear sister? Don't they say that troubling times bring family closer?"

"No family I know has standing orders to hang their cousins from trees and torture them to death," Sarael said.

"It *is* a different kind of love," Conthal agreed. "Perhaps, from this tragedy, we can reforge our bonds and start fresh? Make what was wrong right?"

"There is nothing that needs to be *made right*, except you need to call off your zealots and your sorcerers." Sarael's skin went gray and a faint hint of white light gathered around her irises.

Dalanar edged toward the door.

"My dear, how do you expect my sorcerers to practice without using your Servants as subjects? You wouldn't want them to involve *innocents*, would you?"

Sarael's pupils blazed white and she scrunched her eyes shut with a gasp.

"That's enough, Conthal. You've done enough," Gardanath said.

The sorcerer raised his eyebrows in a show of polite confusion, but returned to stand next to Dalanar. When Sarael opened her eyes again, the glow was gone.

"Now," Gardanath growled. "Someone tell me what happened to Quin."

Sarael stroked the young woman's hand and sat beside her. "She's reacting to Dalanar's geis or his grounding power through her. This sickness is something I've never seen before. She's dying."

Dalanar stiffened and stepped over to the bed. "This was not my intention."

Barrand rumbled deep in his throat, but made no move when Dalanar took Quinthian's wrist. The handmaiden's pulse was weak. Her face haggard and swollen. He pulled the blanket aside to reveal the handprint on her shoulder. A black and pulsing bruise had replaced the pale scar he expected. It somehow retained his magic and lay on her chest, radiating into her heart and brain and Throkar only knew where else.

Conthal stepped closer to examine the mark. "That would be interesting to study. You'll have to run the calculations for me later. I'm curious how you intend to rectify the situation."

Dalanar tightened his jaw at the rebuke. *Run the calculations* — as if he was a lowly apprentice and not a full master. Clearly, though, he'd done something wrong. Why had the power not dispersed?

Tempting aromas of roast lamb and almond rice, fresh bread, artichokes with butter, and red wine drifted from the kitchens. She could wait until after he ate, surely. He glanced at Sarael. Her energy was spent on healing herself, and she was now exhausted. The handmaiden would have difficulty dealing with the poison ... *his* poison ... until the avatar's grace regenerated. He cursed softly and summoned his magic.

Energy seared across Dalanar's nerve endings like the burn of acid, setting his skin and bones on fire from the inside. It boiled his blood, stoking the Fever that made him sweat and shiver.

He laid his hand over the print on her chest. Dalanar wasn't hot enough to burn her yet, at least, not to leave blisters. He mentally sketched a formula that might be suitable. The power had to be drawn from the woman's body without doing further harm. Simply reversing the spell he used to ground himself through her was unlikely to work. He needed to shrink the channel to a trickle, and increase the duration.

He modified the spell and went through the calculations

again. The equation returned energy to the caster. *Interesting*. Potentially useful, to draw power from another sorcerer or ... non-sorcerer? Would they die if he drained the tiny spark of magic most humans possessed? Dalanar set the question aside for later. The altered spell should work, although he preferred testing new mechanics on disposable subjects first.

Sarael stroked the handmaid's forehead. "I'm not sure I can keep her asleep for much longer, Seal."

Dalanar was startled to hear the Yhellani use his formal title. He shrugged. "I will control her, if need be."

Barrand growled at him, rage etched in every movement.

"Keep your dog off me, Sarael."

Gardanath drew in a deep breath. "It might save her, guardsworn. Let him be."

"He did this," Barrand hissed.

The big avatar jerked his head in agreement. "You may not war with each other here."

Conthal's lips twitched. "That *was* naughty of you, Dalanar. We must think of some way to repay Sarael for the inconvenience."

Dalanar ignored the comment and focused on the spell. If he failed, he'd endure more of Conthal's sarcastic commentary. Of course, the handmaiden would die without Dalanar's intervention; hastening her death might even be considered a mercy. He closed his eyes and began the delicate process of extracting the power from her essence.

A FAINT BRIGHTENING OF the sky and the stirring of birds in the courtyard alerted Dalanar that dawn approached. He had been hunched over the woman for hours. His skin was on fire and his teeth chattered from cold.

Sarael observed from a chair beside the bed. Her hair was clean, and she wore a pristine white robe. She threw more wood into the blazing fireplace and placed a cup of boiling tea on the table at his side. He nodded curtly. It was improper for him to be served by an avatar. Was she too simple to realize that?

"I've never attempted it, but I believe I can dispel some of your Fever. Would you like me to try?"

He looked up into her face, disconcerted to find compassion instead of loathing. "Why?"

"You *are* trying to save the life of someone I care about. If you heat up much more, I'll have to heal her burns again."

Dalanar suspected her motives, but didn't think she intended to harm him. In any case, the Csiz Luan truce made it impossible for her to attack outright. "What must I do?"

"I need to touch you."

Dalanar winced, but held out his arm. Sarael lifted an amused eyebrow at him, but took his hand in hers. Instead of being cold, they were faintly warm. A sparkling blue light, like dawn on an early summer day, swelled out between their palms. The flawless purity dazed him, and he forgot to breathe. Dalanar's body temperature dropped as if he dove into a refreshing pond.

"Great Lord!"

"Lady, actually." Sarael returned to her seat.

"Would you teach me?"

"Are you professing a change of faith?"

Dalanar almost laughed at the sensation, like emerging from a long illness. Delicious heat swept through him. With renewed vigor, he turned to the handmaiden. She was awake.

The Yhellani looked disoriented and blurry-eyed, but possessed enough spirit to scowl at him again. "Get away from me, abomination." She slid her hand over the sheets as if searching for a weapon.

"You're safe," the avatar murmured. "He's helping you. *This* time."

He deserved that. Even in her weakened state, he was glad her sword wasn't within reach. Her well-muscled arms were traced with a soldier's scars. Possibly only good fortune saved him from harm in Crador.

"Are you done?" Sarael asked.

Dalanar shifted closer, but Quinthian regarded him with suspicion.

"I only wish to know how much poison remains." He shrugged, easing the tension from his neck and shoulders. "I will leave it, if you prefer."

The woman hesitated, turning to Sarael, who patted Quinthian's arm reassuringly. She nodded slowly as if doubting her decision.

The handmaiden tensed when Dalanar placed his hand on her chest, covering the mark again. His finger slid over her collarbone to touch the fluttering pulse in the hollow of her throat. Most of the power was gone. She was safe. Time to stand and stretch his aching muscles. Return to his room and his bed. He was even cool enough to eat. God of Knowledge, he could eat!

Quinthian watched him, face relaxed and eyes misty with exhaustion. Their aqua became a deep blue in the dusky light. For once, the Yhellani wasn't angry or frightened, a neutrality of expression he rarely encountered. Her lips were parted and her head tilted back to regard him from beneath dark lashes. She met Dalanar's gaze without wavering.

A desire he hadn't experienced since his youth overcame him. It almost brought him to his knees beside her. He stumbled away, although the urge to caress her soft skin, brush his lips against the pulse of her neck, and feel her body entwined with his was nearly overpowering. He sucked in air and ran a hand through his hair trying to regain his composure.

"Is something wrong? What is it?" A gruff voice from the darkness beyond the bed called. Barrand. Of course, no guardsworn would leave the avatar alone with Dalanar.

Sarael frowned, glancing between him and the woman. Quinthian had slipped into a doze.

"I've done what I can." Dalanar pulled his light robe closed, even though sweat beaded on his neck. "She's healthy and strong, I expect she'll recover quickly." He walked toward the door of the chamber, not waiting for a reply.

Sarael called after him. "Thank you."

DALANAR SOUGHT OUT THE bathhouse adjoining the manor. He was grateful it was empty in the predawn hour.

The sudden rush of physical longing took him by surprise. Decades had passed since he experienced anything like it. Before becoming a sorcerer, he had been warned about the impracticality of the Fevers and the unavailability of potential partners. He had a lover during his novitiate, before he started casting. Everyone did. No one mentioned a return of those feelings. It must be the precipitous drop in body temperature causing youthful foolishness.

Or...perhaps Yhellania was toying with him. It would doubtless amuse the Goddess of Fertility to punish him by forcing such an inappropriate attraction on him. That it was with her handmaiden would only make the situation even more entertaining.

Dalanar cursed Yhellani plots as he stripped off his hot woolen clothes. For the first time in his life, he took a cold bath.

CHAPTER NINE

QUIN WOKE TO SUNLIGHT blazing through the window of a room she didn't recognize. She jerked upright, alarmed, until she noticed Sarael asleep beside her, wrapped in a thick green blanket. The sound of the water churning in the caverns under the city reassured her further. They were in Csiz Luan. Safe.

Conversation in the next room had awakened her. Barrand. Thera. And Gardanath? She sprang from the bed and sank to her knees with a stifled curse. Gods' blood, she was weak.

Quin sat against the foot board and panted. The distance to the voices now seemed daunting. Well, she would go slowly. She got to her feet and lurched across the room, pausing to lean on furniture. Her legs trembled.

Where was the guard for Sarael? Did they expect her to protect the avatar? The last few days had jumbled together in a collection of vague sensations and useless vignettes. Quin grumbled in frustration.

The discussion took on an edge of anger. If they didn't quiet down, they would wake Sarael.

Quin stepped into the main sitting room. She belatedly recognized it as one of the manor's guest apartments.

Thera glowered at Gardanath. Quin knew from her former

guardian's bearing, he was about to stop listening to Thera's arguments.

"You have to let them go," the tiny woman insisted. "They've done nothing wrong."

"A curious assertion, considering one of them put a bolt in your avatar, lieutenant." Gardanath crossed his massive arms over his chest.

"What?" Quin demanded.

The three soldiers turned, and Barrand rushed over to help her to a chair. Thera and Gardanath glared at each other, but no one spoke.

"Who tried to kill Sarael?"

Gardanath sighed in exasperation. "One of Conthal's zealots." He crouched in front of Quin. "You worried us, girl. Made us desperate enough to let that sorcerer poke at you. But he managed to do what even Sarael couldn't."

To her dismay, sensations of Dalanar kissing her neck, his breath urgent as she wrapped around him in the hot darkness, overwhelmed her. That hadn't happened, had it? Where did that image come from?

Barrand touched her forehead. "Are you sure you're feeling better? You look feverish."

Gardanath considered her for a long moment and stood. "There is nothing further to discuss: we will interrogate the engineers. One of their own participated in a plot to execute a guest. Ravendi corps engineers. Unforgivable!"

Thera blocked him when the avatar attempted to depart. She looked like a doll challenging a bear. "They volunteered to help us. They gave up their leave to guard Quin. They filled potholes! How can you punish them for what that Throkari freak did?"

The red creeping up Gardanath's neck subsided. "What?" He turned to Barrand as if for confirmation, but the commander appeared baffled. "Volunteers? You didn't pay them? Any of them?" Gardanath's grim expression softened and he laughed. "Volunteers and at-will soldiers are not bound by the same strictures as contracted mercenaries. This is a different situation altogether." He picked Thera up by the shoulders and set her down beside Quin. Gardanath strode out of the suite calling for Eulesis in a voice that caused the decorative vases to rattle.

"You convinced Ravendi engineers to fill potholes for free? How?" Quin gazed up at them in wonder.

"What was that about?" Barrand dropped in to a chair beside her and indicated the departing avatar.

"He must have thought the person who shot Sarael was bound by contract. They attacked someone who had been invited into Csiz Luan under the accords. You don't maintain your reputation if your troops turn on their patrons." Quin rubbed her hands over her face. "Great Lady! What did he do to the assassin?"

Thera shuddered. "Ravendis decided to handle the situation. Gardanath's squire is never going to scrape the blood and bits out of his formal armor."

"It was bad?"

"It was horrifying." Barrand looked pained.

Quin ran her fingers through her tangled and greasy hair and cringed. Not bathing for days was forgivable on campaign, but in contrast with the fine appointments of Gardanath's home, she felt like a savage.

"Thera, would you help me to the baths and tell me what's happened? How did you raise a volunteer army of mercenaries?"

CHAPTER TEN

ARAEL, YOU HAVE BROKEN my Seal. He's done nothing but eat all day," Conthal chided.

"Bah, you're both just skin over bones. You've been out causing too much trouble in the world." Gardanath laughed and patted his stomach. "I couldn't live on jerked meat and dried rations for long."

Dalanar lifted his glass in salute to those assembled in the evening room, but said nothing. He appeared sated and drowsy. Conthal frowned, but didn't pass up the wine offered to him by a black and red clad server.

Quin stayed as far from Dalanar as possible while keeping him in view. How was she supposed to be civil to him? She shuddered, remembering his attack. The agony. Skin searing. The erotic images that came into her mind earlier managed to be even more disturbing. Quin fingered the hilt of her sword. The rotting truce prevented her from ridding the world of him.

At least Quin felt stronger after she spent the day eating and sleeping. She soaked in the baths with Thera, catching up on the missing time. It amused her that Kalin's rejected proposal was the topic of such heated gossip in the corps. He deserved it for taking after that obnoxious archer.

The thought of Kalin made her smile into her cup. They

hadn't seen each other in months. He promised to meet her at the Summer Festival where they would have three sweet, uninterrupted days and nights to do their part ensuring an abundant harvest. Being the festival queen was the most enjoyable aspect of being Sarael's handmaiden, and Kalin had been Quin's only choice for consort since she assumed the role.

Quin returned to watching Dalanar. His presence felt like a sliver under her skin. Irritating and difficult to ignore. Candlelight cast shadows over the sharp planes of his face, emphasizing hollow cheeks and temples. Of everything she expected of him, an attractive, underfed man eating like a child given a plate of sweets was not among them.

A doe-eyed brunette offered him a tray of grapes. He took a handful and said something that caused the woman to titter nervously before moving on.

Dalanar met Quin's gaze before she could turn away. He raised an eyebrow, but his expression remained neutral. When Eulesis, Gardanath's second-in-command, swept into the room, Quin jumped up to greet her, relieved to escape the sorcerer's stare.

Eulesis towered like a slender sapling above the other women. Despite bearing Gardanath three children, she kept her whipcord shape and her lethal edge. Her graying blonde hair was knotted up in the complicated Enng fashion Quin had never managed to replicate.

"My dear." Eulesis pulled Quin into a rough embrace and kissed her on both cheeks. "You're completely destroying my son. He's down two stone since you rejected him."

Quin snorted. "How can you tell?"

Eulesis regarded her sternly for a moment, but finally grinned and hugged her again. "I'm glad you are well. Where is the man we have to thank?" The tall woman dragged Quin along behind her like a riptide. Eulesis might have been nearing fifty, but there was no resisting her.

The sorcerer stood.

"Dalanar, it's been too long. We three should sneak away with a bottle of spirits and tell tales about our avatars. I'd bet we all have fascinating secrets to share."

"I'm sure it would be enlightening, but I must decline." Dalanar glanced at Conthal. "I'm fond of my seal, but I don't want it placed inside my body in a way that would be difficult to retrieve." He polished the large ring bearing the emblem of the Throkari Tree of Knowledge.

Gardanath roared with laughter. He grabbed Eulesis to his chest and kissed her. "You wouldn't tell them *my* secrets, would you?"

She raised an eyebrow at him. "You would need to give me a ring before you threaten me with it."

"I have something else I can bury inside you, if you like," he rumbled in her ear.

Quin, still in Eulesis' grasp, pulled away, cheeks burning.

Dalanar smiled faintly at Quin's reaction. "I didn't think Yhellani blushed at such things. It's unexpectedly ... charming."

She stalked over to stand beside Sarael.

"I don't have any secrets, do I, Quinthian?" Sarael murmured.

"None that I would ever tell, my lady."

Barrand hovered beside the avatar like a guard dog, bristling at the idea.

During the course of the evening, it became apparent that something, a semi-divine fascination, or perhaps loneliness and isolation, drew the avatars together. They mocked and antagonized, but couldn't resist being in each other's company. To

Quin's disgust, this meant the seconds were obliged to join them, if only to be sure they didn't come to blows.

"You're wrong, Sarael," Conthal said. "Do you still believe stars are holes punched in the night sky?"

"Of course not, but to claim they are worlds like ours is beyond belief. Do they have their own people and gods?"

"They're not all planets, possibly a small number. I cannot say yet if any of them are populated," he admitted.

Sarael crossed her arms. "Preposterous."

"It is the pursuit of knowledge, instead of accepting what has been *known* for millennia without question." Conthal sneered. "If we all followed Yhellania's teachings, fire would be a questionable new invention."

It was late, and several ewers of wine lay empty on the low table between them. The avatars and their attendants reclined on couches and cushioned chairs on a terraced patio overlooking the city. Torches wavered in the warm breeze from the dry, grassy hillsides abutting the fortifications to the south. A far-off guard called a sleepy *all clear*. The gentle flow of water into the caverns thrummed like a mother's heartbeat. The drums of Csiz Luan.

Dalanar held his wine glass loosely and stared out toward the river, apparently deep in thought. He had been unexpectedly quiet, deferring to Conthal except when directly engaged. He ignored Quin after their initial introduction, his gaze sliding past her when he infrequently glanced in her direction. The sorcerer's arrogant disregard rankled. He should at least have the grace to acknowledge her hatred. Quin stayed in her place beside Sarael, quashing the childish urge to place herself in his line of sight just so he couldn't so easily ignore her.

Eulesis cleared her throat in the lull. "A messenger arrived from Lyratrum today."

Gardanath grunted. "Ach, yes. I was going to mention that

once we finished our bickering." He was half-asleep, and more than half-drunk, sprawled with knees wide and arms outstretched in a huge chair.

"How is Morgir doing?" Sarael's eyes widened with concern.

"He's manifest, of course, dragging Laniof's body around, howling at the sky, and trying to find the killer. He's convinced it's a sorcerer because of some rotting handprint in his studio. About what you'd expect."

Dalanar and Conthal exchanged a glance that Quin couldn't decipher. Was that guilt? They *had* been traveling along the road leading from Lyratrum. Why would they want Laniof dead?

"Lyratrum is a mess." Eulesis lounged like a leggy cat on a large divan next to Gardanath. "Morgir hasn't selected a new avatar, and production on our shipments has ceased because all the artists are vying for the position. They've all gone mad along with their god."

Gardanath cleared his throat. "A question for your vast intellect, O founder of universities, speaker in the tongues of worlds."

Conthal narrowed his eyes, but gestured languidly for the other man to continue.

"What could kill an avatar so easily?" Gardanath might have been asking about the color of the sky— vaguely curious, but indifferent to the answer.

Avatars were not destined to die peaceful deaths. Only a cataclysmic event, an army or a natural disaster, could overcome the power of their god to shield them. Fast or overwhelming. Usually both. It took Gardanath three battalions to pry Ravendis out of the head of his predecessor.

How had Laniof died in his studio with no one aware of it, not even his god? A chill ran over Quin's skin. She considered the fire-lit faces around her. Sarael's lips pressed together in a pale line, and her hand shook as she drank her wine. Quin wanted to comfort her, but didn't know how. Maybe fear was the best thing to feel.

Conthal looked sharply at Gardanath and cleared his throat. "The same tool that can create a god can destroy an avatar."

Quin almost dropped her glass, and Eulesis choked.

Gardanath furrowed his eyebrows and drained the rest of his wine. "The staff has returned."

Conthal nodded. "So it seems."

"What staff?" For the first time, Quin addressed Conthal. "Are you saying gods can be created?"

He pursed his lips. "I shouldn't be surprised Sarael kept the knowledge from you."

Quin gave him a withering glare. "Why aren't we overrun with them? Everyone could have their own personal deity perched on their shoulder?"

"By Ravendis' bloody balls, don't even jest about that." Gardanath tossed his cup onto the table with a tremendous clatter. "The last thing we need is a legion of gods running around, riding us like goats."

"There used to be more," Sarael whispered. "So long ago we don't remember their names. I have dreams, I think they're Yhellania's, about empty corridors. Vacant thrones."

Gardanath ran a hand over his smooth head and scrubbed at his face.

"And a new god was created ... recently?" Quin slid to the edge of her seat. "Is that what happened to Laniof?"

"Don't be ridiculous. Laniof is dead." Conthal swirled his wine. The dark liquid spilled over the rim onto his hand. He cursed softly and dabbed his wrist with a bleached cloth.

"Sarael? Gardanath? Is there a new god?" Why wouldn't they answer a simple question?

Sarael wouldn't meet her gaze.

Gardanath shrugged and grabbed a fresh goblet. "Laniof said a shiny new deity approached him with a fabulous treasure not long ago. He declared it an *artistic triumph*. Wanted me to come up to see it. But then Laniof was killed, and now the treasure and the god are gone again."

"The treasure was the staff?" Eulesis said, rising up on an elbow.

"Presumably."

Quin felt as if she was missing half the conversation. "What is this staff? What are you talking about?" How did *they* all know about it? She had never heard of such a thing.

"An old relic." Gardanath grunted. "The important part is that it can kill avatars. Someone who didn't like Laniof has it, and none of rest of us are universally adored."

Quin frowned. "So, the god murdered Laniof with the staff and took it with him when he fled."

"Gods don't kill avatars," Sarael said. Gardanath and Conthal looked pained at the idea.

"If he *is* newly created, perhaps he doesn't know any better."

Sarael shook her head firmly.

Eulesis sat up. "Didn't the Morgiri provide a description?"

Gardanath chuffed. "This is coming from Lyratrum. They sent an oil painting, a poem, and a folded moon beam or some crap representing their sorrow over Laniof's death." He touched Eulesis' shoulder. "Go get those things off my desk, love?"

She slipped back inside.

"Don't your gods know where he is?" Quin asked.

"Of course not. Gods and avatars must be physically present to *see* each other." Conthal filled a cup from the kettle hanging over a lamp and added some powder to the liquid. The tea held the musk of foreign spices.

Quin would have preferred the scent of ale and the company of the other guardsworn. Barrand and most of the others were down at one of the taverns in town enjoying a night off, drinking and having a good time away from the politics.

Eulesis returned, carrying a roll of canvas, and a delicate white object.

"Couldn't find the poem," Eulesis said, placing the hand-sized cylinder on the table between them.

"Ah. That." Gardanath grumbled. "The thing was a monstrosity. I might have burned it. Accidentally."

Eulesis grinned at him and unrolled the canvas.

The name *Astabar* was illuminated in silver and bright blue paint at the top. Below, emerging from a gray background, was an intense painting of a handsome man of about Quin's age. His dark hair fell in unruly waves and indecisive curls to his shoulders. Thick eyebrows shaded lively brown eyes. The artist captured a sense of innocence and antiquity. He had a broad, strong nose that flared at the base over full lips and a light dusting of freckles. He wore a somewhat ragged goatee. There was a tilt to his mouth as if he found humor in everything. Quin liked him.

"Are you sure this isn't the avatar of the new god?" She touched the corner of the portrait.

"If the god selected an avatar we would feel it," Sarael said. "The power balance changes. When he was born, he brought divine energy into the world with him, like a dowry. Anyone with the right knowledge can tap into it. If he invests an avatar, a large portion of the power will return to its source in the divine realm. We would notice the drop."

Quin turned to inspect the tiny marble sculpture. It appeared to be a reproduction of a fighting stick. The staff? What else could it be? Two twigs, off-center from each other, emerged from either side of a central trunk. Intricate designs, which made Quin dizzy and vaguely nauseated, flowed across the surface. She was awestruck by the sculptor's skill.

"Not much to look at," Conthal remarked over her shoulder.

She jumped away, startled. She hadn't noticed him come up beside her; he wasn't Fevered. "Which, the god or the staff?"

He raised an eyebrow at her. "You assume that's the staff?"

Quin ignored him and smirked at Gardanath. "Did they say anything else in their report, or was everything in their poem?"

"Just that Astabar here came to Laniof with a gift, and they made some kind of deal. Next thing the gentle citizens of Lyratrum know, the gift is gone. Astabar is gone. Laniof is dead, and the place is crawling with sorcerers. They're not sure who did what to whom, but they're pretty sure Morgir isn't going to settle down until things are figured out."

"Why hasn't Astabar invested an avatar yet?" Eulesis laid the painting on the table, moving cups to hold down the curling edges. "Doesn't not having one hurt?"

Quin considered the quirk to the god's lips. She tilted her head, examining the picture again. From some angles, it looked like a smile. "He seems to be having a good time. Does anyone know what he is the god *of*? I hope it's something amusing, like wine or gambling."

"How ... whimsical," Conthal said. "Eulesis is correct. He must be reaching the limit of his endurance. Maybe that is why he sought out Laniof."

"Why would he need the help of an avatar?" Quin turned to Sarael and Gardanath.

"He didn't want Laniof. I suspect he wanted the information Morgir buried in his brain. If I'm understanding Ravendis' memories, avatar creation and some of the other important bits of divine knowledge, have to be figured out when they arrive on this plane." Gardanath rubbed a hand over his shaved head and chuckled at Quin's incredulous expression. "What? Not very godly? Tell me about it."

"Where did the staff come from? Did the gods make it?" Quin poked at the marble reproduction. *How did the patterns writhe like that? Was it a trick of the eye or part of the magic?*

Conthal sipped his tea. "It is time for our young companions to leave us."

Quin was about retort when Sarael spoke, "Good night, Quinthian. Rest well."

"But...."

"I believe we have been dismissed." Dalanar inclined his head to Conthal, and started toward the entrance to the main house. Eulesis patted Gardanath on the shoulder and sauntered after the departing sorcerer. With a bewildered look towards Sarael, Quin hurried to follow.

The Ravendi nodded to them before disappearing into the family wing.

Quin stopped in the foyer, trying to make sense of what happened. A god had been created and the avatars said nothing. Why? They were *all* hiding something. Even Sarael. Sweet, earnest Sarael.

Dalanar turned to go. He knew.

"What's going on?" She spoke before she changed her mind.

The sorcerer paused. "A great deal, I'd imagine. We don't consort with uncomplicated people."

Typical Throkari answer.

"That's not what I meant."

"Perhaps not. Sleep well, Handmaiden Quinthian." He bowed and turned toward the blue suite.

Quin scowled after him and fondled her sword hilt. Damned truce.

She was a simple soldier. She knew how to fight. She knew

how to endure. She'd never asked to be surrounded by complicated people mired in deep plots who shared the minds of gods.
She hadn't wanted to be handmaiden, however much she loved
Sarael. Nevertheless, as the Yhellani second, she deserved to
know the truth. Lies of omission were still lies.

The silence echoed, and she didn't want to be alone. Quin
wished Kalin was with her. She sighed and crossed the marble
floor to the forest suite.

Quin was depleted and needed more time to recover from
the illness. She couldn't think about this anymore tonight.

She greeted the guardsworn posted at the entrance and crept
past Barrand where he slept near the door. He sat with chin
propped on his fist, snoring through his battered nose. She entered her assigned room and collapsed on the bed. She dreamed
of dead gods and unfathomable plots.

CHAPTER ELEVEN

ONTHAL GLANCED UP FROM his journal, pen poised over the page when Dalanar entered. A glass retort containing a milky green liquid boiled suspended over a lamp and dripped clear fluid into a jar next to the avatar.

"Did you find any trace of our wayward godling?"

Dalanar set his saddlebag down beside the door and grabbed a light robe to fend off the chill of the room. The thick draperies were closed against the intense sunshine, and the only heat came from the fireplace. "Nothing ... except an enclave of your cultists to the south."

He had spent another fruitless day riding around the outskirts of the city attempting to locate Astabar. Conthal predicted that the god would try to reach Gardanath, now that Laniof was no longer available to teach him how to invest an avatar.

During the brief time Astabar was their *guest* after his birth, they learned he was the god of illusion and trickery. He hid for fifteen years; he wasn't going to be found unless he wanted to be. A worthless expenditure of time and effort. At least Dalanar manage to avoid becoming Fevered by using only the slightest trickle of power. He could still eat normal food.

Conthal wasn't surprised. "We prefer 'Tree of Knowledge Fellowship'." He made a note on the page. "And?"

"They've served their purpose. At this point they may be scaring off our quarry, more than helping further a practical goal."

"Did you bother asking if they've seen any sign of Astabar?"

Dalanar sank down in the armchair opposite his master. "They tend to become incoherent when I talk to them. They'll only really listen to you."

"You are far too fastidious. They are a tremendous help to the cause."

Dalanar grunted. It wasn't a cause he supported. His grandmother was yet to be born when the avatar established the doomsday faction of the Throkari religion. Conthal claimed the Fellowship was a way to keep the more excitable believers occupied. He took the idea too far. "Perhaps you can send them away now?"

The avatar set the pen aside and regarded him with a piercing stare. "Why do you care?"

Dalanar shrugged. "Gardanath will track the assassin to the camp. Having them crucified on the gates of Csiz Luan would be a waste. And, as I said, they may scare off our friend."

Conthal laughed. "Compassion, Dalanar? I thought I ground that out of you thirty years ago. Needless to say, Gardanath already knows I am involved."

Dalanar stiffened and was about to reply, but Conthal interrupted.

"Have you made any progress in finding a solution to my Yhellani problem?"

"You have access to Sarael now. What more do you need?" Truthfully, Dalanar had put Conthal's request from his mind once she had arrived in Csiz Luan.

The avatar regarded him coldly. "The truce prevents me from any direct action. Throkar is adamant about that. I need her outside the gates."

Dalanar rubbed the back of his neck. "The Yhellani Summer Festival takes place soon. She has no choice but to travel to the Chapterhouse or risk the harvest. We could arrange an ambush of the procession. Take the avatar prisoner."

Conthal tapped his desk thoughtfully. "I've forbidden the Fellowship from attacking Yhellani en route to the festival. The chance of them killing key participants is too great. I cannot reverse my decision or risk losing their confidence."

Dalanar searched his memory for everything he knew of Yhellani customs. He knew the basics, but the topic had never interested him enough to delve deeply. A dim recollection surfaced from a decades old lesson. "The only outsiders granted permission to attend are candidates to become the festival king ... avatars of other religions are not excluded from competing in the selection, by the way." He tilted his head at the man. His master would never participate in a fertility rite, but Dalanar felt obliged to make the suggestion.

The avatar shuddered. "*You* are going to petition to be the Yhellani Summer King?" Conthal laughed, a sound that started low in his chest, and grew louder until he had to wipe away tears. "They will go mad at the mere suggestion. This idea intrigues me."

Dalanar gave Conthal a small smile. "Since I am overcome with the handmaiden's wit and charm, I shall offer myself up as her consort. They'll be so busy trying to protect poor Quinthian from me, they won't see you coming to destroy her mistress."

"The handmaiden will refuse you. Yhellania certainly won't believe you."

"I'll be convincing." Memories of Quinthian in the predawn light, eyes misty, skin soft and warm beneath his fingertips, flickered through his mind. He shook them off. No sane person would expect the woman to select him. The idea was absurd. He just had to appear sincere enough that Yhellania wouldn't bar his entrance. Whether a candidate had any hope of succeeding was never called into question. They encouraged pathetic romanticism.

Pounding reverberated against the door, and Dalanar rose to open it. Gardanath and several soldiers waited in the hall, and the huge man stalked in without invitation.

Conthal stepped around his desk with a smirk. "Do come in."

"We caught a co-conspirator to the assassin who shot Sarael," Gardanath said.

The Throkari Avatar smiled thinly. "And you wish me to reward him for services rendered?"

Gardanath glared at him. "I have no use for assassins. The only thing lower than shooting someone in the back is poison. You want it out with a rival, come at them straight with blade or magic." He grumbled deep in his massive chest. "It's nearly a perfect chance these are your people acting under your orders. I accept that. But I need to be sure this was not an attempt by the same enemy who killed Laniof."

Conthal's face went flat at the mention of Morgir's avatar.

"Can you tell me with complete confidence that you prompted this attack?"

The slender man shook his head. "I cannot. My opinions on the matter are well known. However, I have not ordered any particular individuals to commit any atrocities in some time. Present company excluded."

Gardanath contemplated them gravely. "I want you to geis our prisoner. To find out whom they represent. If it's Throkar, fine, I expect that. If it's someone else, we need to learn what's going on."

Conthal turned to Dalanar. "I believe this is where I order you to perform an atrocity. You've been entirely too smug about escaping your Fever, and eating your way through our host's pantry."

Dalanar nodded without expression. He had become Conthal's pet monster; no better than a guardsworn with a cudgel for the avatar's purposes. It was the price Dalanar once willingly, even eagerly, paid for power and prestige. He sighed inwardly and went to retrieve a set of heavier robes.

THE PRISON BLOCK CROUCHED at the far end of the training and assembly field below the manor. A handful of Sarael's guardsworn practiced on the yellow sands. The Yhellani wore sleeveless white vests and tan kilts, but in the heat, they had been soaked through with sweat.

Dalanar located Quinthian without difficulty. Her Ravendi braids singled her out from the others. She sparred with Thera, the small woman who acted as Barrand's lieutenant. The handmaiden's left arm showed obvious weakness when she hefted a quarterstaff, and she stopped to rest several times. Thera pointed them out as they drew closer, and Quinthian squinted in their direction, leaning on the staff.

How *did* one court an enemy and appear convincing? And a Yhellani Guardsworn with more reason than most to despise him. To be honest, Dalanar didn't have experience wooing allies either. Before he began casting, he and his few lovers selected each other for convenience rather than any particular attachment. Such things had been of little interest in the twenty years since.

His scheme didn't seem so clever in the afternoon sunlight. Why did she have to be Iyana's daughter? The image of Quinthian's face, eyes half-lidded, with dawn light coloring her hair cerulean blue, came into mind. Her soft skin and pulse under his fingertips. The gentle rise and fall of her chest. Watching him, unguarded.

Perhaps Dalanar should get her a new sword. The one she used in Crador had no doubt been damaged during their encounter. Didn't suitors typically offer gifts? And, it was unlikely she could afford something appropriate to her station. A present like that would make his interest appear genuine. He made a mental note to inquire after the best weapon merchant in the city.

Dalanar turned away as they approached the prison and caught Conthal considering him with amusement. He chose to ignore the expression.

THE CHILL INSIDE THE building was a shock when they entered. It set off Conthal's cough, and they waited several minutes until the avatar's breathing calmed. Dalanar was glad he brought heavier clothes. His silk-lined wool tunic and pants layered with an assortment of thick robes kept him warm after drawing power. Staying comfortable in winter or cold rooms was particularly difficult. The Golden Darkness, with its geothermal heating, was a blessing for sorcerers and vital for attending to Conthal's illness. They had been away too long.

Cells lined both sides of the hallway. Most empty. Halfway down, the guard unlocked a room larger than the others. A stone archway surrounded the door, but the room's walls were white washed plaster. A high barred window let in generous afternoon light, and slate tiles containing several drainage channels covered the floor. An interrogation room.

A man, shackled in irons at wrists and ankles, sat at a small table. He was dressed in a bright green tunic, intricately embroidered brown vest, and black trousers. No callouses from fieldwork or military duty marked his hands. A clerk or merchant— some kind of townsman. The prisoner didn't lift his head until they were inside the room.

His shoulders sagged until he saw Conthal. "Great Lord!"

"Don't start," Conthal said.

The man quieted, eyes sparkling with joyful tears.

Gardanath looked between the two, with a nauseated grimace. "I suppose that says it all, but I need to be sure."

Conthal approached the table. "What is your name?"

"Aadavel, Great One." He bowed, nearly touching the floor.

"You serve Throkar?"

"I do! With a full heart and complete devotion." Aadavel managed to grovel lower.

"I'm going to have my Seal test that devotion. Do you dispute my right to do this?"

The man paled as he gawped at Dalanar. "No." He could barely speak.

"Don't fight him. I hear it's less painful that way." Conthal walked to the door and rested against the frame.

Gardanath crossed to the opposite side of the room, as far from them as the space allowed.

Dalanar closed his eyes and drew power. It rushed in, soaking into the spaces between his bones like water pouring into a bowl filled with pebbles. It rushed to his head making him dizzy with the intensity. The formula for the geis was rote to Dalanar. He did the calculations needed to factor in the man's weight and size in seconds. He had lost count of how many people endured the spell within his arms. A hundred? A thousand? How many more would he be asked to interrogate?

The accomplice made small mewling noises when Dalanar lifted him into the geis embrace. Dalanar had grown strong from restraining unwilling subjects. He crossed one arm over the cultist's pelvis, the other across the chest and neck. He set his thumb along the man's jaw, the position for the first stage of the spell. Painful, even at the lowest intensity.

Energy shot through the prisoner's head, completing a circuit in Dalanar's arms. Unlike the Yhellani Handmaiden, no mental block had been erected and there were no natural defenses. Dalanar received a pure stream of thought: fear, awe, complicity, and pride. Surface images, inconclusive.

Dalanar paused to give the man a moment to recover. Over the years, he discovered this was the best way to obtain the clearest information. The room still rang with the echoes of the man's screams, and Conthal removed his hands from his ears.

"Great Lord, I'll tell you anything. Please ... stop him." Aadavel whimpered.

"Where is your devotion to Throkar, Aadavel? If there was any other way, we would use it," Conthal assured him blandly. A small smile twisted his lips.

Dalanar moved his hand up to the second geis position and began again. The man's body convulsed in agony, but Dalanar held on without difficulty. Conthal's orders. Direct orders flickered through the cultist's memories. He obeyed the command to kill any Servants who attempted entry into Csiz Luan. Issued after the death of Laniof. No indication of other influences.

Dalanar's mind filled with the sweet mysteries of another's life. He drank them in. At last, he relaxed his hold, letting Aadavel rest. A faint smell of urine permeated the room.

As he was about to release the sobbing man, Quinthian stormed in, slamming the door into the wall. Her rage flared against Dalanar's senses. The connection he established with the handmaiden in Crador sizzled to life between them. He had begun to think the spell had not been successful; another error to add to that evening's tally.

"What are you doing, Gardanath? How could you allow this?" She wrenched the table aside to confront Dalanar. The noise was overwhelming in the small space.

Conthal stepped up to Quinthian from behind and grabbed one of her upraised arms, and the back of her neck. He whispered a word into her ear. The handmaiden stopped, held nearly immobile by the avatar's power. She panted and her eyes flashed, but her body remained limp. Dalanar needed to learn that spell.

He caught a few fragments of her thoughts. Images of Conthal and himself suffering gruesome torments. Impressively creative. Unexpected in a Yhellani.

"This is an accomplice to the woman who shot Sarael," Conthal told her silkily, moving in close behind her. "There may be others. They may be working for the people who killed Laniof. Aren't those good reasons to use the proper methods to obtain information? Can we risk not knowing the truth?" The avatar let go of her, leaving a light pink burn in the shape of a handprint on her wrist. "My Seal was about to give us a report on the findings, do you wish to listen?"

Dalanar realized he still held Aadavel and lowered the man to the floor. "He's what we expected," he said. "A Throkari cultist from town, using the opportunity to harm Sarael. His lover was on leave in Crador. She sent word about the Servants' plans, and they arranged the attack. No evidence of nefarious outsiders."

The handmaiden slowly turned her head toward Gardanath. "You encouraged this ... assault? Allowed it?"

Gardanath straightened. "I did."

Horror and betrayal crossed her face before she managed to force her expression to impassivity. A muddle of impossible to interpret emotions buffeted Dalanar through their connection. He hoped her mind wasn't always such a chaotic mess.

"How do you live with yourselves?" she asked.

"The handmaiden needs lessons in the way the world works," Conthal remarked with some amusement to Gardanath. "I expected her time with you to have tempered that naïveté."

The scarlet-clad man shook his head. "She's been keeping bad company."

The woman gritted her teeth. "Maybe the world is tired of your sick games. I know I am. Why don't you let us be free of you?"

"Do they want to be free, Quinthian?" Conthal indicated Aadavel who crawled over to lie at his feet, still bound. Blisters marred the man's face, but he sobbed for Conthal's approval.

"Did I do well, Great Lord?" he mumbled. "Did I serve Throkar?"

"Oh yes, Aadavel, you did well."

The man curled into a fetal position and lost consciousness.

"Release me. I'll go." Quinthian sounded weary. She stumbled when the spell freed her and she shuddered. She didn't look at any of them as she left the room.

Gardanath let out a gusty sigh and turned to the others. "I'll be hanging him in the morning."

Conthal dismissed the unconscious man with a wave. "As you will."

Dalanar needed to ground himself into rock to begin cooling down. He placed his hand, fingers splayed, on the freezing blocks by the door. He shoved the remains of his power into the crystalline structure of the stone. The solid mass of energy would dissipate as light and heat over several days. To non-sorcerers it appeared as a glowing handprint.

GARDANATH PARTED FROM THEM when they reached the entrance of the prison, leaving them to return to the manor. No sign of the handmaiden.

"Your orders were fresh in his mind," Dalanar said, pulling his black robes closer about him. The sun provided little warmth so near the horizon.

"It was obvious Sarael would come here," the avatar agreed.

"I didn't need to geis him. You knew."

"It was needed to appease Gardanath. He'll believe the results of your spell, and not investigate further. If he continues searching for a deeper conspiracy, he may discover things I don't want him delving into about the staff and the godling."

They walked toward the manor in silence.

At the steps, Conthal paused. "Ride back to the encampment. Find out if they've seen or learned anything about Astabar, and then send them away."

"You've set your cultists watching for a god?"

"Not as such. He is unlikely to appear to them in raiment of glowing blue. He might steal their supplies and horses, though. That, even they would notice."

"It would be better if you went," Dalanar said.

"I know." Conthal turned and walked inside.

CHAPTER TWELVE

BARRAND RUBBED A CALLOUSED finger against the rim of one of the delicately painted ceramic plates on the table, and whistled. "Mercenary work pays well. You think Sarael would consider hiring us out for a few months? On the off-season."

Quin surveyed Gardanath's sunlit Evening room. The table was set with cups and plating from the finest galleries in Lyratrum. Flowers from the abundant spring cascaded from vases in the corners; their heady scent made her miss the gardens of the Chapterhouse. Growing up as the avatar's ward opened these doors to her, but she hadn't been around enough to become accustomed to them.

She laughed. "Would that be the off-season where we're plowing, or the one where we're reaping, commander?"

He chucked her on the shoulder. "Ha! Either one would do."

While Barrand admired the fine appointments, Quin wandered over to stand in the morning light that swept in an open window. Below, the Afris shimmered as it flowed past the bend and started the long descent toward Enng. The mountainous coast of Utur was a smudge over the water to the west. Not even the widest river in the world kept the Throkari sorcerers away from civilized people.

"How much longer are they going to be?" Barrand grumbled.

As he spoke, the double doors of the room thumped open with such force the plates jumped, and Kalin erupted inside.

"Quin! They just told me you were here."

There was the briefest impression of gold curls and red enameled armor, before the giant pulled her into an enthusiastic embrace. She clung to his neck.

The sound of Gardanath clapping to summon the servants, and the conversations of the others, reminded Quin of where they were. She let go, and he lowered her back to the floor.

"Kalin," she breathed. A feeling of ease filled her like a summer afternoon, his broad face and warm brown eyes the first reassuring thing Quin had seen in days. She studied him. Alone, he was imposing, taking after the impressive build of his avatar father; in the plate armor of the Ravendi elite, he was a monument to destruction. "What happened to you? Did you grow again?"

He grinned and knocked on the breastplate. "Promoted."

"Now you smell worse than ever. I hope you're not staying for breakfast." She turned away from him with a sniff, but couldn't suppress a proud smile. It faded as Dalanar approached.

Kalin frowned at the sorcerer. "You're the one who attacked Quin. Left her for dead in an alley." He stepped between them as he snapped the guard away from the hilt of his long sword. The sound echoed in an unexpected lull.

"Enough, boys." Gardanath's booming voice filled the room. "Let's at least play nice before breakfast. I need a good meal in me before we get truly nasty." He slapped both men on their backs, although he only let his hand linger on Kalin's.

He laughed as he blew on the fingers that touched Dalanar. "I keep forgetting. You can fry bacon on your skin.

"Kalin, go change out of that rusty iron, and return prepared to be polite to my guests."

The armored man looked like he wanted to protest, but remained silent. With a glance at Quin and a long, flat stare at Dalanar, he departed.

"He's grown astonishingly since I saw him last. Do you keep him penned with the cattle?" Conthal said as he took a place to the left of Gardanath.

Gardanath beamed. "He's the biggest of my boys. Still thinks with his sword, but has potential. However, I believe you're referring to Agreos. He was coming up when you last honored us with a visit. It's been some time."

Conthal inclined his head in agreement. "I remember dark hair."

Gardanath fondly regarded Eulesis, who draped herself into the chair beside his. Her honey-colored hair was streaked with gray and fell in waves down her strong back. "He's my first blond. Apparently, the trick is Enng blood lines. When you live as long as we do, Conthal, you learn these things." A flash of sadness crossed Gardanath's face, but he looked away to signal the servers.

"Actually, you're the only avatar to produce progeny. You've been so generous about it we can scarcely begrudge you the honor. It's been fascinating watching you single-handedly populate Dacten over the centuries. Wouldn't you agree, Sarael?"

Sarael turned chill blue eyes on Conthal but said nothing.

"Such irony: The Avatar of War has children, while the Avatar of Fertility remains barren."

"It was ever my choice, Conthal," Sarael told him sternly.

"Oh, right, your condition. How sad." The sorcerer tried to appear sympathetic, but failed.

Gardanath glared at the man. "I'm also the Avatar of Trade and Diplomacy and I'm very good at it. Right, Eulesis?"

The woman beside him gave him an arch smile. "At times.

Although, I believe it was I who demanded your services as a concession during the negotiations when we met."

"So you did. You were wild, fierce, and the youngest herd boss the Enng ever elected. But I was the mediator." They grinned at the memory. "I wasn't going to turn down a beautiful woman demanding to bed me. I couldn't insult a clan leader like that."

Sarael turned with a jerk and led Quin to the other end of the table.

Barrand sat beside Dalanar, but disregarding courtesy, edged his chair as far toward the end of the table and Sarael, as space allowed. The sorcerer didn't deign to notice as he sent the tea to be reheated.

Kalin rejoined them before the eggs were served. Quin only caught a whiff of metal and soap, as he slid into place beside her and squeezed her hand under the tablecloth. His uniform was the brilliant red and gold of the Ravendi elite guard, with the clean straight lines of the mercenary legion. He had belted on his sweat stained fighting broadsword and dagger, not the ceremonial confection he wore earlier. She approved.

In a moment of quiet, Kalin nodded respectfully to Sarael, who sipped her tea and chewed on a piece of toast.

"The Summer Festival is approaching, Mother Sarael. I'm looking forward to seeing Tyrentanna in bloom, and to the honor of being Quin's consort again. What is the theme—"

Dalanar rose and regarded Quin. "I wish to be chosen as your king at the Summer Festival."

The room went silent. Even Gardanath stopped mid-bite and stared at the sorcerer with an expression of clear astonishment.

Quin emitted a sound that was half-cough, half-laugh of dismay. "What?" Was this some new form of torture? "You're not invited."

"You will allow me the same opportunity to court you as any other suitor." Dalanar looked dubious about there being competition. If he attended, he might be right.

Quin glanced around the room, expecting someone to announce that this was a joke. Only Conthal looked amused. "And if I don't agree to this ... arrangement?"

"I will order that every festival king be hunted down and slaughtered until you die." His expression was flat. Emotionless. The death of Yhellani meant nothing to him.

Quin stared at him in speechless horror.

"You are not required to select me, but I insist the decision be an honest one."

"Are you mad?"

"For this to be fair, you must remain celibate until the festival. For obvious reasons, I cannot compete for your affections in that way."

She shook her head. This was absurd. "I'm already bound—"

"Release him."

"How dare you?" Quin balled her fists in the tablecloth.

Kalin slid his chair back. "I don't surrender my place, and certainly not to you. What lunacy is this?"

"Then it is fortunate you look fetching in red." The sorcerer didn't spare him a glance.

Quin leaned toward Dalanar. "I'll refuse to participate before I ever choose you."

Sarael gasped.

"You'll risk blight on the harvest and a drought for the next year because you won't consider me? Isn't that a little ... *selfish* ... for a Servant of Yhellania?"

Quin sputtered.

Kalin turned to Sarael. "Surely Yhellania will not stand for this pollution of the ritual."

"My child," the avatar said, "mortal evil is an issue for mortals to contend with." Her tone was serene, but she crushed her toast in a white-knuckled hand.

"Isn't the invitation open to everyone, Sarael? Officially? Open to those who come in peace and love?" Conthal's voice was cloying with sincerity. "I'm certain Dalanar's intentions are nothing if not loving."

"Threatening to kill my consort is not peaceful," Quin said.

"As long as you are willing to evaluate Dalanar on his many fine qualities before you make your decision, not one golden hair will be mussed. This need not be disagreeable."

Quin trembled as she resisted the urge to draw her sword. "And how do I prove that I made an impartial decision, if I choose someone else?"

Conthal's smile turned predatory. "That *is* a conundrum."

"Do something, father." Kalin didn't take his eyes off the Throkari.

"Ach, boy." Gardanath scratched at his beard as he pondered. "Dalanar, there must be some concession you would be willing to take instead of going and ruining their little party. You'll be the frog in the festival bower, and you know it."

Dalanar considered Quin and finally flicked a contemptuous glance at Sarael. "If Sarael crawls to the Golden Darkness and pleads with Conthal to forgive Yhellania for destroying the Tree of Knowledge, I would release my hold on the handmaiden."

Fury and disbelief blinded Quin. The chair toppled over as she surged to her feet and unsheathed her sword. Sarael and Barrand slid away from the table. A dish broke. Tunnel vision closed around Quin's targets of Dalanar and Conthal. The Throkari Avatar hadn't moved, but a black glow seeped from under his eyelids, a sure sign the god was present. Dalanar's outline wavered with heat.

"Sit down, all of you. Sit down!" Gardanath ordered. No one moved. "Need I remind you, you are under truce? SIT. DOWN."

Quin slid her sword into its scabbard with a snap. A pale maid helped restore Quin's chair and place setting. She sat stonily, refusing to look at Dalanar or the dimly glowing man beside him, who now made her skin prickle.

Gardanath peered at the sorcerer over his wine glass and chuckled. "Dalanar, in all my years in diplomacy that's the most audacious opening demand of a negotiation I've ever encountered. Going straight for the giant metaphysical rift between your religions. That has a certain ... style."

Sarael sniffed.

"But I must point out your position is weak coming from a man who can barely keep from setting himself on fire before finishing tea. You understand you have to be able to touch the handmaiden in question?"

"I'll prepare myself," Dalanar said.

"Not that we need any prurient details, son, but since becoming a sorcerer, have you ever managed to *prepare* so thoroughly? I speak for us all when I suggest this is not only relevant to the arbitration, but high in our minds in concern for Quinny ... and yourself, of course."

A vein throbbed on Dalanar's forehead. He didn't answer.

"Ah. Well. Perhaps Sarael needn't ready that trip to Utur so soon."

Kalin smirked. He took Quin's hand again and rubbed his thumb over the base of her palm.

A pinprick of fiery pain began inside the scar on Quin's shoulder. She prodded it with her fingertips. Was Dalanar doing something? The sorcerer narrowed his eyes at their joined hands and the pain increased. Quin gritted her teeth and stared back, unrelenting.

"I can think of only one solution to the whole thing." Gardanath gestured for wine.

Everyone turned to face him with different levels of hope, suspicion, and amusement.

"We'll all attend the Festival. Have a reunion, like in the old days." He drained his cup, a trickle of red liquid spilling into his scar. "We can witness the handmaiden refuse to take a consort, causing the crops to wither and die, or reject a Throkari wizard and see the world consumed in a fiery tantrum. I, for one, am not missing the spectacle."

Dalanar frowned at Conthal and the pain in Quin's shoulder evaporated. "*The old days*?" he muttered.

"Someone might be targeting avatars," Barrand protested. "It's too dangerous to bring everyone to the Chapterhouse."

"I scarcely expect to attend and not pay for such fine entertainment," Gardanath said. "The services of the Ravendi mercenary corps are yours for the duration. A gift. We would be no safer here than we will be there, surrounded six deep by guards, if that is your wish."

Eulesis gaped at him, but recovered quickly, her eyes calculating. "We may need to shift some troops from Byzurion."

An alien leer slid across Conthal's face as he considered Sarael and Quin. The black glow in his eyes grew more intense as the excitement caught Throkar's attention.

"You are most generous," Sarael said, twisting a napkin around her fingers. "I don't understand the sudden interest in the festival ... from any of you."

"I practically raised little Quin. As a proud poppa, I want my girl to be well-treated." Gardanath's voice was teasing, but held an edge of caution, and he cast a significant glance toward Dalanar. "This will be an excellent way to revive the old traditions. The avatars used to gather at the yearly festivals. There aren't many of us and we don't have much opportunity to meet and commiserate."

"*What have you to whimper and moan about, mortal? If you were my avatar I would have exorcised that self-pity from you centuries ago.*" Their attention snapped to Throkar, where he glared out through Conthal's eyes in a burning haze of black light.

The god examined the room regally. His presence pulled the air from Quin's lungs and the strength from her bones and sinews. Unwillingly, she lowered her head. Had she not been sitting, she would have fallen to her knees. The household staff wailed as they prostrated themselves where they stood. Only the other avatars remained unaffected.

Throkar sneered as he caught sight of Sarael. "*Yhellania still has the village idiot, I see.*" He slid off his chair with inhuman grace and stepped closer to her.

"*My avatar is a scholar of profound intelligence and learning. He founded the University of Dacten, established an enclave for sorceries at the Golden Darkness, and learned the language of the world. Ravendis chose the greatest general and tactician history has ever known, however querulous he's become in his old age.*" He peered into Sarael's eyes. "*Are you in there, Yhellania? What was the best thing your avatar did before you took her? Tie her shoes?*"

"I am a healer, Throkar, not a general, or a scholar," Sarael replied coolly. "At least I haven't been driven insane by having to share an overcrowded brain with an egotistical despot. Tell us, what have you done with that vast knowledge to help ... anyone?"

Throkar snarled at her and swung away, turning toward Quin. The full impact of the god's attention was almost too much to bear, and a small sob escaped her. She couldn't lift her head, but saw him watching out of the corner of her eye.

"Leave her alone." Sarael rose up, prepared to intervene.

He made no move to touch Quin. "*You can do better than this, Dalanar.*"

"A trifle, Great Lord."

"*You have other obligations. This is a distraction.*"

"Politics."

"*Change the politics.*"

Dalanar tilted his head, but said nothing.

Throkar receded abruptly, allowing them to move again. Conthal began coughing his deep, chesty cough.

"Ah, it's always refreshing when one of our godly overlords stops in for a visit." Gardanath fumbled for his wine glass as one of the servitors scrambled to his feet and rushed to fill it. The avatar's hand shook.

CHAPTER THIRTEEN

QUIN WATCHED DALANAR RIDE out of the gate from her vantage point in the trees. He was up to something; she just didn't know what. This was the third day he ventured out alone. Her friends in the wall guard reported he remained out until mid-afternoon, and returned empty-handed.

She had tried tracking him from the walls the previous day, but he disappeared into the forest for hours. The Throkari sorcerer was not out for the pleasure of a morning ride. You needed to possess a soul to enjoy something like that.

Today, Quin followed. If he was doing something related to the staff or another attempt on Sarael's life, they needed to know about it. She wasn't foolish enough to engage the man, although she was tempted. Without the element of surprise on his side, Quin thought she might have a chance. She wasn't completely recovered, though. Another time.

Gardanath set aside the land around the fortress as a preserve for his soldiers to use for training and maneuvers. During a less peaceful past, he tore down the old city and moved the inhabitants inside the walls of Csiz Luan or under them. The area now remained protected from settlement, unchanged for centuries. She drilled there as a youth and knew the hidden paths and eerie ruins. While Dalanar kept to the ramparts, she traveled parallel to him on a game trail sheltered by trees. She caught sight of his black clad form from time to time through the woods and let him stay ahead.

He rode a Nag. Quin had never seen one before. Like their owners, they were repellent and expensive to maintain. The beasts resembled horses; deep, mottled brown coats, and long equine heads. As a defense against the tree-dwelling predators that shared their native range, Nags grew chitinous plates that ran along the ridge of their spines. The heat-resistant armor allowed even Fevered sorcerers to ride. They were opportunistic scavengers with sharp teeth and eyes shifted forward on their flat faces. Disquieting.

When the city angled west, Dalanar continued south, veering to meet up with the forest, but keeping to the grasslands. Quin cut over to the woodland boundary, and waited until he rode out of sight to make certain he couldn't hear her. She followed the hoof prints that creased the dirt at the edge of the grassland.

The sorcerer passed out of the land familiar to her. The city was a smudge in the distance, shining in the sunlight reflected from the river beyond. Huge clouds mounded up in the bright blue sky, and wind lifted and fluttered the leaves.

When Quin checked again, the trail had disappeared. She cursed her inattention. He must have slipped into the bushes at some point just behind. It couldn't have been far. Quin dismounted and tied her mare under a protected ledge hidden by brush.

Quin retraced her path, searching for the tracks. She found a number of them. Either he had been here several times, or he was meeting others. She stepped under the quiet canopy of trees and followed a faint animal track.

At the top of a low rise, Quin heard voices below her. She dropped to her stomach and inched forward to look over the ledge.

The land dropped into a well-concealed ravine. One flank had suffered a collapse at some point in the past and now grew trees as tall as the surrounding woods. The larger end of the gorge formed a rough square with three sides cut from the earthen walls about a hundred paces across. Several tents were pitched in the depression, surrounding a firepit ringed by log benches. A handful of horses stood hobbled near the opposite wall of the canyon.

"I speak for Conthal when I say he wants you to leave now."

Dalanar faced a loose circle of eight people. They wore un-remarkable shirts and trousers in plain browns, grays, and blacks. Neither rich nor ragged. They carried weapons, and handled them with confidence. Their disheveled appearance suggested that they had camped in the gorge for some time.

"How can we be sure you speak for him?" One man stepped forward. A symbolic branch was drawn on his forehead.

Quin froze. Tree cultists. She inched backward and rolled over onto a dusty boot. A blade whistled and she threw herself against the shoe, knocking the wearer off-balance. Quin leapt up, drawing her own sword.

The bald man facing her dressed like the others: unexceptional clothing in worn earth tones. He was Quin's height, but had fifty pounds on her in a solid barrel of muscle around his torso. The cultist bared his teeth, revealing a missing incisor. He held a short sword in one hand and a knife in the other.

Quin eased into the ready position with her broadsword. This, she understood, and she ached for a real fight. She tensed and relaxed her shoulders and started circling, waiting for an opportunity to strike.

She faked a small stumble and the man pounced. He swung his sword to cut across her side and jabbed at her belly with the dagger. She blocked the sword and whipped the tip of her blade around in an arc to slash at his knife hand. He cursed and dropped the dagger. Quin pushed him away and thrust at his unprotected ribs. He managed to sweep the blow aside, but she recovered into a defensive position too quickly for him to retaliate.

The bald cultist came at Quin again, this time using his bulk. He rushed her, swinging his sword in a series of darting strikes. She parried, blocked, dodged, but the rush forced her back. She couldn't afford to break concentration long enough to turn. How close was the edge?

He kept coming. She braced herself, and dropped into a leg sweep, while parrying one of his blurred swings. The move surprised him. He stumbled and collapsed. Quin twisted out from under him as he rolled over the brink. In a last effort to avoid the drop, he grabbed her ankle. They fell.

The landing knocked the air out of her lungs. Quin staggered to her feet, panting, and raised her sword. If she hadn't been so terrified, the pained surprise on Dalanar's face would have made her laugh aloud.

The bald man she had been fighting wiped blood from his lip. "She was spying."

"You could not have chosen a less opportune time for this," Dalanar said through clenched teeth. The sorcerer turned to the group. "Let's not be distracted. Have you seen the man Conthal asked you to watch for?"

"I seen her before," a woman said, pushing the others aside to stand just outside the range of Quin's sword.

"How do we know you come from him, again?" a pinched-faced man in green demanded. "Maybe you're a Yhellani slop-sucker, trying to trick us into leaving."

Dalanar closed his eyes and exhaled. "I am Conthal's Seal. I bear his ring with the emblem of the Tree of Knowledge. I represent him, when he isn't able to come himself."

Most of the Throkari looked confused.

"How can we be sure you're not just some Yhellani who stole the ring?" The man in green squinted up at Dalanar, obviously impressed with his own cunning.

"Throkar would strike down any Yhellani who touched this seal." Dalanar glanced at Quin out of the corner of his eye.

Was that a flash of amusement? Quin resisted the urge to stare at him.

A mousy man, who appeared to be the leader of the group, slid off the log and joined the others. He slapped the ashes off his pants and inspected Dalanar and Quin. "I doubt Conthal'd want us to leave without completing our mission. We're here to kill Servants, and we ain't killed a one. We got a shot off, but that just lost us two well-placed sympathizers. We've nothing to show for this." He indicated the campsite and their unkempt appearances.

"Conthal was impressed with your attempt on Sarael. You have his thanks."

"And yet, he didn't come himself?"

"You forget yourself," Dalanar snapped. "He's the Avatar of Throkar. He doesn't have time to ride around visiting everyone who serves the god."

"We want to stand out. Be deserving."

"Conthal gave you an order. If you disobey, you will call down his wrath upon you."

"With respect, *Dalanar*, if that's who you are," the leader said. "You've given us an order, not him."

A vein throbbed on the sorcerer's forehead.

"Ay. What do we do with her?" the bald cultist asked again.

A wiry man with a large ax came to stand next to the woman and inspect Quin. "She does look familiar."

Irritation flashed across Dalanar's face. "She grew up here."

"But we didn't," the leader said.

They turned their attention to Quin.

"I recognize her!" One of the women crowed. "She's Sarael's girl. Her handmaiden."

"Leave her be," Dalanar commanded. They ignored him.

The cultists moved closer, surrounding Quin, forcing her to stand beside Dalanar. She didn't trust the sorcerer not to slaughter her eventually, but he seemed to have longer-range plans than killing her today.

"If you *really* served Conthal, I'd think you would know her," the mousy leader said with a self-satisfied expression. "I have a plan Conthal will like. We'll hang the spy from a nice big tree and make extra sure she's dead. After that, we'll go. You can report we killed an important Yhellani, and you achieved your goal of making us abandon our lovely campsite."

"It is forbidden to kill the handmaiden. Depart now, and leave her unharmed, or I will destroy you."

Quin stared at him. The Throkari had orders not to hurt her?

"I don't believe you're who you say you are, *Father Dalanar*. I may just turn in two heads to Conthal: A Yhellani and an impostor." He sneered and gestured for his people to attack.

It felt as if the air around Quin erupted into flame. She gasped at the heat roiling off the sorcerer as he drew in power. It blew back the hair of those closest to him and singed exposed skin.

Dalanar's robes crackled with static and billowed around his body as he lifted a hand out to the leader. He pressed a finger to the man's forehead, and an ember buried its way inside. The cultist froze, then screamed, a long, terrible sound that didn't stop.

Black scorch marks appeared on the man's face and clothes. They burst open to reveal a flame burning within him. He glowed like a lantern, bones casting silhouettes through the velum of his skin. That too, caught fire, and he crumpled to the ground as ash and silence.

Three people ran into the woods, begging the gods for mercy.

Quin turned away to defend against a sword thrust. The bald man was undaunted by sorcerer's tricks. The woman who recognized her also joined in, slashing at Quin's side with an ax. Quin rolled under the woman's attack and slammed her out of the circle where Quin and Dalanar stood back to back.

Blessed Yhellania, how had it come to this?

The other three attackers focused on Dalanar: two archers, and a swordswoman.

Sweat poured down Quin's face from her proximity to the sorcerer, but with the first volley of arrows, she appreciated it. They burst into flame and slagged metal before reaching them.

The bald man dodged in with a new series of blows, trying to drive Quin out of the area under Dalanar's protection. Her unexpected move from their first encounter wasn't going to work again. He was agitated, though. His strikes, instead of being controlled, drifted further from his body.

His much longer reach, typically a disadvantage for her, gave Quin the opening she needed. She pulled away slightly, letting him follow her, first with his sword. Before he recovered forward, she slipped under his guard, drew the dagger from behind her back, and plunged the blade up into his heart.

He arched in surprise, his arms dropping over her shoulders as if they were about to embrace. She pushed him off, but her dagger stuck. She left it.

Quin brought her sword up in time to block an ax swing,

but the edge of her blade cut into her cheek from the force of the blow. She sprang away and landed next to Dalanar.

The sorcerer grabbed the tip of his attacker's weapon. A burst of light spiraled up the metal to flash against the woman's hand. She gasped, but didn't release her hold. The cultist yanked her sword free, cutting Dalanar's palm.

The archers sent another flurry of arrows at his head, timed with a lunge from his opponent. He spread a paper-thin disk of searing light between his outstretched hands. The arrows disappeared into it first. The swordswoman had already committed to her thrust: the blade entered, followed by her arm. Nothing appeared on the other side. The woman screamed.

Quin didn't see what happened next, as the cultist attacked her again. Quin hated ax users. People who chose axes as a weapons were fundamentally broken. Where did they get the idea that hewing humans down like trees was acceptable?

Fighting against one was harder, too. An ax could shatter a broadsword if used to block an attack. Quin needed to redirect the force of any contact or dodge it completely. This fight would ruin the edge of her blade. She'd have to spend hours working the nicks out.

Quin held her sword point high, with hilt low to keep it out of range of her opponent.

The woman shook out her scraggly hair and gave Quin a malicious grin. "I've killed your Servants, girl. Dangled them like fruits in the trees, and watered the roots with their blood. Their faces get red and pinched, and they make angry little squealing noises when they die." She let out a braying laugh, but her eyes never left Quin's face.

Quin said nothing. Getting emotional over the taunts of an enemy in combat was suicide.

A bead of cooling liquid trickled down her cheek, and the air felt suddenly chill. Quin had drifted too far from Dalanar. It opened her up as a target for the archers. She retreated into the circle of his warmth before they could react.

The woman advanced, swinging the ax to strike across Quin's shoulder. She danced aside and guided it down with her hilt. The move blocked her opponent from reversing the motion and coming up with an underhand swing at Quin's stomach. She chanced a flick of the sword's tip at the cultist's throat, but missed.

Quin lunged and used the pommel to strike the woman on the hand, trying to force her to release her grip. The cultist howled with rage and swung at Quin's head in response. Quin side-stepped, and tried a clumsy swipe at the woman's ribs. Her error earned Quin a solid blow to the side of the sword. Her hand tingled, but the blade didn't shatter.

They circled, breathing heavily. Quin flexed her fingers inside her leather glove, trying to regain sensation. Stupid. She had to be more careful.

A piece of molten metal fell on her shoulder, and she yelped and twitched it off. Another arrow destroyed.

The woman came at her again. She twirled the ax so fast the blades blurred. Impressive display, but not an attack. Quin sneered in disgust. She didn't even have to block. Although the pattern created an imposing barrier, it was purely defensive. Quin spotted an undefended gap. The base of the ax stayed stationary, while the head moved around it.

Quin braced herself and lunged for the opening. The result was spectacular. The ax head snapped off and flew into a tent, as her sword buried itself deep in the woman's chest. The broadsword bent and broke with a painful metallic clang and her arm numbed up to the elbow from the shock. The cultist's eyes widened and blood spurted from her lips.

Quin whirled around, panting with reaction, preparing to confront a new opponent. Only Dalanar and Quin remained. He glowered at her and turned away.

Smoking corpses and twisted remains littered the campsite. To hear about the Throkari sorcerer's power was far different from seeing it played out before her in a brutal firestorm. Quin didn't have a chance of killing him alone, or in any kind of a fair fight.

Dalanar's cheeks were ruddy and his black hair dripped with sweat. Waves of heat and steam coiled around him. He paced among the corpses, whispering over each of the bodies.

Fear stung her when she looked at him. Was this even close to the limit of his abilities? What could Conthal do with the powers of an avatar combined with those of sorcery? She swallowed hard. How could they protect the Yhellani from these monsters? Quin closed her eyes and pushed away the despair, the hopelessness. She'd talk to Sarael and Barrand. There had to be a way.

CHAPTER FOURTEEN

QUIN RETRIEVED HER DAGGER, careful not to touch the dead cultist. Handling corpses was Throkari business. She gingerly checked over the fallen and the remaining equipment to find a replacement sword. Quin found one at last in a tent near where Dalanar had fought.

She turned to leave and stumbled over the swordswoman, her arm and shoulder burned away. It was only the sorcerer's curiosity that had kept Quin from sharing that fate in Crador. Nothing but blackened bone, and the odor of charred meat.

The figure opened her eyes, and Quin staggered back in revulsion.

"Help me," the woman whispered.

Images of the cultists she had slaughtered at Yhellania's command blinded Quin for a moment. She was not an executioner.

Dalanar strode over, grabbed the weapon from Quin's lax hand, and plunged in into the woman's heart.

"Check her pulse," he commanded.

Cringing, she touched the fighter's neck. Nothing. Quin wiped her fingers against her trousers as she stood.

The man wrenched the sword from the body and threw it to the ground. "Let that cool."

"Why—"

"She was already dead. Did you want her to suffer first? You certainly weren't about to waste any of your precious healing on a Throkari." He narrowed his eyes at her, contempt palpable.

"Why didn't you let them kill me? Those were your allies."

"I'm not done with you."

The hazy sunlight snuffed out, and he scowled at the sky. Quin glanced up. Dark clouds threatened rain. The air tingled with anticipation and smelled of the sweet pungency of damp soil. Dalanar groaned.

The sorcerer turned and inspected the largest of the tents.

"Shouldn't we head back?" Quin asked.

"I'm not holding you here."

She remembered the bubbling skin in the alleyway, where her saliva burned him. "You're afraid of the rain."

"Are you afraid of fire? No. Yet you respect it. You take precautions not to be injured. I am too Fevered to ride, and I wouldn't be able to avoid the storm in any case." Dalanar unpacked the saddle bags from his beast and led it under a ledge that had been converted into a stable.

Despite her apprehension, Quin found herself curious about the man. If she couldn't kill him outright, she needed to figure out some other way to destroy him. Sorcerers were a mystery to her, but perhaps if she spent time with him, he might reveal a weakness. Quin assumed, as long as she didn't attack, he would leave her unharmed. For now.

Quin found a place for her mare among the Throkari animals in the cave. Dalanar's Nag was tied away from the other mounts. The creature eyed her with far too much intelligence. She circled around it to feed her horse oats and water from the cultists' supplies.

The rear wall had been filled in with brick and stonework,

now crumbled and pierced by encroaching vegetation. It resembled a shrine, although nothing like Quin had seen before. Rows of niches ran from floor to ceiling. Twenty? The one closest to the entrance held the accoutrements of the Throkari religion: sacred branch, bound book, and incense. Were these niches *all* dedicated to gods? Quin gaped at them. There were only four … five gods? Where were the avatars of the others? People couldn't have forgotten them; what deity would allow that? It didn't make sense.

On the wall, beside the niches, Dalanar had grounded himself in the stone. The outline of his large hand, long fingers splayed, glowed black and red on the rock face. It was not the precise reproduction of a hand. His fingerprints and fine wrinkles weren't visible. But there was a dark gap at the base of the middle finger where he wore his seal, and a crescent moon shape marred the center of the palm, with several creases radiating out beneath.

It matched the one burned into her shoulder, four fingers and a thumb curling across her collarbone, the index finger resting against her jugular vein. Quin ached with the memory of pain. At first, she hadn't understood how people identified the glowing handprints sorcerers left on stone, but they were as distinctive as the people who created them. Quin would be able to recognize Dalanar's mark for the rest of her life.

WIND AND ASH BUFFETED her as she stumbled from the cave. Thinking of the man turned to char, Quin spat grit out of her mouth and brushed ineffectively at the dust, skin crawling. An iron kettle now boiled over a fire beside the largest tent. Dalanar, enveloped in blankets, leaned out past the canvas flap and measured some of the water into a large cup. He swallowed it and ladled out more.

Heat poured off him, even through the layers. The sorcerer's eyes were glassy, but not unfocused, and his teeth chattered occasionally. He ignored her while he drank cup after cup of boiling water. Dalanar looked ... pathetic.

"What?" he snapped.

"I had no idea."

He didn't respond.

"I'd feel some sympathy, but—"

"Don't."

The first drops of rain thumped to the ground around them, and Dalanar retreated into the tent. Quin paused. She should leave. Staying near him was an invitation to disaster. He might not attack her, but could she honestly say the same of herself? In her current state, it would be suicide. But she might never get a chance like this again. Quin took a deep breath and ducked inside after him.

The interior was the size of a small bunkroom. Blankets and padding stretched across two cots to form a large bed. A chest had been placed beside it as a makeshift nightstand. A tiny table, served by creaky wooden chairs, occupied the last space near the door.

The sorcerer's body heat already warmed the interior. Quin chose a seat where she could keep watch for returning Throkari. Dalanar sat rigidly on the bed, carefully not touching the rumpled sheets. The canvas thrummed to the beat of the wind and the pale yellow of the material stained everything inside a sickly color. The light faded as the rains came. Neither of them spoke.

Quin regretted her decision almost immediately. What was she doing sharing a tent with the Throkari Seal— the abomination responsible for the deaths of hundreds of Servants? Her mother? Did she really think to discover a way to destroy him? Douse him with a bucket of water. She sighed. Just get past his touch that burns his enemies to cinders from the inside, heat that turns arrows to ash, and a disk that reduces limbs to dust. And water might hurt him, but not kill him. Attempting to get rid of him would endanger too many people, and the Yhellani couldn't afford to lose any more guardsworn.

Bored with her gloomy deliberations, Quin cleared her throat. "You must have a *few* Throkari admirers. Why do you want to be *my* consort?"

"Your impeccable timing and restraint, no doubt."

He no longer clenched his teeth, and the strain on his face had faded.

It was hot inside the tent and Quin shifted closer to the door. "Why is Conthal letting you do this? He can't approve of you courting a Yhellani. What if I taint you?"

Quin was surprised to hear a soft chuckle from the dark figure on the bed.

"How can the *innocent* taint the wicked, Quinthian?"

His sarcasm rankled. What exactly did he think *her* guilty of? He was the one who gloried in his status as the Butcher of Narnus. She was just a soldier. Even as a guardsworn, she had never harassed Throkari priests or threatened school children. "If I make you repent your evil ways, he'd lose his Seal."

"You don't make me think pure thoughts, but I'm looking forward to your trying."

Quin snorted, and shifted in the uncomfortable chair. She sat for a long time, considering. Dalanar's interest wasn't personal, no matter that he tried to pretend otherwise. What could he gain from attending the Summer Festival?

The position of consort offered no power. The royal couple reigned for three days over the festival to bless the crops and ensure a bountiful harvest. His most important duty was to conceive a child with the queen. She shuddered. The king also judged the games and competitions. He sat beside Sarael for many of the events.

Quin chewed her lip. Was Dalanar planning to murder the avatar? Not possible, even with his tremendous power ... unless he had the staff that killed Laniot. They *were* traveling along the Road from Lyratrum. Ravendis' enforced peace might be the only thing keeping Sarael alive. Fear ate into her stomach.

A tool that slayed avatars and made gods. She flinched. Quin wasn't ready to think about that.

Could it be anything else? Would he try to murder *her* in some spectacularly demoralizing way in front of the gathered celebrants? He said the cultists weren't supposed to kill her. She had never been harassed or harmed by the Throkari before Dalanar's attack in Crador, not even when she was posted outside Csiz Luan. Her presence in the corps certainly wasn't a secret. With how much the Ravendi gossiped, the news probably traveled up and down the Great Road within days of her arrival. She'd assumed Gardanath assigned people to guard her without her knowledge, but maybe precautions weren't needed. Nobody had wanted to risk worsening the famine.

Having the sorcerer at the festival would have a devastating impact on the celebration, though. He was the darkness in their nightmares. When the story circulated, few of the devoted would attend. This year's festival was going to be a disaster. Would the *Seal of Throkar* consider ruining a party a worthy use of his abilities? That didn't make sense. He was too full of self-importance.

She must have been lost in her contemplations for some time, because the rain had let up to a soft patter when the man shifted on the bed.

"Did you never want to ask me about your mother?" Dalanar's voice was gentle, nothing resembling his usual mocking arrogance.

The breath caught in her throat. "No!" It sounded more like a plea than a refusal.

"Why not?"

"I can't trust you not to lie, and I won't listen to you gloat about her murder."

"I am the only one who knows what happened."

"You killed everyone."

"You wouldn't know unless you asked."

"I won't." Quin jerked the tent flap open.

The vegetation dripped in the aftermath of the rain, but the storm had passed. Puddles shone with the last dusky hours of light slipping under the guard of the clouds. The air was still.

Quin stopped. Whatever her opinion of him, he fought beside her. Protected her back. Quin's Ravendi training was too ingrained; she couldn't simply abandon him in the field. "Should I send help?" she offered reluctantly. "They might be able to get a wagon out here."

"I will return on my own when it is drier."

Grudgingly, she added, "Do you need anything? Food? Water?"

His smile was the briefest flash of white teeth. "You should go, Handmaiden Quinthian, or I'm going to think you care."

Quin rolled her eyes and turned to leave, but paused despite herself. Dalanar's blankets fell away. The light through the tent cast intriguing shadows on the planes of his handsome face. He didn't appear as gaunt as when she first saw him in Crador. Apparently, the rumors were true and he had eaten enough for six men the last few days. He looked good.

God-cursed Throkari.

CHAPTER FIFTEEN

WHAT WERE YOU THINKING going after him? Do you want to kill yourself? Is your grudge worth another famine?" Gardanath waited on the steps to the manor. He had his thumbs tucked in his sword belt and was using his full height to tower over her. "Sarael and Barrand nearly shredded the walls with worry. I organized patrols to search for your corpse."

Quin had rarely seen the avatar so angry. She handed the reins of her mount to the groom who shuffled forward uncertainly.

"I didn't intend to fight him. But if I *had* killed him, it would have been worth the risk."

"You can't," he said.

Quin looked away. "I know." She was tired. Exhausted. The surge of energy from the fight and proximity to the Throkari had faded. Sore and hungry, she wanted nothing more than bed. She didn't think she would be so lucky.

Sarael and Barrand stepped out on the landing beside Gardanath. Her commander's face was mottled red, but Sarael regarded her with pity.

"Are you done now, Quinthian? Can you put this behind you?" Sarael's soft voice carried over the still air.

Quin stared down at her feet. The muscles in her shoulders

burned from the exertion of the day's fighting. She shook her head. "We have to understand his power ... him ... to have any chance of defending ourselves. He has to be stopped."

Gardanath grumbled. "I'm glad your insubordination is someone else's problem, girl. Your death won't be my responsibility." He sent her a final disapproving glare and retreated inside.

Quin exhaled. "I'm sorry I worried you. I should have left a message."

"Greetings Sarael, I'm off to spy on Dalanar. Hope to be back before the evening meal? That would have eased our minds." Barrand bared his teeth in a rough approximation of a smile. Very rough. "You're obviously not sorry, but no use ignoring what you learned about the creature. Tell us what happened." He gestured for Sarael and Quin to enter the manor in front of him. "Don't get blood on the furniture."

A simple meal was laid out on the table of the evening room: cold meat, rolls, and cheese. Quin's stomach grumbled. She piled food on a plate and poured a cup of water from a silver vase. The others watched silently as she gulped it down, not bothering to apologize for the delay.

At last, Quin pushed away the dishes and sprawled in the wooden chair. The dried blood that soaked through her clothes itched and she shifted uncomfortably. She described what happened, going over Dalanar's abilities and their consequences with as much detail as she remembered. However ghastly, she wished she had examined the bodies and asked what happened to the archers.

THE DISCUSSION LASTED INTO the night. They considered everything that might counter his attacks, but even with Sarael's help, hadn't come up with much beyond dousing him in water. He must be well-prepared for that contingency.

"What we need is another sorcerer." Barrand grunted and cracked his back.

"To fight him?" Quin rose from the table and paced. Bruises from falling off the ledge formed indigo stains under her skin, and her muscles had seized. The soreness would only get worse if she remained still. Sarael hadn't offered healing. A fair punishment.

"Well, that's one way. Are there any in the corps?"

Quin tilted her head. "Not that I know of. But I've never asked."

Barrand rubbed his nose. "Ah ... I was thinking more to get ideas on how to beat him. What about one of the university types?"

Sarael sniffed. "Conthal's influence is all over the university."

"Someone told me those sorcerers aren't involved in religious politics anymore. We should send someone to ask. It isn't far."

"No, Barrand. There is nothing there to help us." Sarael crossed her arms with finality and turned to Quin. "Leave Dalanar alone. I won't lose you, as I lost your mother."

Why was she being so stubborn? Couldn't Sarael see that Dalanar had to be stopped for the Yhellani to have any peace? Was there something that worried her more than him?

Quin decided to try another tactic. "What about the staff? Can it really create gods?"

Sarael nodded hesitantly and looked down at her hands. "Some years ago, I felt a strange power emerge. Now, I think it was a god being ... born? Too much happened at the same time. We couldn't follow up. It's possible that the staff was used, but I don't know."

Quin stared at her. "A god came into the world and you ignored it? What was more important?"

Sarael turned to Quin, face distorted with grief. "Narnus. I lost your mother and the others. We were under attack again." Tears rolled down Sarael's cheeks. "What could I do? We refused to give them any more Yhellani villages to target. We uprooted everyone. Lost everything except a few fields and the Chapterhouse."

Quin felt ill-equipped to ease Sarael's sorrow; her own grief had long ago solidified into rage. But she placed what she hoped was a comforting hand on the woman's shoulder. Sarael's compassion had nursed Quin through the devastation of her mother's death. Wiped away her tears, and provided a purpose when the world ended. She owed Sarael so much— loyalty, love, protection. She rarely got the opportunity to return the kindness.

Sarael sniffled. "I apologize. I've been feeling sorry for myself today."

Quin hugged her impulsively, something she had never done as an adult. Sarael rewarded her with a beautiful smile, an effect somewhat ruined by a running nose.

Barrand handed her a clean handkerchief.

Quin sighed and began pacing again. "This must be why Dalanar wants to be the consort. It's the only time we gather during the year. A perfect opportunity for a massacre, except ... his presence is going to drive people away. If even a fraction of the faithful attend, I'll be surprised."

"Attacking Sarael there would be suicide. Yhellania would retaliate. He doesn't strike me as someone willing to die for his cause," Barrand said.

Quin traced the leather-wrapped hilt of her sword. "Somewhere, there is a staff capable of killing avatars. Someone used it to kill Laniof. What if it was Dalanar and Conthal? The Morgiri found a sorcerer's handprint. Even now, the rotting staff could be decorating the mantel of their evening room. They want to hurt Sarael, and, out of nowhere, Dalanar is planning to attend the festival this year?"

Sarael frowned. "They aren't the only evil in the world, and we aren't the focus of every plot."

"You're the one I care about. You have to admit it's suspicious. What if Ravendis is the only thing stopping them from killing you right now?"

The avatar paled and sank further into her chair.

Barrand moved to stand between them. "That's enough, Quin."

"It's not enough! Something is going on. Sarael knows more than she's saying. How are we supposed to protect her when she won't tell us the truth?" Quin circled her commander and bent over Sarael, who slumped down, forehead resting on one hand. "Why were you all secretive and anxious the other night? What do you not want us to know about the staff?"

"Quin, stop," Sarael pleaded, not meeting her eyes.

"You've been alive for a long time, but you're still human. The concept of your own mortality can't be that staggering. What is it—"

Sarael jerked up, irises flashing with white fire. Yhellania pushed her avatar aside and emerged within her. Quin and Barrand collapsed to the floor, unable to move with the weight of the goddess crushing them.

"*You overstep yourself, Quinthian,*" the goddess said. "*I will not allow you to abuse Sarael.*"

The pressure retreated enough for Quin to draw a breath. "I'm sorry, Great Lady!" She cringed inwardly. "I want to protect her, and I grew excited."

"*That isn't all you want. You're selfishly set on your own desire for revenge. I hoped you would outgrow that by now. You disappoint me.*"

The rebuke of the goddess tore into her, and Quin whimpered.

"*Leave Sarael out of this. She doesn't have the answers you are seeking. Am I understood?*"

"Yes, Great Lady."

Without warning, Yhellania retreated and Sarael stood before them.

The avatar rushed to Barrand.

Quin wiped blood from her nose. "I'm sorry."

"You're trying to help," Sarael said in a small voice.

A disappointment. Quin rubbed at the center of her chest to ease the ache in her soul. Revenge wasn't her *only* motivation. How could she keep Sarael safe without destroying the sorcerer? Why did it matter what her reasons were, as long as she protected the faithful? But perhaps Yhellania didn't object to Quin's goal so much as her methods. If going after Dalanar directly was unacceptable, that didn't prevent her from finding out about his weaknesses or the staff. Someone else might be able to use that information against him.

Barrand was right; they needed to talk to the sorcerers at the university. Until then, however, she knew someone closer who might be able to help. In the morning, she'd go in search of Ethalion.

CHAPTER SIXTEEN

QUIN FOUND ETHALION HOLDING court in the shade of one of the eight massive towers that held aloft the city's sluice gates. Gigantic winches and pulleys stood ready to lower solid iron slabs down to block flooding river water from entering the Undercity canals. The engineer and his entourage lounged along the edges of the wide slot beneath the iron plate. In Quin's opinion, an insufficient number of chains kept it from crashing down and sheering the people below in half. You couldn't trust anything made by sorcerers.

Thera eyed the group suspiciously. "What do you want here?"

Barrand had insisted the lieutenant accompany Quin. Officially, it was to help in case she hadn't fully recovered from her illness. Unofficially, it was to keep her from antagonizing Dalanar. She didn't protest. There were other people who might provide the information she wanted, and the sorcerer hadn't returned from the encampment anyway.

"They're not so bad. Just off-duty Ravendi. You'll like Ethalion."

The small woman huffed, but followed when Quin wove through the crowd.

Ethalion's scarlet and gray engineer's uniform hung open to reveal a faded red undershirt. His chin-length dark hair framed bright inquisitive eyes. A goblet dangled between the fingers of one hand and a dice cup occupied the other. He puffed furiously at a cigar clenched between his lips as he shook the dice out onto the velvet cloth.

"Yes!" He raised his arms in victory. "I am the BEST dice player in Csiz Luan, probably the entire world!"

His companions groaned as they picked up their wine skins and stalked off. Ethalion leaned back and blew out a long, self-satisfied stream of smoke. His gaze fell on Quin. "Quinny!"

"Still cheating at dice?"

"Your words sting like arrows." He gave her a wicked grin. "How's Kalin?"

"Amusing." Kalin and that damned archer. Why couldn't he have better taste in lovers?

Ethalion sprang up and pulled her into a friendly hug. "Good to see you awake. You looked pretty rough in Crador."

"You were one of the volunteers?"

He shrugged. "Leave was over." The man nodded to Thera with a half-smile. "Lieutenant."

"You cheat?" Thera growled.

"People accuse me of cheating all the time, but I am merely an excellent player blessed by the goddess."

Thera regarded him through narrowed eyes and reached for her sword.

Ethalion danced back. "Tell her, Quin! I'm honest."

Quin placed a restraining hand on the woman's arm. "It's true. At least, nobody has been able to prove otherwise."

Thera snapped the blade back but kept a hand on the pommel.

Ethalion swallowed and took a long drag on his cigar. "What's up, Quinny?"

"Stop calling me that."

He grinned and held out his hands. "I still have blisters from repaving the road."

Quin huffed. "Fine. Call me whatever you want, but I need some information."

"Well, sit down and tell your old friend Eth all about it." He offered his wine skin to Thera. She shook her head but sat with legs dangling over the edge of the gap in the ground.

Quin knelt nearby, tucking her feet under her. There was no way she would sit under the gate.

Ethalion threw the dice into the cup and straightened the velvet cloth. "Game?"

"Really?"

"The Handmaiden of Yhellania vouches for me."

Quin sighed and pulled a coin from her belt pouch. She threw it down on the cloth.

"And you, Thera?"

Eth had a lilt to his voice that made Quin glance between them.

Thera's cheeks turned the color of late summer raspberries. "You have all my money."

"I'll spot you."

Quin expected Thera to bristle, but the woman inclined her head in thanks. *Well, well. Perhaps they shared more than a dice game on the road from Crador.* "Have you heard about Laniof?"

"I hear about everything." Ethalion passed the dice cup to Thera with a flourish. "Guests always go first."

Thera dumped the dice into her palm and examined them critically. With a grunt, she dropped them back in the cup. The muffled sound of their rattle was comfortingly familiar.

"Eight." She announced when they rolled to a stop.

"Very nice," Eth said. "So, what about Laniof? Terrible tragedy. Morgir insane with grief. Lyratrum in turmoil."

Quin nodded. "The weapon. What do you know about it? Where did it come from?"

The man tapped the ashes from his cigar letting the powder swirl in the currents of air rising from the Undercity. "A staff, right?"

"Gardanath called it a relic."

The engineer scooped up the dice and passed them to Quin. She always lost at games of chance, but it was a small price to pay if he could give her any leads. With a cursory shake, she dumped the dice out. Twelve.

"Excellent." Ethalion puffed on the cigar. "I've heard of it, I think. Mostly rumors. There was some excitement at the university some years ago. A scholar found reference to a weapon, lost for ages, which possessed special powers. Not sure what started him looking for it, though. If it's even the same thing."

Thera glanced between Quin and Ethalion. "Why are you asking him?"

The engineer rattled the dice in his hands.

"Use the cup," Thera said.

He let out a put-upon sigh and dropped the dice in the cup. She held out her hand imperiously.

"You are a deeply mistrustful woman, Thera."

"Probably why I'm still alive." She examined the dice again, and passed the cup back with a grunt.

He shook and flipped the cup over with a flourish. Twelve. "I'm interested in old things—particularly weapons. Especially rare ones. I collect them, and sometimes sell them, if the price is agreeable."

"You have no idea who has it? Where it is?" Quin asked.

"Apparently, it was in Lyratrum."

"That's helpful."

Ethalion chuckled. "I'd tell you if I knew. I don't like the idea of someone out there having the ability to destroy Gardanath with a touch."

"Is that how it works? Just touching an avatar will kill them? Does it work on anyone else? Sorcerers?"

The man shook his head. "Haven't had time to investigate. Only found out about the university involvement after the news about Laniof reached us." He gestured to the dice. "Your round."

Quin grumbled, but picked up the dice again. Eight.

Ethalion swept up the dice, puffing thoughtfully on the cigar. Eight. "Still tied." He passed the dice back.

"Are there any sorcerers in the corps? Someone not aligned with Conthal?"

Eth sucked his teeth. "Not sure, but one of the messengers delivered a note to the university a few months back. Said it was the first time she'd seen a sorcerer in person."

"Did the messenger know why?"

"No. Maybe Gardanath is looking into reinforcing those weak sections of the Undercity?"

"We can hope." Quin dumped the dice out on to the cloth. Eleven.

"Quin," Ethalion started and then stopped. He straightened the cloth and didn't look at her.

"What?"

He rolled again. Eleven.

Thera grabbed the dice before he could pick them up. "You're cheating!"

"How could I cheat?"

Thera threw the dice into the slot leading to the Undercity.

"Those were my favorite dice!"

"Obviously." Thera crossed her arms over her chest and glared at him.

Quin shoved the small collection of coins over to him. "What?"

Eth took a deep breath. "I found someone who survived Narnus."

"That's impossible."

HO, WELLIVER!" ETHALION CALLED as they climbed the broad wooden staircase running up the side of a cliff-side tenement.

"Ho, yourself, Eth. Don't bring those thrice-cursed dice up here." An old man sat in a chair overlooking the Afris, soaking in the heat. His linen pant legs were pulled up to his knees and his feet rested in a water-filled bucket. Sweetly-scented blue flowers grew abundantly in boxes lining the rooftop deck, while chubby bees drifted between them. In the river below, tiny ships were being escorted into the caverns by pinprick-sized barges.

Quin let the hot fragrant air fill her lungs and she lifted her face up to the sun. Its pounding intensity eased the pocket of uncertainty knotted inside her chest. Sarael had told her that there were no Yhellani survivors of Narnus ... had forbidden Quin from investigating further, since only Dalanar and Conthal knew what happened. Approaching them for information was out of the question for anyone who enjoyed breathing. But what if Sarael had been wrong? Or lied to stop a heart-broken child from escaping the protection of Csiz Luan to search for answers and revenge.

Welliver nodded to Quin and Thera. "You brought some better company with you today."

"This is Quin and Thera. They're Yhellani Guardsworn."

The old man peered at them through rheumy eyes. "Guardsworn, eh? I never did see a reason to commit to one god, but I suppose Yhellania is as good as any other, if you're leaning that way. Not as demanding as Morgir, nor as serious as Throkar."

"You're not Yhellani?" Quin asked, confused. "What were you doing in Narnus?"

Welliver's nostrils flared like an animal scenting for predators on the wind. "What is this?"

"My mother was there—" Quin began.

"A lot of mothers were there. And children," he snapped. "And foolish old merchants hoping to sell iron pots and ribbons on one last stop before heading home."

"Quin's mother was the handmaiden—"

The bucket tumbled over in the man's haste to stand. Water spread across the pale tiles leaving a dark stain. "Are you mad, Ethalion? You bring the handmaiden to me when those sorcerers crouch in the center of town like spiders tending a web? To *me*, who has managed to slide beneath their notice for over a decade, when they would no doubt enjoy hunting me down for escaping their massacre?"

"Ravendis protects you here," Ethalion soothed. "Isn't that why you never leave the city?"

Even fifteen years later Welliver trembled, air rasping in his throat, at the chance of being discovered. His reaction convinced Quin more than anything else could have: he had been there. He had the answers she needed to finally understand what happened to her mother. What had he seen?

Quin's childhood had been haunted by nightmares imagining the suffering her mother endured. Iyana's body, burned and broken. Dying with nobody to ease her passage or speak the prayers on her behalf. Quin would wake up on the sleeping porch shared with the other cadets, shaking and sweating, trying to stifle sobs with her pillow. Too terrified to attempt sleep again until daylight crept into the cracks around the shutters. The dreams came less frequently as she grew older, but each time she saw the results of Dalanar's butchery first-hand, the night horrors grew more detailed.

This was her only chance of finding out what happened, and Welliver's reluctance made her grind her teeth in frustration. He had to tell her. The impulse to hurt him until he relented was nearly intolerable. He had no right to keep this information from her or all the families devastated by the calamity.

Quin relaxed her clenched fists. If she abused or threatened Welliver, it would be no different than geising him. She would not become another Dalanar to get what she wanted. She could not torture the poor man again by making him relive those memories against his will. "I'm sorry we disturbed you. We'll go." Her voice was husky with disappointment. "If you change your mind, please send for me." Quin tugged Ethalion toward the stairs.

Welliver stared after them, pants still rolled above knees, standing in the puddle of water, his face a sickly-gray mask. Quin nodded and started to follow Thera down the stairs.

"Wait," the old man called.

Quin paused.

"I didn't see how your mother died, but I did see her after everything else was gone."

"What?" Iyana survived the destruction? Everyone had assumed she died during the cataclysm or just before. Quin couldn't swallow around the tightness in her throat.

"I saw her helping Dalanar. They were running towards the center of town. Where it started. I don't know what they were doing, but she was helping him." He straightened and his jaw hardened. "That's all I have to say."

"How—"

Welliver hobbled into the house and slammed the door. The sound of the bar being thrown was final.

CHAPTER SEVENTEEN

ELLIVER WAS LYING. QUIN didn't know what
he had to gain by telling her such cruel and obvious falsehoods, but no doubt the Throkari
were involved. Maybe Dalanar found him and threatened to torture him unless he dishonored Iyana's reputation. Making her
appear to be a participant in the destruction of Narnus. Helping
Dalanar? Lies!

Quin stormed down another alley, baring her teeth at a tea
seller who moved aside too slowly. She wasn't sure where Thera
and Ethalion had gone. Didn't care. Had they called to her as
she ran past them down the stairs? What was Ethalion's part in
this? It was well-known that he and Quin were friends, and it
was true that Eth usually heard about everything happening in
the corps or the city. Did they place Welliver there as bait,
knowing the news of a survivor from Narnus would eventually
make it to Quin? Were they that treacherous? They *were*
Throkari.

The old man was so frightened, though. He *had* been in
Narnus during the catastrophe. She believed him ... about that.
Trauma marked people. Soldiers from the corps who had endured atrocities sometimes reacted that way when reminded of
their pasts. But why would Welliver say such a thing about her

mother? Did he simply misinterpret what he saw? Iyana's body was covered with sorcerous burns. Had she only been cooperating until there was a chance to escape?

And why would they be moving toward the *center* of the devastation? Dalanar caused it. Wouldn't he already have been at the source? There was so much Quin didn't understand about sorcery, the staff, Narnus. She needed answers. If the university held those answers, she would find a way to get there—with Sarael's permission or without.

Quin paused to regain her breath and peered through a stone archway into a circular courtyard. Planters and benches alternated along the walls, and a basalt statue of Ravendis, sword arm raised in triumph, adjudicated over the yellow sand filling the center. Gardanath's private training ground. Quin barely remembered the walk through the city, or passing through the main gates. Her feet carried her unthinkingly to the place where more of her sweat, tears, and secret angst had been spilled than any other in Csiz Luan. Growing up, the avatar had always been there dispensing advice and bruises in equal measure during their weekly training sessions. Quin turned away. She was old enough to be solving her own problems.

"Well, Quinny, are you coming in?" Gardanath sauntered into the center of the small arena. He wore a plain brown kilt and an unbleached tunic. Sweat plastered the linen of the shirt against his skin. In one hand, he held a dull practice blade, and in the other, a half-empty wineskin. None of the usual hoard of attendants clamored for his attention.

"Where is everyone?" Quin asked as she entered.

"Bah. I'm not so decrepit I can't escape my toadies when I've a mind to." Gardanath held up his weapon. "Metal out, girl. I need a better target." He glared at the hacked apart remains of what had once been a straw practice dummy as if its destruction was a personal insult.

Quin drew her sword.

Gardanath took a swig from his wineskin. "What's got you in a lather today? Dalanar back already?" He smirked and began circling, forcing Quin to move to stay out of range.

"Can you think of any reason my mother would *ever* help Dalanar and Conthal?" The question held all the fury, bitterness, and confusion she'd felt since hearing Welliver's accusation.

The avatar's astonished laugh echoed off the courtyard walls. "Your mother was Yhellani to her fingertips and so devoted to Sarael she thought the sun only shined at her command. What is this foolishness?"

"Ethalion found a survivor from Narnus. The man *claimed* that he saw my mother helping ... *them* after the city was destroyed."

Gardanath wiped his chin with a sleeve, before slapping Quin's sword with a perfunctory blow. "Ethalion, eh?" He lunged at her suddenly, and Quin danced back clumsily.

"The only way Iyana would help those two would be to protect you or Sarael, or if she thought she was. If it's true—"

"It's not!"

"If it *is* true, maybe they tricked her." Gardanath shoved the stopper back into the bottle and slung the strap over the statue of Ravendis' arm. "Let's see how soft you've gone since you left the corps."

Gardanath came at Quin with an aggressive finesse that always astonished her. He dodged and twisted with crisp precision. He seemed to know where Quin was going to strike before she did and responded without hesitation.

The third time he landed a blow that sent Quin sprawling, she raised her sweaty and shaking arm in surrender. "Rest!"

Gardanath never lost their practice bouts. A few times, she had come close to besting him, which was better than most could claim. He never coddled.

Gardanath laughed and drove his weapon point first into the sand. "A few more sessions like that will true you up. Glad Barrand didn't let you forget *all* your training."

"I just nearly died!" Quin sagged onto a bench, panting.

"That was days ago." He grabbed the wine skin and settled on the bench beside her. They passed the wine between them, drinking in silence.

Quin's shoulders relaxed as the alcohol eased through her. It felt natural to be beside Gardanath, muscles burning from a vigorous training session, and bruises slowly staining her skin. The best of her time with the Ravendi. She smiled at the memories.

"Better," he said. He popped the joints in his neck and slouched back against the wall. "I knew an Idgari general once I hated beyond reason. She killed more of my troops during the attack on Idgar Castle than I lost in a year before. Blue eyes and a figure to make a man's hands sweat. Ran into her some months after the siege. Seems she hated me almost as much, but damn did we get along fine in bed."

Quin squinted at him suspiciously. "I don't understand your point."

"Ach, don't act innocent. You and the sorcerer. One thing I've learned about Yhellani: if you're not 'worshiping the goddess', you're thinking about it."

"And the Ravendi are different?"

He grinned. "We think about fighting, too."

"This is nothing like you and your Idgari."

"Is this love?" He looked bewildered.

"No. There will not be a bed."

"Pity." Gardanath sighed lustily. "I met her before my investment, of course. We had two fine, strong daughters. Long dead now.

"Things were simple before I became an avatar. I was a general. I had a family. I knew Throkar would come for me at the proper time, and those I loved wouldn't pass through the gates before me. That was the natural order."

Quin listened quietly, afraid to move lest she break the moment of intimacy between them. Gardanath had never spoken of the time before his investment. She hadn't known he was married when it happened. Had his family been proud or terrified about his change?

"Having a goddess take over half your head alters everything. Corrupts everything. You cling to the remaining scraps of being to prevent *them* from taking it away. Before the investment, life was a bounty wasted at leisure. After...." He laughed harshly. "That's what has us spooked by this staff, Quin. We've become used to letting go of everything but ourselves. The damned thing deprives us of even that.

"It could be different for Sarael. Now, don't prickle. I mean no offense. I'm just saying she was simple when she was taken. Yhellania didn't want to rip her servant's mind into pieces, I'd guess. But Ravendis and Throkar don't care as much for that as for their shiny prizes."

He drained the wine skin and held it absently by the strap. "Things were good back in the day...." His voice trailed off, lost in his thoughts.

Quin had never considered what becoming an avatar meant for Gardanath or Conthal. They always existed. The Ravendi had been a celebrated general before his investment, and he was selected later in life than the others. How did he survive his loved ones growing old and dying generation after generation?

Maybe Sarael had been wise never to bear children. She initially worried about passing on her illness to her offspring and asked her handmaidens to take her part in the festivals. But perhaps Sarael knew such endless loss would be too much to bear.

To share your mind with a god. Not to share, to sacrifice. Horrifying. What part did they give up? Memories? Feelings? For someone like Gardanath, it must have been devastating. Why would anyone accept such an offer? No wonder they were mad.

Gardanath shook his head and glanced around as if worried he had been overheard. "You didn't come here to hear an old man maunder on about things that happened before your grandmother's grandmother was born. What is it?"

"We need help. *I* need help."

"For a price, anything is possible." He winked at her.

The sun hung low over the city, casting everything in a harsh, bloody light and sending green-tinted shadows into the cracks and crevasses of the stonework.

"Do you know any non-Throkari sorcerers? Are there any in the corps I could talk to?"

"Bloody little good comes from magic. Don't want that sort in my business, and I don't want my soldiers thinking they can depend on them. Why do you want one?"

"Dalanar is up to something to do with the Summer Festival, but we don't know what, and we don't know how to fight him. We also know nothing about the staff. Ethalion said someone at the university discovered it. Maybe they know more. We need to send someone to ask the sorcerers for help, but Sarael won't let anyone leave. She's being unreasonable."

"That's Sarael for you. Can't tolerate change. Badgered her for years, trying to get her to choose a new handmaiden after Iyana's death. Sarael refused, even with the famine. Only women from your family are handmaidens, and that was the end of it.

Things are happening too fast now. She's frozen."

"The festival is only a month away. We don't have much time. Would you talk to her? Get her to unbend and let us do our job to protect her?"

"Ha! Get an avatar to unbend? That'll cost you." He paused dramatically. "At least pretend to give Kalin another chance after the redhead debacle."

"Pretend?" Quin asked dubiously.

"You did reject him."

"I turned down his marriage proposal, because we don't have any children. The Yhellani would riot if I married before I got pregnant."

"Foolishness." He snorted. "And the redhead?"

"You know what archers are like. He's been punished enough."

HUNGER DROVE QUIN TO the kitchens. She was always ravenous after training, and had missed the midday meal. Dalanar sat at the scarred work table. Despite the heat blasting from the ovens lining the walls behind him, the sorcerer showed no signs of discomfort. He chewed a piece of dried beef, and held a slender book open in the other hand. He looked up when Quin peered through the doorway.

He had made it back. It was appalling to feel responsible for Dalanar, even so, a small burden eased from Quin's mind when she saw him. Any worry was absurd; he was devastatingly capable of defending himself. Military loyalty could not be ignored, however illogical or inappropriate.

Dalanar set his book aside. "A delightful surprise to see you again so soon, handmaiden." He spoke without the slightest hint of sarcasm.

Quin grunted. Did Iyana think she was helping the Yhellani

by working with him? Dalanar's question in the tent haunted her. Did she want to ask what happened? Desperately. But never from him. She checked the position of her sword before entering.

The cooks at the far end of the room glanced up from their tasks with wide eyes, and pursed lips. No doubt worried a fight would break out in their tidy kitchen. Fire and blood spattering the shiny copper pots. Quin savored the image.

Dalanar shifted in his chair. "To what do I owe this pleasure?"

"There's no need to carry on this farce when no one can overhear us."

The sorcerer nodded and selected a branch of burgundy-colored grapes from the bowl beside him. "You look parched. Do you want some fruit? They are exceptionally sweet this year."

"I want you dead."

"I may not be overly familiar with such things, but I don't believe that is the way one typically greets an admirer."

Quin balled her fists and bent over until their faces were a hands-breadth apart. "What do you want?" The heat from his body made her skin prickle with remembered pain.

Dalanar rose and stepped around the table to stand before her. Quin resisted the urge to retreat. She yearned to grab her dagger, and plunge the blade into his stomach. She was fast, but was she quicker than his magic? It would be worth Ravendis' wrath to rid the world of him.

"I can't simply be a man desiring an attractive woman?"

"Not between you and me."

He gave a soft laugh. "That is true, Quinthian. There is nothing simple here." He looked into her eyes and she was transfixed again by the blackness.

A mixing bowl clattered in a stone wash basin. She jerked guiltily.

He smiled. Quin fled.

CHAPTER EIGHTEEN

KALIN WATCHED QUIN CLIMB the stairs on her way up to the manor. She stared down at her feet, rubbing her shoulder like a veteran with a weather-wise ache. The aftereffect of Dalanar's tainted mark and brutal attack. Kalin clenched his hand around the hilt of his sword and squeezed until a blister ruptured. He would make the sorcerer suffer in return. At least Kalin was there to help her now. She didn't have to deal with the monster alone.

"Hello, Quinny."

She started in surprise, and had to tilt her head to meet his eyes. He moved down until he matched her height. Her smile didn't smooth the slight crease between her eyebrows.

"Hello, K." Some of her usual humor returned, brightening her expression.

Quin wasn't aggressively beautiful, like Eulesis. Didn't have his mother's brashness or bold grin. Quin had a subtle allure, like the scent of a flower on the night air. She viewed the world with large, thoughtful eyes, and an unshakable sense of justice he envied. The Yhellani cadet who knocked him into the sand with her training blade still held his heart.

Kalin took her hands. "Come with me."

Quin peered around hesitantly. People stared at them,

some whispering. Kalin shrugged. He had been the topic of gossip for months. He couldn't remember a time he wasn't. Being Gardanath's son singled him out for a level of scrutiny other Ravendi didn't have to cope with.

"They're jealous we're together. Best looking soldiers in Csiz Luan."

She rolled her eyes. "How do you fit all that ego in your armor?"

Kalin tugged her hand again, and led her on the faint path encircling the hill on which the manor perched. The outcrop of land sloped on one side, but formed a sheer rock face on the other. It left room between the administration buildings and the inner walls of Gardanath's compound for a small park.

Kalin pulled her down one of the trails. Ocher and brown pine needles from seasons past softened their footfalls. Sunlight slid through gaps in the branches, and the beams reflected off motes of pollen. The smell of hot sap saturated the woods, broken by whorls of cooler, mossy air from a trickle of a stream.

"Everywhere I go people are whispering about Dalanar and the festival." Quin caressed the thick bark of a tree.

"If we didn't gossip, we'd have to spend the time drilling. You know that." Kalin raked his fingers through his blond curls and leaned against the tree beside her. "I've missed you."

Quin wrapped her arms around him and laid her head on his chest. She fit perfectly under his chin. Kalin brushed his lips across her temple.

"Remember the place we used to go?" He stroked her side and nuzzled her below her ear.

Quin studied him, eyes half-lidded, as if the dappled sunlight was too intense. "I remember."

The mossy depression, formed by an uprooted tree, lay behind a finger of rock close to the wall of the manor compound.

They found it a necessary retreat as youths needing to escape the watchful eyes of their captains, and later, as a way to be alone for more intriguing pastimes.

Everyone complained about Gardanath's obsession with capes as part of the Ravendi uniform. Kalin was grateful for the frivolous thing as he spread the cloth over the ground.

Quin frowned. "We shouldn't do this. I shouldn't put you at risk. Dal—"

"Shh. No one has ever found our spot. If he does, I'll kill him." He unbuckled his sword belt and threw it down beside them. Quin laid her weapons on a pillow of moss. She still used the dagger he gave her at their first Summer Festival.

"Now." Kalin hooked a finger in the waistband of her pants. "I want to see what he did to you." He unbuttoned Quin's vest and slid the fabric down her arms, exposing the smooth skin of her stomach. A halter, knotted at neck and waist, bound her breasts and half-hid the scar. Kalin traced the edge of her ribcage as he reached behind her to pull the ties loose.

Quin studied his reaction, lips pursed. She obviously expected more than lustful admiration. He forced himself to inspect the handprint over her collarbone.

The mark possessed a misty quality, appearing to have a depth beyond the surface of her skin. Not precisely black, but it consumed light like a rainy twilight. Kalin tried not to let the disquiet show on his face. "That's something."

She cuffed his shoulder.

Kalin laughed and kissed her neck and breasts lavishly in apology. She tugged at his uniform, and soon they were wrapped in the cloak, their clothes scattered around the clearing.

By the gods, he'd missed her. Nine months was too long to be apart. Despite what some people assumed, they had no vow of fidelity. With her responsibilities and their lengthy separations, such a demand would be unreasonable. She was Yhellani. But Quin. His Quin. He loved the smell of her hair. How she fit against him. The gentle tug of her teeth on his earlobe. Her long, long legs.

"Yhellania," Quin whispered. "Give us your blessing."

Kalin smiled at the Yhellani prayer. He'd missed that, too.

Quin moaned, low and sweet, when he ran his hand up her spine. She pushed him onto his back, and he forgot to think about anything else.

"How did this start with him?" Kalin asked later. He held her close, her body nestled against his, an errant sunbeam warming their grove.

Quin grumbled and laid her cheek on his chest. "The meddling of the gods, as far as I can tell. We assumed he and Conthal were returning to Utur on the Great Road, so we turned toward Crador. I found Dalanar at an inn. The result was ... unpleasant. And now these threats about the festival. He's as deranged as his master."

Her words were flippant, but he could see the truth. Quin was no better at hiding her emotions than an Enng cadet, even after Gardanath's coaching. He also doubted the sorcerer was insane. They were quiet as Kalin unraveled her braids, loosening the strands and spreading her hair over their intertwined bodies. He delighted in the silken warmth.

At last, Quin spoke, "they're up to something, but what? I can't figure out what he would get out of being the consort. Or how to stop him."

"Are you sure his interest isn't sincere?"

She scowled. "He's been celibate for twenty years. Sarael gave him the gift of banishing his Fever. What does he do? He eats. He doesn't pursue a lover. He's not interested."

"That must offend your sensibilities. To pass up the opportunity for sex?" He smirked. "How unnatural."

"He is a Throkari," Quin said flatly.

Kalin chuckled and continued untangling the soft waves of her hair. "What are you going to do?"

"I don't know. I fought beside him, and his powers are terrifying. He can reduce people to ash with a touch." She shuddered and curled closer. "Sarael won't let us do anything to protect ourselves. To learn how to defend against him. He could be planning to make the festival a bloodbath."

"His plans are ruined. Gardanath is bringing in the corps and the other avatars. They won't allow anything terrible to happen."

"His plans *should* be ruined. If being allowed to attend was their goal, then why is he still acting like he wants to be the consort?" She fell silent, running her hands idly over his chest. "Kalin, what if he intends a repeat of Narnus?" Quin impatiently wiped her eyes with the palm of her hand.

Narnus. This time with Quin murdered instead of her mother; the Chapterhouse and its people burned down to the bedrock.

He sat up and gathered her into his lap. She must have kept this speculation from Sarael and the others. Kalin rocked her, whispering soothing, and meaningless words. He smoothed her hair and tried to ease her mind in the only other way he knew how.

ONE BENEFIT OF THE mark Dalanar placed on the handmaiden was the ability, when focusing, to sense in which direction she was located. Unbidden, he also detected the surface residue of strong emotion and an occasional whisper of thought or intent. It was the trickle of background noise blossoming into a rush of passion that jolted him out of his quiet study.

Dalanar gasped at the sensation, startling a man who swept

nearby. The custodian retreated around a corner and emitted a nearly inaudible whimper. Dalanar slammed the book shut. Quinthian was disobeying his one command, his one threat, and no doubt with that mop-headed cow Gardanath sired. He had no desire to experience her religious ... frolicking through the connection, thus his completely reasonable request that she abstain. Why had he trusted a Yhellani to behave with any self-discipline?

Another shudder made him pause in the door to the blue suite. He closed his eyes and focused on the bond between himself and the woman. Her presence pulled like a loadstone—beneath him and to the east.

"Is there another floor of rooms under this one?" he snapped at the man who had timidly started sweeping again.

"Nn-no."

"What is located in that direction? Below the manor?" Dalanar pointed toward where he felt her strongest.

The man arched away from his finger. "The wall of the compound, the park, the tailoring district—"

Dalanar jerked his head. Ravendis' truce didn't apply to personal grudges between two men over a woman, he decided. The Throkari weren't at war with the Ravendi. There would be no political confusion when he tore Kalin's guts out of his body and made him eat his own liver.

After several minutes of searching, Dalanar found the trail behind the administration building. Large shrubs grew across the faded path, and he resisted the urge to burn down the entire grove as he shoved though the boughs. He muttered curses about nature and the benighted things that lived outdoors. The trails twisted and overlapped, making the park seem larger than the space it occupied.

Dalanar followed the sensation of drowsy contentment to a

corner by the wall and paused. He heard voices, muffled by moss and mounded earth. Instead of the insipid pillow talk he expected, they discussed Narnus.

He froze.

Narnus.

Bodies crushed and torn. Hundreds dead. A thousand? He didn't know. Everything covered in gray ash. Iyana's face, her skin streaked where tears washed away the fine dust. The burn marks from his geis on her cheek. Eyes like sunlight on a glacial lake, watching him with bravery and defiance.

Dalanar's wrath faded and his shoulders slumped. He should be pleased the Yhellani Handmaiden wept in terror over his machinations. When he was younger, he would have laughed about it with Conthal. Since Narnus, he realized making people cower in fear was a hollow victory. It didn't mean you were worthy of respect.

He drew in a deep breath and walked back the way he had come.

One disadvantage to the mark Dalanar placed on Quinthian was that he couldn't silence the feedback of strong emotion that passed through the link. When her quiet tears turned to renewed passion behind him, he gritted his teeth and attempted to ignore it.

CHAPTER NINETEEN

T HE AVATARS GATHERED AFTER dinner, more out of habit than a desire for each other's company. Another storm had blown up, and they remained inside all day. The enforced proximity soured their tempers; conversation was stilted and tense.

Quin crossed her arms, stared out the window, and wished she could be anywhere else. She spent the afternoon failing to learn basic Yhellani healing practices; mixing poisons instead of antidotes, twisting bandages, and poking herself with needles while sewing sutures. All under the sarcastic tutelage of Father Jol.

Remembering the recipes was easy; Quin had a knack for recalling things she read. Knowing some formulas didn't grant the patience or skill required for healing, though. She drained her wine glass and poured another cup from the pitcher.

Quin settled deeper into her chair and glumly considered the others. Sarael was distracted and quiet. Gardanath had gone well past drunk, and Eulesis occupied her usual spot at his side. They whispered to each other, and Quin was quite certain she didn't want to hear their conversation. Dalanar read at the desk, while Conthal paced, watching the rain sheet across the darkened city.

With a resigned sigh, Sarael broke the silence, "We need to do something about Morgir."

"What would you have us do about a god, dear sister?" Gardanath twirled a dagger between his fingers.

"He isn't regaining his senses. You heard the last messenger. Someone needs to intervene."

"Are you suggesting one of us should go? With a staff-wielding, avatar-murdering maniac wandering around?" Conthal's bow-shaped lips twitched up. "I don't believe Throkar would allow it. I imagine your gods love you almost as much."

Sarael grimaced as if she just swallowed one of the medicines Quin attempted to blend earlier. "I'm going to send Quinthian. She will represent us and offer Morgir our condolences. As handmaiden, she can also try to persuade him to select a new avatar."

Quin struggled to hide her jubilation. A chance to be free of Csiz Luan—the avatars, Dalanar, the gossip. She could visit the university to seek aid.

Gardanath jerked his head. "Superb idea, Sarael. If you don't mind, I'll send Eulesis to pass along our sympathies. We'll invite Morgir to come to the festival, too. If paranoia is preventing him from investing someone new, we'll make certain the Chapterhouse is the safest place on the continent. He'll have no excuses."

Quin's excitement faded. Eulesis was a fine companion, but would she object to Quin's plans? She eyed the blonde curled up on the large chaise beside her commander. Eulesis winked.

Conthal watched the exchange suspiciously and turned to regard Dalanar. "I would not want to be remiss in offering our condolences on such terrible loss. We should make this a collaborative venture. I offer up my own handmaiden, as well. Won't the world shudder in wonder at our solidarity?"

"No!" Quin gripped her cup so hard, small indentations

formed. To be quartered near the man was bad enough, but to travel with him? Which god hated her?

"We are well aware of your prejudices, handmaiden. My Seal has treated you with the utmost courtesy since you arrived, even with your constant goading. Indeed, he has gone out of his way to heal and assist you, despite my advice to the contrary. How are you behaving differently than the Throkari you accuse of zealotry?"

Quin gaped at him. Conthal thought being rude was somehow equivalent to butchering innocent healers? Completely mad. "He can't attack me because of the truce."

"Well, girl, sending a united group is going to make a bigger impact on Morgir's scrambled brain than just two of you. If your apprehension about traveling with Dalanar is safety, I suggest we agree to extend the terms of the accords until the matter with Morgir is sorted out." Gardanath laughed. "Pretend Ravendis is watching over your shoulder, waiting to turn you into meat pie if you step out of line."

Conthal inclined his head at Sarael. "Are we agreed: no fighting, until Morgir picks his new avatar?"

Sarael glanced at Quin. "We are agreed."

"We're agreed, too! Eulesis, no matter how badly they behave, you can't bend them over your knees and spank them."

Eulesis groaned.

It would be bad enough traveling with Dalanar, but slipping away to the university would be difficult if Quin had to make excuses to the others. She considered what Gardanath said. "We don't need to return together, correct? Our pact only lasts until Morgir selects a new avatar, and then we're free to do what we want?"

"That is a unique way of saying you intend to attack my Seal at the investment ceremony."

Dalanar gave her a speculative look, but didn't seem worried.

Gardanath rubbed his chin. "No, I suppose you're right. To keep you two in company any longer than that would be unnecessary and cruel. You probably have all manner of religious matters to attend to before the festival anyway."

Quin pretended not to notice Sarael's warning expression.

Dalanar cleared his throat. "Any sorcerer traveling into Lyratrum in the current climate is risking an immediate death sentence."

"You're an ambassador for the Throkari. That should provide immunity." Irritation flickered across Conthal's face.

"I'm not sure a god, mad with grief, is going to stop and check my papers."

"You're one of my cleverest students, I'm certain you'll figure out something." Conthal paused, considering. "Your specialized knowledge will prove useful in locating the killer, as well. We certainly can't let someone with the ability to indiscriminately murderer us wander the countryside. I believe that should be your primary goal."

Dalanar closed his book with a thud.

The geis. They intended to torture people until they found their answers. A tingle of loathing ran across Quin's skin.

Gardanath grinned at Dalanar. "Virgins at the Summer Festival are supposed to wear white robes. You should have some made while you're in Lyratrum. I doubt you own anything suitable." He eyed the man's dark gray and black clothing.

Quin and Dalanar were the only ones who didn't find the comment amusing. Even Sarael smiled gently.

Dalanar stiffened. "That won't be necessary."

It would be a relief to get away from where Quin's personal life was the subject of constant jokes and table conversation. Growing up as the first Yhellani to join the Ravendi corps got her teased mercilessly. The seasonal rituals and the sexual habits of the Yhellani were grounds for a lot of ribald commentary. But the speculation, now Dalanar was involved, lost its humor. The mercenaries of the corps were hardly chaste; it simply wasn't part of their doctrine. She'd never learned what the Throkari church taught. Don't let it interfere with your studies? Quin didn't care. She just wanted some semblance of privacy.

FATHER JOL CLUTCHED AT the reins of his sagging horse in the center of the bright courtyard as Quin and Sarael emerged from the manor. He lifted his chin defiantly, while his elderly gelding pulled toward a fringe of grass just out of reach.

Dalanar and Conthal stained the pale cobblestone with their shadows and their dark clothing stood out in stark contrast to the reflected sunlight. Gardanath and Eulesis waited erect and precise to their right, already having completed their final instructions.

Quin felt Dalanar's eyes on her as she descended the steps. She pretended to ignore him, but his gaze made it feel like the seams of her clothing stood up against her skin. It must be the spell connecting them.

A groom lounged in the shade of the eaves, holding the lines to their mounts and pack horses. A few women in Ravendi colors eased gracefully around the animals and gear, ensuring everything was in place. An air of foreboding pressed down on Quin's senses, despite the sunshine and fresh breezes carrying the scent of hay and river water. The horses shifted, their tack jingling.

"What is this, my child?" Sarael asked Jol as the two women approached.

The priest tightened his lips into a firm line. "I am going with Handmaiden Quinthian. She cannot go alone with that ...

Throkari." Jol's voice was higher than normal, and it carried in the morning air.

Gardanath and the others, attracted by the comment, drifted closer to listen.

"I will not allow that ... *Servant* to accompany us." Dalanar crossed his arms and stared at the Yhellani.

Jol shivered and his skin went gray, but he didn't move.

"Father, this isn't necessary," Quin said.

"I cannot, in good conscience, let a member of my flock travel with such evil. Your soul is unprotected, Quinthian."

She usually thought of Jol as nothing more than a petty bureaucrat, not a devout Servant. Despite their antipathy, he was ready to endanger himself because he feared for her. She was humbled.

Dalanar looked at Quin and shook his head in amused disbelief. "You're not a *Servant*, are you. Is this man your village priest?"

Quin had never regretted her decision not to take the vow of Service before. To subject not only herself, but Sarael and poor brave Jol to this ridicule, because of her stubbornness. She couldn't meet their eyes. She turned away from Dalanar in disgust, but the tall man moved closer.

His warm breath caressed her neck. "Apparently, there's still time for you to convert to a better religion. One that values knowledge and learning. *We* would never forbid you from discovering any secret you wished." He stared down at the smaller man. "Stay, *Father* Jol, I will take over her religious education. You've obviously failed thus far."

Conthal's hoarse laughter turned into a fit of wet coughing.

If Sarael and Quin hadn't held onto Jol, he would have launched himself at the sorcerer. Quin placed her remaining hand on Sarael, as it looked like she might attack the Throkari herself.

Gardanath's booming voice interrupted any continued conversation. "Enough! The plan was for Eulesis, Quin, and Dalanar to go, and by the goddess' blood, that's who'll go. No conversions! We've ample trouble with people wandering around murdering avatars without stealing each other's handmaidens. Agreed? Of course it is. Now go!"

Quin whirled on Dalanar. "Stay away from me, abomination!" Blood pounded in the corners of her eyes and her throat closed. Quin stumbled to her horse, and the beast shied and tossed its head as she mounted. She inhaled deeply to steady herself. After making the heart and hand devotion to Sarael and Jol, and saluting Gardanath, Quin rode out the gate.

THIS IS GOING TO BE delightful. Thank you so much!" Eulesis gushed to Gardanath, swinging up on her own mount.

"Ach, don't let their bedroom games interfere with the mission."

Eulesis chuckled throatily, before following Quin, chivying the pack horses along behind her.

Gardanath's comment sent Conthal into a paroxysm of silent laughter and froze Sarael into a pillar of disapproval. Jol had a greenish cast to his skin.

Conthal slapped Dalanar on the back as he mounted his Nag. The sorcerer nodded and followed the women.

Gardanath noticed Sarael's displeasure. "What are you frowning about? Your kind is worse than soldiers with your Summer Festivals, and Winter Festivals, and holiday this and that. You're like rabbits, the lot of you. It would do the both of them good. Dalanar's an uptight prig who hasn't had a decent ... eh ... release in who knows how long. Maybe never. And Quin, well ... I've seen how she watches him."

"He killed her mother," Jol said. "He's an animal."

"Maybe it's time for her to let Iyana be dead, and move on. Maybe Dalanar had reasons. Did Quin ever ask?"

Sarael gasped. "I forbade it."

"Of course you did," Conthal's voice dripped with hostility.

"Nothing good comes of knowing that kind of thing. It would only hurt her."

"If she learned the truth, you couldn't control her with her hatred."

"I don't do that! I want what is best for her."

"Don't you?" Conthal asked.

"Would you two stop? Rotting void, I grow tired of these same arguments!" Gardanath's voice echoed through the courtyard.

They stared at him in offended silence.

"Bah." He wiped a hand across his scarred beard. "Let's go drink until our gods have to flee our liquor sodden brain meats."

Sarael turned frostily and retreated towards her rooms, followed closely by the Servant.

"Conthal? Or is Throkar riding you hard today?"

Conthal stopped muttering about village idiots and managed a tepid smile. "I have some research I must attend to. Perhaps another time."

Gardanath sighed, and walked up the stairs toward the darkened foyer alone.

CHAPTER TWENTY

IT WAS THE END of a long and miserable first day. The situation was worse than Eulesis imagined. Bedroom games could be amusing, but Quin and Dalanar were engaged in an outright war. If this was traveling with them while a truce was in effect, she wanted to be several countries away when the terms ran out. From the way they surreptitiously watched each other, hatred wasn't the only thing on their minds.

Eulesis tossed her thick braid over a shoulder and inspected the young woman. Quin was chopping wood for the evening fire. She wore a simple vest that bared her arms. As she swung the ax, her muscles flexed. At least the girl hadn't gone soft as a guardsworn. The familiar network of the shiny scars of a fighter glinted across her skin, and a gray stain was visible on her chest: the sorcerer's mark that nearly killed her.

Although fostered in her household, Eulesis didn't know the handmaiden well. When the child arrived at twelve, she joined the cadets, and soon became too involved in corps life to have time for a surrogate family. If anything, the death of her mother made her harder and more driven. Then came missions and postings. Eulesis rarely saw Quin. She was surprised when Kalin introduced her as a lover. With the throngs of people passing through Csiz Luan, it would have been possible for them never to meet.

"Why does Quin call you an abomination?" Eulesis asked Dalanar, as she poked at the smoky fire she was trying to keep lit. She kept her voice low, but Quin clearly overheard, as the intensity of the swearing and the hacking increased.

Dalanar laid his hands over the soggy wood and smoldering branches and crushed them out. He brushed them aside leaving the rocks that lined the pit. He considered them for a moment, then closed his eyes and whispered.

A buzzing started in Eulesis' head that was soporific and alarming. The earth stretched up and the gods reached down and they touched somewhere in her middle ear. Something important merged and crumbled.

Quin snarled at the sorcerer. "How dare you?" The woman stalked towards Dalanar, hissing like an enraged badger, covered in enough twigs and leaves to resemble a dying bush. She hefted the hatchet meaningfully.

Eulesis was about to remind her of the treaty, when the woman dropped the ax and ran into the woods. The muffled sound of Quin becoming violently ill drifted into the clearing.

The rocks in the firepit glowed with a cheery, red heat, and a rabbit, skewered on an iron spit, roasted above it. From the smell, it had been cooking for some time. A waxed canvas tent had been erected between two of the larger trees near the edge of the campsite. Dalanar's?

Eulesis spat dirt and pine needles out of her mouth. She lay on her side with her bedroll tucked under her head and a cloak spread over her shoulders. The fire made it too warm for a blanket, and she was sweating.

"What happened?" She flipped the cover to the ground beside her. Eulesis tried to focus her eyes as she checked the position of the sun. It had moved an hour or two closer to the horizon since he started his demonstration.

"An abomination," Quin said as she drooped onto her pack. She wiped her mouth on a rough cloth she pulled from a pocket.

Dalanar offered Eulesis a cup of water, which she accepted with a grateful nod. His hand had been recently bandaged. She raised an eyebrow.

"Quinthian was not as gracious. Unsecured liquids can do me a great deal of injury at the moment, as she well knows."

Quin peered up at the clear sky, perhaps wishing for rain.

"Yes, that would be the abomination, although the Throkari prefer the term theurgy. Some people can be affected quite strongly." He tilted his head toward Quin.

"You're abusing knowledge and power you have no right to use. You don't know how it alters the world or the gods. For what? A fire?" Quin clutched her stomach.

"I demonstrated a concept. One that may prove useful to us in the future."

They stared at the rocks that showed no sign of dimming. He poked at the rabbit with a long knife causing some of the juices to drip and sizzle. Dalanar set a pot of water to boil. He pulled his thick robes shut and leaned closer, warming his hands.

Eulesis wiped sweat off her forehead and shifted away from the heat. "You could melt Rynd with enough of those things."

"Rynd couldn't afford me."

Quin scowled. "You never do anything just to help people?"

"If it's advantageous."

"For them?"

"For me."

"So, that's magic," Eulesis said to forestall more bickering. She had heard rumors about sorcerers, but never seen magic used. She wasn't even sure how many sorcerers there were. Ten? Twenty? Dalanar probably wouldn't answer such a question. Gardanath preferred to keep magic away from the corps; although she suspected he had a sorcerer on the payroll somewhere.

"No, that is what *Servants* consider abomination. The language of the gods is melded with the language of the earth to make changes to the fundamental nature of being. You doubtless don't understand. There are other kinds of magic, as well." Dalanar glanced away from the glowing stones to raise an eyebrow at Quin's shoulder. "We don't want another demonstration of the geis, do we, Quinthian? Although, it is one I'm particularly skilled at."

Quin ran for the underbrush.

"Alas, Gardanath would view it as a violation of our truce, however tempting," he called after her.

"Most people try to entice the women they want into bed by being nice to them," Eulesis murmured.

Dalanar held her gaze, face expressionless. His eyes were disconcertingly dark.

"I'm the murdering, torturing abomination her nursemaid threatened her with to make her stay in her cradle at night. I am the one they said slaughtered her mother, her friends, and her fellow Servants. I've haunted her nightmares for fifteen years, Eulesis. How many poems and flowers would it take for her to open her arms and bed to me?"

"And did you do those things they say?"

"Some of them ... Most of them."

"Then why don't you leave her alone?" she asked in exasperation.

"She reminds me—" Dalanar jerked his head and turned to her with a bitter, self-mocking smile, his face and body closed. "She amuses me." He stood, poured some of the boiling water into a ceramic cup, and stalked off into the forest.

Quin returned, and grabbed a wine skin as she threw herself down. "Did he leave for good?"

"I don't think he does anything for *good.*" Eulesis stared into the firepit and rubbed at her temples, trying to ease the tension. "He's capable of anything."

"Yes."

Eulesis considered her next words. "Don't choose Kalin at the festival. Keep my son away from this." She didn't look at the young woman, but out of the corner of her eye, she saw Quin flinch.

The handmaiden nodded once in the gathering dusk.

CHAPTER TWENTY-ONE

QUIN WOKE WHEN EULESIS pressed a gentle hand to her lips. The moon had inched less than a hand's breadth across the sky since she closed her eyes. Was it her turn to take over watch already? She glanced around. Dalanar was back, leaning against a log, legs stretched out in front of him. They *were* traveling with the rotting sorcerer; it hadn't just been an unfortunate dream. Despite his relaxed pose, an air of tension filled the clearing, bringing Quin fully awake.

She slid from the bed, grabbing her sword belt in a smooth motion. She pulled on her boots while watching the fringe of forest to the west toward Csiz Luan. Quin strapped on her weapons as she joined the others by the fire.

"How many," she whispered.

"One." Dalanar was back to drinking the boiling water.

Quin turned to Eulesis in confusion. "One? Did they signal reinforcements?"

Dalanar continued as if she hadn't spoken. "He is a sorcerer, but I don't know him. There aren't any sorcerers I haven't met."

"Should we pour water on him to make sure?" Eulesis asked.

The man shot her a sour glance. "He'll move to avoid us. I've pushed him around the forest for several hours, trying to get close enough to identify him. He's clever. I want you two to drive him into me. I'll incapacitate him and find out who he is and what he wants."

"Geis?" Quin gritted her teeth. "Why don't you just talk to him?"

"While he's casting spells in my face? The last thing we want is a magical duel, Quinthian."

"I don't know, that might be exciting."

"Right," Eulesis said. "What do we do?"

They agreed to prod the watcher away from the campsite and toward a long bluff Dalanar pointed out on a rough map he drew in the dirt. It was situated half a league from the Road to the east. Dalanar would circle behind, and pin him to the wall like a moth.

Eulesis poked at the firepit with a stick. "Where is he now?"

"Two hundred paces, directly south."

"He hasn't attacked. Why don't we invite him in?" Quin asked again. "There's no evidence he's aggressive."

"Why hasn't he approached? He's spying. We can't trust his intent isn't violent when confronted."

"It must be obvious we realize he's there."

"And he hasn't come forward. That isn't honorable behavior. Is this what the Yhellani Guardsworn teach you? Are you *all* so trusting and fatuous?"

"Please, tell us everything you know about honor, Dalanar. It won't take long."

"Children!" Eulesis snapped in a harsh whisper. "Argue later. Focus on the issue at hand."

Quin glared at Dalanar and hoped the lurking sorcerer sent a blast of magical fire into his too handsome face.

"I'll go first." Quin settled her brigandine more comfortably on her shoulders. Without a backward glance, she headed into the woods, somewhat to the right of where Dalanar indicated the spy lay watching. Eulesis would go left.

Once away from the campsite, Quin waited for several minutes until her eyes adjusted to the gloom. The forest bowed under the weight of its years. Little in the way of undergrowth impeded her, but the roots grew large and tangled, especially around the bases of the trees. Dead leaves piled up in places, crunching and slithering underfoot. The scent of moss, dirt, and the faint, sweet odor of leaf mold tickled her nose. Crickets droned in competing choruses that peaked and fell without regard to each other's melodies.

The quarter moon dimly peeked past the high canopy, providing enough light that Quin avoided bashing into trees and kept some semblance of direction. Why didn't she bring a hand lamp? It was Dalanar's ludicrous idea to sneak around even though they were obviously trying to find the watcher. A lantern would have worked as well. His mind was too contorted with schemes and conspiracies to begin to have an honest plan about anything.

She had an idea. "Hello, sorcerer? We don't want to hurt you. We only want to talk," she called out as she walked parallel to the camp. She paused, listening for a reply. Nothing.

A boot thudded to her right and just ahead. Quin turned toward the sound and followed, being careful not to stumble over the knotted roots covering the ground. They uncoiled like rope in the darkness, and occupied her attention to avoid twisting her ankles. The trees grew closer together and herded her south-east.

She stopped, trying to get a bearing on her quarry. Quin's heart raced and she took deep calming breaths. The shush of a cloak being dragged across a pile of leaves came from farther on and to the left. The strange gallery of trees must open up ahead.

Quin wiped a trickle of moisture off her forehead, and started down the lane again. She stayed to one side and searched for an opening between the trees. Each one sent numerous small offshoot branches from their bases. Brambles and undergrowth now formed a tangled mess in the remaining gaps, out of character for this forest. If she didn't find a way out soon, she would make her own exit.

Someone tripped on a root to her right, but no movement accompanied the heavy thud. Quin drew her sword. The chorus of insects stopped to listen. She pressed her back to one of the oaks and scanned the gloom.

"Show yourself," she demanded. Someone watched from the darkness. Playing with her. Making her skin prickle. Damned sorcerers. She heard nothing except the sighing of the wind shifting a canopy of trees in the distance.

This was a horrible idea. Why did she agree to this nonsense?

She needed to escape the unnatural corridor. Quin hoped she could penetrate the deception by normal means and not require magical ones—*before* whoever was out there decided to attack.

Quin inspected the brambles. Barrand would be disgusted by her hacking vegetables with a sword, but she swung at them viciously. There was no resistance, and she narrowly avoided burying the blade in her leg. The brush between the trees didn't exist. She spun around, weapon raised, ready to fend off an attack. None came. Only the occasional chirp of a brave cricket disturbed the hush.

Quin had the sensation of something going awry, even of panic, but she didn't understand where those feelings originated. Nothing threatened her. As odd as the circumstances were, and as wrong as their plan had gone ... *She* wasn't panicking, was she? Sweat trickled between her shoulder blades. Where was Eulesis?

The moon skimmed the horizon when Quin stepped warily out of the illusory grove. From outside, it was nothing more than a rough circle of trees at the edge of a small meadow. The escarpment tore away from the forest floor and towered like the wall of a fortress. The dew on the rocks smelled silty and flat.

She paused to listen again, hoping the enemy sorcerer was still nearby. Instinct told her that he was gone.

Quin hurried along the cliff, trying to locate the meeting place. Whatever she thought earlier, Quin prayed Eulesis and Dalanar hadn't been caught in similar traps.

When she was well past the last point they would have intersected, Quin went further. They hadn't made it. The woods were quiet, she realized. No crickets. No chorus of insects. No wind. The stillness made her ill with anticipation. The prior anxiety hadn't lessened, and she felt scattered. She needed to focus. This must be a spell, like the illusion of the brambles.

First, stay in control. Second, return to camp and try to locate the others. Third, if she couldn't do it alone, help Dalanar kill this rotting sorcerer. Quin shivered. As she turned, blinding blue pain seared through her scarred shoulder and sent her crashing to her knees.

"Dalanar!" The name was forced from her lips as the image of the campsite from his perspective burned in her mind.

The god, Astabar, stood in front of the sorcerer, blazing with blue light. Gone were the laughing eyes and good-natured lift to the lips from the portrait. This was a god fully manifest on the mortal plane, no avatar between himself and the insignificant humans around him. His presence created a vacuum that pulled everything toward him including the light from the night sky. He touched Dalanar's temples and the sorcerer screamed.

CHAPTER TWENTY-TWO

Q UIN COLLAPSED TO THE ground clutching her shoulder. The pain went on, but lessened to a manageable level after a few seconds. Sweet Yhellania, they chased a god and now he was angry. How was she going to rescue them?

In the vision, Eulesis sprawled unconscious near the log they used as a seat earlier, her pale hair turned bloody red in the sorcerous firelight. Had the god tortured her? Was Quin next?

Where did that image come from? Sarael said the mark on Quin's shoulder was a link with Dalanar. Could he see what Quin was doing? She'd demand an explanation later. But certainly, if any negotiation was possible, she'd be overjoyed to trade Dalanar for Eulesis.

Quin struggled to her knees. After a few deep breaths to keep the panic, her own this time, under control, she headed towards the campsite. There was no way to outrun a god. She would try to talk to him and welcome him on behalf of Yhellania. Dalanar probably said or did something offensive. Quin wasn't sure about Eulesis. She could be impulsive; Kalin took after her.

When light from the firepit filtered through the trees, Quin stopped and sheathed her sword. She dusted off her leather brigandine, and tried to make herself presentable. She took the gold medallion representing Yhellania, and her position as handmaid, from her belt pouch, and slid the chain over her head. Quin only wore the necklace on official occasions, as jewelry was forbidden in the guardsworn. Things didn't get any more official than meeting a god.

When she was ready, Quin cleared her throat and stomped toward the clearing. No doubt Astabar already noticed her, but if he was distracted tormenting Dalanar, she wanted to make clear her visit wasn't intended to be a surprise.

His power pressed down on Quin and made breathing difficult as she approached the circle. She hoped to get within eyesight before collapsing under the weight. Walking felt like wading through deep water, but she pushed forward.

Dalanar knelt before the god, his face peaceful. Astabar's touch against the sides of the sorcerer's head might have been mistaken for the gentle caresses of a lover, if it weren't for the pain echoing within Quin's shoulder and the intense blue light emanating from the god. That cold power contained nothing loving or gentle.

Quin continued until the black spots in her eyes and the urge to prostrate herself grew intolerable. She backed up a few paces, and sagged to her knees, head bowed.

"Great Lord Astabar, I bring greetings from my mistress Sarael, the Avatar of Yhellania. Will you hear me?" The deference in Quin's voice wasn't feigned.

For a long time, nothing happened. Then the searing ache in her shoulder faded, and Dalanar slumped to the ground, unmoving. The god turned his fiery blue gaze on her, and Quin collapsed, face pressed into the rocky soil. He moved closer, crushing her deeper into the earth until she was certain a crater formed around her.

"Truly?"

Quin wished she could see his expression. The wry lilt to his tone matched the painting. She nudged a small stone out of her mouth and took a chance. "Well, perhaps not, Great Lord. However, you were the subject of lively conversation before we left Csiz Luan. I'm sure Sarael would have sent her greetings if she'd thought of it.

"Once you're finished torturing my companions, I've no doubt they will gladly lie and offer you greetings from their avatars, as well."

The god chuckled and turned away, relieving the pressure on her enough that Quin was able to sit up. His laughter made her inexplicably joyous. She couldn't help but join him even while wiping the blood from her nose and lips where the rocks cut them.

"I merely wished to introduce myself to whoever did that." He pointed down at the firepit. "Reality shifted around me many fathoms away. It's a disconcerting feeling when you're not entirely part of this reality to begin with."

"As I've said myself, Great Lord. You only needed to ask. We would have told you."

"I know this man." Astabar turned to gaze down at Dalanar. "He is ... intriguing. This was his doing? A master sorcerer who can speak the language of the world?"

Alarm traveled up Quin's spine. Why would Astabar care about Dalanar? "Yes, Great Lord that is what I've heard. He's the Seal of the Avatar of Throkar, and a priest of the Throkari religion. He is an evil man. He's murdered countless innocent Yhellani and tortured even more."

The god turned blue-lit eyes upon her. They had less impact, and she could stay kneeling. "You are fond of that word, torture, but plainly you don't know what it means." He pushed Dalanar over onto his back with a foot, and studied him in the light.

"The position of Seal, is an assistant to the avatar? It's administrative? What happens to Throkari priests when they leave the order? He's pretty, don't you think?"

"Great Lord, you should ask him these questions. He'll provide the correct answers. I don't wish to mislead you in any way with my ignorance."

The god inclined his head. "But is he pretty? Would you mate with him?"

Quin stared at Astabar in incredulous horror. Even here, in the middle of the woods, talking with a new god, her personal life was still being discussed. "No!"

Astabar's face fell. "Oh. Why not? Is it something easy to fix? I don't like his eye color, myself. But I think I can change that."

A different kind of horror arose inside Quin. "You're searching for an avatar," she whispered.

The god regarded her with surprise. "Of course. What did you suppose we were talking about?"

She covered her mouth to prevent a scream from escaping. "Not him! Please, Great Lord, not him."

"I'm sure you're nice as an administrator for Sarael, but I'm not certain your opinion can be trusted on these matters. I'm going to ask the other one."

Quin could no longer speak. The god's will made her mute.

Astabar bent over the sprawled Ravendi. He touched the soldier's temple with a finger and her eyes flashed open. She buried her head in her arms.

"Now, Eulesis, tell me about this man."

The compulsion in the god's command was so intense, Quin felt the urge to tell him everything *she* knew about the sorcerer. Only the forced silence prevented her from listing every crime he had committed.

Eulesis levered herself up and slumped against the log,

drawing her knees to her chest. She refused to look at Astabar. In a faltering voice, she began, "Dalanar is the Seal to Conthal. Thirty-nine years old. Manifested sorcerous powers in infancy by setting the family home on fire. Chosen to go to the Golden Darkness at eight for training. Appointed Seal and ordained to the Throkari priesthood at twenty-three. He became a full master at twenty-seven. Obedient to the avatar, although not necessarily a devout Throkari. Details of his personal life are unknown, but assumed to be similar to other sorcerers - no lovers and few friends."

The report shouldn't have surprised Quin, considering Gardanath's network of informants, but some of the information was new. She frowned at the woman. Why hadn't they told her?

"And would you have relations with him?"

Eulesis' mouth dropped open.

Astabar stalked over to the unconscious man, lifted his head up by the hair, and tilted Dalanar's face toward her. "Why is this a difficult question? Do humans find him attractive or not?"

"Yes, Great Lord. However, most fear or hate him, and that counters any desire they might have for his appearance."

He considered her answer. "I shall think on this. We may have to work on his behavior."

The god touched Dalanar's forehead, as he had with Eulesis, but the sorcerer didn't stir. Astabar peered up at Quin. "What's wrong with him?"

Quin shrugged. Astabar turned to Eulesis who shook her head. He poked the fallen man's temple again. No response.

"You, fix him. You're the healer." The god pointed at Quin.

Suddenly able to move and speak, Quin scrambled to her feet, legs tingling and numb. She hobbled to her saddlebags, and pulled out the healer's kit Jol prepared for her.

Maybe something pungent for him to smell or drink to wake

him up? She remembered the poison she inadvertently made and paused. His death ... her revenge. She felt soiled even thinking about killing a defenseless enemy. *Two cultists, bound by Yhellania's will.* She shook away the image. If it meant protecting the Yhellani who would suffer at his hands in the future, that was worth risking death and banishment to the godless void for breaking the truce, wasn't it? She dug through the small bundles of herbs. The ingredients she needed were missing. She sighed and pulled out the hartshorn salts. Might as well try them first.

Quin crawled to the sorcerer's side and cracked open the wax seal on the vial. The acrid scent made her eyes water, and she waved it under his nose. No reaction. "Great Lord, does he have a heart beat?"

Astabar huffed. "Why don't you know these things?"

Quin extended a hand above the prone man. Ripples of heat distorted the air around him. "He's too hot for me to touch."

The god pressed a fingertip to Quin's face and one to Dalanar's. "There. Now you can fix him."

Fever no longer spilled off; Quin moved closer.

Eulesis cursed. "I didn't pack enough food for this. Is he alive?"

Quin checked for a pulse; it beat powerfully in his neck. He needed to shave. That simple, human detail made her pause. He was an obscene monster who had stubble on his cheeks and liked grapes.

Dalanar caught her wrist and slid it away from his throat. "Trying to select the right spot for your dagger?"

She jerked out of his grasp. "You finally have an admirer."

The sorcerer gingerly rose to a sitting position opposite Quin and braced himself on one arm. His complexion was chalky. Dalanar's eyes widened as Astabar drew closer.

Quin suffered a surge of dread that wasn't her own, although observing Dalanar, she wouldn't have known it came from him. He faced the god without visible reaction. She covered her shoulder protectively. Would that bolt of blue agony pierce her through their connection again?

"What happens to Throkari priests who leave the priesthood?" The light in Astabar's eyes faded, revealing the brown of the painting. His divine presence retreated, pouring into the figure of the man before them.

The effect was disconcerting. Where the world once curved around him, now it paid no more attention to him than any other rock or tree. At least Quin could function again.

Dalanar glanced at her in confusion and rubbed the back of his neck. "Everything depends on how they leave the order. If the laicization is voluntary, the Preceptors may recommend a symbolic banishment from the Throkari temples for a year and a day. They must give up their access to the libraries and schools, and of course, not participate in the other activities of the priesthood and church. If the banishment was involuntary, it depends upon the offense."

"What about apostasy?"

Dalanar choked. "Astabar, what are we talking about?"

"I want you to be my avatar."

The sorcerer's arm buckled and he fell over. Dalanar didn't try to sit up.

"I've been here many years now, and met many people, but in you, I perceive great potential. You are also not already claimed by a god. Additionally, people will like you better working with me than whatever it is you're doing now to make you ugly."

Eulesis failed to stifle a snort of slightly hysterical laughter.

"Think about it, Dalanar. How much more can Conthal teach you? How much could you learn from me?" Astabar sounded completely reasonable. "Those libraries don't contain the knowledge you seek." The god tapped a finger to his head.

A near erotic rush of longing coursed through Quin from her connection with Dalanar. She regarded the sorcerer with disgust. "Really?" She rolled her eyes. "You are such a Throkari."

Dalanar tore his gaze away from the god and stared at her in mystification. "What?"

"Never mind." Quin grabbed her sachets of herbs and re-packed them.

"I would also change your eye color, but we can talk about that later, when you are feeling better." Astabar straightened from where he crouched next to Dalanar.

A god no longer occupied his space; he appeared to be a normal man. He was a little taller than Quin, dressed in scruffy and disreputable dark clothing. A number of dagger hilts peaked up from various places in boots, belts, and sashes. Whoever painted his picture glossed over his attire.

Quin stared at him. "You're a thief and not even a good one. Look at you!"

Astabar laughed his merry, contagious laugh. "Delightful girl, I am the god of thieves and illusions, and ... a few more things. I represent both the good thieves and the bad ones. It wouldn't do for me to live like a king when some of my followers survive on pennies."

Eulesis glanced from Astabar's disheveled hair and alley-stained clothes to Dalanar's well-groomed and tailored precision with a gleam of delight in her eyes. "I can't wait to see this."

CHAPTER TWENTY-THREE

QUIN SLEPT AS SOON as she pulled the rough wool blanket over her shoulders. She wasn't sure if Astabar's powers had anything to do with it, or the compounded events of the day exhausted her. The sorcerer started eating before she closed her eyes.

At dawn, Astabar decided they would stay at the campsite for another night. Dalanar's condition hadn't improved. The Throkari protested, but his skin was clammy and his eyes didn't track together. No one dared object to the god assuming command of the group.

Quin woke again in late morning. Dalanar still slept, one arm thrown over his face to block out the sunlight streaming in from between the tree branches high overhead. He had removed his shirt during the night, exposing well-defined arms and shoulders. Faint traces of dark hair began where he held the blanket across his chest. How did a sorcerer develop muscles like that?

Eulesis cleared her throat delicately behind Quin and mimicked Astabar. "So, not ugly?"

Quin flushed and turned away. "Where is our new friend?" she asked too quickly.

The woman chuckled and tilted her head to look at the

man with an appraising smile. She shrugged. "He was gone when I woke up. Not exactly reliable as a sentry."

Eulesis crouched down beside the firepit and hooked a clean pot into an iron tripod. She set oats and fresh water to boil. "These rocks are quite useful."

Quin grunted and folded her blanket in her lap.

"Do you think he'll take the offer?" Eulesis paused in stirring the porridge.

"Wouldn't you?"

"Never." She shuddered. "I've lived with Ravendis for nearly thirty years in the closest way possible that didn't involve her climbing inside my head. I don't know how things are for the others, but Ravendis is a cruel and demanding tenant."

Quin stared at the sleeping man. "He may be a fool for it, but he's already lost. Astabar knows his weakness. The worse for the world. Another deathless, unkillable sorcerer. I hope Astabar makes him suffer in ways Ravendis can only dream of."

"Maybe not unkillable any more," Eulesis said carefully.

Quin met her eyes. "Maybe not."

Eulesis stood and drew her sword. "Ready for your morning prayers, heathen?"

Quin snorted, but joined in the slow series of forms and drills the Ravendi used as their daily devotion to their goddess. The meditations quieted her mind, and provided respite from the turmoil of the last few weeks.

Quin had asked her mother once about the Ravendi meditations. They sat on the steps of the Chapterhouse at the end of the Summer Festival, watching as the last of the celebrants climbed the switchbacks out of the valley. Someone sang a sweet ballad that echoed off the limestone walls and even the birds quieted to listen.

Quin could barely contain her excitement. Ballads and birds

were the least of her concerns. She had spent the previous three days spying on the unit of Ravendi soldiers Gardanath sent to help the guardsworn protect the festival. Only a few months remained until she turned twelve and would be sent to Csiz Luan for training. Finally!

"They pray to Ravendis every morning. They do these drills with their swords. Have you seen it?"

Iyana smiled and gently pulled Quin's hair back from her face. "I've seen it," she said.

"And sometimes they fight each other as part of their prayers. Did you know? They sometimes go really fast. Do you think I'll be able to do that?"

"I think you'll be able to do anything you set your mind to, little tiger."

Quin grinned at the nickname. "But will Yhellania be angry that I'm praying to Ravendis? Do I have to mean it?"

Iyana leaned back and looked up at the blue sky, the sun making strands of her dark blonde hair flash with gold. "You needn't worry. All the gods know you belong to Yhellania. But remember, it was Ravendis who convinced Gardanath to take you on. So, you should probably mean it just enough that she doesn't think you ungrateful and send you back." Iyana tickled her and Quin laughed with all the joyous enthusiasm of a wish about to come true.

Iyana was dead before Quin turned thirteen.

Astabar returned before they finished, a brace of rabbits slung over his shoulder. He gave the women a pleasant smile as he checked on Dalanar. The god drew out one of his long knives. Quin expected the command to help; however, he prepared the animals without a word. He coated the pieces with oil and herbs and laid them on the rocks to cook.

The scent of roast meat filled the clearing and Dalanar stirred. Quin and Eulesis shared a private smile as the blanket dropped to his waist when he sat up.

The sorcerer peered at them with a blurry, confused look. He noticed the cooking meat and Astabar's grin, and they no longer existed.

"I should have said *weaknesses*," Quin muttered.

The god handed pieces of rabbit to Dalanar who devoured them with single-minded ferocity. Astabar offered a few slivers to Quin and Eulesis as an afterthought. When the bones were stripped clean, he passed out ceramic bowls of gruel sweetened with honey, and Dalanar ate that, as well. The man had an astonishing capacity.

"Quinthian, check him. Is he better?" Astabar commanded.

Although the air in the clearing was stifling, Dalanar pulled on a fresh shirt. The fine cloth was pressed, and tailored to emphasize his wide shoulders and narrow waist. Throkari black, like his other clothing, it hung over the loose, linen pants he seemed to prefer when the weather was warm.

He regarded Quin warily as she approached.

"Sitting would make this easier," she said.

Reluctantly, he lowered himself to the blankets. She stared into his eyes searching for any improvement. His gaze flickered down to her chest and then returned to stare.

"What?" She put her hand to her breast and touched her medallion.

"Your badge of office? I didn't realize you had one."

"I can't wear jewelry as a guardsworn. Look straight ahead."

"I wasn't aware Yhellania could afford anything so fine."

"You arrogant, inbred—" Quin reached behind her for the dagger. Astabar placed his hand over hers, trapping it.

"Dalanar, I begin to understand why this fine woman

doesn't like you. You have no finesse. No charm. What you meant to say was, 'What a lovely pendant'." The god leaned closer. "That *is* quite nice."

The acquisitive gleam in his eyes made Quin nervous, and she tucked the necklace inside the shirt next to her skin.

"It's old," she told him defensively. "A gift to the Order from the queen of Terrisea for healing the crown princess. I suppose each Seal is given a new ring?"

Dalanar held out his left hand and examined the heavy gold signet on his middle finger. An image of the Great Tree was cleverly engraved into the face creating the illusion that it floated above the surface. "This is my second one. Sorcerers are hard on metals, especially fire casters." The man looked embarrassed.

A feeling of unreality overwhelmed Quin. She was comparing badges of office with Dalanar while camping in the forest with a god, and she'd only wanted to kill the sorcerer *once* during the conversation.

Quin sagged to her knees, head spinning, and vision muddled. She rubbed her forehead to dispel the dizziness. Maybe she hadn't recovered from yesterday, either. Was that a flicker of concern she saw in Dalanar's expression? She shook her head to clear it.

Astabar turned to Eulesis, eyes alight with interest. "What is your badge?"

Quin realized she didn't know. "It must be useful, like a weapon or shield."

The Ravendi mumbled something. Dalanar wheezed with his dry chuckle.

"What?" Astabar asked.

Eulesis grimaced. "It's a big garish medal, with a bright blue sash. Gardanath makes me trot the rotting thing out for formal presentations to the corps. I look like a prize pony at the clan fair."

Quin choked back a laugh. "That ribbon is your badge as second-in-command? I thought it was some weird uniform."

Eulesis sighed. "Gardanath and his uniforms."

Dalanar pressed his hands to the sides of his head and doubled over. Astabar hissed at Quin, and she edged closer to the sorcerer. He didn't acknowledge her.

She reluctantly put her hand on the back of his neck and massaged the tense muscles as Sarael had shown her. She muttered a small prayer for help in healing and hoped not to be struck down for blasphemy. Nothing happened.

"What did he do to you?" she whispered in Dalanar's ear.

He continued to rub his temples and didn't reply.

"It was like a geis ... although different somehow."

He tilted his head to peer up at her with narrowed, unfocused eyes. "How do you know?"

Quin shrugged. "Isn't that what your spell does?"

"No. You shouldn't have felt anything."

She saw his focus turn inward. "Don't worry about it now! Did he geis you?"

"If geis is a rapier, what he did is a rusty plow. Something is ... damaged."

Quin stared at him for a long time then lifted his chin until he looked at her. His eye whites were bloodshot and his nose bled. The blackness of his irises made it difficult to tell if his pupils were dilated, although they tracked correctly again.

"I only have some basic herbal knowledge, and a few prayers," she reminded him. "And I have no desire to spend my afterlife attempting to explain any prayers I submit on your behalf."

"Doesn't Yhellania offer compassion and forgiveness?" he mocked softly.

"Compassion is easy. She's still working on trying to pardon you for joining the Throkari priesthood. She has years of forgiveness to go before catching up to current events." Quin considered. "Could Astabar heal you? He's one of the few gods who doesn't wish you dead."

Dalanar recoiled. "I don't want him near me. He's a butcher." The blood from his nose reached his lip and Quin handed him a spare bandage.

"Can you do any magic? Theurgy ... to fix yourself?" Quin felt dirty saying the word.

"Quinthian, my brain is broken. I'm afraid to turn my head too quickly in case gray liquid starts spilling out of my ears. The last thing I want to do is channel the power of creation through it. The other magics are not particularly useful for healing."

"Would you accept a Yhellani prayer? I doubt it will work for you, and we could both be struck dead. She's already annoyed with me, however ... I can *try*."

"Angry with you?" His lips twitched into a brief semblance of a smile. "Let's test those herbs first. I know some herbalism. What do you have?"

Quin pulled her pack closer.

They concocted a bitter, nasty-smelling tea they hoped would help stop any bleeding within his brain. He managed to swallow it without too much gagging and lay down on top of his blankets. He lapsed into a light doze.

Astabar fretted. "Is he better yet?"

Quin regarded him with astonishment as she rose from kneeling beside the sorcerer to stretch her legs. "Whatever you did hurt him badly. Don't do that to people."

The god scoffed. "He uses that spell all the time."

"He shouldn't. It's monstrous."

"Eulesis is fine." Astabar gestured to the soldier, who was oiling her leather armor. The woman winced.

Quin frowned and bent to prepare some willow bark tea for

her. "If you won't listen to me, talk to Dalanar before doing it again. Goddess help me, perhaps there's a trick that will stop you turning people's brains into pudding. Maybe he can teach you."

How had her life gone astray to the point she just advised someone to take lessons in the proper way to geis? Quin compromised her values within days of meeting Dalanar. It used to be easy to separate right from wrong. Now she was having to decide which choice was least bad. What was happening to her?

CHAPTER TWENTY-FOUR

Astabar paced the length of the clearing, unable to remain still. Quin and Eulesis tried to ignore him, but he tended to forget himself and leak divine energy, making him impossible to overlook.

Eulesis relented first. "Astabar, we should go hunting. He's going to be hungry when he wakes. We're still paying off the butcher from the last time his Fever broke in Csiz Luan."

The god's smile of gratitude blinded them. Eulesis put aside her leather and drew a bow and quiver of arrows from one of the packs. Quin ducked her head to cover a grin, recalling her comment to Gardanath about archers. She had forgotten it was Eulesis' preferred weapon.

"You will stay and watch him," Astabar commanded.

"Yes." She sighed and sat where she could observe the sorcerer, unable to resist the compulsion. Still asleep.

Quin pulled her bedroll closer to Dalanar. The man's head rested on one arm and the corner of a folded blanket. His nose had stopped bleeding, but a little dried blood remained on his upper lip. His face held a sickly gray undertone and shined with perspiration. It was a hot day; that could be normal. She wished a real healer were with them.

Quin *should* be learning how to be a real healer. She unpacked the kit to examine the contents and found a thick sheaf of notes in Father Jol's small, precise hand. Pages of advanced herbalism, prayers, surgical instruction, and field techniques. A quick read of the invocations made her snort as they appeared to be more for preserving her soul than helping a patient. The other information was invaluable. Quin was indebted to the man again.

She had never studied Yhellani Servant prayers. The devotions and simple appeals she learned as an adherent were far different from the ones Jol provided. These were specific. They required lists of attributes, some weirdly irrelevant, be included in the supplication. For healing a stomach ailment, the prayer needed to incorporate the time of day the symptoms began; the height of the patient; how many children they had; and their favorite season. Why would Yhellania care about such things? Baffled, Quin turned to the next page.

"You can read. That's heartening. I wasn't looking forward to attempting to teach you."

Quin eyed the sorcerer over the top of the papers. "I'm sure you meant 'Good afternoon, Quinthian, may I have more tea?' At least, that's what I assume someone suffering from brain damage would say to the person holding the medicine."

Dalanar rubbed at his upper lip. He scanned the clearing. "Where are they?"

"We sent momma bird off to find food for the hungry chick."

Dalanar raised an eyebrow. "He commanded you to help me?"

"No. Just watch. I can watch you die, as long as I do so attentively. I would be *fantastically* attentive about that. You should reconsider how offensive you wish to be."

"Habit," he said. "If it is not too great an imposition, Handmaiden Quinthian, may I have another cup of your delicious tea?"

His florid speech held no hint of the mockery he obviously intended. Quin tilted her head to one side. "You managed to hide your sarcasm through an entire sentence. I'm impressed."

The corners of his eyes creased and a flicker of a dimple appeared on his cheek. Dalanar had dimples? When had he ever smiled enough to earn laugh lines?

Quin relented and ground up a new batch of herbs. She stirred several spoonfuls in hot water from the kettle set near the rocks and handed him the mug. She figured the vile stuff would be a suitable punishment. "Why do you care if I can read?"

"Literacy is the foundation of the Throkari religion."

"We're not supposed to try to convert each other."

"True." Dalanar took a long swig of the tea and spit it out. "What did you do?"

"I substituted a few things based on my *reading* to make it more effective. You can thank Father Jol."

The sorcerer gulped convulsively. "I will find a special way to thank him, directly outside the gates of Csiz Luan."

"When it saves your ungrateful—"

Eulesis sprinted into the clearing. "Incoming." She turned and fired twice into the dim light under the forest canopy behind her. She threw the empty quiver and bow aside, and unsheathed her broadsword. She glanced at Dalanar, who levered himself unsteadily to his feet. "Rot."

The clearing wasn't appreciably defensible, although one corner backed against a cluster of trees and denser brush that appeared difficult to penetrate from behind.

Quin shoved the medical pack into Dalanar's hands and drew her own sword as they retreated.

"How many?"

"More than five." Eulesis voice always maintained the same cool tone, even in combat.

"What happened?"

"Stumbled on a robbery."

"Where is Astabar? Isn't that his thing?"

"Off chasing a deer."

Footfalls pounded on the loamy trails leading to the campsite, and several figures crashed into the glade. The brigands retreated, no doubt fearing arrows.

"I might be capable of performing some simple magic," Dalanar said. He slumped against a stump, barely able to stand.

"Don't be foolish. Unless you're about to die, don't waste the effort we've put into healing you." Dalanar paled and Quin worried he would faint. "Sit down and pray."

"What can Throkar do?"

"Not Throkar. Pray to Astabar."

The bandits must have realized Eulesis no longer held the bow, because they timidly emerged from the trees. They wore the loose knee pants and vests of the hill country villagers who lived in the area, but were a mix of ethnicities from Ryndi to Enng.

The leader was a huge Uturi woman with the same dark coloring and haughty expression as Dalanar. They could be siblings. Her hair was fingertip short and a scar ran down one of her perfect cheeks. Muscles bulged on her arms, making Quin wonder if crime was a sideline to a blacksmith position in a town or village somewhere nearby. If she left no survivors, who would know?

A motley assortment of four women and two men, wielding a variety of swords and daggers, made up the rest of the group. While their weapons weren't good quality, they were sharp and well cared for. No one carried an ax, Quin noted with approval. None of them appeared inexperienced.

The leader swaggered over and stopped out of reach. She planted the tip of her massive great sword in the dirt. Her followers arrayed behind her.

"You're outnumbered," the woman said in a musical voice.

"So, it appears," Quin said.

"Your companion killed three of my people."

"You were harassing travelers."

"That's our job."

"Not in Dacten."

"Quinthian," Dalanar said mildly, "are you trying to keep us *out* of a fight?"

Quin clenched her teeth at having to capitulate. "Take what you want from our things, and leave us alone." Those members of the band not eager to engage nodded at the offer.

The giant's mouth twisted into a contemptuous smile. "Who will pay the blood price for my dead?"

Eulesis scoffed. "Superstitious nonsense."

The woman's laugh was deep and throaty. "One of you must fight me until I spill enough of your blood to satisfy the spirits of the slain. Not him, though. He's half-dead already."

"That's barbaric." Quin examined the leader, calculating her abilities. With that strength, she'd swing her monster of a sword like a pine switch, but would she be precise? Being a blacksmith didn't make you a fighter.

She whispered to Eulesis, "Do you recognize her? Was she ever in the corps?"

The blonde frowned. "No, but we're not the only ones who need soldiers or train them."

"You're the best. Someone like her would go to you first. How about you, Dalanar? She's Uturi. I presume there are non-magical guards at the Golden Darkness. A relative?"

He sneered. "No."

"I'll fight her," Quin said, taking off the light shirt she had on over her vest.

Eulesis opened her mouth to protest, but Quin shook her

head. The woman had already fought and been pursued through the forest. Quin was rested. It could make the difference.

The bandit leader leered at Eulesis. "Sending the girl to pay your debt? Thought you had more mettle than that."

Quin stopped Eulesis from heading out to confront the woman, sword half-drawn.

"Pray to Ravendis for me?"

Eulesis nodded.

Quin turned to Dalanar. "Are you praying to Astabar? Get down on your knees. We need him back here."

"Throkar is going to strike me blind for this."

"Are your friends praying for you?" The dark-haired woman smirked at them as Quin walked on to the field. "How sweet. You must be very religious."

"You have no idea."

"I don't need gods: I have this." The bandit swept her giant sword into position with a flourish.

Quin started toward where her armor lay on the fallen tree.

The Uturi blocked her path with the sword. "You won't need that. I want you to bleed."

They saluted and began to circle. The woman was a foot taller than Quin, rivaling even Kalin. She had the shoulders of an armored guard and the broad, heavy hips of a wrestler. It felt like standing next to a mountain.

The woman opened with a lightning fast strike at Quin's face. She barely brought her blade up in time, but managed a solid block. The anguished ring of metal almost deafened her. The great sword tapped off Quin's broadsword and changed into a thrust that scored a bloody furrow under her sword arm.

Quin jumped back with a hiss. Her flesh stung, but the cut hadn't severed any muscles or tendons. Where had this woman learned such finesse with a great sword? She handled it like a rapier. Well, Quin fenced too. They could be wielding logs; the principles were the same.

She dropped into an *en guard* position. The woman laughed heartily and tried to decapitate Quin with a backswing that was a blur of black and rust red. Quin ducked, rolled, and came up at the edge of the loose circle made by the brigands. They hooted and jeered as they pushed her back.

Quin lunged in, hoping to pierce her opponent's undefended chest. The woman twisted to the left, and swept Quin's blade aside like a twig. Quin circled away. She hoped to tangle the giant up in her own feet, as the woman turned to track Quin's movement. The bandit was too agile.

Quin was sick of fighting people who didn't have the decency of carrying regular swords. The great sword would ruin the broadsword with those direct encounters. Her fights were about how well she avoided real combat, and it began to rankle. She intended to have words with Gardanath.

The brigand peered down at her with an indulgent smile. "Focus on your work. I don't want you dead, just bloody."

"Much appreciated. Where did you learn to fight?"

"Here and there. Ready for another wound?"

"Not if I can help it."

The bandit stabbed her in the leg.

Quin gasped in shock. She hadn't seen the woman move. Reaction dulled the pain and narrowed her focus to her opponent. She needed to end this. The bandit was faster, stronger, and more skilled. Maybe that could be used against her. With good reason, the woman didn't think Quin capable of hurting her. Enough to let her guard down? Quin had an idea, although it meant being stabbed again. She didn't have a choice about that either way.

Hot blood gushed down the inside of her leg when she took

a step. Quin sucked in a breath to stop from crying out. Flesh instead of muscle, but the cut blazed with pain.

She raised her blade tip and started circling. The woman sauntered around the circle watching her. Oozing confidence.

Again, the woman flashed forward, thrusting at Quin's stomach. Quin deflected the sword, forcing it to slide along her ribs instead of into her guts. The blade grated against bone.

Quin didn't wait to recover. She caught the woman's sword wrist with her off-hand and held on. The Uturi lifted Quin off the ground, and swung her closer in preparation for tossing her into the ring of spectators. Quin dropped her own sword, grabbed her dagger, and placed it at the woman's throat. She pressed hard. If the bandit did anything but hold Quin aloft, the blade would slice into her jugular.

"Have you spilled enough blood, or should we have some more?" Quin dug the side of the dagger in deeper, until a trickle of scarlet welled up and ran down the metal.

The bandit froze. "We're done."

"Tell *them*."

The woman clenched her fist but relented. "The debt is paid. Take their things and leave."

Quin held the dagger a moment longer before pulling it out with a jerk, and let go. She started when Eulesis caught her before she crumpled to the ground. The pain that Quin had held in check during the fight washed through her and for a moment she could do nothing but lay panting in Eulesis's arms.

The blonde smiled impishly. "You did good ... for a Yhellani." She gently brushed the hair away from Quin's face and scanned the bloody gash in her side with a frown. "Let's get you up. Never show weakness in front of an enemy."

Quin wasn't sure if Eulesis meant Dalanar or the bandits. Probably both.

The Ravendi helped Quin limp over to where Dalanar rummaged around in the medical kit. The brigands had already ransacked their belongings. They'd dumped out the saddlebags and pawed at their clothes and personal items.

The leader bit the inside of her lip as she surveyed the scene. She looked from the rock pit, to Dalanar's Nag, and back to them several times. She must have given some signal, because the bandits stopped looting and backed away.

The giant walked over to stand in front of them. "Why would a Throkari sorcerer, a Ravendi officer, and a Yhellani guardsworn travel in peace?"

"Why would a sword master be leading a gang of bandits instead of working for Gardanath?" Eulesis countered.

"I find uniforms restrictive, and the chain of command pinches like a bad pair of boots."

"We always have work for freelancers."

The woman blanched in recognition. She examined each of them again, lingering longest on Dalanar. "You're Uturi. I'd heard you were formed from the pits of lava and darkness under the citadel."

"You caught me on a good day," Dalanar said.

"I suppose I finally have something to thank a god for. You'll not be too disappointed if we depart early." She gestured for her band to go. The brigands looked confused, but headed into the trees.

Astabar stepped into the clearing, his eyes blazing with blue power. "You can pray to me, Magda. I am your god."

❋

CHAPTER TWENTY-FIVE

EVERYONE COLLAPSED UNDER ASTABAR'S divine force. Quin, who had propped herself up on her elbow while Eulesis tended her leg, and Dalanar bandaged her side, was crushed flat. Dalanar fell onto Quin's sore ribs.

She whimpered. "Move off."

Dalanar managed to adjust his head to rest on her hip. "This is pleasant. You should feed me grapes."

"I'll show you where to put your grapes."

Some of the bandits whimpered.

"No need for worry," Astabar assured them. "I am the god of thieves, which, from observing your recent activities, seems to be you. I'm less about poking holes in people, and more for the sly procurement of things not my own. Nevertheless, there's a place for every kind in my organization." The god peered around expectantly. Besides a few terrified sniffles, silence.

"Great Lord." Eulesis managed to lift her head. "You might want to introduce yourself and perhaps lighten the … magnitude of your presence."

He nodded thoughtfully, and the light faded from intense blue to a soft glow. "You may call me Astabar, or Great Lord. Get up, if you want. The groveling is a bit much."

Magda was the first to her feet and she gaped at him. "Astabar," she stumbled on the name. "Great ... Lord? May I ask a question?"

He gestured magnanimously.

"You're actually a god, and not just an avatar? Never heard of a god of thieves. How—"

"Yes, I've not invested an avatar and am manifest on the mortal plane. I did not exist here until recently, but that is the concern of religious scholars, not simple thieves such as ourselves."

"How are we to pray to you? What can you do for us?" Magda asked.

"Excellent questions. Let us sit and discuss them. We can prepare the deer on Dalanar's clever fire and establish a new religion."

Magda glanced at the sorcerer anxiously and turned toward her gang. They were gone. "But...."

"Oh, they had other places to be. I encouraged them. It's better to start small with a few quality adherents than with a multitude of mediocre ones. As the leader of your own group, you will appreciate my wisdom."

Astabar extinguished the last of his light, revealing delighted, brown eyes. "Would you help me carry the deer over to the campsite? I cleaned it while watching your duel. You're an extraordinary fencer."

Quin pushed Dalanar's head off her lap and sat up, pressing a hand against her ribs. Her thigh was deeply punctured. She and Eulesis exchanged glances. That kind of wound came with a high risk of infection. The gouge on her arm was long, shallow, and easily cleaned. No issues there, although fighting would be painful until it healed. Quin didn't know about her side. She wouldn't be surprised if the bones were chipped. The cut needed attention. "Who has the neatest stitches?"

Eulesis shuddered. "I can make wounds. I'm horrible at sewing them up."

"I've practiced on cadavers, but never the living," Dalanar said off-handedly while searching through the kit.

Quin and Eulesis stared at him in revulsion.

"Conthal wanted to use live subjects. I convinced him otherwise."

"If they needed healing...." Quin said.

"No, Quinthian. Conthal wanted to use captive Yhellani." The man pulled out the packet of needles and boiled thread. "I want better light than this."

Eulesis helped Quin stand, and they staggered over to the firepit. Dalanar was ashen by the time he came to rest beside Quin on the log. They stared at the jumble of their belongings. Eulesis' red, Dalanar's black, and Quin's white and brown clothes mixed with books, armor, and supplies.

"Easy for Magda to figure out who we are," Quin said.

Dalanar picked up a book with torn pages and stared at the bandit, jaw clenched and nostrils flaring.

Magda winced. "Sorry."

Eulesis sighed and set about sorting through the mess. Dalanar had the largest pile with the layers of robes he required for warmth. He grabbed his books, pens, and papers, and began packing them away, smoothing the pages, and folding his garments between them. He had such a peevish expression, Quin nearly laughed aloud.

She touched her side. Blood had already soaked through the bandage. She crawled to her bed, glad it was near the firepit. She considered making a tea to help with the pain. Too much effort. She shivered.

"Don't let your teeth chatter. It shows lack of discipline," the sorcerer scolded her.

As if just realizing what he said, Dalanar stared at her in surprise. "Eulesis...." he called.

The Ravendi placed a gentle hand on Quin's arm. "Tea, pain killer, and stitches."

Quin must have fallen asleep or passed out for when she awakened Eulesis was urging her to drink. The odor of poppy oil steamed from the mug. She drained the cup. Quin lay on her uninjured side, and black blankets ... robes ... draped over her, providing delicious warmth. She touched one. Finely woven wool and something else. Silk? It was the most luxurious thing she ever felt. The cloth smelled of incense, ink, and a faint hint of man. An erotic combination.

Dalanar sat nearby drinking his own tea, elbow propped on a bended knee. He listened as Astabar and Magda discussed their new religion. The god rotated two of the deer haunches on a long spit.

The drugs hit Quin like a wash of spirits throughout her body. She smiled at the sense of well-being and snuggled deeper under the covers. "Shouldn't you be involved in that conversation?" she asked Dalanar.

He raised an eyebrow at her. "Me? I'm a Throkari priest. What would I have to add?"

"Oh, you're still pretending you're not going to be his avatar."

Dalanar dropped the teacup into his lap with a curse. The man leapt up and bent over in obvious pain. He cast her a resentful glare as he grabbed another pair of pants and retreated into his tent to change.

Eulesis chuckled. "Manage to do that again, and he may be unable to perform the duties of the consort."

Quin rolled her eyes.

When Dalanar returned, she stroked the fabric of the robe covering her. "This is lovely. What is it made of?"

"The wool of a rare sheep from the high mountains of Utur. The fiber has unique insulating properties...." His voice trailed off and his dark eyes scrutinized her. "She's ready."

"Good." Eulesis folded the pile of blankets away from Quin's side, releasing the built up heat. The Ravendi split Quin's vest at the seam, and cut off the blood soaked bandages. Eulesis cleaned the wound with water from a basin warmed beside the rocks. Clumps of sodden Yarrow blossoms dotted the surface and released an autumnal scent. The herb would help stop the bleeding and perhaps ward off infection.

Thankfully, the painkiller was effective. Quin barely noticed when the woman wiped down her arm and bandaged it, or soaked her punctured thigh with hot Yarrow-infused compresses.

Dalanar threaded the needles, measuring each length. He ran the tips across the flame of a candle. When he was satisfied, the Throkari knelt by Quin's stomach. Eulesis took up a position at Quin's back to provide assistance.

"Are you sure you're up to this? You're a little unfocused," Eulesis asked him.

He gave a sharp nod. "I saw how you sewed up Gardanath's chin. Let's not do that to our young companion."

Eulesis grunted in agreement. The Yarrow root slowed the blood flow to a trickle allowing them to view the wound for the first time.

"It could be worse," Dalanar said, "A little ragged in a few places, most of the length is neatly cut. Are you ready, Quinthian?"

Quin clenched her jaw and twisted one hand into the folds of the covers, bracing herself. The precaution was unnecessary. The sorcerer was gentle and efficient. He didn't linger placing the needle or drawing the thread through. His stitches were firm. She only wheezed in pain when he secured some underlying muscles.

She relaxed and watched him work in a haze. He was so beautiful. "Who are you?"

He met her eyes, startled. "You know who I am."

"I'm beginning to think I don't."

Dalanar scowled and returned to suturing. "You're beginning to understand the world isn't utterly black and white, but don't think it changes who I am."

"You didn't let Conthal use Servants for his experiments," she whispered.

"Conthal's unreasoning hatred for the Yhellani is a waste of valuable time and resources. Do you understand how difficult it is to keep prisoners alive through repeated torture? Look at you after one fight. You're weak with lost blood and in shock, and they're not particularly bad wounds. You have the advantage of a warm fire with good food, medicine, and people to see to your care. A Servant in a prison cell would die within days. We would need more subjects. However, a few corpses and we obtained the information we required. No screaming. No blood. No wasted time."

Quin was silent. The man was not what she expected. Dalanar was a pragmatist. He sought the quickest, most efficient way to fulfill his goals—whatever they were. He would destroy anyone in his way, but he didn't do it out of the zealotry of Conthal or the tree cultists. That attitude certainly explained his love of the geis. Had Iyana helped him in Narnus? Her mother would need a good reason to do so; she wasn't a fool to be tricked easily.

"You don't hold the same grudge against the Yhellani as Conthal. You don't even agree with him about it. Why do you obey?"

"Why do you obey Sarael when you disagree with her decisions?"

"She's not asking me to murder innocent Throkari scholars at village schools," Quin said.

"And if she did?"

"I would resign."

"I know." His stare sliced into her. "I made a different choice."

Quin watched him while he finished the remaining stitches. She felt an unaccustomed hesitation through the connection they shared: he was lying. She just couldn't tell if he was lying to her or to himself.

Two prisoners lay at Quin's feet executed at Yhellania's command. Could he feel her lie, as well?

CHAPTER TWENTY-SIX

MAGDA KICKED QUIN'S FOOT. "Wake up. Time for training."

Quin cracked an eye open and groaned. She ached in a hundred places, and the sky was just turning the dusky blue of predawn. "Let me sleep. Didn't you get enough blood when you hacked me apart yesterday?"

"Are all Yhellani guardsworn pathetic whiners like you?"

Fierce heat pounded through her, and Quin stumbled to her feet, grabbing for the sword Eulesis left at her side the night before. It was gone.

Magda drew Quin's sword out of its sheath and examined it. "If you want your pig sticker, put on your boots and come with me. You won't need armor." The giant turned and strolled toward the rear of the clearing.

Quin pressed her hand to her ribs, trying to ease the pain. Eulesis and Dalanar slept undisturbed. She sighed.

"Isn't she stupendous?" Astabar rested against the log, flipping a coin across his fingers.

"Just great." Quin pulled on her shoes. She wanted to crawl back into bed, but was curious what the bandit had to say.

Magda waited where they fought the previous day. A patch

of bare dirt free of roots and undergrowth about fifteen feet across. It had seemed smaller. She tossed Quin the sword.

"Gardanath trained you, eh? I'm not impressed." The Uturi woman drew her weapon and began swinging it methodically around, loosening her muscles.

Quin straightened. "Among others. Any faults in my fighting abilities are my own."

Magda barked out a laugh. "You're loyal, but stupid. Gardanath is old. His combat technique hasn't changed since people were using bronze clubs to whack each other in the face. Once you realize that, you can beat any of the Ravendi-trained fighters. Your trick with the dagger is good, though."

"Why are you telling me this?"

"We might be allies for a while. I don't want someone who can't fight guarding my back. I'm going to fix the errors in your education."

"Why aren't you teaching Eulesis? She's Ravendi."

"Eulesis is Enng."

Quin's first impulse was to take offense and refuse. Her injuries reminded her it would be a mistake. To turn down the offer of training from a swords master out of unwarranted pride was idiocy. More grudgingly than she intended, Quin said, "Thank you."

Magda grinned. "It's not *that* bad. I won't hurt you."

Quin returned the smile weakly. "That will make a welcome change."

"We'll start with blocks. I want you to come at me with different thrusts and swings, and I'll show you the correct way to parry. We will do this slowly. You're not up to anything fast for now. Begin."

Quin had trouble standing by the end of the short session, but she grasped the weaknesses in the Ravendi technique. Magda, despite her gruffness, was a patient teacher. She mocked, but was willing to repeat her instruction until Quin understood the lesson. When the woman finally called a halt, Quin was beginning to feel confident.

"Not as hopeless as I expected." Magda sheathed her sword. "We'll keep practicing until I'm sure you won't endanger us with your incompetence."

"Thanks."

The others were awake and regarded them curiously when they returned. Quin gulped down water and wiped her face with a cloth.

"Fascinating," Eulesis said dryly.

"You caught that? Good."

"I'd like to hire her," the Ravendi murmured. "To teach, if nothing else. Gardanath could use some shaking up."

Astabar snarled at her, eyes flashing blue. "Keep your hands off my adherents."

Eulesis ducked her head. "Of course, Great Lord. I apologize."

AFTER QUIN EXAMINED DALANAR, they broke camp. The sorcerer's pupils had returned to normal, although he reluctantly admitted he still suffered stabs of pain deep behind his left temple. Quin took more of the painkiller, but knew she'd be just as uncomfortable lying around as riding. She offered some to Dalanar, who refused.

"We learned long ago poppies and sorcerers don't mix. You can still see the damage above the gates of the Golden Darkness, not that I recommend you visit."

Magda snorted. "Not a hospitable place, even for the locals." The woman tied saddlebags onto a horse Quin hadn't seen before. The Uturi must have retrieved it while she slept.

"Did you find out what happened to your friends?" Quin asked.

"They were getting ready to run back to the hills. Didn't want anything to do with a new god. Cowards."

"But you do?"

"More interesting than banditry." Magda shrugged. "Probably more profitable. If we set things up right, we'll be able to steal from thousands at once instead of just a few at a time."

Quin stared at her.

"You Yhellani could learn something from us."

Astabar grinned at Magda's back as the woman mounted. "Isn't she stupendous?"

To Quin's secret delight, Astabar placed the rocks from the firepit into a cast iron pot without her needing to make the suggestion.

"I take it your Lord Greatness and loyal adherent are joining us on our travels? We're only going to Lyratrum."

"More than ever, you need our help." Astabar was painfully cheerful.

"If you don't kill us first," Dalanar muttered as he swung up on the Nag. He wasn't dressed in unrelieved black. As a concession to the day's ride, he left his cassock unbuttoned, revealing heavy, tan pants. For the first time, his shirt was wrinkled.

Quin winced as she threw the bedroll over her saddle and balked at the effort required to climb up. She surveyed the campsite. Eulesis handled most of the preparations and everything was spotless. No sign of their two-day stay remained, nor any indication of all that happened. Quin led her horse to the big log and used it to help her mount.

She wore a kilt and a sleeveless vest to make tending her injuries easier. The night before, they had decided to sew her thigh wound closed, in addition to her side, since the cursed thing wouldn't stop bleeding. She had pointedly ignored Dalanar's knowing smile as he knelt between her knees, and he soon became too focused on his work to tease her further.

Eulesis handed her sliced venison on a chunk of brown bread. "Are you sure you're ready to ride?"

"The sooner we get to Lyratrum, the sooner we can be free of them."

"You'll be able to tell your children you were present at the founding of a new religion."

Quin grinned at her. "I'll let their grandmother tell them. One religion is enough for me."

Eulesis gripped Quin on the shoulder, but her face fell when she noticed Dalanar. "We shall see. Let me know if you're in too much pain to continue."

Eulesis led the group out of the clearing at a walk, letting Quin and Dalanar adjust to the movement. The cut on Quin's leg was at the front of her thigh, and not touching the saddle, but it was sore and a huge black bruise pooled under the bandage. Riding would be hard no matter what they did.

The Great Road from Utur to Terrisea formed the primary trade route within the four countries it crossed, and was paved the width of two standard carts for most of its length. The river port in Csiz Luan was a popular destination for goods, but farmers and villages along the Road used it for deliveries between settlements.

Policing and maintenance of the Road fell to whichever sovereignty it passed through. The kingdom of Dacten hired the Ravendi corps to do both. This made it even more startling Magda and her group set up in the area to prey on travelers.

When they left the trail and joined up with the main road, they passed several ox-drawn carts rumbling toward Csiz Luan.

The farmers greeted them, but didn't make an effort to engage in conversation.

A few hours of travel brought them out of the forest and to the start of the rolling farmland of northeastern Dacten. A refreshing breeze hit them as they crested the last hill, a welcome change from the sweltering closeness under the trees.

From their vantage point, the plains of Dacten spread out before them. The cornflower blue sky was scattered with fringes of white clouds that cast shadows on the fields and tiny villages dotting the landscape for miles. To the south, the capital city, Anagis, was a smudge on the horizon. Quin stopped to admire the view. She hadn't visited the country in years. It felt like coming home.

Dalanar reined in his Nag beside her. "It appears we shall stay the night at an inn. That will be a pleasant change."

"Nothing good comes from staying at inns," Quin said. "I'm hurt."

"You can take baths at inns," Astabar pointed out. "Those are good, and considering how bad humans smell, I recommend them to each of you."

Quin urged her horse into a jarring canter and caught up with Eulesis and Magda.

WHEN THEY STOPPED AT the inn of the village of Fairwald, it didn't take much urging for Astabar to convince everyone to visit the small bathhouse. Even though Quin could only sponge herself off around her injuries, it felt wonderful to be clean.

Eulesis and Quin were still brushing out their wet hair when they left the baths with Magda. A magenta and purple twilight painted the short street in eerie colors. Dalanar and Astabar waited on the porch. A procession for the dead was passing by on the way to the Throkari shrine at the outskirts of the town.

The sorcerer scanned the crowd with increasing irritation.

Dalanar turned to the bath attendant who slouched against the door frame. "Where is the priest? Your Throkari priest?"

The gawky man swallowed. "She got sent away after the last attacks on the Servants in the area. Someone burned down the Yhellani hospital. Some of our people died in the fire."

"Was she involved?" Dalanar asked acidly.

"Can't tell. We just don't want anything to do with your war no more."

"And who performs your Death rituals?"

The man shrugged. "Don't know. Torval is the first to die, since."

Six stout, shrouded figures carried the wrapped body on simple planks. Torval's white-haired widow followed, draped in a moth-worn mourning mantle obviously passed down for generations. It had been elaborately embroidered in purple and red and was much too big for her diminutive frame. The slack-faced woman stumbled along, dragging the hem behind her.

The sorcerer stepped toward the street, but Astabar held him back. "I picked this up for you." The god handed Dalanar a black robe, and a purple silk-lined hood and stole of the Throkari priesthood.

"How...?" Dalanar accepted with a nod, and pulled them on over his clothes. He strode through the crowd and into the place of a Throkari priest beside the widow.

The old woman peered up at him in surprise. He put one arm around her shoulders and took one of her frail hands in his. "I'll take care of everything now. Tell me about Torval."

Quin and Eulesis glanced at each other and hurried after him.

THE LINE OF MOURNERS WOUND around Fairwald and came to an untidy halt at the Death Gates. Word must have spread that an unknown priest appeared to perform the rites, because more people arrived who hadn't been part of the procession. Quin and Eulesis managed to secure a place near the front.

Dalanar escorted the widow to a seat beside Torval's bier. He moved to stand in front of the altar. An incense burner, a large bound book, and a branch lay on an embroidered cloth. Behind the altar, a stone pillar held the shrine: a painted wooden case where the ritual objects were stored when not in use. A purple banner displayed the symbol of the Tree of Knowledge embroidered with silver thread. Dalanar lit the incense and touched the branch, but didn't remove it from its place.

He turned to the crowd. "Today we gather to witness the passing of Torval into the realm of the afterlife. By calling on Throkar, we strive to make this journey an easy one for our departed, for the Great Lord's knowledge is needed to bypass death's final Mysteries. It is his powers that defeat death's opposing will. Torval was a man faithful to the gods, rejoicing in the light and in the dark, respecting the mighty and the creative. He treasured learning and the simple contentment of innocence. He was a man worthy of our respect. Do you join with me in calling on Throkar?"

As one, the people surrounding Quin and Eulesis gave their assent.

Dalanar bowed to the widow, who walked over to where Torval lay. She touched his shoulder, and turned to rejoin the gathered villagers. Quin looked around in confusion; the ceremony typically ended after the bier was lit.

Dalanar lowered his head again, and sang, quietly at first, so Quin couldn't catch the words. His throaty baritone held her still. As his voice grew louder, she realized he used a devastatingly beautiful language she didn't recognize. The words sounded ancient and momentous, like the speech of gods. They were, once heard, out of her grasp, as if trying to remember a dream.

Tears ran down her cheeks at the sheer immensity of a meaning and sorrow she could never understand. She realized the emotion behind the lyrics was being shared with her through the connection with the sorcerer. It poured into her from some unguarded place at his core. Longing, loneliness, regret, passion. Her breath caught.

With a flash of blinding black light, the platform ignited. The pyre burned white, but produced no heat. Within seconds, only a fine pile of ash remained. Dalanar let his voice trail off.

"Throkar has answered our prayers and helped Torval into the afterlife. May he find us worthy when our time comes."

Dalanar gestured for the widow to join him at the altar. The priest opened the tome, and they completed the information on the Death ceremony for the village records. He closed the book and crushed out the incense. The widow hugged him and patted his cheek. Dalanar stiffened at the embrace, eyes wide. With a tearful smile, she joined the other mourners.

Quin stared at him, still transfixed by the intensity of his emotions. How could a remorseless murderer possess a soul? Harbor such vulnerability or doubt? Was this really the man who destroyed an entire city?

THE CROWD STARTED BREAKING up after the old woman and her family departed. A few formally dressed older men and women lingered, waiting for the Throkari to descend from the small hill.

"Uh oh," Eulesis said, nodding at them. "That's either a job offer, or a get out-of-town committee."

Dalanar swept off his hood, and opened his robe as he walked down to face the town elders.

"Father, may we have a word?" A balding, heavyset man spoke first.

The sorcerer inclined his head but didn't reply. They puffed out their chests at his lack of deference.

"You're aware of the circumstances surrounding the departure of our last Throkari priest?" a woman, with an uncanny resemblance to the first elder, asked.

"I am."

"You must understand it was the only way to handle the situation. Things are spiraling out of control between you Throkari and the Yhellani, and our people are getting caught in the middle." The first elder turned to the others for agreement. They eyed Dalanar sternly.

"We appreciate your help. We wanted a good send off for Torval, but I'm afraid we're going to have to ask you to move along." The second elder set her jaw and stared up at him.

"I have no intention of staying beyond tonight," Dalanar said.

The balding man scratched his head. "Well, that's a problem, Father. Word will spread, and by morning, a crowd of people will be hanging around to pester you with their little problems. We don't want anyone to get their hopes up."

"What does this tell you about the needs of your community, elder?"

"Look, Father ... What is your name, anyway? We can't risk another incident. Inviting one priest in is just going to bring trouble."

"Dalanar."

"What?"

The Fairwald elders who recognized him took a stumbling step back.

"You have a choice. I can depart tomorrow, after a delicious breakfast at the inn, leaving a prosperous, farming village behind me, or I can depart tonight, leaving a smoking crater.

I'll let you discuss it among yourselves." Dalanar walked away from the gawping elders.

Quin and Eulesis hurried to catch up as he swept past. Quin limped on her sore leg. Her euphoria and confusion shifted to irritability. Her head ached after the intense emotions, and she felt like she had a hangover.

"Those idiots," Dalanar grumbled. "They chased off their priest and school teacher, and she wasn't even involved in the attack on the Yhellani."

Quin glared at him. This was the Dalanar she expected. "Servants have been *murdered* and *tortured* and they didn't have anything to do with the destruction of your damned tree. *You've* murdered and tortured them. *You've* hurt *me*."

"I know, Quin," he said with gritted teeth.

She stepped in front of him. He stopped, but didn't look down at her.

"We should accept it because we deserve persecution, but a terrible injustice is being done here since your priest was *asked* to leave her post? How dare you be angry about this." Quin stood as close as possible without touching him, willing him to meet her eyes. "I used to think you were mad like your master. Now I've seen how painfully sane you are, you disgust me with your hypocrisy and your cowardly indifference." Quin needed to stop before her impotent frustration and rage manifested as tears. She refused to cry in front of her enemy. She turned and stalked away.

"She liked your singing, though," Astabar assured Dalanar from the shadows.

CHAPTER TWENTY-SEVEN

DALANAR SEETHED OVER BREAKFAST. God-cursed Yhellani with their weak wits and compassion. What did the woman want from him? An apology? As if that would be enough. As if anything he did would be enough. He might cast aside his black robes, swear off magic, and become a simple Yhellani village healer ... Dalanar's mind ground to a stop, and he shuddered. Although, the idea of tree cultists trying to burn down any hospital in *his* care did provide a moment of amused distraction.

Quin sat at the end of the table, ignoring him while eating her breakfast. Astabar tried to engage her in conversation, but she shook her head in response. Her lovely face was bruised and scabbed in places from the fight with Magda, and their meeting with the god. She wasn't weak-witted, he admitted, however she had been raised Ravendi.

He turned back to his food. Not Yhellani. A peasant farmer. Dalanar could become a peasant and it still wouldn't change his past. He had done what he had done. He wasn't proud of it, but wasn't ready to end his life out of guilt, either.

Quin was naive. She deeply believed the Yhellani platitudes about absolution. She claimed to hate him, but she had been yearning to find a reason to forgive him almost since they met in Csiz Luan. Trusting and fatuous. He'd never asked for any exculpation for his many wrongs, certainly not from her. You needed to be repentant to be forgiven, and he was not.

And courting Quin was much harder than he anticipated. She enjoyed rebuffing him. Did his threats mean nothing to her? All she needed to do was play along, and they would both get through the situation with minimal discomfort. Typical Yhellani impracticality.

Things would have been easier if he left her dead in Crador. If she hadn't withstood his geis. If she hadn't reminded him of her mother. Some trembling, simple-headed handmaiden would be with them now as a replacement. Someone he could intimidate and who would let him eat his breakfast in peace. Quin dead in that filthy alley ... Dalanar rubbed at an unexpected pain in his stomach and set down his fork. Now she made him lose his appetite.

"Done?" Magda cocked her head at his plate.

Eulesis laughed. "He hardly ate today. He must be ill."

Dalanar didn't bother to reply. He tossed his napkin beside his teacup and slid off the bench. The common room was cool and empty, surprising for such a prosperous town, but he appreciated being able to eat without interruption. He wrapped his robe tighter and hitched his saddlebags over a shoulder.

The innkeeper appeared as Dalanar walked to the front door.

"Good Father, your mounts are ready for you out back, and our grateful community elders already paid your account."

Dalanar caught Eulesis' eye. The others moved from the table, grabbing bags, and checking weapons. Quin wore a Yhellani tabard over her brown kilt and a brilliant white shirt. Her symbol of office flashed between her breasts. She gave him a haughty glare. Where was the fearful, replacement handmaiden he wished for?

"Bring them around to the front," Dalanar told the man. He would not sneak out of the back of an inn like a gutter thief.

The innkeeper cringed. "Sorry, Father, the elders insisted."

Dalanar yanked the door open. The reason for the quiet morning became clear. A squad of Ravendi mercenaries and local militia prevented a line of people from entering the inn to meet with the Throkari priest. His reputation doubtless kept some away, but the duties they needed him to perform outweighed the trepidation of the others.

Eulesis and Quin came up beside him and looked out at the crowd.

"How long do you suppose this will take?" the blonde asked with amusement.

"I have no idea. I've never done the menial duties of a priest."

"We can still escape out the back door."

He groaned as the villagers spotted him.

DALANAR SET UP A chair in front of the Throkari altar and spent most of the morning hearing the pleas of the community. The Fairwald elders watched sourly, but they couldn't convince the Ravendi troops to arrest Eulesis or her companions for any amount of money. After the elders surrendered to the inevitable, they stationed the soldiers outside the town to prevent latecomers from entering the village. Dalanar approved. The line was long enough.

Most of the issues were administrative. The townsfolk needed events recorded in the record book—births, deaths, marriages, graduations. It was the customary responsibility of the Throkari priesthood, although anyone suitably educated and trustworthy could manage the task. This town took the custom more literally than most, and hadn't updated the register in months. Dalanar intended to locate a viable replacement and explain the requirements before departing.

He sent the few land disputes to the elders, and solved a number of engineering problems. Those Dalanar found stimulating. He helped a builder calculate the proper thickness of the support beams to hold a fieldstone roof and a miller determine the best pressure for the millstones to grind grain.

Quin and the others rested under the giant oak to observe and probably whisper sarcastic comments about his performance. He supposed he should be grateful that they whispered. The Yhellani attracted a crowd herself. Many requested healing, which she attempted to provide, but most gawked in amazement that Dalanar didn't execute her on sight.

A few Ravendi mercenaries stopped to confer with Eulesis, and stayed to visit with Quin. Dalanar heard snatches of their conversations. Discussions of past sieges, their time as cadets, and her involvement with Kalin. At least she had enough sense to refuse the brainless cow's proposal. Dalanar pursed his lips and turned to the next person in line.

A ragged boy of about ten tugged at his robe. "Are you going to kill the Yhellani when you're done?"

"We're traveling under the truce of our gods."

"Is that the only reason you're not going to kill her?" The boy looked dubious.

"No. Although, she's been quite difficult lately." Dalanar glanced over at Quin who was wrapping a bandage around an old man's wrist.

"I thought *faithful* Throkari were supposed to kill Yhellani." Dubiousness turned to disapproval.

This child was accusing *him* of not being devoted to the religion? In his twenty years of service, no one had had the audacity to question his faith, and now every time he turned a corner, someone else was doubting him. Was Throkar punishing him? Dalanar glanced around searching for the child's parents in the crowd. No one stepped forward to take responsibility for the insolent youngster.

"Who told you this? Was it your village priest?" If it had been, he would find her and reintroduce the tenets of the religion. Firmly.

"No. The Tree of Knowledge Fellowship preached here at the oak for a few days. They told us the Yhellani killed lots of people with the famine. They poison children and burn village record books, too."

"Not that I've ever seen," Dalanar said, his distaste for the cult growing.

"They destroyed the Tree!"

Was everyone determined to be contrary today? Dalanar took a deep breath and called up his meager reserves of patience. Educating the young benefited all. "When Yhellania created the world, she was to place it within the branches of Throkar's Tree. She refused to listen to his council, and she made it too big. The world shattered the tree. Some say she did it on purpose to leave humanity ignorant. Some say she made a mistake and it was accidental. Either way, the Yhellani in our villages today weren't riding around on the goddess' shoulders at the creation of the world telling her how big to make it. Your anger is misplaced."

The boy wrinkled his forehead. "How can a goddess make a mistake?"

"That is the ultimate question, isn't it? The question of divine fallibility."

The boy was silent for a moment obviously considering the new information. Maybe it would be enough to turn him away from the teachings of the cult.

"It doesn't matter why," he said at last. "The only way to

punish Yhellania is by hurting her people, and they deserve it for following a wicked goddess." With his decision made, the boy stalked away.

Although he owed Conthal for trying to save his family after Yhellania turned away, that didn't prevent Dalanar from being critical: establishing the cult had been a grave mistake, perhaps the worst Conthal had made during his tenure as avatar. Lies and unreasoning hatred were opposite everything Throkar stood for. Everything that called Dalanar to join the priesthood willingly when only superficial obedience had been required. And the Fellowship grew bolder and more influential with each passing year.

A broad-faced woman approached Quin with a stubborn set to her jaw. Dalanar sat up straighter. This woman came prepared to cause trouble. Another tree cult sympathizer?

"I lost my baby 'cause of you." She stared down at Quin, hands clenched at her sides.

Eulesis and Magda stopped talking and focused on the villager.

Quin nodded slowly. "I'm sorry." She held out her hand. "Tell me about your baby."

Dalanar didn't expect that response, and apparently, neither did the woman. She glared at the handmaiden. Anger, confusion, and misery flashing across her face.

"She starved when my milk ran dry. We all starved. Why didn't you be the handmaiden? You left us to die while you played soldier."

Great Lord, these ignorant peasants blamed Quin for the famine? Had she been dealing with this since Iyana died?

"I am so sorry. I was too young. Yhellania refused to let me become handmaiden until I turned twenty-five."

The woman's face reddened and she tensed as if preparing

to lunge at Quin. "She was so beautiful. So happy. How could Yhellania take her from me? Why did she make us suffer?"

"I don't know." Quin shook her head. "I don't know. I'm so sorry." She held out her hand again, but the woman ignored it.

"Your goddess is cruel." The woman lifted her chin and stumbled down the path back to town, following after the boy.

Quin stared after her, face stricken. She looked at Dalanar, and her expression went flat. He turned away first.

CHAPTER TWENTY-EIGHT

KALIN FOUND HIS FATHER in the manor armory dressed for practice in sandals, tan kilt, and loose white tunic. Even as the oldest of the avatars, he was as strong and imposing as men half his apparent age. Gardanath grumbled about Ravendis, but the benefits of her presence outweighed any imagined inconvenience. He was ageless, powerful, and brilliant.

Gardanath's squire was helping him into a boiled leather breastplate, heaving uselessly against the straps.

"Been awhile since you've seen the field, father."

"I could still kick your puny ass, boy. What do you want?" Gardanath gnashed his teeth at the servant who backed away uncertainly.

"I'll help him. You can go," Kalin told the man as he examined the buckle. The squire fled without another glance at the avatar.

"Coward. He's worried he'll get a beating for letting my leather shrink."

Kalin looked him in the eye, and yanked hard on a strap. "I'll fix it."

"Damn," Gardanath wheezed and pushed the armor down, settling the padding on his shoulders.

Kalin jerked the straps into place on the other side.

"Out with it. You've come to moan about your love life. I told you not to take up with the archer." Gardanath chuckled, but Kalin only mustered a grimace.

Kalin crossed his arms over his chest. "Why don't you do something? I can't bear thinking about that monster touching Quin."

"What can *I* do?" Gardanath paused while wrapping the sword belt around his waist.

"Well ... Ravendis. Tear him apart! Destroy him."

"Ravendis? That red bitch is laughing her ass off." Gardanath scoffed.

"Make. Her." Kalin's hands clenched until his knuckles turned white.

"*We* don't make the gods do what *we* want." Gardanath draped an arm over Kalin's shoulder. "I've lived a long time. I've seen this kind of thing before. He'll grow bored, his sort always does. It won't last."

"I won't let this start." Kalin's voice was bitter.

"Don't do anything stupid."

"Are you encouraging this?"

"There's more at stake than your love life."

"You're using Quin as a pawn in one of your games?"

"Damn it, boy! I didn't put her on the board. She's there now, and the last thing I, or she, needs is you thrashing around knocking over the pieces. By Ravendis' blood, I swear I will try to protect her. Stay out of this."

Kalin sagged onto a low stool. Why was this happening to him? To them? Just as things were working out, that creature hooked his claws in Quin and dragged her into some game of one-upmanship with his father.

He rumbled deep in his chest. Kalin was not going to let this happen. Dalanar might frighten children into hiding under their beds, but he refused to be cowed by a bogeyman's reputation. The sorcerer was only a man, and men could be killed.

Gardanath squinted at him. "Don't do it, Kalin."

"What?" he snapped.

"Whatever it is you're planning. I'm not ready to lose you, boy."

His father's ancient green eyes held such sadness he almost relented. Images of Dalanar hurting Quin with his scalding touch, forcing her into a game she had no way to win, filled him with fury. It drove any thought but murder from his mind.

"If you love her, stay away from the festival. You'll make the situation worse. Let her pick someone else. Someone Dalanar can't accuse her of favoring."

Kalin gave him a flat stare and stalked from the room.

CHAPTER TWENTY-NINE

IGH CLOUDS MOVED IN after lunch, as they prepared to depart the village. However, the temperature remained warm, and Dalanar didn't anticipate rain. He opened his robe to let the breeze blow through his clothes. The ache at his left temple persisted, but the day was pleasant, so he tried to ignore it. He hoped the sharp agony wouldn't return.

"What is the Golden Darkness like, Dalanar?" Eulesis asked, riding next to him. "I've never been to Utur."

Dalanar pressed his fingers against his temple and squinted as he faced the woman. Why was everything so painfully bright? "It's smaller than you might expect for a citadel with such a pompous name. A sorcerer who fancied himself a poet built it about four hundred years ago. Set into the side of a volcano, using ancient lava tubes to form the foundation of the layout. A lake of the lava inside the mountain illuminates the interior. It *is* a golden darkness. We also use it to provide heat to our living quarters. Conthal and I live there, several of Conthal's advanced students, and the school and staff. Since we never have more than a few children at a time, it isn't crowded."

"Aren't you worried about an eruption? You could die in your beds like boiled sausages," Magda said.

"The architect was a geomancer, an earth caster, of some skill. He drilled vents below the citadel to act as an overflow if the magma rises. Lava would leak out the sides and only raise the temperature within somewhat. Fortunately, they have not yet been needed."

"You showed your powers early. Why didn't they send you to the school when you were younger?" Eulesis asked.

"My father was a sorcerer. My mother, a noblewoman from the Uturi capitol. She knew I would go eventually, but wanted to keep me around as long as possible. He helped contain me. I lived in stone rooms with cheap furnishings, until I could control myself."

"Not Conthal?" Quin's voice was full of revulsion.

"No." Dalanar snorted at the idea of the avatar doing something so vulgar and human.

"The whole thing with sorcerers not having children is a myth?" Eulesis sounded skeptical.

"Not entirely. The Fevers make sorceresses barren. Males are able to father children, but once we start casting, things become complicated. However, it takes years of training before we begin to perform even the simplest spells. By the time we turn twenty we're expected to have exorcised those youthful indiscretions and be ready to settle down to the serious practice of magic."

"Is magical ability hereditary?" Magda asked.

"We don't know for certain, but it seems to be a component. Conthal wanted to do a study by requiring the Throkari sorcerers to have children. He couldn't get anyone to participate. No one would put aside their experiments long enough to impregnate a partner."

The expression of disbelief on Quin's face made him laugh. Yhellani did not comprehend someone choosing celibacy and magic over a lover. There were no Yhellani sorcerers.

Eulesis arched an eyebrow. "He didn't order you to do it as Seal?"

"That was not part of my oath."

"How can there be so many Throkari? You're buried in your books all day," the Ravendi teased.

"True, Eulesis, but we demand perfection in our studies, even if it takes all night."

"The Yhellani are more numerous because we do it right with so many people." Quin smiled sweetly.

"Rabbits!" Eulesis said, imitating Gardanath's booming pronouncement on the religion.

Eulesis and Magda burst out in guffaws. The two women had taken an unexpected liking to each other, even after their fraught introduction. Probably since they shared the same sense of humor. Soldiers.

Dalanar looked at Quin and sweat prickled under his collar. Her long, muscular legs were exposed by her kilt, the straps of her sandals winding their way up her calves. He remembered being between her knees while stitching up her thigh and shifted uncomfortably. Dalanar pushed the images from his head in disgust. He was not some randy youth with his first lover. He pressed at his temple trying to ease the throbbing.

Three days since he was Fevered, and he didn't yet trust his mind to handle the strain of casting. The headaches persisted and perhaps, worsened again. Using magic to regain his Fever might be worth the risk, if it would suppress the damned, maddening lust.

Damned, *inappropriate* lust. He was supposed to *act* as if he wished to bed her, not think about the sway of her hips when she walked or how a genuine smile—never for him— transformed her face. He'd joyfully eat dried rations to get the woman out of his head. Her soft skin, and parted lips in the faint light of dawn ... he groaned. Yhellania had devised a fitting punishment for his crimes.

Quin cast a wary glance at him.

Astabar rode up. "Are you well, Dalanar?"

"As well as can be expected...." He nodded at the god ... *for a forty-year-old man reliving the extremes of youth.*

FARMLAND STRETCHED FROM HORIZON to horizon and villages pressed against the road every few miles. They passed several within hours of leaving Fairwald, but none of the party expressed an interest in stopping.

As the sun approached the low hills, throwing long silhouettes in front of them, Quin called a halt at the gates of a small hamlet. Dalanar couldn't see what caught her attention. It was an insignificant place of three or four public buildings, perhaps a tavern, a smithy, a community mercantile, and a meeting hall. A handful of small unattractive houses squatted around the outskirts of the village square. It didn't possess a gathering tree or Throkari altar, indicating the population was fewer than seventy in the town, and surrounding farms.

They all stared at the handmaid.

"Some Servants are staying here. I need to talk to them."

"How can you tell?" Eulesis asked, dismounting and leading her horse to the gates.

Quin looked pointedly at Dalanar. "I'd rather not say." She grabbed her bag of herbs. "This won't take long. I'd like to refresh my supplies and have them tend my leg. I'll ask for advice about your head, but for obvious reasons, I want you to stay out here."

Dalanar swung off his Nag and stretched his legs. He searched for anything on the fieldstone gates or in the small trees that might indicate the presence of Yhellani Servants in the settlement. He found nothing.

Quin hobbled into the packed dirt square forming the common area between the buildings. She limped worse than before, and fresh blood blossomed over the old stain on her tabard. Why didn't he insist on checking in Fairwald? A woman spinning yarn at a wheel on a doorstep, pointed Quin toward the building Dalanar identified as the meeting hall. After a painful walk, the handmaiden disappeared inside.

Astabar sidled up to him. "I wonder what she's telling them about your injuries. That you're weak and unable to use your power?"

Dalanar snapped his head around to face him. "What do you want, Astabar?"

"I don't want you ambushed by over-zealous Yhellani seeking a chance at revenge."

"I thought you liked Quin."

"I do! I don't want you to hurt her. However, I know how she feels about you. Shouldn't you be aware of what she's up to where your life is concerned?"

Dalanar looked over at the meeting hall. While *she* was bound by the truce, this would be the perfect opportunity to recruit other Yhellani who were not. He could not defend himself, and she knew it. An arrow from the darkness, and Conthal would need a new Seal.

He turned and stalked toward the village square ignoring the calls from Eulesis and shaking off Magda's half-hearted attempt to grab his arm.

If he caught Quin breaking the truce, it would embarrass Sarael and delight Conthal. He paused at the entrance to the meeting hall, but only heard faint noises from within. He slipped inside. A small foyer was separated from the main room by a heavy curtain used to block drafts. He pulled the door shut behind him.

"Oh sweetness," an elderly woman's quavering voice said to his right. "Look at that! A handmaiden shouldn't be fighting. Your blessed mother was such a gentle soul, and your grandmother didn't know which end of a sword to hold. Here you are poked full of holes like an old dish rag."

"Mother Noria." Quin sounded exasperated.

"Where are the babies? Iyana had you her first year as handmaiden. You've been performing your duties for three. What happens if you die? Who will inherit? Isn't Gardanath's boy capable of getting a child on you? He seems willing enough, and his father doesn't have any such trouble."

"Noria!"

Dalanar pictured Quin's flaming cheeks and smiled briefly.

"Nor, I don't think Quin came to us for help with her duties as handmaiden." The silhouette of a stooped old man holding a basin passed behind the drapes.

Only the vague outline of the room was visible. Windows lined the walls, flooding the space with bright afternoon sun. In the far end, a small podium held the village journal and displayed a simple embroidered hanging of the Tree of Knowledge. Benches hunkered in rows before the lectern. Near the door, carved wooden chairs surrounded four tables. Quin lay on one, shirt open, and kilt pushed up her thigh. The sorcerer couldn't see either wound from his position.

Five Servants occupied the room with Quin. The two elderly ones who had already spoken and three young ones. Journiere healers. A dark-haired woman with olive skin sorted through Quin's bag and refilled the herbs from a much larger pack at her feet.

"Now, Mert, I'm just saying what everyone is thinking. It's not we don't love you, dear one, but we worry about Sarael.

She depends on her handmaidens. Being a guardsworn puts you at a greater risk. And no babies. Now, I've said my peace." The old woman raised her hands in surrender to Mert, who grimaced at her.

Quin inhaled sharply at something the old man did, and they were quiet for a few minutes while he worked. The students gathered around to observe. Mert directed the redheaded young man to start on her thigh.

"Quin, you said you have a patient with a head injury? We could examine him...." Noria offered.

"That isn't possible."

"Oh, the poor duck. Is he still alive?"

"His mind was damaged with a geis. We've been using a tea to stop bleeding in the brain, but he's having bad headaches."

"Dalanar?" Mert asked.

Quin started.

Noria scoffed at the old man. "Not in years. Whatever else you may say about him, his victims recover ... if they survive. Was it Conthal or someone new?"

"Dalanar doesn't break their wits? I'd heard...."

"Maybe in his early days. When I talk to survivors now, Conthal did the damage. Not saying it isn't painful, and those burns! At least people wake up again." Noria glanced at Quin's chest and creaked to her feet, eyes wide. "Is it you? I've seen Dalanar's handprint enough times to know it. Great Lady!"

"No, Noria! It's not me."

Mert gawked at her. "He didn't kill you? Did he recognize you?"

"Not at first. About my patient? How do you treat Conthal's survivors?"

The Servants frowned at each other. "We don't have a treatment. They either heal on their own or die. We're curious about your tea, though."

"But...." Quin sounded distraught.

"I'm sorry, sweetness. Is it a lover?" The woman patted Quin's hand.

"Noria," Mert warned.

Quin didn't speak for a long time. Mert brought out needles and thread, and mended some of the stitches on her side. The red-haired youth kept hot cloths pressed against her thigh. He was being a little too enthusiastic about the task, and Dalanar began to tingle with power. Even that tiny surge of magic sent a stab of agony into his brain, and he almost cried out. He bent over, trying to pant silently until the pain subsided.

When Dalanar recovered enough to listen, Mert had completed a prayer over Quin. The sound of a pure chime faded from the air. Yhellania wasn't irritated with the handmaiden any longer.

Quin sat up gingerly, retying the strings of her vest and pulling her kilt down. "I want you to do something for me," she said.

Dalanar stiffened. He had been about to leave, feeling foolish for listening to Astabar's taunts.

"We'll do anything," Mert assured her.

"Don't attend the Summer Festival this year." The entire room was rooted in uncomprehending silence.

"Don't go?" The boy's voice cracked.

"Get word to every Servant and the faithful. Have small community celebrations. Don't go to the Chapterhouse."

"Why?" Noria asked.

"Conthal and Dalanar are coming to the Festival with the rest of the avatars. I don't know what, but they are up to something terrible. I may not be able to stop them, but I will not give them the Yhellani in one place to make it easy."

Dalanar pressed a hand to the bridge of his nose and closed his eyes. He didn't know what Conthal planned either, but the avatar wasn't going to like this.

With a jerk, the curtain in front of Dalanar parted, leaving him standing face to face with the youth.

The boy gasped. "Dalanar!" He turned and ran.

The hall erupted into chaos.

Noria launched herself at Dalanar, white hair and fists flashing. Mert grabbed a bulging sack and began throwing handfuls of herbs into his face. They both yelled for the children to run. Dalanar sneezed.

The boy seized Quin's wrist and jerked her toward a door in the front of the hall Dalanar hadn't noticed. The girls joined in. Quin resisted and tried to attract their attention over the screaming.

Dalanar managed to turn the old woman around into the geis hold, simply to keep her from scratching him with her sharp nails. She went still in anticipation. She barely came up to his shoulder.

"Stop! I'm not going to harm you." He yanked the bag away from Mert. "Control your students! They're going to hurt Quinthian."

Their eyes were wild with unthinking panic.

Dalanar pushed the old woman to a chair and walked toward the door where Quin had managed to resist being pulled through. Seeing him coming, the journieres shoved Quin to the floor and piled on top of her.

"You can't have her!" They sobbed and cringed away from him, but would not let him touch Quin without sacrificing themselves first.

Great Lord. It was one of the bravest things Dalanar had ever seen. He half-turned at a noise behind him. Magda, Eulesis, and Astabar slid into the back of the room.

"Eulesis, would you get Quin out from under the Yhellani before they kill her?" He retreated to the windows, arms crossed. He glared at Astabar as the god wandered over.

Magda and the Ravendi rushed to the pile and lifted the crying Servants from the handmaid. Quin rose to her feet, wiping tears from her own cheeks. She held an arm across her ribs.

The Servants hugged each other and stared at him like lambs caged with a wolf. He looked away.

Noria stomped over to stand in front of Dalanar, scanning him up and down with a snarl. "We must appear the fools to you. You could have blasted us to ash and taken what you wanted, no matter what we did. But we'll fight you to protect our own. You remember that, Throkari." Her voice was harsh and unquavering; her body trembled.

"You were very courageous. No one has ever attacked me with fingernails or medicinal powders before."

She started in surprise. "Ha! You won't soon forget us, I'll wager. Why didn't you geis me, sorcerer? Didn't think an old healer like me would have something for you to learn?"

He blinked at her. She was offended he hadn't geised her?

Noria looked up into his eyes, focusing first on one, then the other. "Drink your tea and pray to your god. Ours won't help you." She tilted her head. "I can't imagine who would be brave enough to geis you, but they need to die."

Astabar snorted indignantly. "I didn't know the Yhellani were so bloodthirsty."

"Conthal is plenty bad. I don't want to clean up the messes from someone else, too."

Dalanar couldn't think of a reply.

The old healer turned to leave, but paused. "Can I make a request?"

He lifted an eyebrow at her.

"When you're with your master, you do the geising."

"I will take it under advisement." Conthal believed *these*

216

people were a threat to the Throkari? Where were the master-minds plotting the fall of the church? How long had it been since his master actually associated with any who weren't his prisoners? Dalanar sneezed again. Perhaps the Servants planned to infiltrate the citadel and blow their noxious powders in through the vents.

Quin ushered Mert and the students over to the benches. Noria joined them, shoving the old man over to sit beside him. They still stared at Dalanar warily and went still when he approached. They didn't flee, however, which he took as an improvement. He leaned against the podium curious as to how Quin explain his presence.

"I am sorry about scaring you. *He* was not supposed to come in here." Quin gave him a sour scowl. "Laniof was murdered, and the other avatars met in Csiz Luan. Yes, including Conthal and Sarael. They sent us, under a truce, to convince Morgir to invest a new avatar."

Quin was so painfully sincere. So serious. He couldn't resist the impulse to tease her, just to see how she would react. He hadn't lied to Eulesis; the handmaiden did amuse him, and that was something he hadn't felt in a very long time. "Quinthian, you didn't tell them the best part. The avatars are going to attend the Summer Festival this year to witness us being bound as the king and queen." Dalanar put his arm around her shoulders. Her jaw clenched and her body went rigid.

"Who has not had a chance to set a compound fracture?" Quin's voice remained pleasant.

"Remember the truce," he murmured into her ear.

"I doubt retaliation for groping me counts as breaking the truce. I'll be certain to ask Eulesis about it as they're setting your arm."

He patted her shoulder, but removed his hand. She was

probably correct.

Mert eyed Dalanar with dismay. "Oh, Quin."

"Remember what I said earlier. I meant it." Quin frowned at them.

"Won't be any babies from him," Noria grumbled just loudly enough for him to hear.

Mert insisted on examining Quin again. The Journieres stared at Dalanar with terrified faces. The dark-haired girl shuddered with sobs, although she was eerily quiet. Noria handed her a cup of tea, and Dalanar hoped it contained something to make the girl sleep.

He wasn't used to being around Servants and dealing with the effect of his presence. It was ... uncomfortable. He would have preferred to leave, as he was sure everyone involved would agree, but Astabar kept him trapped in the hall.

"Did you notice how they attempted to protect Quin by covering her up with their bodies? An unusual practice." Astabar stepped in front of Dalanar when he tried to walk to the door. "What is it you do to Servants when you find them?"

The girl cried harder and started hiccupping.

"This is not an appropriate time to discuss this," Dalanar said.

"They are quite frightened of you, and you've been nice to them. Why is that? Is this one of those reasons women consider you ugly?" Astabar turned to the girl who wasn't crying. "Do you think he's pretty?"

The Journiere flinched at the question, but was unable to resist the compulsion in the god's voice. "He's pretty, but...." Face pale, she swallowed hard, and joined her sister in crying.

"I didn't realize the Yhellani were so emotional," Astabar said.

Noria came to stand in front of them. "Is this another Throkari sorcerer?"

"I certainly am not!"

"Then why are you torturing my children? Leave, and take Dalanar with you."

Quin slid off the table, holding her ribs again. "I'm sorry, Noria. We'll go." She pulled Mert into an embrace, followed by each of the students, kissing their foreheads and wiping the tears off their cheeks.

She hugged Noria. "Please, do as I ask."

"Oh, I'll pass the word along, but I'll be there myself. I wouldn't miss seeing this for the world."

Quin grumbled in frustration.

"I'm old. If I'm going to die, I'd like it to be exciting."

THE HANDMAIDEN LED THE way outside, Dalanar close behind her.

"Why didn't you stay by the gate?" she growled. "We could have avoided the whole incident."

He didn't bother replying.

The tension eased from Quin's shoulders as they rode further from the hamlet. At last, she sighed. "I suppose I should thank you for not killing anyone."

"Why would I kill them?"

"They attacked you. They're Servants. They're Yhellani. Pick one."

Dalanar rubbed at one of Noria's scratches. "I was too terrified they'd tear my head off to fight back."

She gave him a withering glare.

"They were trying to protect you from one of the worst monsters imaginable. It was incredibly loyal and brave. How could they hurt me? There was no need to retaliate. Despite what you may believe, I don't randomly slaughter Servants."

Quin didn't respond for a long time, but finally nodded.

"Are your injuries improving?" Dalanar asked.

"My leg was infected. Mert called on Yhellania for me. I needed some new stitches in my side. You probably saw."

He didn't deny it. "Is your private life usually subject to public opinion?"

"Yhellani don't have private lives, the handmaiden even less than others. I'm used to it. Mostly. It's been bad lately."

Dalanar shook his head. "How do you tolerate everyone interfering?"

"Do we need to have another discussion about your hypocrisy?"

"That isn't personal," he lied.

"I can't imagine anything *more* personal." She held her ribs and turned in her saddle to give him a hard look. "Do you understand what happens at the Summer Festival, Dalanar?

"Well enough," he said. There was a banquet. He assumed a significant amount of time would be spent praying for good crops, or fertile fields, or whatever tedious thing they did. At some point, the king and queen retreated to the bower where they had their union. A tingle went down his back. What if Quin chose him? He shook the thought away. She wouldn't. Besides, the charade was not intended to get that far.

Quin snorted with amusement. "If you want to be consort, you'd better be up to it, old man." She turned around and Dalanar knew she was smiling smugly at his ignorance.

Astabar drew closer. "Handmaiden, what happens at the Summer Festival? What would Dalanar need to do?"

"Shouldn't you know this, being a god?"

"I'm new." He winked at her.

"Sex," she said. "The Summer Festival for the king and queen is entirely about ensuring the crops are fertile. There's a feast and the union toast the first night. A few events on the afternoon of the second day they can attend for a break. Most of the faithful consider it a better omen not to see them until the blessing of the farmers after sunset the third day. Otherwise, they're expected to be doing their best impression of rabbits."

Eulesis chuckled.

Astabar gaped at Dalanar. "Quin would let you do that? *Can* you do that?"

Eulesis laughed harder.

"The handmaiden knows my conditions," he replied curtly.

"But can you do what is required, Dalanar? Maybe you should encourage Quin to choose a younger, more experienced man. The crops are vitally important. Should we be risking them on your abilities? You can still attend the festival with your master. Maybe you can meet a nice human your own age?" Astabar sounded genuinely anxious. He turned to the Yhellani. "Have you tried explaining about the harvest? We can't risk another famine."

Quin's amused expression faded. "I'm sure he knows."

Dalanar looked away. After Iyana died, there had been twelve years with no Summer Festival. No blessing of fertility from the goddess. The harvests were barely sustainable. Few children had been born. Starvation and death followed. Conthal no longer encouraged his zealots to disrupt Yhellani festivals; the stakes were too high.

Dalanar straightened. "Regardless, *my* personal life is not open for discussion." The idea of Kalin as the consort annoyed him. He should have killed the Ravendi whelp in the forest that day in Csiz Luan. He was getting lax. Without thinking, he pulled in his power and let it sizzle across his fingertips.

Stabbing pain in his temple made him clutch his head. With a guttural cry, he fell to the ground.

CHAPTER THIRTY

QUIN HANDED DALANAR a cup of tea, and he managed to hold it to his lips without spilling the hot liquid. A distinct improvement.

After two days at a campsite near the road where he fell, and an overnight at the first inn they came to once they risked moving him, the sorcerer sat up in bed able to feed himself. How could Quin be ambivalent about his recovery? She wanted him dead, didn't she?

She took the cup and replaced it with a slice of bread and cheese. Quin was helping Dalanar even without the compulsion of a god. Was it possible her mother had reason to do the same?

Dalanar nodded to her and ate. "I'm ready to leave today."

"We need to hurry or we won't make it to the festival. Although, that might be for the best." Quin smirked at him. "There's a bath house in the garden. Call for Astabar if you need help."

"Why don't *you* help me, Quinthian?" Dalanar lowered his voice to a seductive murmur. "I'll show you I'm up to fulfilling the role of the Summer King. I want to set your mind at ease." He patted the bed beside him. "We wouldn't wish to risk the wheat."

"Are you feeling all right?" Did he have lasting brain damage from the attack?

"Better than I've been in days."

"You've been half-dead."

He inclined his head in agreement.

Quin decided to attribute his comment to those strange things people say when they get concussions. She'd known someone in Malesini who had been hit so hard with a shield he called everyone 'mother' for two days and insisted swallows plotted against him.

She gave him a weak smile. "Astabar."

The god leaned in through the doorway.

"Help him to the baths, please. I advise you not to let him prove anything to you."

THEY PASSED THE BORDER from Dacten into Terrisea on the second day after leaving the inn. The guards took one look at Eulesis and ushered them across without the usual spate of questions. Gardanath's influence spanned the continent.

They kept up a slow, steady pace that didn't strain Dalanar's endurance, but tested their patience. Astabar hovered over the sorcerer like an expectant father, and used his ability to compel the others to provide him the utmost comfort.

The god never put any pressure on Dalanar. Him, he wooed like a Yhellani youth with his first goddess-touched infatuation. He provided gifts, told amusing stories, and whispered secrets too low for anyone else to hear. Those disturbed Quin the most.

She managed to overhear one of their conversations, but they spoke a language composed of numbers and odd words she didn't understand. The discussions filled Dalanar with a weird joy she felt through their connection. Afterward, he would sit by the fire rocks scratching formulas into the dirt while muttering. Astabar gazed on with equal measures of covetousness and pride.

Despite the coddling and attention, Dalanar wasn't healing.

He had frequent episodes of crippling headaches, although no more incidents of erratic behavior.

They made camp early after crossing the border. The sun barely touched the tree tops, but Dalanar was nauseated and hunched over with pain. Magda and Astabar helped him down from his horse, and led him to a small copse of trees beside a tiny stream. The god began his nightly routine of unpacking the fire rocks from the iron pot. Quin set up the kettle to boil water for the tea.

Eulesis glared at Astabar. "Well?"

He looked up at her, startled.

"Hasn't this gone on long enough? It's time you fixed him."

Dalanar groaned weakly in protest.

Astabar raised his hands helplessly. "He is worse each day, it is obvious. I have no doubt he'll die in terrible agony within a week unless something is done."

The teacup fell from Quin's limp fingers and shattered at her feet. Dalanar dying in excruciating pain? Everything she prayed for since childhood. Justice for her people, for her mother's death. She should be elated; she was tired. Quin studied Dalanar's gray face as he propped himself up against a tree.

The Throkari squinted at her. "There is a certain romantic irony to that kind of ending. Regrettably, Quin, I'm not a romantic." Dalanar looked at the god, visibly bracing himself for an unpleasant answer. "And what can be done, Astabar?"

"I have provided all the help I can ... from the outside. Become my avatar."

Dalanar let his head rest against the tree trunk and closed his eyes. "Quinthian, what would you have me do?"

"I would rather you die than live forever as a sorcerer and an avatar, going mad like Conthal." Quin crossed her arms over her chest, goose bumps rising on her skin.

"Eulesis?"

"You will find death preferable."

Astabar huffed at them.

"Magda, do you have an opinion to add?" He cracked an eye at the tall Uturi.

"If my death were eminent, I'd grab for any hand offered."

Dalanar chuckled, but cut it off, rubbing his head. "I made a vow to the queen of the Summer Festival that I would be there for her. It would be rude of me not to attend."

"She quite understands these things. You needn't worry," Quin assured him.

Dalanar turned to the god. "What do I need to do? How do I become your avatar?"

Astabar stared down at the ground. "I don't know."

Quin blew out the breath she held. Astabar hadn't found out how from Laniof.

"How can you not know? Isn't that a fundamental god thing?" Magda narrowed her eyes at him.

"I came into being knowing many things." Astabar sounded defensive. "Those having to do with humans aren't Old Knowledge. Information about you must be passed between us in mundane sorts of ways."

"I don't understand. What is old knowledge?"

"*Old Knowledge*," Astabar corrected, emphasizing the words. "The Universe created the gods. It also created the laws and patterns that guide its working. Since we are essential parts of that plan, we instinctively understand it. That is Old Knowledge.

"However, gods created *this* world and you humans. We made up many silly and unnecessary rules that apply only to you. You're not a part of the Universe's pattern, so when we are born, we don't already understand you. And truthfully, you are very odd. This is why I was trying to learn how to make an avatar from Laniof ... before he was killed."

"Huh." Magda frowned, clearly unimpressed.

"You were with him when he died?" Quin asked.

"I had many things to do in the city that night and we parted early. I would not have let this happen if I were present!"

Quin wasn't sure she wanted to know what errands would send a god like Astabar into the city at night.

"What did Morgir think of you?" Eulesis took another cup from a pack and handed it to Quin. The kettle boiled over, water spurting out in hissing splashes.

Quin shook herself and slid the pot from the heat. She added some of the mixture of herbs they created for Dalanar to the cup and doused them in the hot water.

"Morgir ignored me, but this is not unusual. He has long been unappreciative of my gifts. And his avatar was strange, even for a human." Astabar gazed over at Dalanar, who unenthusiastically sipped the tea Quin handed him. "You will be the *best* avatar."

"I hate to be the one to point out the obvious, Great Lord," Quin said, "but if you don't know how to make an avatar, and he'll die within days, how do you intend to learn in time?"

"You're going to Lyratrum to convince Morgir to invest a new avatar, yes?"

"Yes, but reports say he's inconsolable with grief, he has no heir to Laniof, and the city is in chaos trying to find the murderer. It might take weeks to sort out."

"I have determined we will have three days once we arrive. After I witness the process, I can do the same with Dalanar."

"If you do as well as you did with the geis, there will be

nothing left of your avatar."

Astabar beamed. "Dalanar has faith in my abilities."

Dalanar cast Quin an aggrieved look and gulped the rest of his tea.

CHAPTER THIRTY-ONE

A PALL OF SMOKE BLANKETED the city of Lyratrum as they crested the hill overlooking the gates. Csiz Luan reflected the martial mentality of the god who resided there, with orderly streets, training fields, and precise architecture. Lyratrum embodied Morgir's fundamental philosophy that rules inhibited creativity.

The city rambled up the sides of twin hills, bridging a shallow ravine that contained a picturesque waterfall. Half-hearted fortifications encircled Lyratrum. Quin suspected they were just an excuse to display the magnificent marble friezes that portrayed Morgir bringing art to humanity at the creation. Gates of wrought iron covered in gold-leaf depicted the celestial sphere, which Morgir spun from the light of stars. Inside the walls, the buildings were a riot of colors and styles that clashed and wandered drunkenly up the hillsides. Clever sculptures of every imaginable material stuck up from town squares, rooftops, and windows. It was eerily quiet. Smoke came from a burning warehouse in the lower factory district, instead of the stoked furnaces of the crafting houses and studios.

Eulesis grunted. "We need to get these people working. We have contracts for their goods to fill. Why are no wagons leaving? What are they doing?"

"I'd like to point out again, my entering the city may cause some difficulties. Morgir might still be feeling prejudiced about sorcerers. I am fairly well-known here." Dalanar's face was ashen and drawn. He insisted on riding late into the night, and resuming before dawn to reach Lyratrum that evening. His hands trembled, and he could barely hold the reins.

"Wear my tabard. No one will recognize you," Quin offered sweetly.

"I'd rather die."

"Hmm."

"Enough, children!" Eulesis snapped at them. "We go straight to Morgir and try to get his attention, as we agreed."

"I believe I can help with Morgir, if he proves intractable," Astabar said.

"We may need you to stop him from turning Dalanar into a fine mist once he realizes a sorcerer is in town." The blonde turned her horse and started down the cobbled road toward the gates of the city.

"I'm not sure I can prevent that from happening, but I am quite charming and can talk quickly." Astabar smiled at Dalanar and followed Eulesis.

Quin tapped her tabard with a finger. "I would be happy to lend it to you."

"You are a cruel woman," Magda told her as they rode past the sorcerer. "I like you."

THE GATE GUARDS INSPECTED THEM carefully. Despite Dalanar's worries, they didn't recognize him as anything beyond a Throkari priest.

"Going to try to become the next avatar, Father?" The guard nudged her partner with an elbow and gave the sorcerer a bold wink.

"What are you talking about?" Eulesis asked testily. "We're here to meet with Morgir."

"You and everyone else. Morgir has to choose a new avatar, right? So, people are following him around hoping to be picked for the job."

The Ravendi rubbed her forehead.

Quin rode forward. "We come on embassy from Gardanath, Sarael, and Conthal. Please escort us to His Greatness."

"How do we know—" the first guard started, but her partner punched her in the shoulder before she finished.

"Look at them, fool." The second guard curtsied to them with a flourish. "Welcome to Lyratrum, Your Graces." She stared at Dalanar. "Father, I must warn you that Morgir is being ... extreme when it comes to sorcerers at the moment."

"Thank you. Would you provide us with a guide? I always lose my way trying to find the Gallery."

"Right away, Your Grace. I'll summon one of the apprentices."

The guard pulled a red cord, and a series of bells and chimes that ran over the courtyard and into the city rang exuberantly. The first soldier led them to a stable and found workers to care for their mounts and gear. Astabar warned them about the iron pot full of theurgically-enhanced rocks.

When they returned to the gate, a knobby-kneed girl of twelve or thirteen waited, talking to the guard. She wore a dun-colored smock that fell to mid-thigh, brown shorts, and untied boots. Her dark hair was woven into a long braid. A fine white powder coated her, giving everything about her an overall tint of gray. She was at one moment a gawky child, the next a blossoming young woman, and she straddled that line awkwardly and with ill-ease.

She tugged at her smock, but relief crossed her pretty features when she recognized the Ravendi second. "Lady Eulesis!

You got my note. Thank the colors!" She sighed dramatically.

"What note, child? Was it a poem?"

"By the first colors, no! I tucked a note inside my sculpture of that horrible staff. You didn't find it?"

Eulesis glanced around at the others. "No. Who are you?"

The apprentice bowed and tripped as she stepped on a boot-lace. Quin caught her before she fell.

"I'm sorry," she said, her face blazing. "I'm Rylir. I'm one of the apprentices who work for Morgir in the Gallery." The girl turned and shyly beckoned them to follow her as she crossed the gatehouse courtyard. She led them through a gaily painted tunnel with an ivy motif and up winding streets lined with narrow houses and workshops.

The traditional Lyraturi construction of workshop and showroom on the first level, with an outside staircase leading to second-floor living quarters, was the predominant style. It was a point of pride that each was in some way unique from its neigh-bors. Architecture from foreign countries nestled in between the other buildings. A normally white plaster Malesini-style house was painted dark turquoise and covered in disks decorated with animals. An Uturi mountain cabin had been recreated in marble and glass instead of the expected logs and sod. Magda and Da-lanar exchanged expressions of disgust at the impracticality of the materials, and swept past without another glance.

The girl flitted ahead of them, disappearing around bends and down alleys.

"Rylir, wait." Quin motioned for the apprentice to return.

They moved at Dalanar's pace; the man refused to rest, but neared collapse. At the next open square, Quin grabbed his arm and forced him to sit on the edge of an ornamental fountain. He obeyed without argument. Astabar sat next to him, muttering something too low for Quin to overhear.

Rylir appeared at their side. "Oh, Your Grace, I didn't realize you were ill."

He waved her off with a hand.

The girl noticed Astabar for the first time, and her eyes widened. "*You*! Thief!" She poked him in the chest with a finger. "Are you a killer, too?"

"Hello, Rylir." He grinned up at her. "I *am* a thief, but not a murderer. I am sorry about your master."

The girl deflated. "I thought maybe it was you. It might have made everything easier. Are you really a god like Laniof said? You're not at all like Morgir."

Eulesis touched Rylir on the arm. "What did you want to tell us in the note?"

"We need help to sort things out. I didn't expect *all* of you to come." She glanced at Quin and Dalanar, lingering on the Seal with a slight frown. "It's bad. Laniof died weeks ago, and still nothing is getting done. We're defaulting on our contracts. At first Morgir went wild with grief, but now the constant pestering of people clambering for him to choose a new avatar is making things worse. They want to be selected and won't leave him alone. I've tried to convince them to go away, but I'm only an apprentice and they don't listen to me."

Quin asked, "what has Morgir been doing?"

Rylir looked down at her shoes. "He huddles in the Gallery holding Laniof most of the time. He eventually preserved the body, but the smell. Ugh!" She shuddered. "A few times a day he'll demand someone find the murderer. Everyone pretends they're doing something, but they come right back. They're treating the main hall like a village fair. They go in and show off their work to him in the hope he'll choose them. It's disgusting."

"I'm afraid we're going to pressure Morgir to take an avatar, as well," Eulesis said ruefully. "It should calm him."

The girl sighed. "I understand. Let me know if I can help." She frowned at Dalanar again. "Father. Your Grace, I must warn you—"

"Morgir thinks a sorcerer was involved in Laniof's death?" he asked.

"Yes, but ... it's worse. Not only was Laniof geised before he died, witnesses confirmed a rumor that *you* were here at the time. Morgir issued orders for your arrest."

"That seems like something you should have mentioned before we entered the city." Eulesis eyed him coldly.

"Throkari matters. Nothing to do with you."

"But everything to do with our present situation. We agreed to cooperate on this. Is there anything else of relevance you would like to tell us before we speak to Morgir?"

Dalanar gave her a flat stare and remained silent.

"Did you kill Laniof?" Quin asked. She felt his lie through their connection before. Maybe the question would startle him into revealing something.

"I did not," he said stiffly.

Again, Quin got a sense of truth behind his words, but it was clouded. Cautious. What did that mean? Did Dalanar know who was guilty? Had it been Conthal? She grumbled. Quin was no magician to be able to sort out cryptic impressions. Just like a Throkari to make something potentially useful into a confusing muddle. "Was it Conthal?"

He didn't answer. She received no confirmation of truth or deceit.

"I suggest we hurry if we're going to visit without the encumbrance of manacles." Quin dusted off her tunic from where she sat on the lip of the stone fountain. Anger or recovery from the brisk walk returned some of the color to Dalanar's face. He no longer looked like he would faint at any moment.

THEY ALMOST MADE IT to the Gallery before the city guard intercepted them. More people filled the streets, and the soldiers were clearly worried about a conflict escalating out of control.

The captain, a portly man in his fifties, approached them, hands well away from his weapons. "Your Graces," he said, bowing his head. "I am certain this is a terrible misunderstanding, but we have been given the solemn duty of seeing Father Dalanar, Seal of the Throkari Avatar, escorted into the presence of the god Morgir. He is to answer the accusation that he was involved in the death of the Avatar Laniof." The charges came out in a nearly unintelligible rush.

The man stepped back as if expecting retribution, but Dalanar gestured for him to lead. "Please take us to him."

The captain swallowed, and his hands shook as he placed them on his belt. He signaled to his soldiers, who drew up in formation around them, looking more like an honor guard than a prisoner detail.

To her dismay, Quin found herself walking between the sorcerer and Rylir.

Dalanar smiled shallowly. "I've always appreciated Morgiri manners. You could learn something from them, Quinthian."

"I imagine few of them accost women in dark alleyways. You should study them, as well."

"My introductions seem to be frequently misunderstood," he mused.

"The burns make it difficult to be objective."

"Perhaps that's the problem."

Quin scowled at him and turned toward the apprentice. Rylir watched them with huge round eyes, bursting with curiosity. The girl obviously couldn't decide if she should ask questions or run to escape the fighting.

"Why...? How...?" Rylir began, apparently deciding it was worth the risk.

Quin pressed at her forehead with the palm of her hand. "Please. Don't ask." Dalanar's amusement resonated through their link. Arrogant rat.

"You made the sculpture of the staff they sent to Gardanath? That was exquisite," Quin said.

The girl tried to wipe some of the powder off her smock. "I didn't do it justice. It's a horrible thing. I mean no offense, Father."

The man frowned in confusion. "None taken."

As THEY NEARED THE Gallery, artists clogged the intersections and narrow passageways as they dragged around their most impressive masterworks. They argued about whom had the best piece, jostled each other, and joined the end of the long queue that likely began at Morgir's studio. Quin felt sorry for the sculptors pulling statues on rickety carts over the cobblestone pavement, but they were undaunted.

The chiming of tiny bells and the grinding of gears rumbled through the streets. The crowd quieted and turned toward the top of the hill. If Quin craned her neck, Morgir's Rose was just visible. Silver and brass twisted together to form the petals of a giant lotus. The metal blossom was held aloft by spirals of black iron. It balanced precariously on its stem; a folly certain to topple in the first breeze. Magic. Engineering. Divine will. The flower endured for over five hundred years.

The sound of gears intensified, vibrating in her ears. The flower began to rotate, and the petals unfolded. A faceted crystal sphere, no smaller than a horse cart, emerged from the center.

The last of the sun's rays struck the surfaces and cast monstrous rainbows across the hillside. The already brilliant city became a kaleidoscope of light; the people and buildings splashed indiscriminately. Colors lit up Dalanar's face, making even him look festive. A sigh of pleasure escaped the crowd. The motion slowed, at last, and the prism retracted, covered again by the petals.

The Lyraturi returned to their conversations and jostling, as if nothing out of the ordinary had occurred. Quin shook her head at the lost splendor. Dalanar's gaze lingered on her. Was that a wistful smile? He looked away. Their escort cleared his throat and gestured for them to continue.

When the press of people blocked their way, the guard captain whistled and the soldiers formed a precise wedge that plowed into the crowd. They beat their swords on their metal shield rims causing Quin to cover her ears at the noise. Artisans shouted in dismay as they were shoved aside in the narrow street, but a path opened up.

"I could get used to your being bound as a criminal," Quin told the sorcerer earnestly.

The trail of hopefuls passed through a dim tunnel that scarcely allowed three people to walk abreast when empty, and Quin's group had to proceed single file. One of the artists, a short, stocky woman, was shouldered away by the guards. She bellowed and lunged at Quin and Rylir, heaving them into Dalanar. The sorcerer caught Quin across the stomach and prevented her from falling, but missed Rylir, who tumbled to the ground with a cry.

The attacker swung something dark and heavy. Quin drew her sword and managed to block in time. The echoing wail of fine steel against the metal deafened her. An iron bar? Was the woman insane? Bystanders screamed and shoved for the exits. Quin tried to regain her feet, but stepped on something soft.

Rylir's hand? She lost her footing again. Dalanar's arm across her sore ribs didn't falter. He was as solid as a stone wall at her back.

The woman swung once more, a flickering outline in the dim light from the tunnel mouth. Quin parried and tried to slash the woman's hand, making her release the rod. Quin's opponent avoided the riposte. There was no room to maneuver with the passageway still packed with people. Dalanar moved them to the left, standing over Rylir and preventing anyone from trampling her in their panic to flee.

Quin found places to set her feet. The woman lunged at them with the end of the bar. Quin could only divert the direction of the iron shaft a few inches. Dalanar needed to evade with her, or they would both end up impaled on the rotting thing. Quin swept the rod away with her sword, metal shrieking against metal. Using her other hand and her body, Quin shifted them backward and to the side, out of the path of the charge. Dalanar followed her lead, and they moved together as if rehearsed. The stout woman missed stepping on Rylir, but ran into Magda, who punched her in the face. The attacker collapsed, the metal rod clattering down the emptying tunnel.

Dalanar loosened his hold on Quin. He drew his palm across her stomach, brushing the stitches lightly with his fingertips. He whispered in her ear, "Is that what fighting feels like? You were remarkable." His hand lingered at her hip before he dropped it to his side. He didn't move away. Dalanar's scent surrounded her: ink and incense, a faint hint of salt and sunshine on his skin.

Desire washed through their connection, and it took her several minutes to realize the emotion wasn't hers alone. When Quin finally noticed he no longer restrained her, she stepped aside without looking at him, not trusting herself to reply.

Quin crouched next to Rylir, who regarded them with a baffled expression.

"I thought...."

"Don't ask," Quin said. "Are you hurt?"

"A skinned knee and bruises. I'll be fine." The girl brushed the dirt off her hands and on to her shorts.

The captain pushed his way past the fleeing people followed by his guards. His men dragged the stocky woman out if the tunnel. "I'm so sorry, Your Grace. Geva's been strange since lightning struck her masterwork a few years ago." He held the iron rod out for them to examine. Even in the dim light, it possessed a haunting pattern similar to Rylir's replica of the staff. "I hear it was an incredible piece, but she built on the hilltop. Completely slagged. This is all that's left and she gets a little ... excited when anyone touches it." He handed the metal bar to one of the guards. "Return that to her, would you?"

"Did you see those marks, Rylir? They looked like the staff."

The girl tilted her head. "They're quite different."

Quin gazed after the retreating guard for a moment before turning to follow the others out of the tunnel.

CHAPTER THIRTY-TWO

THE GALLERY WAS A squat, unexpectedly practical structure surrounded by several acres of covered terraces and pillared colonnades. The best arts and crafts the city offered were on display. Manicured gardens of whimsical topiaries, exotic plants, and flowers overwhelmed Quin's senses as they were escorted to the building at the center.

The line of candidates didn't extend to the Gallery entrance. Word of their coming must have preceded them and the way had been cleared. If Morgir was as upset at Dalanar as they said, it was a wise precaution. The artists still glowered and cursed at them as they went past.

The entryway opened into a large meeting hall that ran the length of the structure, and lay open the two stories to the roof beams. Doors to private rooms lined the walls, and staircases led up to the second floor on either side of the great room. The large chamber would need the heat from the twin fireplaces in the colder months, but they crouched dark and unused. Tapestries depicting scenes from the Creation hung from the rafters. A huge stained glass window of Morgir bringing color to the colorless world formed the entire end wall. The curtains of colored light he called down from the sky were depicted by slivers of multi-hued crystal. A scent of decay caused Quin's eyes to water, but she couldn't determine where the smell came from. She tried not to gag.

As Quin adjusted to the light, she noticed a small stooped man with disorderly white hair sitting in the dimness in front of the window. He rested on a large marble bench draped with a gold cloth. At first, it appeared another person sat with him, but Quin realized Laniof's corpse was propped against his side. Bile stung her throat.

Around her, people knelt. She hastened to follow.

The god Morgir opened his eyes, and yellow light spilled out. "Leave us, Captain." The god's voice resounded within her bones and forced Quin to the ground.

Metal and leather creaked as the guards hurried to obey. The door slammed behind them.

"Your arrogance is legendary, Dalanar, but this exceeds even my expectations. You return to the place where you and Conthal fell as jackals on my ... Laniof. Torturing and murdering him. And now you come to gloat over my pain?" Morgir's words reverberated like thunder in the mountains.

"Great Lord, we were not responsible for Laniof's death. I am truly sorry for your loss."

"Witnesses placed you in Lyratrum when he died. A geis was laid upon him, and a glowing handprint left behind. Do you deny you were here, and that you perform the geis?"

"I would like to know who claimed they saw me, Great Lord. And I am not the only sorcerer who knows that spell."

"Answer the question. Your evasions will not work with me."

Dalanar hesitated. "We were in the city to deal with Throkari affairs."

"Why were you here?" Morgir's voice dripped with compulsion. Even Quin felt the need to explain where she was at the time.

"We were tracking the new god."

Astabar grumbled off to Quin's left.

Dalanar continued, "Laniof told anyone who would listen that he discovered a god. We came to investigate."

"Laniof wouldn't reveal Astabar's location, so you geised and killed him?"

"Great Lord, no. He was dead when we arrived. We never had the opportunity to meet with him. Once we learned what happened, Conthal was ... disquieted about the possibility of an avatar-killer wandering the countryside. We turned and headed directly to Csiz Luan."

"Do you have proof of any of this?"

"Someone must have seen another sorcerer."

"Only you and your master."

"How can I prove—"

"I WANT JUSTICE!" the god roared, shaking plaster lose from the walls. "Your death may not bring my avatar back, but it will end these outrageous lies!"

Quin gasped as Morgir raised his arms and brought them down toward Dalanar's head. In a flash of blue, Astabar moved in front of Morgir, blocking him from completing the gesture.

"This man is my chosen avatar. I won't let you destroy him."

"Out of my way! He killed Laniof. You don't understand what that means."

The loss and sorrow in the god's voice wrenched at Quin's soul, and she found herself weeping.

"I don't know," Astabar agreed. "But I won't let you kill Dalanar on hearsay."

"You don't know how to invest an avatar, do you? I won't teach you, if your choice is this murderer." Morgir's eyes filled with spiteful glee.

"You say you want justice, yet you rush to convict on rumors. Dalanar has many enemies, this is known. Who spoke against him? Were they Throkari?"

"Of course not," Morgir snapped. "Yhellani."

Astabar shook his head. "It is indeed a terrible devastation. Living without the cushion of your avatar must feel like being sliced to pieces. However, your people greatly need you. You must come back to them." The blue light faded from Astabar's eyes and he looked at his brother god with profound compassion.

"I can't rest until I know." Morgir spoke so softly, Quin wasn't sure he intended anyone to overhear.

"Great Lord," Quin said diffidently. "If we can prove it wasn't Dalanar who killed Laniof, will you take another avatar?"

Morgir pointed to the sorcerer. "It was him."

"If Dalanar is guilty, he deserves your wrath. But if he isn't, do you want the real murderer to get away?"

Morgir stopped in front of Quin. "Who are you? Why are you here?"

"Great Lord, I am Quinthian, the handmaiden to Sarael, Avatar of Yhellania. She sends her deepest sympathies, and an offer of aid to help you with your current situation."

He eased the divine pressure on the room, allowing them to sit. Some of the light faded from his eyes.

"What does Gardanath have to say, Eulesis? No, not the pretty words. What does he actually think?"

Eulesis turned deep pink. "Great Lord, he said you need to put Laniof in the ground, find a new avatar, and start honoring your contracts. He's also sorry for your loss."

Morgir gave Dalanar a contemptuous glance. "And Con-thal?"

"I am to offer my help in finding the killer and express our sorrow."

"Do you have anything *else* to add, Astabar?" Morgir

turned to the god who had almost faded into the gloom under the staircase.

"Yes. I am sorry about Laniof, and I hope you bury him soon as the room is very small and the smell is very great."

The god considered them, and tugged at his ear in a surprisingly human gesture. "What strange companions."

He gestured for Rylir to rise. "I'm sorry, small one. I didn't mean for you to be caught up in this."

The girl scrambled to her feet and wiped at her smock.

"Have these people treated you well?" Morgir asked.

"Yes. They can't decide if they like each other, but they are nice to me."

"I'm glad of that. I may ask you to show them around while they attempt to prove the sorcerer isn't guilty. Would you be willing?"

"Of course. They're exciting! Did you hear Geva attacked us in the tunnel?"

Morgir stared at them over the girl's shoulder. "Dead?"

"No!" Rylir said. "Magda punched her in the face and knocked her out. Blood was everywhere! I think she has a broken nose."

Quin hadn't noticed the blood in the darkness.

Morgir returned to the bench, pulling in his divine presence. His eyes became a medium gray. It was strange that the god responsible for bringing color into the world chose such a bleak human form.

"One thing we haven't established," Morgir said, as they clattered to their feet. "How long do I give you to find this proof?"

Quin glanced at Dalanar's pale, thin-lipped face. "Two days should be enough."

CHAPTER THIRTY-THREE

ANIOF'S STUDIO CONTAINED A mess of sketches, old paint pots, and canvases jammed into corners. Windows let in the afternoon sunlight and provided ample illumination to see into the cupboards and drying racks that ran along the opposite wall. Judging by the style of the pictures hanging in the few free spaces, Laniof was the artist who painted Astabar's portrait.

The room took up most of the first floor, with the door leading to the main hall on the left. An easel stood at the end, accompanied by a rolling stand that held jars, rags, and brushes. Laniof had hooked his palette under a blank canvas, and it sat undisturbed, waiting for his return. Several brushes, caked with drying red and brown pigment, rested on a mixing tray. Quin preferred the acrid stench of solvent to the smell of corruption in the outer chamber.

Rylir huddled in the center of the room with eyes full of unshed tears.

"If this is too difficult for you, we can ask for someone else," Quin said.

The apprentice wiped her nose with the back of her hand. "I haven't been in the studio since they found his body."

"Where did they find him?" Dalanar asked abruptly.

Quin hissed at him.

"I don't have much time, Quinthian. Forgive me if I'm a little terse."

Rylir moved to the open space beside Laniof's easel and indicated the floor.

Quin paced the length of the room, looking into the corners and cabinets. "How many people were in the building that night? Did anyone hear shouting or screaming? If someone geised him, he might have cried out."

Dalanar stroked the dark stubble on his throat. "A surprising number of people remain silent when geised. Stubborn people."

"A few masters and apprentices stayed late, but they didn't hear anything. Laniof frequently worked through the night, though, and no one is sure when the attack happened. He could have been alone," Rylir said.

Dalanar surveyed the studio. "Where did the sorcerer ground himself?"

The apprentice led them to a marble pillar in one dusty corner of the workshop. The bust of a former avatar perched on top, contemplating the room with quiet disdain. She pointed to the bald forehead. Smooth and unmarked.

Dalanar scanned the sculpture with half-lowered eyelids. "I can feel its presence. With magic, I could bring the mark to the surface." He moved closer. "I'm surprised the bust didn't shatter when it cooled. The sorcerer we're dealing with isn't as powerful as I am."

Eulesis turned to the girl. "Was there anything else? Anything left behind, or last words?"

"No, Your Grace."

Dalanar flicked dust off his black robe. "We need to examine the body. Perhaps we can find a distinguishable handprint from the burns. We must determine what actually caused his death, as well. We've been working on assumptions."

"You're disgusting." Quin shuddered. "I'm not sure I want you to learn how to kill an avatar. How are you going to convince Morgir to give up Laniof's remains?"

The Throkari smiled thinly. "The question is how are *you* going to convince Morgir? He likes you better."

QUIN FOUND THE GOD still sitting on the stone bench in the audience hall. Beside him, Laniof had been laid out, arms placed across his chest, and holding a long glass prism.

Morgir regarded her as she approached, his gray eyes deep with sorrow. "Have you found proof, handmaiden?"

Quin bowed her head. "No, Great Lord. I came with an unusual request, one I would never ask lightly. If I did not fear for Sarael, Gardanath, and even your future avatar, such a thing would never cross my mind."

The god waited, but said nothing.

"To understand what terrible things took place, we need to examine Laniof's remains, Great Lord. How is it possible to kill an avatar in the center of his power? How can we prevent it?"

"You dare ask this of me?" Morgir's eyes flashed brilliant yellow, and Quin was flattened to the floor like a mouse in a trap. Others in the rooms around them fell to the ground. Cries of dismay. Objects breaking.

"I'm so sorry to upset you, Great One!" Quin rolled her head to one side. She tasted blood. Another brilliant idea from the sorcerer. Why did she listen to him?

The pressure let up, and an old man sat in the place the god occupied a moment before. "Take him," he said. "I understand what you ask. Just ... don't defile him. Don't cut into him. And don't let the Throkari touch him."

Quin winced. "We will treat him with the utmost respect. As if he were my own avatar."

"I'll hold you to that, Quinthian."

QUIN HELD LANIOF BENEATH his arms while Eulesis carried him under his knees. She was going to vomit up her last six meals. The Ravendi second kept whispering for her to stay strong and focused. Quin swallowed repeatedly to keep the gorge from rising. Even with her Ravendi training and combat experience, the Yhellani proscription against touching the dead was deeply ingrained. Yhellani handled births not deaths; this kind of thing was the responsibility of the Throkari.

Rylir led them to another room, empty save for a tall work bench and some cupboards similar to the ones in the avatar's studio. The sun had dropped below the horizon, and only weak light filtered in from the hall. The apprentice motioned for them to put the body on the table, and they slid him onto the surface.

She stepped out, and returned a moment later with an armload of candles and reflectors. They set them up around Laniof until he became the brightest spot in the darkened chamber.

"The rules are: no cutting and the sorcerer doesn't touch," Quin told them as they moved closer.

"That's going to be a damned nuisance. I hope you can get yourself under control, Quinthian. You'll need to act as my hands for this."

"Me?" she squeaked, but knew the answer. Who else? Rylir? Eulesis? The woman shook her head in firm refusal. Quin took a deep breath, and regretted it. "Could we open the windows?"

Laniof was a tall man with fair, thinning hair and a scruffy beard. He appeared to be in his thirties, but must have been several hundred years old. Younger than the other avatars. Whatever Morgir did to preserve him, hadn't happened soon enough to forestall some of the early signs of corruption. His skin was greenish-blue and his stomach bloated, pulling at the fabric of his clothing.

He wore an apron. A few smudges of black and brown paint marked the bottom, a dash of red, and the same reddish-brown she had seen on the paintbrush smeared the waist.

"Was he a clean painter, Rylir? Did he change his apron often?" Dalanar asked once they examined his clothes.

"Yes. Each day he requested fresh rags, aprons, towels, and that his brushes are cleaned. Everything. It's one of the things the apprentices do."

"What was he working on? Not the blank canvas." Quin went to the window and gulped in fresh air, ignoring Dalanar's exasperated sigh. She doubted Morgir would forgive her for throwing up on Laniof's body. The sorcerer could wait.

The girl thought for a minute. "I haven't been in his studio for a while. I help another master. Cleary was Laniof's special apprentice. He found ... Do you want me to get him?"

"Let's wait until tomorrow. No need to upset him." Quin gave the girl a reassuring smile she knew looked false. It was upsetting *her* enough for all of them.

Under the apron, the man wore a finely woven tunic, now stretched tight over his stomach. Quin needed to cut the fabric at one seam to slide it off. They discovered no holes in the shirt or in his torso to indicate a stab with a knife or the staff. His chest was pallid, but his back was garishly purpled and bruised.

"Great gods," Rylir gasped.

Dalanar touched her shoulder. "He wasn't beaten. Blood pools when the heart is no longer pumping. Like water settling in a basin."

The apprentice folded in on herself and backed away from

the table. Her breath shook. Eulesis put an arm around her and stroked the girl's hair.

The burns from a geis were obvious: a scarlet stripe across the pelvis, the other across the chest and throat. He died before his avatar healing began to repair the damage. He had been killed minutes ... seconds after the geis ended. There were no clear handprints.

"Whoever did this was shorter than Laniof, surprised him at his easel, perhaps forced him to his knees—not with strength, but with the spell. I think it was a woman." Dalanar glanced over at Quin.

"Will this be enough evidence to exonerate you?"

"No. Help me figure out how she killed him."

Quin and Dalanar went over the body starting from the top of his head, searching for any inexplicable marks. She held apart his fingers and parted hair, exposed the inside of his cheeks and lifted his arms. They rolled him over and found a circular mark at the small of Laniof's back that nearly blended in with the livid bruising.

The sorcerer gestured for Rylir to step forward. "Does this look like the base of the staff you copied?"

The girl peeked at the mark and retreated with a sharp nod.

Quin stepped away with relief. "Good, we're done."

Dalanar smirked. "We're *halfway* done, Handmaiden Quin-thian. We now have evidence to support our hypothesis, but we can't rule out the possibility that something else killed him unless we make a thorough investigation. Remove his pants."

Quin stared at him blankly, and then moaned.

THEY RETURNED LANIOF TO Morgir at midnight. Out of respect, they cleaned his body and dressed him in the fresh clothes Rylir retrieved from his rooms.

"Did you find what you were seeking, Quinthian?" the god asked.

"We confirmed that the staff was used as a murder weapon, Great Lord." She felt defeated and wished there was something useful to report.

"Ah." Morgir turned to stare out the window at the darkness.

QUIN WAS EXHAUSTED AND polluted in a way she had never experienced before. She wanted to scald herself with boiling water. Scrub until her skin fell away. The others walked quietly beside her; even Astabar spoke rarely. Dalanar was pale in the starlight. He held his head with one hand, and pain echoed through their connection. Quin rubbed at her own temple in an attempt to ease the pressure.

Rylir led them to a house on the edge of the Gallery grounds. The style was so similar to Gardanath's manor, Quin wondered if the same architect designed them both. It was smaller, with two wings of chambers, a central evening room, and a dining area between them.

"I asked that a meal be sent for you, and the bath house is ready."

Without another word, Quin headed out past the garden to the baths. She wanted the smell of death off her skin and out of her soul.

Quin was alone in the women's washroom. She dumped water from the boiler into a hammered brass tub and soaked until her flesh throbbed. She stepped out, grabbed salts and soap, and scoured her body. When the wound under her arm began to bleed, she stared at it vacantly, but stopped scrubbing. Quin rinsed off under a cold pitcher of water and stepped back in the bath. It stung, but made the heat more bearable. She buried her face in her knees and tried not to think about what she had done.

When, at last, the water grew too cold, Quin splashed out of the tub and grabbed her clothes. They reeked of death. She forgot to bring something to change into. She cast around for anything to use as a robe, but found nothing. Quin wrapped herself in several of the small towels and hoped everyone was asleep.

A single lamp burned when she peeked through the door. Dalanar sat at a table reading, a cup of tea beside him. The rest of the house was silent. He watched her, unable to disguise the curl of a smile. "I was beginning to think you drowned."

Quin scowled at him. "Concern for a Yhellani? Hardly a suitable pastime for the Seal of Throkar."

"The least I can do for someone willing to befoul herself on my behalf." The man's voice was full of self-mockery.

"For you? No, Dalanar, for Sarael and Gardanath. I'll do anything to keep them safe. I believe you're innocent of *this* crime: I want to find the real killer. Effort on you is time wasted."

The sorcerer chuckled and turned back at his book. "And order was restored to the planes of mortals and gods."

A drop of water ran down Quin's arm and she shivered. "Where is my room?"

He looked her up and down. "I'd imagine wherever you want it to be."

She growled at him.

"An empty room? Your belongings are in that one." He waved vaguely toward one of the doors. "I'm told the Yhellani express gratitude for life after facing death with an act of *unification*. If you need help with your devotions, I would be delighted to assist. In the spirit of solidarity."

Quin stalked toward her room. "Drink your tea, Throkari. Your brain is bleeding again." She shut the door firmly behind her.

CHAPTER THIRTY-FOUR

DALANAR POUNDED ON THE door at dawn, rousing Quin out of a dream of being chastised by a circle of masked gods. She didn't want to crawl out of the warm bed, but was relieved to escape the foreboding image.

Although the room was cool, the sky held a silvery glow that made her think the day would be oppressively hot. Quin pulled on her white shirt and brown kilt. The handprint on her shoulder appeared as a distasteful shadow in the uncertain light. She planned to ask the sorcerer to remove the rotting thing once he regained his power. He owed her something in repayment for the care.

She hadn't braided her hair before falling asleep and it was a tangled mess. Quin cursed as she brushed through the snags, and pulled the heavy strands into a simple tail.

In the dining area, Magda and Eulesis held teacups and watched the sunrise. Dalanar wore a robe over the loose clothes from the night before and swept from room to room. Astabar was missing, as usual, in the morning. They couldn't tell if he slept.

"Nice of you to join us," Dalanar snapped and threw himself in a chair.

"Someone got up on the wrong side of his sorcerous little bed today," Magda said.

Quin ignored him and poured some tea from a painted carafe. A tempting basket of bread, sliced meats, cheese, and butter had been set out on the table. "Did you make him wait for me?"

Eulesis smiled primly. "Only fair, considering you did all the work yesterday. There would be nothing left after he finished."

For the first time in days, Quin felt like laughing. With a nod of thanks, she grabbed a couple dark bread rolls, speared some slices of meat and cheese on to a plate, and retreated to a seat by the fire.

With great dignity, Dalanar motioned for Eulesis and Magda to precede him. They ate in sleepy silence, with Magda and the sorcerer depleting the mound of food, until he eyed the last roll.

"Oh, take it," Eulesis told him. "I've seen that expression on Gardanath and Kalin, and it's just as pitiful on you. You act like you've never been fed."

He lifted his chin and took the bun before anyone could object.

Dalanar dumped some of the herb mixture in his cup and the acrid odor filled the room, making Quin sneeze.

Eulesis pushed away from the table and stretched her legs out in front of her. "How many sorceresses are there, Dalanar?" In concession to the cool morning, she wore a gray wool tunic over her regular uniform of Ravendi red and black.

Food had sweetened his mood. "Seven, although one is too elderly and one is too young to have done this."

"And the other five?"

"Two are Throkari. The first is nearing her mastery. The second is researching something obscure in the mountains of Utur with Conthal's advanced students. The remaining three are affiliated with the university: teaching, or research. Conthal trained two of them. Gridarl taught the last."

"Gridarl?" Quin asked.

Dalanar actually smiled. "Conthal's academic rival in the magical studies."

Quin didn't understand. "They *fight* and the man is still alive?"

"Well," the sorcerer said, rubbing his chin. "They publish papers ripping each other's theories apart. That is mostly bloodless. Gridarl's biggest issue with Conthal is his refusal to teach the Secrets to anyone outside the religion. Conthal is furious anyone openly disagrees with him. As he's the one who established the customs of the institution, he has no one to blame but himself."

"Why would he do that, if he hates it?" Magda cut up the remaining apple.

"He's insane," Quin told her.

Dalanar frowned at them. "He needs intellectual stimulation. Few can compete with him. Gridarl, at least, is a challenge. Conthal finds the rest of us tedious."

"Surely not you, Seal." Eulesis' mouth quirked playfully.

Dalanar barked out a harsh laugh. "Especially me. He sent me away for several years once, for boring him so completely. I accomplished some intriguing research." He sighed.

Quin decided to seek out Gridarl when she went to the university to find a way to defeat Dalanar. If he fought with Conthal, the Seal would be easy for him.

"What are the Secrets?" Quin asked.

"Nothing the Yhellani approve of." The corner of his mouth turned up.

"Abomination." Quin supposed she should be grateful Conthal didn't teach that godless magic to every sorcerer who wandered by. The fewer people to know it, the better.

Her disapproval had to be obvious; Dalanar ignored it. "Today, we need to inquire if anyone saw one of the sorceresses around Laniof. I will try to recover the handprint on the bust. I might be able to identify the owner."

"I didn't realize you could use magic again." Quin ran her fingertips over the leather-wrapped hilt of her sword.

"I've thought of another way that does not require sorcery."

Quin was surprised by the lack of pain through their connection. If Astabar was correct, Dalanar should be days away from an agonizing end. The tea couldn't be working that well. She mentally shrugged; maybe Astabar figured out how to reduce the pain. Or the god lied to get his way. She wouldn't put it past him.

Quin rose from the table. "We should seek out Laniof's apprentice, to find out about the missing canvas. Whatever the avatar was painting might be relevant—if the murderer went to the effort to remove it."

Eulesis belted on her weapons. "Dalanar, give us descriptions of those sorceresses. Magda and I will ask around the Gallery. Rylir may be able to help."

Magda grabbed her great sword from where she had propped it against the wall.

Dalanar shook his head. "Do you need that?"

Magda snorted. "Ask Geva."

SOMEONE AIRED OUT THE Gallery, and the smell wasn't as bad as the previous day. The sun just crested the eastern hill of Lyratrum and was visible through the stained glass. Morgir sat in a straight-backed chair near the marble bench where Laniof lay, now properly draped in funerary cloths. The chair faced the window and the god didn't deign to acknowledge their presence when they paused to pay their respects. After bowing, they continued on to the studio and closed the door.

Dalanar managed to find a piece of unmarked paper and wrote down names and descriptions. Each line of his elegant script began and ended with a neat flourish.

Eulesis picked up the list. "Conthal hates your handwriting, doesn't he?"

Quin was astonished when he winked at the woman.

Eulesis tried to hand the paper to Magda who turned it down with a shrug. "Can't read."

Dalanar stared at his countrywoman with a scandalized expression. Magda lifted her chin as if daring him to speak.

Quin took the note. With her knack, she needed only a few moments review to memorize the contents. "Not a lot of distinguishing marks. Don't you sort have fangs and reek of carrion?"

Dalanar exhaled as he hefted the bust from the pillar to the table with a thud. "I've been informed you poison children and burn village record books."

"I've never burned a record book in my life," she protested hotly.

Dalanar lifted an eyebrow at her, and Quin turned away. When had she become comfortable enough with him to jest?

She slid the paper over to Eulesis. "If you'll start with this, I'll find Cleary and Rylir."

Eulesis gave her a knowing smile. Quin was relieved when the woman didn't speak before leaving the room with Magda.

"Do you need anything from Rylir?"

Dalanar had already turned to the puzzle of the handprint. "Fine metal shavings. A powder, if possible."

She wanted to ask more questions, but he appeared lost in thought, gazing at the statue.

A NUMBER OF PEOPLE moved about the Gallery when she emerged from Laniof's workshop. Some were young enough to be apprentices, and she decided to approach them first. Not wanting to disturb Morgir, Quin followed them outside into the sunlight. The day was warming up as she expected.

A curly-haired boy of about fifteen carried a bin of rags toward a laundry outbuilding. She hurried to overtake him.

His eyes widened as he took in her sword and clothing. "Your Grace." He managed an awkward bow.

"Good morning," Quin said with a smile. "I'm searching for Rylir or Cleary. Where can I find them?"

The boy gulped. "I'm Cleary. Haven't seen Rylir."

"Excellent, you can assist me. Are you finished with your duties?"

He bobbled. "I'll be right back!" He darted off toward the laundry and disappeared within, only to come tearing out clutching a pile of folded cloths and aprons a moment later. The door banged shut behind him, bringing a chorus of shouts from inside.

"I have to drop these off at the workshops, but I can help. Whatever you need!" If anything, he was more excited than before.

Cleary's hair reminded her of Kalin. The boy was slender and fragile, with translucent skin that didn't receive enough sunlight. Colors stained his fingers and Quin assumed he was a painter like his former mentor. He had on the same style of smock and short pants Rylir had worn the day before.

The apprentice ran into the Gallery, and through an open window, Quin saw him toss his bundle into an empty room. He noticed her watching and stopped. She chuckled as he picked them up and slunk into the main hall. He must not have had much to do, as a few minutes later he scampered outside to join her again.

"We need fine metal shavings. Do you know where to get some?"

He deliberated for a moment. "Iron or something else?"

That stumped her. "We'd better ask."

Dalanar hadn't moved from his place, although now paintbrushes, glue pots, lemons, loadstones, and other mysterious things surrounded the bust. He still squinted at the statue. Rylir perched on a stool against one wall.

Quin leaned inside. "Dalanar, what metal do you want the dust made from?"

He didn't move. "Iron."

She waved at Rylir, who peeked up hopefully. Quin cocked her head to the sorcerer. The girl sighed and went back to drawing figures with her toe.

Cleary's eyes bulged and his skin lost the last hint of color. Quin backed him into the hallway and closed the door to the studio.

"That's him." His voice was small and frightened.

"Yes."

The boy made no move to follow as she turned to leave. She took his clammy hand and tugged him out into the sunshine. "He didn't kill your master, Cleary."

"I ... I don't know. He could of, if he wanted. I saw him once. Before I came here."

Oh.

"I'm sorry." Quin led him to a bench. She empathized with the shock of confronting someone with that kind of history. Suddenly, she wasn't in any particular hurry to help the sorcerer.

They sat in silence, enjoying the warmth of the morning light.

At last, the apprentice spoke, "He came to my village when I was six. Some healers visited, you know, Yhellani Servants?"

Quin nodded.

"We lived in Tyrentanna, near the border with Dacten. We got a lot of travelers passing by, though it wasn't a big place. He and his master came the next day. Dalanar said if we told them where the Servants went, no one would be hurt, but we didn't know. They sneaked off. Conthal ordered him to do that thing—the spell that burns—to the elders." The apprentice's voice trailed off and he stared at the ground for a long time.

Groundskeepers were trimming some of the bright green topiary in the shape of fish. The quiet *shnick-shnick* of their sheers helped to keep the images of the boy's tale comfortably distant.

"They made everyone come out to watch. My grandmother was first, and she died almost right off. She screamed, though. I wouldn't let myself cry when it happened, I was afraid he would look at me. Would take me next and make *me* scream." Cleary's words came out in a harsh rasp.

He stared into her eyes, as if daring Quin to belittle his fears. She regarded him solemnly and said nothing.

"Dalanar did it to a few more people and left them with terrible burns. Conthal was angry and wanted to stay and spell everyone in the village. Dalanar convinced his master to leave. He did do that. I didn't cry for a long time, even after they left. It might bring him back." Cleary let out a shuddering breath. The apprentice turned away and tried to wipe his eyes discretely on his sleeve. "Foolish, eh? To be afraid now? And I'm talking about your friend, I'm sorry."

"It's not foolish to fear real danger. Why do you think Dalanar and I are friends? Do you know who I am?"

"Well, Rylir said...." He sounded uncertain.

"Rylir is young, and doesn't understand some things about how adults interact."

Cleary gave her a half-smile that was uncomfortably mature.

She cleared her throat. "Does it help that I'm not doing any of this for him? I need to find who killed Laniof to prevent them from killing Sarael or Gardanath. People I care about. Morgir said he'd choose a new avatar if we can prove Dalanar didn't commit the murder. I believe he didn't do it. We'd be letting the guilty escape if we don't pursue this further." Just because Iyana *might* have helped him, didn't make him innocent or an ally. She needed to remember that, too.

"It helps, Your Grace." He stood and waited for her, impatient to begin once again. "The evil sorcerer wants metal filings, the evil sorcerer gets metal filings."

Quin smiled at his resilience. "He said a powder would be better."

Cleary tilted his head. "What is he using this for?" He led her into the labyrinth of streets in the district below the Gallery grounds.

CHAPTER THIRTY-FIVE

IT TOOK SEVERAL HOURS for Quin and Cleary to visit enough blacksmiths and metal workers to accumulate a handful of iron dust. She hoped they had gathered a sufficient amount for whatever Dalanar intended.

When they entered the workshop, Cleary lingered in the hall until it was clear Dalanar was not alone. Astabar occupied a stool next to Rylir, and Magda and Eulesis were examining the canvases in the cupboards. Dalanar had found something to eat and rested against the table as he drank tea, staring at a painting. It faced away from Quin so the subject was hidden.

The apprentice pushed into the room before Quin could stop him. "What are you doing? Who let you go through the Master's paintings?"

Dalanar turned toward the boy, teacup raised to his lips. The apprentice froze.

"Whom do we have here?" The sorcerer set the cup down, his dark eyes probing. Cleary's face went slack.

Quin moved faster than she thought possible to place herself between the two of them. "Cleary was Laniof's apprentice. He helped me find your powder. I hope it's enough." She held the small pouch out to the Throkari.

"Did you have to go to Csiz Luan for this?"

"You would not believe how meticulously clean the people are here." In a low voice meant only for him, Quin added, "The apprentice and I reminisced about time spent in your company. Apparently, there is a prematurely deceased grandmother you and Conthal tortured for the entertainment of our young friend."

Dalanar's gaze darted to the boy and back. "I don't know him."

"I find it disturbing that there are too many dead grand-mothers for you to keep straight."

"Can we discuss my failure to live up to your standards an-other time?"

"I thought now would be precisely the right time."

The sorcerer gave her an affronted look, and placed the bag on the table beside the bust. He stepped aside, allowing her to view the canvas he had been examining when she entered.

She gasped.

It was a painting of Conthal. He stood in an empty room that conveyed a feeling of unimaginable vastness, and although his figure dominated the frame, he appeared small in the space. His hand rested on the handle of a locked door, but he was turned slightly as if to face something approaching from behind. His hair and robes were perfectly groomed, as always, however his eyes held the hint of madness that lurked behind his cold façade. He stared out of the picture with hatred and power bare-ly contained. Throkar's alien leer was suggested in the curled corners of his lips.

"Sweet Lady. Does he know Laniof has this?" Conthal's soul had been captured in paint. Anyone viewing the portrait would see the truth of the man. Dalanar was neither surprised nor dismayed; he knew his master's true nature. Quin turned away in disgust.

"I don't think so. I'm uncertain when it was done. Not since I've been Seal."

Rylir poked Cleary in the ribs with her finger. "Go check. Don't stand around gawping."

Eulesis paused from pulling out canvases. "Find out if there's one for Gardanath and Sarael. I'd be interested in seeing them."

Astabar grinned. "Mine is most exceptional. However, I am much more handsome and likable than Conthal. It is unfortunate Laniof is gone. I would have wanted one done of my avatar."

"Yes, that would be intriguing," Quin glanced from the portrait to Dalanar.

The sorcerer handed her the picture and returned to study the bust. She examined it again up close, and her skin itched from the malignancy in the avatar's gaze. Quin passed the canvas to Rylir, who checked the number on the frame and placed it into one of the slots in the wall.

"I have brought gifts for each of you, from my nighttime adventures," the god announced.

Quin narrowed her eyes at him. "You stole from the townspeople." Terrific. Even if they managed to prove Dalanar innocent, they'd all be arrested for theft.

"You mistake me, dear Yhellani maiden. I stole very few things. The others are gifts of a kind heart and a willing nature. You will see."

He pulled several small bundles from his threadbare jacket and tossed them to the women in the room. Eulesis received a black handkerchief dripping with elaborate lace work, and Magda a fine whetstone. Rylir tugged at the cloth wrapping and cut her finger on a chisel.

"Hey, this belongs to Master Arnard." She pursed her lips. "I can't keep it. I'd get into trouble."

Astabar laughed as if that was the best part of the gift.

With trepidation, Quin untied her small bundle. It contained a plain, yellow bar of soap. The same kind her mother had used. The intense scent of lavender, honey, and lye drifted up. It stirred up memories of Iyana bathing her as a child. Her smile as she dried Quin with a big towel. Aqua eyes shining with love. Quin's vision blurred.

"Why?" She wanted to throw the soap at Astabar's head, but she gripped it harder.

"You like baths." The god's face almost glowed with innocent pleasure.

Coincidence? No, not with a god. Astabar was toying with them. He pretended to be human, but he was something ... other, and Quin needed to remember that. He was a god, no matter how affable he seemed. Humans were nothing but playthings. These gifts were a message or a way to manipulate them into doing or feeling what he wanted. Quin wasn't going to allow another god to control her.

Dalanar watched her, looking from the bundle to her face with an inscrutable expression. Why couldn't he just leave her alone?

"Thank you, Astabar. That's considerate." She forced a smile and wrapped the soap up in its cloth. The scent was on her fingers. *Mother, I miss you.*

Astabar nodded pleasantly, but there was a shrewd glint in his eyes.

"And for you, Dalanar, two gifts." The god held out a knee-length, blue jacket, dark enough to appear black. It was made of a fine material Quin didn't recognize, but looked warm and soft, with quilted layers like the gambeson she wore under her armor. Delicate black embroidery of vines swirled around the edges and matching, ribbon-covered buttons ran the full length of the front.

The sorcerer took it warily. "Am I going to be arrested for wearing this in public?"

"Not once you're my avatar. You'll need new clothes soon. The vestments of a Throkari priest will be wildly inappropriate for you."

Dalanar touched the collar of his black robe as if suddenly reminded of what he wore. That would be a difficult adjustment for him. Quin smirked.

"My second gift to you: The Preceptor of the Throkari Church in Terrisea is going to perform your laicization."

"You brought Eccuro here for *that*?"

Even knowing Dalanar couldn't use his power, the people in the room retreated from him.

Astabar didn't blink. "You can't become my avatar while you are still a Throkari priest. Since I am confident you aren't going to back out of our agreement, there is no reason to wait. Throkar and I don't want to fight over you like hot-headed lovers. Choose, Dalanar. Now."

The sorcerer opened his mouth to speak, but shook his head. He started again. "I planned to resign to Conthal directly. This will do." He rubbed at the seal on his finger.

Eulesis said Dalanar's position as a priest was honorary, but Quin thought her information was mistaken. He took his duties seriously when given the opportunity. Unexpected.

"Shall we do this here?" Astabar lifted an eyebrow at Dalanar.

The Throkari crossed his arms. "If you wish, Great Lord." His tone was icily formal.

"Rylir, my girl, would you escort the preceptor in?" Astabar pulled a dusty wooden chair out from under a table and set it the middle of the floor in front of the easel.

Quin and Eulesis moved to stand next to Dalanar as the

door opened and a tall man, bleached white with age, entered the room. His only concession to his advanced years was a heavy cane he leaned on with a hand twisted with joint sickness. A traditional purple mantle dangled over the shoulders of his plain black robe, indicating his rank, but on his head, he wore a colorful knit cap, unlike anything Quin had seen before.

"Preceptor Eccuro." Dalanar bowed.

"Father Dalanar. Still have that stick up your ass?" The old man levered himself into the chair, his blue eyes alight with intelligence. Quin choked in surprise and Eulesis had difficulty holding herself upright while laughing.

The sorcerer smiled thinly. "I'm sure you never wondered why you were posted to Lyratrum."

"I knew why I was banished. Conthal didn't like hearing he was a sadistic maniac who was turning our allies against the Throkari with his policies on the Yhellani. I did wonder why I wasn't executed outright, though." He tapped his cane on the floor in front of him.

"At times, Conthal can be convinced of the value of dissenting opinions."

"I suppose I have you to thank for him leaving me alone during those times he's not so appreciative?" The preceptor glanced around at the others. "You keep strange company for one of Conthal's bootlickers." He nodded at the women. "I detect Ravendi and Yhellani. Remarkable."

"As my master commands."

"Dalanar, you must do something about that stick." He winked at Eulesis, who grinned back. "Our young lord tells me he wants you as his avatar. As much as I tried to dissuade him, well ... time for you to leave the fold.

"You got what you asked for, Dalanar. Was it what you wanted?"

The sorcerer stared at him in puzzlement.

"You don't remember?" The preceptor turned to the rest of the room and gave a gruff laugh. "I should be hurt. I was the school priest at the Darkness when he came in as a boy. I confirmed him to the Throkari religion. Asked him what he wanted. Do you remember your reply?"

Dalanar regarded him with growing recognition. "To be as powerful as Conthal."

"And you nearly are. The Seal is the second highest position in the religious hierarchy. A sorcerer, as well. You had ambition for a young lad." He gave a phlegmy cough. "Did it fulfill your wildest imaginings?"

Dalanar looked pensive. "No."

"What do you want now as avatar of a new god? More power? Your own religion?"

Dalanar's lips curved in a wry smile. "To live."

"Immortality?" Eccuro's disapproval creased his face.

"I'll start with living until the end of the week."

The old man's expression changed to one of genuine distress. As much as he disliked Dalanar, the preceptor seemed to respect him.

"Hmm. I assume we can't dispense with these formalities quickly enough. Kneel in front of me, son."

The sorcerer obeyed, his black robe pooling around his knees. He lowered his head before the old churchman, who placed a hand on his dark hair.

"I call Throkar to witness." Eccuro's voice was a resonant bass that must have been popular at lessons or services.

He repeated the request three times and a stillness that prickled against Quin's skin fell over the room. A pressure of attentiveness made her feel like a mouse scrutinized by an owl. Her ears popped and she yawned. The sounds in the building stilled, and Quin wondered what Morgir thought about someone summoning the awareness of Throkar into his home.

"This man seeks release from his vow of service to the church. He has been a faithful child since his initiation and has devoted his life to your teachings. He entered the priesthood, and served as a loyal and submissive servant to you and your avatar. So outstandingly has he performed his duties that another god has come to woo him away—"

Dalanar lifted his head with a jerk. "We can dispense with this part, Eccuro."

The Preceptor shushed him and tilted Dalanar's head down. "Despite his experiences, Great Lord Throkar, his temper hasn't significantly sweetened over the many years. Since the theological road he follows now turns, he begs leave to rejoin the Throkari laity, and surrender the power and obligations conferred upon him by the office of the priestly orders and as the Seal to the Avatar. Does the Great Lord grant this dispensation?"

Nothing happened. Quin shifted uneasily. What if Throkar decided to blast the entire room in displeasure?

At last, a shimmer of black fog appeared around Dalanar's head, and his robes began to smolder. The sorcerer jumped up and threw them off with a curse. He stamped at the small flames until only a few tendrils of smoke seeped out.

The presence of the god had lifted when Dalanar looked up from the charred pile on the floor.

Rylir's mouth gaped open. "Throkar did that?"

Dalanar picked up the robe. "I suspect it was a vote of displeasure from Conthal. Now he must select and train a new Seal. He's probably livid."

"Over this distance? How is that possible?" Quin opened the windows to clear the air.

"Throkar passed along the message." He twisted the ruined cloth into a ball and tossed it into a corner.

Dalanar had on a gray, short-sleeved shirt of silk. Shiny patches of old burn scars marred his pale skin, and Quin wondered where he got them. She assumed a fire caster would somehow be immune. His face wore a mask of calm, but emotions boiled inside him; loss, excitement, fear, anger. The power of the mix dazed her.

Some compassion or understanding must have shown in her expression. Dalanar raised a finger and pointed at her. "Don't say it. I want nothing from a Yhellani."

"You won't get any sympathy from me." Quin put her hands on her sword belt and scowled at him.

Eccuro tapped his cane on the floor. "He's grown worse since I last saw him. Pity. Well, Astabar, he's your problem now. Wear him in good health? What *is* the proper thing to say to a god about to invest a new avatar?"

Astabar laughed merrily. "I like this man very much. Conthal is not appreciative of your many gifts, but I would value you. Come over to my religion. Make up any rank you desire."

The preceptor smiled at Dalanar's rumble of protest. "A gracious offer, Great Lord. I'm content enough where I am for now. The people of Lyratrum are charming, and the duties are pleasant. As long as Conthal stays in Utur, I have a high likelihood of keeping my guts inside where they belong."

"Keeping your mouth closed will go a long way to extending your life," Dalanar said.

"So the letter I'm drafting to the College of Mandrites regarding the increasingly violent activities of the Tree of Knowledge sect is ill-advised?" The old man's eyes glinted with defiance.

The sorcerer turned away from him with a shrug. "I don't

know who Conthal will choose as Seal. You don't like how I handled things, the next could be a Tree cultist. If you're done wasting my time, I'll return to proving my innocence before Morgir grows tired of waiting."

Eccuro waved his hand toward the sorcerer. "You're banished from the libraries, temples, and schools for a year and a day as punishment, and are restricted from performing the offices or wearing the vestments of the priesthood. The first part is for your own protection, Throkar doesn't appear pleased with you."

Dalanar grunted in response.

Eccuro pressed heavily on the cane as he rose from his chair. He turned to leave.

"Thank you for coming, preceptor," Astabar said. "There's always a place for you with me. Pray, and I should be able to hear you. I'll send Dalanar to attend to your needs personally."

The sorcerer coughed behind them.

"Now that is a tempting offer, Great Lord."

His eyes sparkled again, and Quin couldn't let him go without speaking to him.

"Father Eccuro." She met him at the door. "I noticed you're having problems with joint sickness. I have a recipe for a tea that can help with the pain and swelling. I could also offer a prayer for Yhellania's healing."

He scrutinized her. "A Servant? You don't look much like one."

"Of a kind. I serve Sarael."

"The Handmaiden? What are you doing so far from your mistress?" He tutted at her.

"They're afraid to leave Csiz Luan with Laniof's killer on the loose. Someone had to come fix things."

He smiled. "I'll gladly accept your recipe, but I'll pass on the prayer. I can't say my treatment of the Yhellani has always been exemplary enough to survive the scrutiny of your goddess. I'd rather not call on her for judgment."

CHAPTER THIRTY-SIX

TIME FOR YOU TO contribute to the common good, Sarael." Gardanath erupted into the forest suite, slamming the heavy double doors open. Barrand drew his sword and threw himself in front of the avatar with an instinctive lunge. His pulse pounded in his ears.

"Whoa, good man. A little early for combat, eh?" Gardanath raised his hands in mock surrender.

Barrand glared and sheathed his blade. "You surprised me." He stepped aside grudgingly. Sharing the manor with the Throkari drove his instinct to guard Sarael to levels of intensity he hadn't believed possible.

Sarael and the Servants spent the afternoon rolling bandages and processing herbs with several of the Yhellani priests from the local temple. The table between them was mounded with loose-woven cloth that had been boiled in Yarrow root and kiln dried. The avatar watched her adherents with a possessive glow. Barrand was pleased to see Sarael relaxed and happy. Far too rare an experience for her.

"And how would my time be better used, Gardanath?" Sarael tied off a bandage and flipped it into a large sack nearing its capacity at her feet.

"Word of your presence has spread, and the streets are filling up with pilgrims. If you don't go out, I may have riots. I hate riots."

"So soon?" Sarael turned toward the window as if she expected mobs at the gates. Her aura of enjoyment faded. The view from the room showed only the dusty courtyard and encircling wall of the manor compound beyond the garden.

"Ach, no. I'm not going to let things get that far. I know my job. I've picked out a nice orphanage and school you can visit. Wave to the pilgrims. Do some healing. Bless babies. Everyone will be satisfied. An outing into the city would do you and Conthal good."

"Conthal? Why should he go with us?" Barrand couldn't help the snarl in his voice.

"Don't you think a show of unity between the Yhellani and the Throkari would diffuse some of the aggression, at least among the populace?"

Sarael nodded. "When do we go?"

"Now." Gardanath chuckled at their expressions. "I've learned not to give people time to think up excuses when it comes to unpleasant chores. Conthal is waiting in the courtyard. Let's not provide him more reasons to be shrewish with us. He wasn't any happier."

It didn't allow anyone to arrange attacks in advance, either. Barrand approved.

Sarael's chair rasped against the floor as she stood. Around her, the Servants scrambled to their feet.

Father Jol hurried up. "I will accompany you since the handmaiden isn't here."

Jol enjoyed pointing out ways Quin failed in her service to the avatar—even when it wasn't her doing. He complained about Quin until Barrand wanted to pulp the man's ratty face.

"If you wish, Jol," Sarael said.

Sarael's dimple disappeared when she talked to the priest. A sign, Barrand had learned, that indicated how much the avatar disliked someone.

Sarael turned to the Servants from Csiz Luan. "Mother Aeralan and Father Jairit, would you join us? Outreach to a school could benefit the temple."

The young priestess blushed from her plump cheeks to the roots of her chin-length black hair. Her skin blazed in contrast with her white dress. The Yhellani from the city didn't live in fear like those outside the walls. They openly wore traditional Servant clothing.

Jairit nudged her with a broad shoulder and broader grin. "Aeralan has done some outreach at the local schools already, ay? What's your priest's name? Varen?"

Aeralan avoided Sarael's gaze, but her skin deepened to a shade of maroon Barrand thought only redheads achieved.

He didn't approve of Yhellani becoming involved with Throkari, but took pity on the young woman. "How many guards will Sarael have assigned to her?"

"Dear Sister, if I had any chance of hiring this man away from you, I would offer him his weight in gold. Barrand, bring as many guards as you want. I won't stand between you and your duty."

Sarael narrowed her eyes at him, but the dimple was back. "Two, Barrand."

"Five."

"It defeats the purpose of going out among the people if I'm surrounded by soldiers. Two and Gardanath brings guards of his own." She glanced at the avatar for confirmation.

"Three, and you don't use up your power healing others."

Sarael sniffed but acquiesced. She straightened her robe and tried to dust off the dirt and leaf debris that accumulated in her lap. Barrand left Sarael as some of the women attacked her hair with a comb.

By the time they arrived in the courtyard, everyone was assembled. Gardanath had attached a voluminous scarlet cloak to his ceremonial bronze breastplate and wore a crested helm. Cheek guards swept down into points like talons. With a crimson kilt and sandals, he resembled a warrior out of myth.

Barrand stopped short at the sight of him.

"The people of Csiz Luan appreciate a little theater from their gods. They're going to be sorely disappointed with the two of you." Gardanath grimaced at Sarael and Conthal's simple robes. "Don't you have any of those purple hoods your priests wear? You should at least make an effort to stand out."

Conthal lifted his chin. "I am the head of the Throkari church. I don't need vestments to display my rank."

"We could call on our gods to give the people a real show, Gardanath," Sarael said with a mischievous smile.

"Bah. Good thing I'm coming along. You might be mistaken for beggars and escorted from the city."

The big avatar muttered to himself as he led the way to the gates of the manor. Conthal joined Gardanath. Barrand and the Yhellani guardsworn walked next to Sarael while Jol and the Servants hurried to keep up. Ten Ravendi soldiers formed up around them.

Once the heavy doors opened, the noise from the city nearly overwhelmed Barrand. A cheer echoed off the walls when the crowd spotted Gardanath. When they saw Sarael and Conthal there was an intake of breath, and a deafening cry of excitement.

Throngs of people jammed together against the buildings four and five deep, while red-clad mercenaries restrained them. Representatives from every ethnicity, nationality, and religion struggled to catch a glimpse of the procession. Dark-robed Throkari priests crowded in beside blonde Enng herders who still wore their rough horsehide riding gear. A tall Asori scholar touched a handkerchief to his nose and edged away from the Enng, the white cloth contrasting brilliantly with his dark complexion. A few travelers from Rynd, their skin and eyes eerily pale, stood out from the olive and creamy-tan faces of the Dacti.

Tired and dirty villagers jostled among the townspeople. Their clothing was simple and travel-worn, and they stared at Sarael with hungry desperation. What did they needed urgently enough to make the journey?

"Mother Sarael! Lady Sarael!" One woman, braver than the others, attempted to push her way out between the guards. Barrand and Thera stepped in front of the avatar. The mercenaries in charge of controlling the crowds caught the villager and shoved her away.

"Please, my boy is sick. Will you bless him? Heal him?" She was young, but silver streaked her mousy hair, and her eyes were weary. A weather-beaten man pushed up beside her, carrying the limp form of a toddler.

Sarael nudged Barrand aside and gestured for the man to bring the child closer. Gardanath called orders for their guard to stand at attention. Conthal sighed and wandered over to observe.

The boy had some kind of wasting sickness. His arms and legs were withered, and his face gaunt, but his belly was swollen. When Sarael lifted his shirt, dark shapes pooled under the sallow surface of his skin. His internal organs were enlarged and corrupted. The child stared at the sky, unblinking. Yhellania's power couldn't save him.

"Remember your promise, Sarael."

Tears ran down her cheeks. "Barrand...."

Barrand had to turn away and wipe the water from his own eyes.

The mother, seeing their expressions, fumbled to pull the little shirt down over the bloated belly. The father stared uncomprehendingly. He shook his head and grew more distressed with each refusal.

Sarael reached out her hand and touched both the boy and the father, as if by chance. With a flash of power, the feeling of spring sunlight, a warm caress of rain, the smell of lilacs and sweet loam filled their senses. The boy looked between Sarael and Conthal and smiled with no trace of pain. He turned to his mother and father with the same relieved expression. The boy sighed and closed his eyes. His small chest stopped its painful rattling and didn't rise again.

Conthal stroked the child's cheek. "I have intervened with Throkar on your son's behalf. His soul will bypass the Mysteries without challenge. He need not undergo the Death ceremony, unless you wish it."

The father stared at the limp boy in his arms with no reaction.

Anguish tore across the mother's face, but she sank into an awkward curtsy. "Thank you, Lady. Thank you, Lord." She repeated herself, backing away, and tugging the man along with her.

Barrand ached to help them. To do something to make it better. The silent crowd parted for the couple, and they disappeared down a side street.

Gardanath let out a gusty sigh. "You know, Sarael, that wasn't what I had in mind when I suggested a few miracles. Can we avoid killing children from here on out?"

Barrand stepped between the avatars. "We don't question how you make war. Don't question how Sarael uses her gifts."

The Ravendi squinted at him. "I see. Well, far be it for me to criticize your mistress' healing." Gardanath slapped Barrand on the shoulder and chuckled. "Shall we continue? Hordes of screaming school children await our progress breathlessly."

The man's words made Barrand strangely uncomfortable. He glanced at Sarael. Her eyes were red-rimmed and her face blotchy, but it didn't diminish her radiance.

She touched Gardanath's arm. "We need to set up a clinic at the manor. I must attend to these serious illnesses. While I'm here, I can do some good."

"You'll get more cases of soldiers with the rot than anything else."

"My Servants can care for the less serious issues."

"To a soldier with rot, there is no more serious issue."

Sarael actually laughed, a joyful tinkling sound that made Barrand's heart beat faster.

"Between the Ravendi military and the Yhellani faithful, I'm surprised you haven't infected each other out of existence," Conthal said.

"We have exceptional medical care. That *is* what the Yhellani do."

AN ASORI MERCHANT CALLED to Sarael from a street corner where the crowd thinned. The woman wore a rich robe of sapphire and emerald. The colors were a welcome change from the dull, monochrome palette of most Dactite and Terrisean clothing. A tiny prism hung from the woman's neck on a delicate silver chain. The crystal caught the light and cast colored rainbows on her skin. An adherent of the artist god. Did she make the robe? It was unlike anything Barrand had ever seen.

Sarael paused before the woman, her attention drawn to the brilliant hues.

"Lady Sarael. Please, help us! My brother is dying. I brought him as soon as I learned you were here."

"Where is he now?"

The woman gestured to someone behind her. Several men at the edge of the crowd lifted a litter with a blanket-covered figure. They set him at the women's feet.

Sarael knelt and tugged at the blanket. The patient was a heavyset man, who looked like he normally enjoyed health and prosperity, but now his skin sagged and dark rings circled his eyes. Bruises mottled his face, and his eyelids and lips had a purple cast even Barrand knew was serious. Sarael examined his hands. They shaded to black at the fingertips. Even his nail beds took on the deep, purplish hue.

The avatar touched the woman's sleeve. "Did you make your robe?"

The woman stared at her nonplussed. "We just opened a shop. I sew and sell, and he dyes the fabric. He figured out how to produce the brilliant colors." The merchant pressed her fists to her mouth. "The dye isn't coloring his hands."

"What does he use in his tints?"

"I- I don't know." She dropped to her knees next to the litter and took the man's other hand. "I don't care about the dyes or the colors. I just want my brother. Can you help him?" she whispered.

Barrand started in surprise. For the faithful of the god who brought color to the world to say such a thing was blasphemous.

"I believe he's poisoned with something in his vats: this isn't a natural illness. I'll try to purge the toxins from him. But even if this works, he'll become sick again if he can't find the cause."

Conthal shifted closer. "This is another one for me, Sarael."

"Let the woman work, Throkari. Plenty for you to do later," Gardanath called to him.

The slender avatar shrugged and stepped aside.

Sarael spun out glowing threads of magic until they encircled her with light. She closed her eyes and directed the spiral of energy into the man's body, submerging it inside him from head to feet. Power poured in but did not emerge. Sarael frowned thoughtfully. She untied his shirt and listened to his heart. After a moment's consideration, she sent the cascade into him again. Now light gushed out, soiled a putrid gray. The avatar cocked her head in satisfaction and let the energy circulate through her.

The crowd pressed in, quiet with awe. Guards held them back. The guardsworn scanned the faces searching for any sign of hostility.

Barrand watched Conthal. What did the man think when he regarded Sarael? Did he see the village maiden, the avatar, or the hated destroyer of his precious tree? Was it possible for him to see beyond his loathing to the good she brought into the world? Did he imagine killing her? Barrand gripped his sword tighter.

Conthal noticed his attention. "I am studying sources of magic not based upon sorcery. Gardanath refuses to demonstrate his divine power, thus I am left with the others. My opportunities for observing Sarael are ... limited."

When the light emerging from the Morgiri man was the same clean essence as the arc surrounding the avatar, she reeled it in. The world seemed darker and dirtier despite the sun shining above the building clouds.

The patient opened his eyes and thrashed around in weak confusion. The woman kissed his cheeks, and then turned back. "Thank you, Lady Sarael."

"He is frail. A great deal of damage was done, and will take time to heal. Keep him away from the vats until he's recovered."

"Send a list of the ingredients in his dye to the alchemy professors at the university. They can provide advice on what is toxic and how to safely handle the chemicals," Conthal said.

"Thank you, Lord Conthal."

She pulled a wrapped bundle out from under her brother's knees and handed it to Sarael. "We don't have much money yet, but we do have our material. Please take this with our gratitude."

Gardanath bumped Conthal with his elbow. "That healing ability is quite useful to have around, wouldn't you say?"

"Too much, and you'll put my priests out of their jobs."

"Bah, Throkar takes us all in the end. It's only a matter of how fast we get there."

The avatars and those parading after them surprised the regular citizens. It lent a holiday air to an otherwise dull day. People closed their shops to step out and watch, and the more excitable ran ahead to tell their friends. The whole situation made Barrand nervous, and he wanted to call it off. Conthal was too civil; Barrand's teeth itched in anticipation of an attack or humiliation.

Sarael stopped to heal a few more people. Their illnesses much less serious than the first cases, and Gardanath smiled in satisfaction.

"You can stay in Csiz, Sarael. You're welcome and you could do your healing in safety." Gardanath walked beside her and spoke quietly.

"That is generous and tempting. At times I want nothing more than my own home."

"But?"

"The people who need me most can't travel. I must be out with them, not tucked away behind walls." Sarael smiled at a child waving from the edge of the crowd.

"They would know where to find you if you stayed in one place."

"Someone always knows where to find me. The Throkari haven't made us so desperate yet."

Gardanath shrugged. "The offer stands."

CHAPTER THIRTY-SEVEN

LEARY RETURNED WITH AN over-sized journal containing the record of the avatar's completed paintings, their title, subject, reference number, and location, if on display. The portraits in the studio weren't the only ones, or even the most recent, just significant to Laniof in some way.

The boy laid the book down on the table farthest from Dalanar's work area and opened to a crumbling page. "The picture of Conthal was done about eighty years ago. No record of Sarael. There was one of Gardanath, but it wasn't in the assigned slot."

"I'm sure this is fascinating, however irrelevant to our current goals," Dalanar reminded them testily.

Quin's stomach growled. The morning meal had been hours ago, and they could all use food. "Rylir, where can we find something to eat?"

Even Dalanar glanced up from the bag of iron filings.

"I'll have a meal brought in from the kitchens. You're our guests."

"What you mean, is that we're not supposed to leave," Dalanar said.

She smiled sheepishly. "Not all of you, Your Grace."

"Guards?" he asked.

"Nooo. Morgir described what he would do to you if you tried to go. I had to ask what some of the words meant, and it sounded really painful." She hopped off her stool and hurried for the door. "Shall I request lunch?"

"Bring plenty of extra. Dalanar eats enough for three." Eulesis called after the girl, and Quin hoped Rylir heard. She didn't want to be hungry the rest of the day.

Quin wandered over to the easel at the front of the room and examined the drying paint on the palette. She picked up the brush caked with rust-colored pigment.

"Cleary, what was Laniof working on before he died? Was it a portrait of someone you knew?"

The apprentice skirted gingerly around Dalanar and joined her. "A woman, I think. He was drafting in the rough shapes when I went to bed. I didn't see any of his preliminary sketches." He flipped through the papers that lay scattered around the desk. Cleary stopped and took a deep breath. "Laniof wouldn't let me touch his drawings before. Now, I guess I need to ready things for the new avatar. May as well do this right." He started gathering them into a neat pile.

"What happened to the canvas? It couldn't have been this one," Quin said.

"The blank one was on the easel when I found him ... in the morning."

"The killer didn't want anyone to see his painting. What would she have done with it? Burn it? Here or somewhere else?"

Eulesis wandered over. "I'd get out as soon as possible. Morgir would have been in shock from the death of his avatar, but she couldn't predict how long that might last or when he would manifest."

"Were the doors of the room locked?" Quin asked.

Cleary scrunched up his face in thought. "Only the one to the outside. The one to the main hall was ajar."

"She might have used one of the fireplaces," Quin said.

Eulesis scoffed. "Too obvious."

"He worked on large canvases. I wouldn't want to be caught with one when Morgir showed up."

"Wouldn't hurt to check."

The fireplaces in the Great Hall were dark and unneeded in the late spring weather. A pile of fine ash hid behind the grate of one of the otherwise clean hearths. Quin grabbed an ornate poker and sifted through the cinders. The wood from a picture frame compressed several layers of canvas beneath it, preserving a fragment of color. She slid the charred sliver onto her palm.

"I can't figure out what this is. Maybe in good light."

Eulesis stared in disbelief. "Completely unprofessional."

"A hired killer? A sorceress?" Quin grimaced with distaste. "Don't tell Gardanath or Dalanar. That's too awful to contemplate." She recalled the sorcerer turning the cult leader to ash with a touch to the forehead and shivered.

"Do you believe the idea hasn't occurred to them, Quin?" Eulesis considered her with equal parts pity and amusement.

"Oh."

The blonde touched Quin's cheek. "I don't know how you keep your naïveté. It would be charming in anyone else. You're handmaiden to Sarael, and I suppose she prefers you that way, but you need to grow-up now, and quickly." She dropped her hand to Quin's shoulder. "Gardanath, Sarael, Conthal, Me, Dalanar ... We are not *nice*. We've done things you would find repugnant. Some of us may love you, but that doesn't mean we won't use you for our own ends. Games are being played that have lasted longer than you and I have been alive. They won't hesitate to throw us away if it suits their needs. We're their best *pawns*, Quin. Don't forget that."

"Sarael is different!"

"Sarael is kind. That is the only difference." Eulesis ran a hand over her hair. "I'm not saying this to offend you. I want you to survive being the handmaiden. You don't understand how we fight. You haven't cultivated a deep enough distrust of people to do that."

"What is the game? Whom should I watch for? Is Dalanar—"

"Now that Dalanar is either going to be dead or a new avatar, he may be the last person you need to worry about for a while. I don't know what else to tell you. I don't have the answers, either."

Quin stared after Eulesis as the woman reentered the studio. Too naive? She had been on campaign with the Ravendi mercenaries for several years, fought in bloody battles, and witnessed the aftermath of attacks on Yhellani Servants. *She* was too trusting and innocent? Ridiculous!

"I kept my avatar out of their games, and he was murdered anyway." Morgir appeared beside her. "Was I wrong to do so?"

"Great Lord," Quin started in surprise and hurried to bow. He regarded her with empty, colorless eyes until she thought of a reply. "Was he happy?"

"Yes. Although, he might have enjoyed the company of other avatars. Eulesis isn't wrong. They'll tear you to pieces between them. You may have seen horrors, handmaiden, but that doesn't prepare you for the intrigues." He inspected the scrap in her open palm. "What is this?"

"The remains of Laniof's last painting. Burned in the fireplace."

"Ah. Any more evidence?"

"Not yet."

"You would not be averse to Dalanar's death. Why work so hard for this?"

"He didn't do it."

"He's guilty of many other things."

"Yes, but not this."

"Laniof always liked naive people." Morgir gave her a significant look.

"Have you selected a new avatar yet?"

"I see no reason to hurry."

It occurred to Quin that someone was missing. "Where is Laniof's second? Why haven't we met them?"

"It wasn't necessary for him to have one. If you're not involved in those games, you don't need a pawn to move around the board." He nodded with a slight smile, and returned to the gold-draped corpse. Was he teasing?

DALANAR STUDIED QUIN WHEN she walked into the studio. "Are they having you work to pay for our upkeep? I'd definitely complain to Sarael about that."

Eulesis handed her a rag and Quin realized she was streaked with soot. She placed the charred canvas on the counter and wiped herself off. "This is the only fragment left."

Dalanar moved one of the candles with a reflector closer and they leaned in. Wispy streaks of yellow and red ran across a field of mahogany brown. The same color as the paint dried on the brushes.

"Hair?" Quin looked at the others for confirmation.

"Possibly fur, like the trim on your tabard," Dalanar said. "What is that? Fox?"

Eulesis winked at Quin. "Probably rabbit."

"Sable. This looks more like hair, though. Fur would change color down the length of each strand."

"Who are the redheaded sorceresses?" Eulesis pulled the list out of her vest.

"Ordanna and Mirindra," Quin said without hesitation.

Dalanar stared at her.

"I'm right, aren't I?"

Eulesis scanned the parchment and nodded.

The sorcerer sputtered. "You only glanced at the list this morning. How did ... You memorized it?"

Quin enjoyed the man's chagrin; he was always so annoyingly composed. "It's not hard. Can't you do the same?"

"You have an eidetic memory," he accused.

She shrugged. "It's just a knack."

"Great Lord Throkar, why was such a gift wasted on a Yhellani?"

Quin smiled sweetly. "That must have been a terrible hardship for you when learning magic."

Dalanar pressed at his temples.

Eulesis grinned at them. "This afternoon, when Magda and I continue our questioning, we'll focus on those two. Red hair is uncommon enough in Tyrentanna she will have left an impression."

"Now, let us find out if this has been worth the effort." He lifted the bust off the table and set it on the stool Eccuro vacated earlier. Dalanar opened the pouch and sifted the dust through his fingers. He poured the fine powder into his palm, and with a deep breath, sprinkled it over the bald head of the figure until gray metal coated the top. As he added more, Quin realized that the aspect of a hand emerged in the center. The granules collected over the print, while in other areas they sloughed off when they grew too thick. The sorcerer tapped the side of the marble figure, and in a powdery rush, all but the metal filings in the handprint cascaded to the floor.

Dalanar's smug satisfaction pulsed through their connection as he inspected the mark. The sensation faded into disappointment.

"What?" She walked over to stand beside him. The handprint warped like a shadow projected against a wall. Unidentifiable. His method would have worked if the sorceress used a flat surface to ground herself. There was no way to prove it wasn't his mark.

Astabar sighed. "Most unfortunate."

Dalanar glared at him. "Can't you do something?"

"I am doing something. I'm keeping the pain under control so you can prove your innocence instead of writhing in bed wishing you were dead. Beyond that would be cheating."

The sorcerer groaned and wandered over to a window. He chewed on a knuckle.

Cleary paused sorting papers. "What is he trying to do?"

Quin knelt beside him and picked up one of the piles. Drawings of an elderly man. "Sorcerers leave a glowing handprint behind after they use their power. He tried to recover the mark to prove it's different from his own."

"I saw it."

She rubbed her shoulder. "They're memorable."

Cleary was about to say more, when Rylir tossed open the door and led in three servants loaded down with trays of food.

They laid out platters of fire-roasted vegetables and corn, smoked chicken, and hot rolls with a sharp, creamy cheese. Quin didn't miss the stale bread and salted meat of the guardsworn traveling rations. Dalanar's mood didn't affect his appetite, and he was already filling his plate. She caught his eye and smiled at his slightly embarrassed expression.

As she ate, Quin examined her companions. How did someone stop being naive and trusting? How do you assume the worst about people you love? Do you expect they've already done the most terrible things you can imagine? Easy to believe of Conthal and Dalanar, possibly Gardanath, but never of Sarael. How do you prepare for intrigue when your life primed you for open warfare? Black and white not shades of gray. Was Dalanar right?

She considered him. The man rested against a bank of the slotted cabinets, a cluster of grapes held in one hand. He appeared undressed without his black robes. Vulnerable. Quin doubted he was cold. He wasn't Fevered, but he looked uncomfortable. Dalanar noticed her attention and returned it suspiciously.

For the first time she didn't turn away. He expected the worst of people. She doubted he was capable of love, but he treated everyone with the same level of distrust. He was raised by Conthal in a world of so many shades of gray it must have been practically twilight. Intrigue surrounded him like a murky fog. If he survived, maybe she would ask his advice. Ironically, he might be the least invested in the outcome and the most qualified to answer.

"What do you want, Quinthian?" Dalanar stepped in front of her, blocking her view of the room.

She met his gaze. "You're right. What you said that night about my thinking of the world in black and white. You're right."

He blinked. "I may have been unnecessarily harsh."

"Or not harsh enough. I'm also naive, trusting and a plaything for Sarael."

"Mmm." Dalanar rubbed the back of his neck. "Eulesis?"

Quin nodded. "And Morgir."

"Painful."

"At least he didn't flash his eyes at me."

"And?"

"You are the least naive, trusting, black and white person I know."

"I'm still a plaything?"

"A puppet."

"What are you?"

"I'm a pawn."

Dalanar threw back his head and laughed the first genuine laugh Quin ever heard from him. Her heart beat faster at the sound. No. Not Dalanar. Why did Yhellania *still* torment her like this?

"Gods have mercy, Quin. What do you want from me?" His voice was low and slightly hoarse.

Heat surged through their connection, and, although Dalanar didn't move any closer, he reached for her with his desire. Sensations washed over Quin, and she closed her eyes at the intensity. Images pressed against her mind: Dalanar kissed the corner of her mouth, and moved lower to the angle of her jaw and the pulse at her neck. Quin wrapped strong legs around his hips, and she pulled him down to meet her hungry lips. A soft purr escaped from deep inside her chest. Dalanar caressed her breasts, taking the tip of one, then the other into his mouth. He flicked each crest with his tongue until she arched in pleasure.

Quin took a shuddering breath and bumped against the easel. Dalanar caught her wrist and wouldn't let her retreat further. "What happened? You said you knew when Astabar geised me. Do you still sense ... things?"

She twisted her arm out of Dalanar's grip. "The connection isn't broken—at least from my side. I can feel you. Sometimes."

"Now?"

"Don't be angry with *me*. You were the one who cast the spell."

"What did you feel?"

Quin tried not to, but she blushed. Dalanar looked away.

"Can I turn it off?"

The sorcerer shook his head. "No. When I regain my powers I'll figure out a way to disable it."

"Let's prove your innocence. Then you can fix this."

Dalanar gave her a weak smile. "You're quite blasé about being able to read my emotions."

"The images are engrossing, as well. I worried I had gone mad when I woke up in Csiz Luan with pictures of you naked lodged in my mind."

Dalanar swallowed hard.

CHAPTER THIRTY-EIGHT

EULESIS, MAGDA, AND ASTABAR went out after eating to question the next shift of guards about the sorceresses. Dalanar, Quin, and the apprentices sat in uncomfortable silence over the remains of lunch.

Rylir slid off her stool and started collecting the dishes. "Do you want to see the replica of the staff I made?"

Dalanar handed her his plate. "Might as well. I'm out of ideas."

He avoided looking at Quin as Rylir led them up the stairs to the second level of the Gallery. The sorcerer was controlling his reactions. The connection between them held an echoing emptiness. His presence in that intangible place had been warm and solid; she now felt cold and exposed.

The small apprentice room contained workspaces for four. Rylir's corner held a narrow worktable, shelves, and locking bins mounted on the walls. A rotating platform and a stool dominated the center. A marble block rested on top, a few chips already taken out.

Quin expected a shy, sweet child like Rylir to sculpt animals or nature scenes. She was wrong. The work on display captured the violence of combat as if the girl was Ravendis' daughter. *A soldier caught mid-swing made one last parry against an overpowering opponent. Blood soaked clothes. Feet slipped on offal. Limbs were shattered and limp. Bodies torn, armor broken.* Frozen in pristine white marble, making the madness of war seem more alien and absurd in contrast.

"Rylir," Quin whispered.

The girl pulled at her apron. "Do you like them? You're a soldier, are they realistic?"

Quin inspected each masterpiece speechlessly.

The connection with Dalanar opened and she jerked upright.

:: Say something to the girl.::

Quin gaped at Dalanar in surprise. He could *speak* to her? He still refused to meet her gaze.

"Rylir, these are ... stunning. How do you know...? You've captured the brutality of war perfectly."

The apprentice beamed. "I study the guard practice every morning. And I talk to our veterans."

"You're already a master, Rylir. Why are you in with the apprentices?" Dalanar examined another sculpture. *A warrior lay dying against a ruined tree. He tugged weakly at the arrows piercing his chest in a fruitless effort to save himself.*

The girl shuffled her feet. "I'm not. I make plenty of mistakes. Master Arnard says I'm years away from even Journiere level."

Dalanar grunted. "Arnard is envious. You need someone else to evaluate your work. Did you show these to Laniof?"

"Of course not! I wouldn't bother the avatar with apprentice projects." Rylir opened one of the cabinets and pulled out a larger copy of the staff. She set the sculpture on top of the marble block between them. "This is full size."

Quin took an involuntary step back. The parts of the smaller model that made her queasy before were magnified in the larger scale. The design with its alien pattern and symmetry drew her in and trapped her in a maze. She followed paths with her gaze, tracing the motifs, trying to find the end. Quin attempted to look away. She retraced the path again. The room dissolved around her. The conversation between Dalanar and Rylir sounded muffled. Quin inhaled and centered herself, as if before combat, and tried to focus on one of the statues of fighting on the table. She retraced the pattern again.

The link with Dalanar was silent. She didn't know how to call out to him, or even if it was possible. She retraced the path again.

What about the shield she used to block his geis? It lay discarded in a corner of her mind, dusty and battered. She dragged it over to where the motif seared into her brain. When the path began again, she braced herself behind it. The barrier shattered, but Quin turned aside at last. "Would you put that away now, Rylir?"

Dalanar regarded her with a blend of curiosity and hunger, yet nothing leaked across the bond. She was grateful for his discipline.

She viewed Rylir with new respect. The child could not only view the object, but also recreate it several times. Quin wouldn't be capable of that, even had she possessed the artistic ability.

"A lot of people found the staff upsetting. That's why I made the smaller one." She returned it to the cabinet.

"How are you not affected?" Dalanar asked.

The girl shrugged. "I felt a little strange at first. But then, it was just fascinating."

"It's powerful, even as a reproduction. Could it be used...?" Quin let her question trail off.

"The original gained substantial power from the material it was made from." Dalanar returned to studying the sculptures, hands clasped behind his back.

"What now?" Quin asked.

::Show Morgir the statues.:: Dalanar spoke inside her mind. Aloud he said, "I don't know."

"Will that help prove your innocence?"

"No." :: He needs to see them.::

Rylir tilted her head at Quin.

"Rylir, which of these is your best?"

The girl mulled the question for a moment and pointed to the man with the arrows, dying beside the tree.

"Would you mind if I showed Eulesis? She may want to commission something for Gardanath ... if you're not willing to sell one of these?"

"Oh no, I couldn't!"

"Can I show her?"

Rylir chewed her lip, but picked up the statue and placed the cold marble in Quin's hands.

THE APPRENTICE TRIED TO hurry them through the main hall and into the studio, but Quin lingered. The Gallery swarmed with people. Hopeful artists waited in line to show Morgir their best work. The god sat in his usual place beside Laniof's draped body. He stared blankly at petitioners as they trundled by under the direction of the guards and masters.

"I need a word with Morgir. Would you excuse me for a moment?"

Rylir made a wordless cry and grabbed for the sculpture, but Dalanar stepped in front of her to inspect a painting displayed by a young woman in line.

Morgir barely acknowledged Quin when she bowed before him, although several of the artists glowered.

"Great Lord, we found that the scrap of canvas represents auburn hair. Two sorceresses have that coloration. We're now seeking confirmation they were in the city."

"This is your proof, handmaiden?" Morgir's eyes flashed. He glanced down at the sculpture in her hands and stilled. She held it out for him to see.

"Who ... Rylir? Where is she?"

Quin beckoned the apprentice over and the girl came, dragging her feet.

"What is the meaning of this, small one? Where is your master?"

"Why did you show him? Now I'm in trouble. He'll send me away!" Apprehension filled Rylir's eyes.

"It'll be fine. I promise," Quin whispered.

A lithe man with strangely large hands, and the pale complexion of the Rynd joined them. "Great Lord?"

"Master Arnard, please explain this sculpture to me."

"Not one of apprentice Rylir's better pieces. Her proportions are off, and her careless chisel work cracked the marble of the tree. Her pre-work sketches were amateurish and sloppy. All of her projects have similar failings. She is not living up to the promise she showed when we brought her to the Gallery."

Morgir stared at him, and finally motioned for Quin to hand him the statue. He examined it from every angle.

"Rylir, some of what Arnard says is not wrong. Much remains for you to learn. However, he is mistaken about your promise. You have gone far beyond our expectations."

The girl gaped at him in disbelief.

"This is unquestionably a level one mastery project, but I fear you're too young for the title. To rush such things would do you more harm than good. We shall promote you to Journiere, and continue your education under a number of different masters."

Rylir fell to her knees in front of him and lowered her head. "Thank you, Great Lord. Thank you."

"Oh tush, small one. Stand up." Morgir patted her shoulder.

"What a captivating subject. Show me the rest of your work." He placed the first piece on the fabric-covered bench beside him.

QUIN AND DALANAR RETREATED to the studio as Rylir darted up the stairs to retrieve more of her statues.

Cleary crouched on the floor, still sorting Laniof's papers.

"That was ... kind of you, Dalanar." Quin grinned. If intrigue ended with good people rewarded, maybe it wouldn't be such a bad thing to learn.

Cleary looked up in surprise.

"Her master's jealousy obviously held her back," Dalanar said.

"You're extraordinarily imperious, even inside my head."

"I learned from an expert."

Cleary jumped to his feet. "What happened? Is Rylir all right?"

"That would be Journiere Rylir to you, Cleary. Dalanar tricked her into showing Morgir her sculptures."

"The tricking was Quin's doing. She won't be a pawn much longer."

The boy wouldn't face Dalanar, but his forehead wrinkled in confusion.

"We'll let Rylir tell you. She's thrilled." Quin winked at the apprentice.

Dalanar stepped closer to the boy and frowned down at him for a long moment. Quin's smile faded. Cleary froze like a trapped animal.

"The village of Valgate."

Cleary moaned, but didn't move.

"It was your grandmother I geised? She was strong. I couldn't break into her mind."

The apprentice turned to look into Dalanar's black eyes, his face resigned. Expecting the horror had come for him at last. Quin prepared to leap between them.

"I'm ... sorry, Cleary. I'm sorry your grandmother died."

The apprentice bolted from the room, slamming the door hard enough to shatter the window. Quin started after him. He ran across the green swath of lawn and past the Gallery arcade, then darted behind a hedge and disappeared.

Dalanar was rubbing his temples and leaning against a work-table when she returned to the quiet room.

"You're doing your good deeds before you die. You're giving up?"

"I intend to enjoy a few more excellent meals, as well."

"That's it?" How could he give up? They had barely started their investigation. It seemed out of character for someone who endured being celibate for twenty years just for the ability to do some magic. Of course, that might be why he lacked the will to live.

"I don't know what else to do, Quin. If you have any ideas, I would hear them."

"I'm an ignorant Yhellani peasant. You're Conthal's best student. Think of something!"

For several minutes, the murmurs of conversation from the main hall were the only sounds.

Quin wasn't about to give up so easily; she still needed to find the killer. She climbed onto the stool beside Dalanar. "How close are you sorcerers to each other? Are you friends? Rivals? Lovers? Do you correspond? Like the same food and entertainment?"

"How is this relevant?"

"If you only stay in the same type of inn, or eat the same food, we can visit those places and ask if they've been seen. Tell me about them."

Dalanar shrugged. "Ordanna and I were close, at one time."

Quin raised an eyebrow.

"Conthal trained her at the Golden Darkness, although she never became Throkari. She left before we started the Secrets. Conthal was disappointed and Ordanna was angry, but she knew the requirement and refused."

"Is she capable of murder?"

"She's a sorceress raised by Conthal."

The assumption inherent in that simple statement made Quin's heart ache. How many sorcerers had Conthal indoctrinated in his unnaturally long life? How many thought nothing of killing Yhellani?

"What about Mirindra?"

"Mirindra studied under Gridarl. I'm not sure of her abilities. There is a certain rivalry between the university sorcerers and the rest of us. They regard us as religious fanatics. We find them unskilled and weak."

"Is Ordanna as powerful as you?"

"No. Neither one is."

"Any type of inn you lot prefer?"

"The warmest."

"Where would you stay in Lyratrum?"

"I know of a few places. I will note them down."

The sorcerer found a piece of parchment and wrote out the list. The sun shone through the windows behind him casting the planes of his face in high contrast. Shiny black hair fell into his eyes, and he kept trying to sweep it into place with one hand. Wasn't evil supposed to be ugly? She shook her head.

"With the Fevers, sorcerers have difficulty being with normal people. Can they match body temperatures with other sorcerers?"

Dalanar smiled faintly. "It has been tried."

"And? Was the experiment successful? You and Ordanna didn't try in the name of advancing knowledge?"

"I'm still not a Yhellani."

"What does that mean?"

"It is none of your concern."

Quin puffed at him in exasperation and amusement. "Do either of them have any idiosyncrasies that would make them stand out? Bathe in the blood of kittens?"

"Beyond the casting diet, no. If I wanted to be inconspicuous, I would keep my Fever down. Use limited power."

"You were close once, but not now? Did you have a falling out or was it simply because she left?"

"That is also none of your concern."

Quin glared at him. "How can you be certain it isn't related to this situation? You *were* implicated in the murder. Maybe she holds a grudge."

"You imagine Ordanna killed Laniof as revenge for my breaking her heart? How melodramatic, Quinthian. I certainly don't need to go so far afield to find people who wish me ill." He inclined his head meaningfully at her.

"Perhaps you hadn't noticed, sorcerer, I'm trying to assist you. Why don't you help instead of mocking me? If you don't want my aid, I have better ways to spend the afternoon."

She pushed away from the table and stalked over to where Cleary had been sorting the papers. Maybe there would be something useful in the piles. Dalanar didn't move.

With clanging bells and creaking metal, Morgir's Rose bloomed. Rainbows fluttered over the gardens like butterflies. Quin paused, the sketches forgotten in her hands. It reminded her of the Chapterhouse in full bloom. Happier times. Before the sorrow. She sighed when the spray of light faded, and she returned to the reality of a workshop filled with death and suspicion.

Dalanar walked over to stand beside her, his boots clicking

on the marble tile. He lowered himself to the floor and stretched one long leg out in front of him. She rocked back on her heels in surprise.

"Have you ever experienced a high fever, Quin?"

"I suppose. Yes." She had been sick for days during the siege in Malesini.

"How did you feel?"

What did this have to do with anything? "Weak. Shaky. My body ached."

"Did you want to participate in any of your rituals?"

Quin snorted. "Goddess, no. That was the last thing...." Oh.

"I've been Fevered for twenty years."

"You don't become accustomed?"

"Not that I've noticed."

"You would make a terrible Yhellani."

"Thank you."

Quin chuckled. Twenty years. She would be praying for Yhellania to end her life.

"This is why no Yhellani become sorcerers," Dalanar said.

It was true, although she never understood why. Quin thought it was because a sorcerer would need to seek training from Conthal, but if he had a rival, the instruction was available elsewhere.

"Why *are* there no Yhellani sorcerers?" she asked seriously.

"We don't know. There is no record of a Servant or even a Yhellani adherent with the ability. Too much sex rots the brain."

"Then the Ravendi wouldn't become sorcerers, either."

"You have a point."

"Was the Summer Festival threat a bluff? Are you telling me this as another good deed to add to your soul?"

"I am not Fevered, and I am not bluffing, Quinthian. However, if I'm dead, you no longer need consider me for the position of consort." The intensity of his regard made her stare down at the papers. A shiver of energy ran over her skin. Damn him. The images he shared with her came to mind. He may have been celibate for years, but he was no inexperienced youth.

"You and Ordanna were never ... intimate?"

"We were during our novitiate. Once we began casting, that sort of thing becomes irrelevant."

Quin wanted to ask why he supposedly took an interest in her, if he had been so happily chaste. She didn't want to call him on his contradiction and risk that intense scrutiny.

"We had a falling out. She insisted that I teach her the Secrets after she refused to become a Throkari priestess. She wanted me to disobey Conthal."

Quin whistled. Gutsy. "You were the Seal by then, weren't you?"

"Yes."

"She expected you to betray Conthal? Even *I* realize that's absurd."

Dalanar rubbed at his ring. "Ordanna didn't always pay attention to other people. She was too focused on her own goals."

Ordanna must have been lousy in bed. No wonder he hadn't cared if he never had another lover.

"I refused, of course. She went on to study with Gridarl. We meet occasionally. Assemblies for sorcerers are held at the university where we present research. An odd affectation, but Conthal enjoys it. She appears satisfied with her life now. I don't know what would lure Ordanna or Mirindra into doing something like this."

Quin thought over what he said. If Conthal wanted the staff, he could easily bribe Ordanna with the Secrets. If Dalanar knew of the plan, he was a good liar and foolish to reveal the information, but it *was* possible.

Who else would pursue the staff? Whoever made the new god, of course. For whatever mysterious reason. The other avatars? Why would Sarael want it? She wouldn't even let Quin find out how to destroy Dalanar; she would hardly allow someone to kill Conthal with the staff. Gardanath? His city was the place avatars went for asylum. And his contempt, even outright hatred, for the gods was painfully clear. He wouldn't make a new one. Possibly, as a weapon: a curiosity? Not something he could want enough to kill Laniof to claim. Eulesis? To protect Gardanath? Again, would it be worth killing Laniof and devastating the economy while trade from Lyratrum shut down? Dalanar? He was ambitious, as Eccuro said. Maybe he wanted to be the next Avatar of Throkar. If Conthal were murdered, whom else would the god select? However, he renounced his vows and swore to become the avatar of another god. If he was responsible for this, his plans had gone horribly wrong. Perhaps one god was as good as another.

"You're plotting."

"You're mistaken." Quin stood and dusted herself off. "Where are these inns? I'll go check them out."

Dalanar gazed past her at the door to the gardens. Afternoon sunlight slanted through the windows and drove the shadow of a figure against the floor and wall behind them.

Cleary wore a pained expression and approached as if walking on ice. His skin looked raw and swollen from crying, but he kept his head raised. He held a scroll of canvas.

Silently, the boy unrolled the painting. Quin half-expected Laniof's redheaded woman, and it took a moment to decipher the image. A sorcerer's mark had been rendered realistically in the center, glowing red, the creases of the hand, outline of the fingers, and shape of the palm limned in light. Around it, reflected as if in a broken mirror, were pieces of the hand in different colors, warped, and reshaped, until it formed an exquisite flower. The handprint didn't belong to Dalanar. Proof.

"Why?" Quin asked.

"Someone needed to help Rylir." He let the roll curl shut and he handed it to her.

"Thank you, Cleary," Dalanar said.

The boy stared at the sorcerer blankly. He jerked his chin at them and left the room.

CHAPTER THIRTY-NINE

TO ACCOMMODATE THE PEOPLE and trade that came through Csiz Luan, the warehouses and poorer tenements had been shifted to the caverns. An interesting idea, but the thought of living or working underground made Barrand uneasy. He needed the sun and wind on his face.

Barrand and the others followed Gardanath down one of the pedestrian tunnels leading to the undercity. It spiraled down though rock hollowed out like the shell of a snail, depositing them beside a large canal. The cavern was immense, although the rough ceiling hung oppressively low. Limestone sheeted down, forming chambers above their heads. It muffled sound, but the calls of the bargers, water dripping and splashing, and the dull thrumming of the river still reverberated in the vast space. Oil lamps burned at regular intervals, and some natural light slipped down through grates in the street far above. Shiny condensation slicked the walls. Waterways crisscrossed and intersected. Bridges were built to peak high over the canals, allowing the passage of the barges being poled along with skillful precision. A complete nightmare.

Barrand turned to Gardanath. "Don't you get a lot of earth shakes here? How many collapses have you had?"

"A handful." The big man waved the question aside. "Not many died, but we've had to close a few corridors. Keep meaning to have some of Conthal's minions come back for a look, but I don't feel like bankrupting the Ravendi at the moment."

"Surely, the children don't live down here. It wouldn't be good for them."

"Space is expensive on the surface. I'd rather use the money to provide them with food and clothes instead of paying outlandish rent."

"It's not right," Barrand said. "Children need fresh air and sunshine."

"We don't imprison them down here. They get plenty of time up top, whether they want it or not. For most, this is home and what they prefer. But don't judge the caverns on one area. These are just the canals from the port. The residential and business areas are nicer."

Barrand pressed his lips together in disapproval.

THEY CROSSED A SERIES of bridges over channels of silky black water until they came to an area of docks and warehouses. The stony roof slanted upward until it became lost in gloom, and no longer gave Barrand such a feeling of oppression.

Laborers unloaded and restocked barges at floating piers. Bales and crates were piled onto low-sided carts pulled by ponies or humans. Protests rang out when a boat cut in front of a line of vessels waiting for berths. A Ravendi guard, patrolling the area, harangued the captain and pushed him off, not allowing the workers to unload him.

Sarael turned to Gardanath with a quizzical expression. "You allow private barges? I thought they all belonged to you, and were hired out to the ships moored on the river."

"Bah. They've started bringing their own. I didn't think to create a law forbidding it, so now I'm stuck until I have the time to change it."

Conthal chuckled and Gardanath glared at him. "What?"

"I am amused they managed to circumvent the Avatar of Trade in his own city. I thought you had everything regulated ... and taxed. You certainly out did yourself negotiating with the sorcerers who built this underground lair."

"You tax sorcery?" Sarael's eyes glinted mischievously.

"Dear sister, I tax everything." He winked at her. "You owe me for the healings you performed."

"That's divine magic!" she protested.

"Magic is magic." He laughed. "I suppose we can figure out some exchange. We'll discuss it later over wine. No use being uncivilized."

They left the canals and warehouses behind, and the caverns gained elevation as they climbed into the residential area. Here the evidence of magical intervention was obvious. Walls were unnaturally smooth and passageways straight.

Brick and pebble masonry blocked off side caverns, forming shops and houses, the wooden doors and window shutters opening onto public areas. A Morgiri artist had painted the walls with the seeds of a variety of mosses, algae, and ferns. Magnificent living murals composed of different colors and textures spread through the corridors. One of the plants, glowing with pale blue light, illuminated the sides of the paths and hallways, in addition to forming the highlights of some of the designs.

Not all the buildings were made from living stone. Free standing structures filled the centers of the larger caverns, utilizing every inch of space. It was surprisingly dry and warm. The smell of smoke and cooking pervaded the air, escaping through chimneys in the ceiling. Not as bad as Barrand expected.

AT LAST, THE ORPHANAGE came in to view on one end of a large natural cave. The complex consisted of several doors and three levels of windows carved into the sides of the cavern. Two additional buildings had been built against the rear wall, where the rock was too weak to excavate. A courtyard at the center provided enough space for the children to assemble. A handful of guards stayed at the entrance to keep the trailing people from intruding.

Twenty orphans waited in rows. They wore a uniform of black short pants for the younger, and trousers for the older, with blue or white smocks. The older ones sported the purple waist sashes of students and were attended by Throkari priests. Caregivers in starched red vests accompanied the ones too young for school. They appeared well-fed and clean. A rarity for any orphanage Barrand had seen. Ravendi orphans were cared for in Csiz Luan. It was a contract with the mercenaries Gardanath took seriously.

Barrand stared. "There are so many. Were the Ravendi exempt from the famine?" Children older than four or younger than sixteen were as rare as spots on a Nag.

Gardanath shook his head. "These are *all* the Ravendi orphans in that age group. We thought it best to raise them together."

An iron-haired administrator joined them. Despite a limp and the scars of old victories, she stood as massive and solid as a Ravendi elite guard. The perfect preparation for taking over an orphanage. The woman didn't actually salute Gardanath, but came close.

"Welcome, lords, lady to the Tree of Knowledge Home and School."

Conthal choked in surprise and coughed with suppressed laughter. Gardanath smiled benignly and ignored the irritation of the Yhellani.

Rage built inside Barrand at the insult. The avatar's little jokes grew more offensive each day, and neared the limit of what he would accept without challenge. They were being poked and prodded, manipulated for Gardanath's amusement. A guest could only take so much in gratitude to his host.

Sarael touched his arm. "It doesn't matter."

He gazed down into her blue eyes and it didn't.

"Thank you, Telen." Gardanath slapped the woman on the back, barely moving her. "How goes orphan management?"

"A thrilling challenge each and every day, my Lord." Her voice rumbled like a cave-in.

"We would expect nothing less from our young. You know I pay them to vex you."

"I am aware, my Lord."

"Excellent. Let me introduce my companions. This pale, grim little man in beggar robes is Conthal. Not much to look at, but he claims to be the head of some religion or other. The peasant girl with the dirt on her nose and the attack dog believes she can cure people with magic roots and berries. Sarael."

"Do you want me to escort them off the property?" Telen asked.

"That won't be necessary. Perhaps they'll be useful as an object lesson for the children. As a warning."

"You are wise beyond your years, and that is saying something, ancient one—"

Conthal interrupted. "If you are quite finished amusing yourselves, perhaps we can meet the students?"

For once, Barrand found himself agreeing with a Throkari. Gardanath was far too clever and self-indulgent.

Telen gestured to the staff. The children had prepared a formal presentation for their visitors. Several older students rushed over with chairs. The Ravendi guards arranged themselves around the courtyard while the guardsworn took up positions behind the seats.

The teachers joined the audience. Aeralan sat beside a dark-robed man in the last row. They held hands, concealed under draped sleeves. Barrand growled deep in his chest, and the priestess glanced up in surprise. The Throkari locked eyes with him, but turned away when the play began.

Thera stomped on Barrand's foot. "It's none of your affair, commander," she whispered.

He scowled at her, but when she pushed him toward the end of the row away from the lovers, he relented and moved. Thera blocked his view of the couple.

Barrand expected a retelling of the destruction of the Tree of Knowledge. Instead, the children reenacted the legend of how Ravendis chose Gardanath to be her avatar—after his army slaughtered the previous avatar, cut him to pieces, and burned the remains in an enormous pyre.

The children exuberantly played out the huge swaths of death and devastation caused by the attempt. They flung long crimson streamers across the stage to represent the blood of the fallen, until little bodies tangled in red silk covered the ground.

At last, the boy and girl representing Gardanath and Ravendis stood alone amid the piles of giggling corpses.

"You are the greatest general the world has ever known. You have defeated my avatar and shown you know the meaning of war. I want you for my own, Gardanath."

"No, Ravendis! Look at this blood and death. Look at the cost of war." The boy gestured grandly at the bodies.

"I represent more than war. I also hold the keys of peace. Only when negotiation fails, does this follow. You and I shall build a trade empire that spans the continent. We will bring peace as easily as war." Ravendis' red wig slipped to one side and she tugged it back into place.

The boy stroked his chin. "Uhm ... Yes, your vision will bring peace. I am old and wise, and I understand these things have value. However, I will also have a strong military, in case the peace fails. Yes, I shall be your avatar!"

The girl drew her wooden sword and tapped the boy's head. Someone threw flash powder and the bright light blinded the spectators. When their vision returned, the children were standing up to bow.

The audience applauded. Gardanath forced a grin. "Well, if that doesn't bring back memories."

The orphans beamed. Gardanath shook hands with the younger Gardanath and bowed to the girl who played Ravendis, which made her snort.

"We worked hard to make gifts for you this week." Telen gestured to three of the youngsters. The avatars rose to meet them.

One of the older students, a boy of twelve, bobbed before Sarael. He held out a bouquet made from fabric scraps tied to slender green twigs. Each blossom was unique and joyful. Like a bunch of wildflowers.

"We wanted you to carry the flowers of summer with you wherever you traveled no matter the time of year." Sarael took the bundle with tears in her eyes.

"This is ... this is lovely. And thoughtful." She wiped her face with her free hand.

The student grinned. His teeth glowed against his dark olive skin. He passed her a folded yellow cloth that opened to become a long apron, inexpertly embroidered with small sun symbols.

"Since you wear white, and it's hard to keep clean when

you're healing and mixing medicines, we made you an apron...."
He trailed off trying not to stare at the dirt on the front of her
robe.

Sarael laughed, "I wish I had one this morning. Thank you."
She touched the boy's shoulder and the tiniest spark of light
flickered between them. Barrand doubted anyone else noticed,
but Sarael did something to the child.

A bronze-cheeked girl of about five bowed before Conthal
and held up a purple scarf. Different types of fabric had been
half-sewn, half-tied together to form the length. The avatar solemnly placed the ghastly thing around his neck.

In a sing-song voice she said, "We made you this scarf because the teachers said you get cold and have to live in lava or
you'll die."

The girl beside her groaned.

Conthal smiled and ruffled the child's dark curls. "I am
touched by your concern. This scarf will help make it unnecessary for me to spend any time inside the lava."

The girl shoved a small yarn bound book into his hands. "We
all drew pictures or wrote things we thought you would like."

The avatar's eyebrows lifted and he opened the cover. Barrand drifted closer to peer over his shoulder with Sarael and
Gardanath. A childish drawing of Conthal's visit to the school
graced the first page. On the next, a volcano erupted. The third
showed a sorcerer setting a Yhellani Servant on fire. Sarael
jerked, bumping against Barrand.

"I like this a great deal." Conthal gave Sarael a sly smile.
"Would you care to study it when I'm done, sister? The pictures
tell an inspiring story even you could understand."

"They wrote it for you. I would be intruding."

The last child, nervous about the tension between Conthal
and Sarael, bowed stiffly before Gardanath.

"We made a scarf for you to wear under your armor because Telen says it's starting to pinch." The girl handed him something that resembled a loosely woven rope more than an item of clothing.

"She did? Well, thank you for the lovely and considerate gift!" He wound the cloth around his neck several times. A few of the children tittered. "Mmm hmm." He peered at them suspiciously.

Telen called them to order with loud claps. "Now I'm certain our honored guests wish to meet you, but we aren't going to mob them like troublesome little beasts. Line up by class, as we discussed. Teachers, if you will?"

The Throkari priests herded their charges into groups by a mystical system indecipherable to Barrand. Several small children led Sarael to a chair to one side. Despite the best efforts of the caregivers, the youngest orphans in the school swarmed her.

Someone brought the infants out for Sarael's blessing, and she rocked a sleeping baby while listening to several children babble about the flowers. Her aura glowed like moonlight in the dim cavern.

Barrand wanted her to stay in Csiz Luan. Safe behind the walls. She could visit children like these, and teach them the pictures they drew in ignorance were about real people. The glow of contentment would surround her every day.

The older students gathered around Conthal and spoke with him in turn. He considered their questions and comments with grave courtesy. What were the children asking the head of the Throkari church?

Jol and Jairit hovered beside Sarael to assist her with any need, and Markus and Thera guarded close by. Barrand felt secure leaving for a few minutes.

Several of the aides stationed at Conthal's side glared at Barrand as he approached. One of them wrote on a lap desk. Transcribing Conthal's answers, to share with the school later, or to add to the temple libraries. Gardanath finished his discussion with Telen and sauntered over to Barrand.

"How do you become a sorcerer?" asked one boy.

"The main component is an innate ability. It is similar to another sense, like hearing, or sight. If you are born without it, no one can explain the color red or the sound of the wind. The rest is discipline. Years of study in mathematics, physics, theory, and control. This occurs before the novice even begins casting."

The boy slouched away.

"Is Dalanar coming today? Will he do magic?" a clear, piping voice called from the end of the line. Someone attempted to hush him, but Conthal heard.

"I sent him on an errand, I am sorry to say. He would have enjoyed meeting you."

A girl in pigtails gaped up into his eyes as if trying to spot Throkar. "What's it like to have a god inside your head?"

Conthal smiled tightly. "Somewhat crowded, at times." He turned to the next child.

"That's not an answer," she insisted.

The avatar stared at her. A cold stillness swept over the man and his nostrils flared. One of the priests tried to pull the girl away. The sudden change sent a chill across Barrand's senses, as if a dark cloud covered the sun. Was he mad, as Quin thought? Barrand prepared to intervene.

Conthal took a deep breath and his face relaxed. "When Throkar invested me, I learned *everything* in an instant of time so small it is beyond comprehension. I understood the inner workings of the universe. Then, that knowledge was hidden from me. No human has the capacity to contain it. Over the years, I have rediscovered portions through study." He clenched and relaxed his jaw. "Throkar set up a ... residence inside my head. He occasionally comments or offers advice, and can be quite opinionated. He prefers I eat my eggs hard-boiled and only use blue ink." The children giggled. "He can also take control of my body and make his views known directly."

Barrand had never heard the experience described so candidly. It sounded ... awful. Sarael rarely discussed Yhellania's presence. He wondered if the goddess inflicted any peculiarities on her. Barrand would never be disrespectful enough to ask, but maybe if he mentioned Throkar's demands she might tell him about Yhellania's.

Gardanath crossed his arms over his chest. "Orange. Ravendis loathes the color. I can't eat anything orange. I own nothing orange, and she'll have tantrums if she sees too much of it around the city. We had to pass an ordinance about building colors to make her shut up. I'm thankful it isn't the color blue."

Barrand looked up at him with a half-smile. "I'm glad my hair is gone to gray, I'd hate to be the focus of her ire."

The avatar laughed.

"Are you married? You should marry Mother Onia. She's nice and she thinks you're handsome." The small child with the clear voice had reached the front of the line. An attractive brunette standing behind the students went pale and found the floor fascinating. The children broke out in giggles and fits of gagging.

To Barrand's amusement, Conthal shifted uncomfortably and his eyes darted around as if seeking intervention. None came. Even his attendants leaned forward to hear the answer.

"Well ... That's kind of Mother Onia to flatter such an elderly man. Sadly, Throkar does not want me to marry. If I were to marry her, she would no longer be your teacher. What if someone like Gardanath took her place?"

The children cried out in mock horror and shrieked at Gardanath's fierce expression. It impressed Barrand that the Ravendi Avatar was beloved by the orphans. He had some good qualities.

"That's a load of horse shit," the avatar muttered. "The gods don't care who we fuck. You should remind Sarael of that, too."

Barrand sputtered, positive feeling toward the man gone. He turned away to avoid having to reply. Some of the older students clustered around Sarael, despite disapproval from their teachers. Maybe a few of them weren't lost. His heart eased at the sight.

The lineup of questioners ended, and the children retreated into the school for dinner. The shadows deepened, and Barrand glanced up, surprised. Several of the teachers scurried around refilling the oil lamps that were beginning to sputter and die.

Aeralan and the priest, Varen, socialized with some of the caregivers. The heat from their shared glances raised the temperature in the cavern. Conthal noticed them, as well. He stared at the couple for several minutes, and gestured to the woman beside him.

"Transfer him."

"Father Varen? He's popular with the children, my Lord."

"And the Yhellani."

The priestess studied Aeralan. "The school healer. I didn't realize it had gone so far."

"Rynd."

The woman winced. "Yes, my Lord."

Barrand suffered a pang of sympathy for the fools. Bad enough to start something, but to flaunt their bond in front of Conthal? The priest was lucky the avatar didn't skewer him over a flame. Nevertheless, Rynd was beyond desolation. Nothing but ice caves and lichen for eight months out of the year. The capitol city was ten mud huts, three of which were abandoned.

"I don't like it either, but isn't Rynd out of proportion for the crime, Conthal?"

The avatar turned toward him with something approaching surprise on his face. "Are you addressing me?"

"Yeah."

"And you're saying my punishment for a Throkari priest fraternizing with a Yhellani Servant is too harsh?"

"Yes."

"I wasn't aware you had been granted permission to speak to me, let alone advise me on Throkari policy."

"I believe you need guidance on the decent thing to do."

"What would you suggest as the *decent thing*?"

"Send him to another school in some civilized country."

"How is that punishment? If it's too accommodating, she'll simply follow him. I doubt Sarael has plans to discipline the Servant. Therefore, I am burdened with providing a lesson to both of them to make up for your laxity."

"He'll die."

"We have a temple in Rynd. None of the penitents has died however much they may want to. Why don't we ask him which he would prefer: my judgment or yours?"

"What kind of a choice is that for a Throkari priest? He can only answer one way to please you. Any mercy is up to you," Barrand protested.

"I *am* being merciful. Tell your Servant not to leave the city, dog. Removing the temptation would resolve the problem, as well."

"You're a hypocrite. You'll send your Seal to the Summer Festival to be consort to the handmaiden who despises him, but your priest can't be with a Yhellani who loves him?"

"Politically advantageous alliances have always been above the rules established for the common people. Perhaps if Father Varen had come to me first, I would have given him permission."

Barrand stood motionless as Conthal turned his back and

walked away. He ached to draw his sword and plunge it into the man's heart. To feel the avatar's hot blood gush down his arms and drip off his elbows. To drink in the man's last breath as it rushed out steaming in the night air. He would spit on the corpse and leave it face down in an unnamed alley. A bead of sweat rolled down Barrand's neck, and his armor bit into his shoulders in places the padding had worn thin. There was the faint scent of copper, but he didn't know where it came from.

Gardanath put a hand on his shoulder. "Your blood is burning. It's calling to Ravendis and I'd rather you didn't wake her." He looked Barrand up and down. "Those aren't the feelings of a Yhellani. Are you seeking to convert?"

"Of course not."

"Go to your girl. Maybe she can calm you down."

Barrand straightened. "Lady Sarael is not my girl."

"Shh, Ravendis is cranky when she wakes up."

Barrand stormed by Aeralan on the way over to Sarael. "A word with you, Mother? Alone."

She followed him, but her gaze lingered on Varen.

Of the nursery-aged children, two infants remained outside. Sarael held one and Jol the other, as Telen and several caretakers chatted nearby. The avatar wasn't about to surrender the sleeping baby any time soon, and Jol smiled as he jiggled a wooden rattle for the child in his lap.

Barrand maneuvered Aeralan to a place just out of earshot from the others.

"Your indiscretion has gotten Varen posted to Rynd, and you targeted for death."

Her forehead creased. "Conthal?"

"Yes, Conthal. He noticed you making eyes at each other."

"But, we didn't do anything! How could he have known? Did you tell him?"

Barrand stared at her.

She bit her lip. "What are we going to do?"

"Say good-bye, and forget him. Don't leave the city until you're an old woman or we manage to kill Conthal. Stay away from the Throkari. All of them."

"How can you be this unfeeling?" she whispered. "I love him!"

"I want you alive. We can't afford to lose any Servants, no matter how foolish."

Aeralan's eyes widened in disbelief. She hurried away and disappeared into one of the buildings.

Thera wandered over. "You always find ways to charm the ladies."

"I'm good at it." Barrand rolled his shoulders and cracked his neck in an attempt to loosen his tense muscles.

Conthal and his attending priests joined the expanding circle around Sarael. His calculating leer, as he watched the Yhellani Avatar, made Barrand fume.

Conthal turned to the school administrator. "If we are done here, we will visit the temple for devotions. I request the accompaniment of as many of your Throkari staff as you can spare for several hours."

"My Lord, school is over. They are free to go with you. To deny them the opportunity would be cruel."

"Conthal, they could just worship you here, you know," Gardanath said.

The avatar managed to sneer down his nose at the taller man. "Formalities must be observed."

Telen bowed to Conthal. "Thank you, my Lord, for your kindness and your attention to the children."

"I enjoy meeting the young. Thank you for providing them with admirable care. They are clearly well-treated."

Gardanath nudged Conthal before he turned away. "You're always welcome to bring a guest for dinner at the manor. I suspect Mother Onia would be delighted to receive an invitation."

Telen snorted. "That boy is a troublemaker cut from your cloth, 'Nath. Onia's mortified enough without you bringing it up again."

"I hope he doesn't banish her to Rynd," Barrand muttered to Thera.

Conthal glanced at him. "In this case, I believe mercy is called for. I can scarcely punish every adherent who finds me attractive."

Gardanath and Telen chuckled while Conthal led the way toward the cave entrance. One of his attendants knocked on a side door of the school, and a cluster of black-robed teachers filed out to join the procession.

"If it were me, the little shit would find himself stuffed in a chest for a few days," Thera said.

Barrand wasn't sure if she referred to the student or the avatar.

CHAPTER FORTY

RYLIR TELLS ME YOU have evidence a sorceress killed Laniof." Morgir stood before them as they knelt in the Gallery hall.

They were to make a formal presentation of their proof and presumably receive punishment should they fail to convince the god. Masters, Journieres, town elders, and other notables filled the chamber. Preceptor Eccuro had made the trip back to be a witness, along with the Ravendi trade faction, a vibrant woman named Josa, and a Yhellani Servant Quin didn't recognize, Maloud.

When Eulesis and the others returned with their findings in the late afternoon, they retreated to their guesthouse to change and rest. Although, they confirmed a redheaded woman left the city within hours of Laniof's murder, there was no way to determine which of the sorceresses it had been. The runner they sent to the inns Dalanar suggested returned with the same information. A woman with red hair stayed for several days. She kept to her rooms, and departed the night of the murder. No one managed a good look at her.

"Great Lord." Quin straightened her tabard and shifted her sword to one side. "Many people may not be aware of the handprint sorcerers leave behind after they perform magic."

"Handmaiden Quinthian, why are you presenting this evidence instead of the accused?"

"I am the last person to have any motivation to lie or distort the facts to preserve this man's life. For everything I know he is guilty of, this crime is not one. There is another reason I will demonstrate."

"Very well." Morgir returned to his bench and gestured for her to continue.

"When a sorcerer does magic they become obscenely hot, and after he or she completes their casting, they must cool down. They do this by forcing the excess heat into stone. This leaves a distinctive imprint in the shape of a hand, different for each person. Until recently, I didn't understand how the Servants I traveled with knew which sorcerer made a mark. I have intimate knowledge of it now." Quin removed her tabard and tunic to reveal a thin undershirt. She slid the narrow strap off her shoulder, and pulled the material down to expose the dark gray handprint.

"This is Dalanar's mark. He branded me with it in a filthy alleyway in Crador, and I nearly died. Does anyone doubt my word when I swear that this is his?"

Morgir and the three witnesses rose to inspect the scar, while the audience craned their necks to see.

Eccuro rapped Dalanar on the knuckles with the cane as he passed.

Quin picked up Cleary's canvas, now stretched over a frame, and slid it onto an easel.

"When Laniof's killer finished casting, she burned her mark into a marble bust in his studio. A more powerful sorcerer, like Dalanar, would shatter the stone, but she didn't. The glowing print attracted the attention of one of the apprentices. Cleary created this amazing painting beginning with a reproduction of the handprint. This mark is nothing like Dalanar's."

Quin stood beside the image for Morgir and the others to inspect the differences.

"You keep saying a sorceress did this. Why do you assume that?" Josa asked.

Quin summarized their investigation starting with examining the body. Maloud's face wrinkled in revulsion.

"Most of this doesn't lead to anyone we can say is guilty without a doubt. We'll need to keep searching for the killer, but Dalanar did not kill Laniof."

Morgir fathomless gray eyes probed each of them. "This is weak, Dalanar, and you well know it. How you have managed to gain the advocacy of a Yhellani Handmaiden you left half-dead in an alley, and an apprentice who dreams of cutting your throat is miracle in itself."

"I believe the character flaw lies within *them*. I did nothing to deserve it."

Morgir pulled at his ear. "The first honest thing you've said." He turned to the representatives of the other gods. "Witnesses, if I blasted the damned sorcerer into pieces, would you object?"

"I might need to file a complaint with the College of Mandrites ... at some point." Eccuro tapped his cane on the floor.

"He's an abomination responsible for countless horrors. Killing an avatar wouldn't be beyond him." Maloud sneered. "I don't understand what he's done to the handmaiden, but she's clearly under his influence."

Josa confronted the others, hands on hips. "What are you talking about? The evidence points in another direction. Great Lord, I would protest!"

Morgir sighed. "Ah Josa, we can't have that. I wouldn't want Gardanath angry with me. He would embargo. It would be disastrous."

The god turned to Quin and Dalanar. "I accept the evidence that you weren't involved. You're free to go. Quinthian, put your shirt on, this isn't one of your festivals." Morgir began to shuffle back to Laniof's body.

Quin called after him, "Great Lord, what about the other part of our bargain?"

The room quieted as Morgir glared over his shoulder, his eyes rimmed with yellow fire. Her breath caught.

"Great Lord, you said you would invest an avatar," she reminded him gently.

"I will not be rushed!"

Astabar walked forward. "Morgir, you've had weeks. It is time to choose."

"Laniof...."

"Laniof is gone."

A vindictive gleam sparkled in Morgir's eyes. "Dalanar."

"No, Great Lord, I will not be your avatar." The sorcerer ducked his head politely, but his voice was firm.

The room buzzed with scandalized whispers.

"Choose someone who will make you happy. An accomplished artist. A kind soul. Lyratrum is filled with them." Astabar smiled and patted Morgir's arm.

The god shook him off and spun to face Laniof's bier. Rylir's small, brutal statues were poised, mid-action. Frozen in perpetual death. Morgir straightened and turned. "Rylir."

"No!" The sound burst out of Quin as she lunged forward. She didn't know how to stop the god from selecting an avatar, but the need to protect overwhelmed her ability to reason. Dalanar wrapped an arm around her waist and held on.

Rylir stepped shyly out of the crowd and tugged at her shirt.

"Small one, I find myself in need of a new avatar. I'd like you to take Laniof's place."

"I can't, Great Lord. I'm only an apprentice." The girl peered around at the gathered people and blushed at the attention.

"You're a Journiere now, remember? A remarkably talented one. I think you're just what Lyratrum needs. Fresh blood, new ideas."

Eulesis moved closer to Quin and Dalanar, tears rolling down her face. Quin had never seen her cry. The sorcerer placed a restraining hand on the woman's arm, but she didn't try to interfere.

"You really want me? What do I have to do?"

"I really do, Rylir. You'll be perfect. I'm going to ask you a question. I want you to answer honestly and completely. I will take care of the rest."

Astabar watched with a predatory expression.

Should Quin turn away or force herself to witness?

"Rylir, will you be my avatar?"

"Yes, Morgir, I will be your avatar."

Eulesis covered her ears.

Morgir kissed Rylir's forehead. The girl's eyes opened wide, and she screamed. The sound resonated in the hall and through Quin's brain, containing power of its own.

Quin pressed her hands over her ears and buried her head against Dalanar. He wrapped his arms around her, and turned until he blocked some of the sound, but didn't stop watching. The sorcerer was used to hearing people scream in pain and terror, she supposed, and he would be next to experience it. He must be curious.

The screaming stopped. It felt like an eternity, but was only a few minutes. Rylir knelt on the floor of the hall. Surprisingly, Morgir remained beside her. The girl slid to one side and would have fallen, but the god swept her up and carried her to an empty guestroom across the hall from Laniof's studio.

The people who hadn't fled the screaming waited for his return.

"I will remain manifest for some time, while Rylir adjusts to the new connection. I've never had such a young avatar. Her brain wasn't as fully formed as I expected." Morgir returned to his seat beside Laniof's body and stared out the window. The attendees glanced around at each other, confused, and began filing out into the darkness.

"Poor baby," Eulesis whispered beside Quin. "How much damage did he do to her?"

"Dalanar, I know how to make you an avatar now. Are you ready to leave?" Astabar grinned broadly, as he joined them. "The pain in your head is about to become worse than I can control."

"Did Morgir hurt Rylir? Is she all right?" Quin demanded.

The god shrugged. "She'll have a bad headache for a few days, but her brain is not bleeding. You should give her some tea as a gift."

Quin stumbled numbly after Astabar as he led the way to the entrance of the hall.

Preceptor Eccuro winked at Quin. "Thank you for the herbs, handmaid. Watch yourself with that one."

She stared at him sightlessly and didn't understand if he referred to the god or the sorcerer.

Not even the balmy night could ease the chill in her core.

CANDLES ILLUMINATED THE GUESTHOUSE when Quin and the others entered, and tea and pastries had been laid out for them. No one ate.

"It was our fault Rylir was chosen, Dalanar." Quin threw herself into a carved chair and put her head in her hands.

He regarded her from his usual place at the desk, but said nothing.

"Did you know what would happen when we showed Morgir her work?"

"How could I?" he asked.

"Did you guess? Did you calculate the odds? Did you think it was a possibility?"

"It was a possibility."

"Why do I listen to you? Why am I so gullible?"

"You were helping a friend who needed assistance. If it also ends up helping us, why is that bad?"

"We made a child into an avatar! That's hideous."

"Morgir made a child into an avatar. We didn't force the decision on him. There were many talented adults to select from. The Avatar of Morgir is not only our friend, but owes her position to our intervention. Everyone benefited."

"That sick game."

"You were doing well, moving pawns around."

Astabar stuck his head in the door. "Come along, Dalanar. Say good-bye to the ladies. We need to go to make it in time."

Eulesis and Magda hugged.

"You're going, too, Magda?" Quin asked.

"I'm the new High Priestess or whatever. Remember what I taught you, girl. Take care."

Quin hugged the large woman, and turned toward Dalanar. Embrace him or stab him? Neither option seemed appropriate.

"We will meet again soon," Dalanar said, as he rose from his seat.

"You'll be the avatar of a new religion, why would the Summer Festival mean anything to you?"

"I have a newfound concern for the health of the harvest."

The door shut with finality, and they were gone.

"You missed your last chance to knife him. The truce ended after Rylir became the avatar," Eulesis said.

"Astabar stole my dagger. I hope he left it somewhere I can find it before we leave."

Quin retreated to her room. Exhausted and empty. There was no gray area in a little girl being made into an avatar. The world was still as black and white as it ever was. Even with her best intentions, she had been a part of setting the child up.

Oh goddess, please help Rylir. The terrible pain she suffered.... Quin shuddered at the memory of the scream echoing in her head.

Quin lit the lamp on her night table with a candle, and began to undress. She sagged onto the bed and kicked off her boots. In a neat pile on her pillow, concealed in the darkness, lay one of Dalanar's fine black robes. She touched it, pressing the soft, silky cloth into its folds. Abomination, she thought wryly.

Quin swept it aside, and her dagger fell to the floor. Funny, Astabar. She drew the robe over herself and lay against the pillows. Her mind raced, and she didn't expect to sleep, but the scents on the material soothed her.

The Astabari arrived at their destination near dawn and began investing Dalanar as avatar. Quin woke as the universe exploded inside her head. She felt the screams tear her throat into shreds.

CHAPTER FORTY-ONE

ALANAR AND ASTABAR DRIFTED beside her in the vast cosmos, but they weren't aware of her presence. They moved purposefully, while she slipped and grasped at nothingness trying to find traction. Matter and energy spun and heaved around her, yet she heard nothing. Her own heartbeat silenced. Terror leached the awe from Quin's bones. Was this the godless void? It couldn't be. Astabar was there, getting further ahead, and she couldn't move.

"Yhellania, help me!" Still no sound, but small ripples spread out from her. Quin thrashed around. The waves didn't reach beyond her fingertips.

She tried again, praying fervently. "Goddess Yhellania, deliver me from this abyss. Please, I'm your devoted servant!" The ripples went no further than before. Black dots appeared in her vision. Was she breathing? Would she pass out? Quin couldn't think. The two tiny figures flickered within a cloud of colored gas and stars. Maybe she needed to call to the god who was present.

"Astabar, help!" She strained to focus her thoughts. "Please!" Another surge arced away from her, going further than her earlier attempts, filling her with hope.

It fell short.

"Astabar! Dalanar! Damn it, help me! Rot you both." The wave shot out again, but this time a silvery beam of light flashed directly between Quin and Dalanar, moving almost faster than she could follow. Their link was visible.

"Dalanar! You scabrous, god-cursed abomination. Don't you leave me here to die, inbred, maggot-infested, sheep-molesting sorcerer." Quin sobbed with relief as the connection lit up with silvery light and the figures grew larger.

A spark flashed the other way down their bond, and Quin felt Dalanar's amusement. "I've never touched a sheep that wasn't willing."

When Astabar and Dalanar drew close enough, Quin grabbed their hands in a grip that probably hurt, but she refused to let go. She didn't care if they were gods or avatars, and capable of blasting her to pieces. Death would be preferable to drifting alone.

"Please, Astabar, send me back." Quin finally saw him clearly and shuddered. The man, Astabar, was a thin shell worn by the essence of the god. She avoided looking at the ethereal blue figure at once as large as a sun and small enough to occupy the same space as the puppet husk.

She turned to Dalanar. Although his hand felt solid, he blazed with searing color from within a translucent image of himself.

Her body only emitted a pearly light with dull colors that pulsed faintly. "Is this my soul?" Quin despaired. What had she done wrong? How was Dalanar's so pure and breathtaking?

Dalanar squeezed her fingers. "It's just power."

"Isn't he magnificent?" Astabar crowed. "I am certain he is more powerful than Conthal. Throkar will gaze upon him and whimper with envy. An adequate repayment for their scheming."

"Why am I here, Great Lord?" Quin grasped her surroundings at last. She knew more about the universe than she even imagined existed. Was she sharing Astabar's mind? Was she *inside* Astabar's mind?

The god stopped and considered her. He inspected the silvery band that wavered and flowed between Dalanar and Quin, and poked it with a finger.

Her *being* stretched away from her body. She gasped and grabbed her chest, although she couldn't place where the sensation came from. Dalanar recoiled, and they both cried out. Astabar tsked.

"Dalanar's spell did more than he intended. He linked your essence instead of whatever he was trying for. Sloppy, Dalanar. Come along, we need to finish this before your bodies die."

In a panic, Quin grabbed Astabar's hand again. They accelerated, moving through time.

"I promised I'd show Dalanar the beginning of the world. I'm embarrassed to admit it began in a committee. The whole process was quite mind-numbing."

The gods assembled in a giant chamber of light. Most of them held no distinct form; they wavered like mirages. Their presences tugged at a deep place in her mind, giving her a faint chill of recognition. Faces seen once and forgotten. The only ones Quin saw clearly were the gods she knew: Yhellania, Ravendis, Morgir, Astabar, and Throkar. They convened at a table set apart from the main room. Other, formless figures occupied seats beside them.

Although appearance was irrelevant there, the gods mostly looked like those incarnations Quin was familiar with. Yhellania lurked inside the shell of Sarael; Throkar within Conthal. Oddly, Ravendis resembled a painting Quin admired once in Byzurion, a woman with blood-red braids and flaming eyes, instead of Gardanath. All just veils covering unfathomable cores. What did Dalanar see?

Morgir placed a model of the world nestled within the branches of a tree down on the table before them.

"Your tree is absurd, Throkar," Ravendis sneered from her place next to Yhellania. "Why give our creations life but no drive to achieve? If you provide every answer they will remain perpetual children."

"To not offer the best education possible would stunt their growth. They would have to start from the beginning whenever they wished to accomplish anything. A waste of time." Throkar steepled his fingers and glared at the red goddess.

Several of the spectral figures spoke, their voices garbled echoes Quin did not understand. Why couldn't she see or hear them?

"Without the tree they will suffer. Yhellania, why do you want that?" Morgir raised an eyebrow at his sister.

"No compassion exists without suffering. No redemption without evil." Yhellania straightened and turned to Astabar. "Why are you smiling, brother?"

"It is easy to steal from the complacent. It is also easy to steal from the dispossessed. My children will thrive either way."

Morgir frowned. "No one needs theft when the world is stable and safe. Only if Ravendis sows discord and war, will there be any necessity to steal."

"If the people lack drive, if they are spoon fed everything, they'll lack the impetus for war, certainly. They'll also lack the motivation to trade, to explore, to create, perhaps procreate." Ravendis slid forward in her throne. "Or worship us. Why would they? They would never have anything to be grateful for. Why are we creating them, if not for that?"

Astabar grinned. "We're bored."

Again, the ghostly voices. Objecting. Annoyed. Apparently, Astabar had that effect on gods, too.

"The universe made us for a reason and we must fulfill our purpose. We cannot do this waiting alone among the stars," Morgir chastised them.

"Their veneration shall give us power, but consider how fascinating they will be. Minute flickers of godhood to manipulate and study. Unending experimentation." Throkar stroked his chin.

Yhellania appeared disgusted. "They aren't toys."

"Your goals are nobler, sister? You want their misery to earn them rewards after they die. To let them sit at your feet and abase themselves for eternity? It is well I am the god of death. I won't stand for such nonsense. You can make birth as ghastly as you want, the afterlife will have dignity."

Astabar began drawing Quin and Dalanar away, leaving the scene behind.

"Did that answer your question, glorious vessel of my appearing?"

Dalanar frowned. "It did, although I wanted to witness the actual creation of the planet."

"Why couldn't I see them all? Hear what they were saying?" Quin peered over her shoulder at the retreating image.

Astabar shrugged and looked away. "Even the gods have rules we must obey, and showing you this skirted the edge of ... legality. My brothers and sisters no longer exist for humanity. If you began to worship, or even acknowledge them, it would extend them power. Power they aren't present in the mortal plane to harness. It's a mess until that god is forgotten and we manage to bleed off that energy."

"What happened next?" Quin asked.

"We bickered for a few centuries over the details, and then Yhellania destroyed the tree. We redesigned what we could, but humanity had been created. Another two hundred years of squabbling on top of the angry recriminations."

"Did she do it on purpose?" She glanced at the god, before shivering and looking away.

Astabar shrugged. "I think she did. You'd have to ask her."

They stood in a vast library. Quin recognized it from the painting Laniof made of Conthal. Their footsteps echoed into the darkness high above them, the sound unmuffled by rows of overloaded bookcases. Each sagged under the weight of scrolls, papers, and bound volumes. Quin fought the urge to sneeze. She tasted grit in her mouth and licked her lips to try to clear it.

She still clasped her companions' hands. Quin wouldn't risk letting go, even if the situation appeared safe for the moment. Dalanar's was firm and comforting. Calloused at the fingertips where he held the pen. His ring pinched her, and Quin shifted her fingers. Astabar's hand was oddly featureless, smooth, and soft. Like a child's.

"I promised you knowledge. Are you ready?"

Dalanar's eyes widened. "Do I get to keep it?"

Astabar laughed. "No."

The sorcerer's gaze grew flinty.

"Perhaps I can offer you a deal?" The god turned to the man beside him.

"What?" Dalanar growled.

"The knowledge from one book a day for the rest of your exceptionally long life. For that day, you will know the text completely. Each day after, it will be as if you simply read it, and your memory will fade as such."

"Am I allowed to choose the topic?"

"If you please me. Still a better deal than Conthal got from Throkar?"

Quin wondered what he meant.

Dalanar rubbed his chin. "Do I have a choice? Can I back out now?"

"Oh no, you and Quinthian would die if you changed your mind at this point. Not that I wish you harm, but you're fundamentally altered and need to complete the transformation."

"All right. One book a day. *Mutually* agreed upon."

Alarm bells went off in Quin's head. "Astabar, what do you mean? Why would I die? I'm not your avatar."

"Of course not, sweet, gentle girl. However, you have undergone a similar transformation.

"Would you like your first book, avatar?"

"Yes. I want the subject to be casting."

"I know just the thing." Astabar winked at Quin.

"A *primer?*" Dalanar's hand trembled, and he tightened his grip.

"It contains an excellent section on linking and binding. The handmaiden would have appreciated your taking the study more seriously as a student."

"Is this how things are going to be between us, Astabar? If they are, I would prefer to die."

"You would kill Quinthian, too?"

"Make her your avatar. Kill me."

"I don't want her. She isn't shiny enough. Although, she is a bit brighter than I expected. Is that your doing, as well?"

Dalanar sighed and rubbed the back of his neck with his free hand. "Possibly."

Despite her own situation, Quin smiled. Things weren't going to be easy for Dalanar. Eulesis probably didn't expect her prediction that the sorcerer would wish he were dead to come true during the investment. Quin gave him a prim nod and gloated to herself.

"Dalanar and I are going to fight over the best parts of his brain now. This will no doubt be tedious. Let's send you home. Rest well."

Quin's hands slipped out of theirs and she caught sight of Dalanar's aqua green eyes. Eyes like her mother's.

DALANAR STARED AT ASTABAR. They were back in the seedy, airless tenement in the no-name town the god led them to after leaving Lyratrum. Magda was asleep on the rickety bed. A single oil lamp burned on the scarred and battered table. He couldn't tell how long they had been gone.

"You were supposed to depart from this plane." Dalanar's voice sounded rough. He wondered what the neighbors thought of the screaming. Although, considering the neighborhood, they were used to such things.

The god shrugged. "I emulated Morgir. He hasn't moved on to the next plane."

"Rylir is a child. My brain is quite capable of handling your divine presence."

"What's the hurry?"

Dalanar shook his head and turned away. Magda sat up, causing the ropes of the bed to creak in protest. She watched them curiously.

"Did you fix my brain while you were deciding where you wanted to live?"

"Everything is perfectly healthy. You have the recuperative grace of an avatar now."

Dalanar called his power, and the sweet sensation tingling across his fingertips filled him with exhilaration. Heat flooded his veins. He welcomed the chill of air on his skin.

The god slouched against the scarred table and folded his arms over his chest. "How long until the Summer Festival?"

"Two weeks."

"Will you be able to remain unfevered enough to be with Quinthian?"

Dalanar narrowed his eyes at his god. "Yes."

"I can't believe you're trying to frighten Quin into choosing you as consort. That is a contemptible thing to do."

Dalanar barked a laugh. "Are you going to act as my conscience, Astabar? A thief?"

"You have an empty spot in your brain where most people put their morals, maybe I'll move in there. Spacious. Rarely used."

"No objections from me. I don't need it."

Astabar regarded him silently for a moment. "It won't be like you envision."

"What do you know about it?"

"I've seen your sordid imaginings. If you think Quin is going to do any of that with you after threatening her loved ones, you understand less about human nature than I do."

"This is none of your concern."

"Do you believe Iyana would approve?"

Dalanar turned on the god. "*Shut up*, Astabar."

"I'll leave things for now, Dalanar. We're not finished discussing this."

CHAPTER FORTY-TWO

"COME IN," A MELODIOUS voice called out at Quin's knock.

She swung the polished wooden door open apprehensively. Her only exposure to sorcerers had been Dalanar and Conthal. One unduly influenced the other in their case. Gridarl was Conthal's greatest rival. She had no idea what he would be like. Quin gestured for Eulesis to enter first.

Gridarl's office was in a stone tower in one of the corners of the university complex. Through the windows, the palace glittered in the distance and the city of Anagis spread out between them. A patchwork blanket of neighborhoods. Old walls separated the districts like tree rings showing the city's growth.

The room itself contained enough charts, glass instruments, and strange artifacts to rival a Malesini junk market. The odd collection sprawled over tables, and overflowed from cabinets until the far end of the office couldn't be seen from the entrance.

"Well, don't keep an old man waiting. Come in." The voice sounded from a corner that possibly held a desk.

Eulesis shrugged and pressed past the piles on the floor, forging a path through the debris. Quin followed.

Another door led to a chamber containing nothing besides

an untidy bed. Strangely spare after the disorder of the main room.

A gangly, Asori man, with a few remaining tufts of white hair regarded them from behind a massive book. He reminded Quin of the marsh birds in Tyrentanna. He must have been doing too much casting, as his bronze skin sagged from his twig-like arms. The deep creases of laugh lines softened his warm brown eyes.

"Master Gridarl?" Her throat still hurt from the damage done screaming through Dalanar's investment. At least her voice had returned, however raspy.

The man stood with a bow that emphasized his resemblance to a bird. "To what do I owe the honor, Eulesis? I'm afraid you'll have to introduce me to your friend. She has the wild-eyed look of the god-touched. Is this why you've come to me?"

"This is Quinthian, the handmaiden to Sarael."

The sorcerer peered at Quin and shook his head. "No. No, that isn't it. What is that?" He pointed to her shoulder.

She covered the scar with a hand. "Dalanar's mark."

"In a person? That was rather cheeky of him. May I see?"

Quin hesitated but shifted aside her collar. She'd indulge him—anything that might encourage the old sorcerer to help them in return.

The man brought out a magnifying glass and pulled her into the light from the window. He shifted Quin back and forth for several minutes while she waited in mystified silence. Gridarl prodded her with a finger, and a wave of warmth streamed through her and down the connection. He poked her again.

"Stop that!" She jerked her shoulder away.

:: Gridarl?:: Dalanar's thought reached her. :: What are you doing at the university, Quin? You should be on the way to Csiz Luan.::

339

"Dalanar is an avatar now," Quin told the old man, trying to distract him.

"Oh? Did he finally kill Conthal and take his place?"

Quin gasped. "What? No!"

"Is he the Throkari Avatar or not?"

"He's the avatar of a god named Astabar."

"Pity. The zealot needs to go. At least Dalanar doesn't foam at the mouth during debates. Poor job, there though," he said, indicating her shoulder. "Not sure what he was trying to accomplish. Do you know?"

Quin shook her head.

"Well, I'll ask him next time we meet. I doubt you came to listen to me criticize my colleagues, in any case. What can I do for you?"

Eulesis chuckled. "When Dalanar told us about you, we were surprised Conthal hadn't killed you. Now, I'm doubly amazed."

Gridarl's brown eyes twinkled. "I'll be dead soon enough. He'll miss trying to keep up with me. The current crop of sorcerers is lackluster. Weak and slow. He's in for a boring generation. Watch him. He'll get into trouble with nothing better to do."

"We have several questions, Master Gridarl—" Quin started.

"I still don't understand why you're glowing." The sorcerer pulled Quin around to another window and glanced at Eulesis for confirmation. "Do you see?"

"No...." she said.

"Hm. Continue."

"Were you informed about the murder of the Morgiri Avatar several weeks ago?"

"A sorcerer was involved, yes? Any progress in finding the killer? Obviously, this is of grave concern to the Collegium of Sorcerers."

Quin unrolled the canvas revealing the handprint. "This is the mark of the sorceress who used the staff of the Tree of Knowledge to kill Laniof. Whom does this belong to?"

The man reluctantly took the scroll and examined it with his magnifying glass. "Wasn't Dalanar accused?" Gridarl retreated to the seat behind his desk.

"He was *wrongly* accused. You know who made this handprint," Quin said.

"I should check with my colleagues for confirmation. This is a serious charge, and I wouldn't want to be mistaken."

Eulesis slapped her hand on the desk. "Ordanna or Mirindra? Surely, you know the difference between their marks."

"Are either of them at the university now? We must retrieve the staff. It can kill the avatars. We can't allow that kind of power to remain at large." Quin put all her fear and frustration into her plea.

Gridarl chuckled. "Oh, it can do much more than that, handmaiden. Since Dalanar has become the avatar of a new god, you must appreciate its ability to create gods. Far more terrible, is its power to destroy them."

Eulesis gasped and bumped into a shelf. A brass bowl fell to the floor with an echoing clatter. Her face drained of color and she pressed one hand against her lips.

"No." Quin stared at the sorcerer, not understanding. "The staff can kill the avatars and create gods. That's what you meant."

"We used to have a well-stocked pantheon. The staff, as you call it, killed them off."

"How do you know? How do you know about this at all?" Quin demanded.

"One of my research projects discovered Throkar's Branch a number of years ago. Conthal and Gardanath realized there

341

had to be a way to kill gods, since so many of them were missing from the pantheon mentioned in the old texts and ... in their memories, I suppose. They issued a challenge. I had access to the university libraries, Conthal to the temple records, and Gardanath to his trade network. I happened to find the reference to the Branch.

"Gardanath sponsored an expedition to locate the object. Lamentably stolen almost immediately and has been lost since. Until recently, that is. Oh yes, I know quite a lot about it."

"How does it work?" Quin whispered.

"The Branch summons a god onto this plane, bringing their divine power into this world with them. You're familiar with the destruction of Narnus? It can be used to kill an avatar, and later the god, when it manifests. The power stays behind when the god is killed, providing a tidy boost for those remaining."

Quin couldn't breathe. This was what Dalanar and Conthal intended from the beginning. They planned to bring the staff to the Summer Festival and use it against Sarael and Yhellania. Their ultimate revenge. Killing Quin, Servants, or even Sarael meant nothing. Dalanar admitted it in Fairwald. No one advised Yhellania when the world was made. Only the goddess had been responsible for destroying the Tree of Knowledge; only she could pay the price. Quin needed to warn Sarael and Gardanath.

Quin abruptly realized what he said. "Narnus? What do you mean? Dalanar and Conthal destroyed Narnus."

Gridarl grinned appreciatively. "Of course, they *want* you to believe that, however, even they are not so powerful. Somebody used the branch to summon your new god in Narnus. Every sign points to that being the cause of the destruction. Not sorcery."

Quin sagged against the wall. Welliver said that Iyana and Dalanar had run towards the center of the destruction. He hadn't been lying, and neither was Gridarl. It was clear from his expression. Everyone else had been. They were lies of omission, but Sarael knew. Yhellania, Gardanath, and Sarael. Telling her not to pursue her mother's death. Not to probe into what happened at Narnus. Letting her believe the simple explanation that Dalanar and Conthal were to blame. The avatars didn't want anyone to discover that the gods could be created, or more importantly, destroyed. They knew about the staff and its capabilities. They lied.

Quin's heart ached. "Why, Eulesis?"

"We're pawns." The older woman still looked pale.

"Gridarl, who does this handprint belong to? We need to know where she took the branch. Sarael's life is in danger. Yhellania's existence is at stake. We don't have so many gods we can afford to lose another one."

"We seem to do well enough." He scoffed. The sorcerer regarded their strained, terrified faces, and softened. "Don't consider this an official ruling. She deserves a fair trial before you turn her over to the Morgiri or anyone else."

"Fine! Who?" Quin's feelings of betrayal and fear were turning to anger and impatience.

They needed to go. The procession from Csiz Luan would be leaving for the Chapterhouse shortly. Once Sarael left the protection of the city, the truce no longer applied. They might attack her at any time after passing through the gates. Did they intend to wait until the festival? To make the Yhellani watch their avatar and goddess die? Quin prayed that Conthal's cruelty outweighed convenience.

It was a week until the festival and it would take eight days for Eulesis and her to reach traveling by road. They could make it, if they cut overland and switched horses as they rode into the night.

"I believe ... Ordanna, although I'm not making an official statement."

Of course. Conthal knew how to bribe her. She had wanted the Throkari Secrets enough to attempt to convince Dalanar to betray his master. Killing Laniof would mean nothing to her.

"Is she here?"

"No. She was doing a research project at the coast...." The old man's voice trailed off unhappily.

"We need to go, Quin." Eulesis started threading her way around the piles toward the door.

"One last thing." Quin slid the painting of the handprint into the oilskin case Cleary had given her. "How does a non-sorcerer kill a sorcerer?"

Gridarl gaped at her, and his complexion deepened with rage. "Get out."

Quin cringed. She had not meant to be so blunt. "I'm sorry! The Throkari sorcerers attack Servants ... we're just trying to find ways to protect them."

Gridarl drew himself up to his full height, displaying the imposing figure he must have been in his prime. "There are hundreds of Servants and a limited number of sorcerers. I may not approve of the Throkari, but once I tell you how to kill *them*, perhaps you'll decide the world is safer without any of us. I do not trust the religious mindset. It is not a risk I will take."

Quin had no response.

"THAT COULD HAVE GONE better." Eulesis eyed her as she mounted. "Are you ready for this?"

Quin gave her a bleak stare and kicked her horse into a trot, heading off the university grounds and toward the Chapterhouse.

CHAPTER FORTY-THREE

THE TRIP TO CSIZ LUAN was uneventful and went by more swiftly than Dalanar wanted. He wasn't ready to face Conthal after a mere six days of adjustment. Things had changed too momentously. The others unquestionably felt the shift in the power levels of the world; they wouldn't be surprised there was a new avatar. Only Conthal knew it was him.

By becoming the avatar, Dalanar ruined years of his master's planning. At least he kept the god out of the hands of those who created him. Better than letting Astabar fall under the influence of Throkar's enemies. Something could be salvaged, surely. There was still a net gain of energy, after all.

"You meant to kill me?" Astabar raised an eyebrow at Dalanar.

"Yes, for your power. As long as you didn't invest an avatar, you were vulnerable to the staff." No point lying to a god who shared his mind.

Astabar was silent for several minutes. "That would work. Conthal is probably quite disappointed in you."

Dalanar rubbed the back of his neck.

"If he has the staff now, he can kill you first, and then destroy me." Astabar pointed out helpfully.

"We'd better hope he doesn't. He'll be angry enough to use it."

The gates of the city stood open, and a line of farmers and travelers waited to enter.

"Festival day?" Magda suggested, twisting to check the pennants flying above the walls. They were red. Yellow flags hoisted on the ramparts served as an invitation to gather.

"I doubt they would plan another event so close to midsummer," Dalanar said.

A crush of people filled the streets leading to the manor, and Dalanar used his mount to press apart the crowds. He missed his black robes. Nobody recognized him now.

"What's going on?" Astabar called out to a harried guard.

"Ay, what isn't going on? The 6th battalion's been recalled from Byzurion for the Summer Festival, and they're staging to leave. The avatars are meeting at the manor. Pilgrims is here to see 'em, and Lady Sarael is doing healing and such. Where have you been?"

Dalanar blinked in surprise. Gardanath planned to bring a thousand soldiers to the festival? That seemed a bit ... excessive.

Magda grew impatient and, with a voice audible for several city blocks, yelled over the noise, "Stand clear for the incarnation of Astabar. Newest of your gods." To Astabar she whispered, "Can you do the light thing with his eyes?"

Astabar grinned wickedly and took over Dalanar's body.

Dalanar was shoved aside and could only observe as the god shifted him around like a marionette. He felt wrapped in wool, hearing and sight hazy, flesh numb. From this perspective, trapped inside his own head, Dalanar finally saw the god's thoughts and memories.

It *was* a shared mind; Dalanar had begun to doubt. He walked through images of their meeting in the forest. Astabar recognized him from when he and Conthal attempted to hold the god prisoner. Dalanar foolishly supposed Astabar didn't remember. Despite their unfortunate past, the god found the aura Dalanar's power generated—and the theurgy—too great a lure to resist.

In a rush, control returned, and the scents, tastes, and sounds of being in a body overwhelmed Dalanar. He grabbed the reins and tapped his heels into his Nag's flank, urging her into the empty path created by the parting crowds. People reached out tentative hands to touch his boots or jacket. He pushed her into a trot.

"I didn't think you could do that from the outside," Dalanar said.

"Why is that?"

Dalanar opened his mouth to reply, but had no answer.

The gates of the manor swung open for them. Gardanath, Conthal, and Sarael waited on the steps leading up to the main house. Kalin, Barrand, and a few others lurked around their betters.

Gardanath appraised them as they dismounted. "Do you agree to honor the accords of Csiz Luan, Astabar, and hold your avatar and adherents to them?"

The god bowed with a theatrical flourish. "I do, mighty Gardanath. No hitting."

The big avatar scratched at his short beard. "Well boy, you sure caused a stir, but I can think of no better avatar for our new god. You going to introduce us to your little friend?"

Dalanar stiffened at Gardanath's comment. Considering how he and Eulesis felt about the gods, it wasn't a compliment. "Great Lord, as you know, this is the Ravendi Avatar, Gardanath."

"Yes, the man I was coming to find when I became distracted with my new toy. I will seek your guidance later on some of the finer points of the investment."

"Great Lord, I am at your disposal."

Dalanar nodded to his former master. "The Throkari Avatar, Conthal."

"I have not forgotten." Astabar's voice turned chill. "I hope our *current* acquaintance can be mutually advantageous."

Conthal inclined his head. "Since you stole my most valuable asset, it would behoove us to work together to utilize that benefit."

"The Yhellani Avatar, Sarael."

"Quinthian speaks highly of you, although I worry about the Summer Festival. Is it wise to base the health of the crops on the activities of one couple? Things can go wrong."

Sarael's lips quirked. "We've never had an issue before, Great Lord. The Summer King and Queen always manage their parts quite well."

Astabar was about to say more, but Dalanar interrupted, "Great Lord, would you speak to Gardanath now regarding your questions? I have some things to discuss with Conthal."

The god hesitated. "I will talk on this further with Sarael."

"I'm sure she'll be delighted. This remarkable Uturi is Magda. She is Astabar's first adherent, High Priestess, and is responsible for cutting Quinthian into several more pieces than she began with. I wouldn't recommend offending her."

Sarael and Barrand examined Magda with horrified expressions.

"What happened? Where is Quin?" the guardsworn captain demanded.

"Thanks, Dalanar," Magda grumbled.

He turned to follow Conthal into the manor.

Kalin blocked his way. "You're an avatar."

Dalanar returned his stare.

"Avatars can be killed."

"Excuse me."

"Dalanar, if you touch Quin, I will kill you."

"Kalin, if you interfere, you will die. I'm past childish threats. I'm stating a fact. I don't even care if you suffer first, you will simply be dead. For your mother's sake, stay home."

The younger man's face contorted with rage, and he gripped the hilt of his sword. "I don't fear you."

"No. It takes imagination to be afraid. That doesn't make you brave. It doesn't make me any less dangerous. Quin cares for you. Why would you want to hurt her by killing yourself doing something stupid?"

"How do you know what she thinks?"

"We did spend a great deal of time alone." He gave Kalin a knowing smile. "Did you ever consider that your threats arrive too late?"

Kalin shook his head. "Not with you."

Dalanar shrugged. It had been worth a try, for Eulesis. He brushed past the soldier.

"Watch your back, Astabari. That staff is around somewhere, and I'm searching for it."

"As is everyone else," Dalanar muttered.

Conthal pushed off from the wall where he waited. A smile played at the corner of his lips. "The jealous lover?"

"He doesn't want me to have what he considers his. This is a property dispute."

"He may believe he's protecting her. That was your plan."

"It might have started that way, now he is too blinded by his hatred of me to care."

"You have that effect on people."

Dalanar smiled briefly and opened the door for Conthal.

Old habits. What was the courtesy between two avatars? Conthal drilled his students on the appropriate etiquette for every situation. Meeting with royalty, peasants, and gods. The lessons glossed over how to behave after resigning your post as Seal to become the avatar of the god you plotted to murder with your master.

Conthal slid behind his desk, and Dalanar took his familiar place in the chair at one side. A hint of iodine and tea lingered in the air, bringing back memories of his weekly visits to Conthal's office as a boy. They spent hours discussing his progress, debating, and planning projects and research.

"I saw Eccuro."

"Yes, I assumed. Still fomenting rebellion and discord?"

"It's subsided to angry letter writing. He seems content."

"I should have hung him from the gates of the temple in Utur."

"Perhaps. However, now you have a devoted and popular Preceptor in Lyratrum, ministering to the heathens. If anyone is going to attract followers there, it's him."

"More likely he'll convert to something else. He's half Yhellani already." Conthal's lips curled into a sneer. "What happened with Morgir?"

"He selected a girl of about thirteen. Sweet, talented, naive. Her name is Rylir. I expect Eulesis will extend the invitation for them to attend the festival. She is too young for Morgir to occupy her brain. We'll have to deal with him being manifest for a number of years until she matures."

"Is that why Astabar is here instead of moving the furniture around inside your skull?"

"I hope Gardanath teaches him how to complete the investment. I'd prefer him to be tucked away quickly. He has access to all my memories and talks entirely too much."

Dalanar worked the ring off his finger. A white line and an

indentation remained where the band pressed into his skin. He set the seal down in front of Conthal. It rolled onto its side with a quiet clink.

Conthal inspected the ring. "The metal is thinning again. We would have needed to replace it soon."

The man slammed his fists on the desk and hurled the contents to the floor. Glass shards and ink sparkled in the firelight. The heat from his hands seared the wood, and the air filled with the acrid scent of burning lacquer. "What were you thinking, Dalanar? Fifteen years of searching for him, and you ruin everything!" Conthal gritted his teeth.

Dalanar started in surprise. Their conversation had been going well.

"It was that, or death." Dalanar shifted in his chair. He kept his tone reasonable. Sometimes he could calm the avatar by appealing to logic.

"Astabar blackmailed you?" Conthal croaked out a laugh.

"That's an apt summary."

"Explain!" He pounded his fists into the desk again, and the wood cracked.

"He injured me attempting a geis. The agony was too great even to draw power. He said I was dying, and the only way to live and regain my abilities would be to become his avatar."

"And you believed him? The God of Trickery and Illusion?"

The heat of anger inched up Dalanar's neck. His master's sneer always got a rise out of him. "What were my options? A Servant confirmed the damage. Since she was accustomed to dealing with your victims, I assumed she was an expert. I could scarcely ask the handmaiden to pray on my behalf. Morgir arrested me for the murder of Laniof. He would have killed me if Astabar hadn't intervened. No chance to request he verify."

Conthal stared at him with relentless gray eyes for an interminable moment. He swept his robes aside and settled back into his chair. The Throkari turned to the sideboard and poured tea from the kettle. "You've been busy. How did you force one of Sarael's minions to look at you?"

Dalanar took a deep breath. He and his master had always avoided open confrontation. Before Astabar, it would have meant a pointless death, now that he was an avatar, what would happen?

Dalanar thought about Mert and Noria and chuckled. "She attacked me with her fingernails while her partner hit me with herbs. They were trying to protect the handmaiden."

Conthal didn't laugh. Dalanar waved the question aside. "Have you selected a new Seal?"

"No. It will take years to train a replacement. I'm quite cross with you."

Dalanar bowed his head in acknowledgment. "Now we are both invited to the festival, there is no reason for me to pretend I wish to be consort."

Conthal tapped the ring against the desk. "Everything is going too perfectly to stop. They have tied themselves up in knots trying to predict what you will do if rejected. They believe the handmaiden will select you to protect the Yhellani flotsam."

"She certainly hasn't given me that impression."

Conthal laughed. "Sarael's suffering is delicious. No. You owe me this."

Dalanar narrowed his eyes at the man. "We will end the ruse before the selection ceremony." As difficult as Quin was, he had a ... fondness for her. There was no reason for the handmaiden to be miserable over a non-existent threat.

His master waved his words away. "I doubt we need continue it so long."

"What are you planning?"

"I won't ruin the surprise. You will appreciate its irony."

Dalanar clenched his fists under the table and stifled a retort. Conthal loved to scheme, enjoyed late nights plotting, but he rarely shared his plans. His former master's habits wouldn't change because Dalanar became an avatar.

"What did Astabar do to your eyes?" Conthal asked.

"What?"

"Your eye color. If I'm not mistaken, they resemble the handmaiden's. Did you not notice?"

CHAPTER FORTY-FOUR

T HE CHAPTERHOUSE IN SUMMER was still the most beautiful thing Quin had ever seen. Although no one lived there, it held the heart of the Yhellani religion, and she remained astonished the Throkari never managed to destroy it.

The house and gardens lay nestled in a strange basin amid the rolling farmlands of central Tyrentanna. The myth claimed Yhellania scooped out the hand-shaped gorge and sprinkled the ground with wild seeds from her hair. She watered her garden with tears of joy over the beauty she created, and it blossomed with every one of Morgir's colors. In the summer, when the rays of the sun illuminated even the darkest recesses, each plant produced a flower with a unique scent.

The first Yhellani Avatar erected the Chapterhouse in the palm of the valley. The two-story lodge dominated the celebration meadow. Emerging from either side of the main structure was a series of small, A-frame shelters built on platforms carved by Morgiri artisans. They circled the inner rim, nestling in trees and skimming over ponds. Rock, vegetation, water, or sky formed the walls of each.

Quin sighed, able to relax at last. They arrived a day early. Her horse snuffled the mud-churned grass of the trail leading down into the vale. The procession from Csiz Luan had already come through. She glanced over at Eulesis. Dirt spattered her riding clothes and dark circles ringed her eyes. Quin no doubt looked similar. "Let's go find the Ravendi encampment."

Scarlet-clad guards patrolled the road, punctuated with guardsworn in brilliant white tabards. The Yhellani smiled with relief when they spotted her, and the message passed swiftly that they arrived.

Quin groaned. "I don't want a formal presentation. I want a bath and sleep."

The women peered over the switchbacks, down the side of the steepest part of the cliff. A huge dais of marble in front of the staircase to the lodge formed the focal point of the meadow. Sarael, identifiable by her flowing white dress, descended the steps trailed by Barrand and Thera. They squinted up toward the road, shading their eyes against the late afternoon sunlight. Gardanath strode across the field, dogged by a flock of Ravendi soldiers. Quin didn't see the other avatars.

Eulesis managed a tired grin. "You won't be able to avoid them. I, however, am going to abandon you at the next bend. Wipe the mud off your face."

Quin found a semi-clean corner of her shirt and scraped the dirt off to the Ravendi's satisfaction.

"Good luck, girl." Eulesis took a side path down to the valley floor.

The woman passed by ranks of brightly colored tents as she headed toward the Ravendi banners crowded into the east end. Far too many of the faithful had come.

QUIN STOOD WITH A hand on her stirrup for several minutes after she dismounted beside the dais. Her legs ached and tingled from the long hours in the saddle.

Barrand held the bridle and inspected her. "We thought you ran off. We weren't worried, though. Father Jol volunteered to be the next handmaiden."

Quin surprised herself by laughing. "He'd be good at it."

"Need help?"

"Give me a minute. My legs are asleep. What's happening? Everyone behaving?"

"Eh. Kalin and Dalanar are stepping on each other's toes. Gardanath wants to paddle them both. Morgir showed up with the toddler this morning. Conthal is ill-tempered. Sarael was irritated you didn't make it to Csiz Luan. At least until Morgir explained about sending you to find the sorceress."

Quin stared at him. "Anything good?"

"Dalanar finally stashed Astabar inside his head, and less is going missing around the camp. The god is displeased Dalanar is harassing you about the selection. He's been berating him constantly." Barrand shrugged. "It's something?"

Quin squeezed his arm, then squared her shoulders and turned toward the gathered avatars. Rylir, Morgir, and Dalanar had arrived. Quin winced. No way to avoid them.

Quin knelt before Sarael with head lowered. The Yhellani Avatar kissed her forehead and sent sunny power washing into her. Quin remained tired, hungry, and dirty, but the aches, the bruises, the cramps from her wounds and long ride faded away. She sighed in relief at the absence of pain.

She loved Sarael and, looking into her kind eyes, Quin desperately wanted things to be the way they had been before. Those were the longings of a child. She knew the truth, and it changed the situation between them, however painful.

The avatar's gaze grew distant. A sign of her speaking to Yhellania. Sadness crossed the woman's face, and she wiped a stray hair from Quin's eyes. "I'm sorry," she whispered.

"Nice of you to join us, Quinny," Gardanath's booming voice interrupted. "We were wondering if the guest of honor intended to make an appearance. I assume you brought my second with you?"

"She fled for the baths. She's far wiser than I." Quin climbed slowly to her feet and faced Rylir and her god.

The girl tugged on her shirt. The plain apprentice smock had been replaced with a knee-length tunic of silky fabric embroidered with exotic birds and flowers. Tiny crystals flashed at the edges, casting little sparks of color when she moved. Clearly, the best work of the Morgiri artisans. The young avatar appeared healthy—no longer the sallow-faced, limp creature Quin left behind in Lyratrum.

Rylir squealed and threw herself into Quin's arms. "I'm so excited! I've never been outside the city, and to come to the Yhellani Summer Festival! I didn't know you were the queen, and Dalanar says you're going to pick him as king. I'm thrilled for you both!" The girl squeezed her again and beamed.

Better than having Rylir's hatred and blame for setting her up to be the avatar. Doubtless, that would come later.

"I am relieved you are doing well. I was worried about you when we left."

Rylir laughed a sweet, bubbling sound. "I'm an avatar now. It will take more than that to hurt me."

Quin nodded to Morgir. "Great Lord, perhaps we can discuss what happened at the university later?"

"I want a name, handmaiden."

"Yes, Great Lord, that's what I'm afraid of."

Morgir went still, as if considering forcing her. Rylir took his hand. "We can wait, Quinthian." She sounded older than her thirteen years.

More out of curiosity than a desire to speak to him, Quin

glanced at Dalanar. She felt awkward and shy. There was so much between them; she didn't know how to sort things out. Tomorrow, she would have to choose her consort. After that, she might have to fight him while defending Sarael and Yhellania. And now, he had her mother's eyes.

"Why did he pick that color for you?" she asked.

"I'm not certain he did it on purpose. You were caught up in things, perhaps it bled over."

"They don't match mine. They're more like Iyana's."

A flush crept up Dalanar's cheeks. He didn't reply.

Quin floundered for a different topic. "How is Astabar? Settling in?"

"He is a noisy occupant. Opinionated." Dalanar rubbed the back of his neck. "I've been informed that it is customary to offer a gift when one begins a courtship. I hope you will find this satisfactory, if a little late." Dalanar held a sheathed sword out to her with a slight bow.

Quin hesitated. He would no doubt view a refusal as a sign she was rejecting his proposal. She balked at the idea of accepting another present from her mother's murderer. But maybe he had been unjustly accused of that crime, as well.

What did a sorcerer know about swords anyway? He had probably been swindled into buying an iron blank at the Under-city market. She'd throw it away as soon as he departed. With a grimace, she took the weapon.

Quin knew she was wrong the moment she touched the hilt. The grip was wrapped with thin strips of leather woven in an intricate pattern. A Kestrial sword. Gardanath's personal smithy. It was worth more than Quin could earn in a decade as a mercenary; she would never be able to afford anything half as good as a guardsworn.

She slipped the blade from the sheath and gasped in appreciation. The metal shone like water over silver. Flawless, but plain. Possessing none of the silly flourishes popular in the corps. Grasping the pommel felt as if she held the hand of an old lover. Comfortable and familiar. The fit and balance were perfect. Quin would have chosen this sword herself.

Sorcerers were wealthy, of course. They charged exorbitant fees to provide magical aid to those able to pay: governments, nobility, merchants. However, this was an inappropriate and ostentatious gift. Did he intend it as an insult? A jab at the poor Yhellani?

With an ache of longing, Quin slid it into the scabbard and held it out to him. "I can't accept this."

Dalanar looked down at the weapon curiously. "What use would I have for a sword?" His eyes contained a glint of amusement. "Don't break this one."

"No one will think less of you for withdrawing your petition. You're busy with a new religion."

Dalanar frowned.

"You're not Throkari anymore. You don't have to do this."

The dark man stepped closer and lowered his voice. "Do you really want me to withdraw?" He tilted his head and stared into her eyes. A trickle of his attraction burned into her core and sizzled along her spine.

Quin froze. What did she want? He caused so much suffering ... was still conspiring with Conthal. How could she possibly desire him? She did. Her stomach knotted and she looked down at her scuffed boots.

"You're evil," she whispered.

"Yes."

"Then stop. Stop hurting people. Stop obeying him."

"I do not wish to hurt you."

Anger and frustration boiled up inside her chest. "This

whole situation is hurting me. Giving me this false choice is hurting me." Quin wanted to pound his head against a rock.

Dalanar stiffened and stared over her shoulder. "I will be at the selection ceremony tomorrow, Quinthian. Remember what I said."

She turned away from him in disgust.

"Gardanath, may we have a word with you?"

His boots clicked on the stone as he sauntered over with a boyish grin. The avatar was such a massive man, sometimes her mind fogged over bits of him in her memories, making him smaller and more manageable. His armor flashed in the blinding sunlight, and her breath caught at the sheer amount of violence he represented. Truly, the embodiment of war.

Sarael and Barrand joined them by the steps leading up to the Chapterhouse.

Quin lowered her voice to avoid being overheard. "Conthal has the staff, I'm certain of it. That's why they're here. They plan to use it to kill Sarael. When Yhellania manifests, they'll destroy her."

Sarael looked dubious.

Barrand said, "We'll triple the guards around her."

Gardanath hesitated. "What makes you so sure? Did you see him with the staff?"

"No, but the evidence is clear. He helped discover the branch. They know what it can do. The murderer wants something only Conthal can provide: The Throkari Secrets. Conthal and Dalanar simply needed the opportunity to kill Sarael and Yhellania. What other reason for their sudden attention to the Summer Festival? It makes sense."

"It is a possibility. I'd hate to focus on the Throkari, and miss a threat from someone we're not expecting." Gardanath rubbed his chin. "Even if it is them, Conthal is not above employing others to do his work. Guard Sarael, but I'll keep the troops deployed as they are."

SARAEL AND BARRAND LED her up the stairs. The main building was the only part enclosed by traditional wooden walls and glass windows. Servants in sparkling white robes fluttered around like butterflies, preparing flower arrangements and decorations. A crew hammered together the bower canopy, a whimsical Morgiri confection resembling an iron willow tree. It would be placed in the grotto for the first night. Quin's stomach churned with acid.

Quin turned to climb the staircase and noticed the rough sketches of Dalanar and Conthal. The scraps of yellowed parchment were tacked on the wall. She had seen them so often they had become nearly invisible. Some Yhellani artist captured the planes of Dalanar's face and his deep, penetrating eyes, but the rest was not particularly accurate. The Butcher of Narnus. It hadn't been him. Quin shook her head. What was the truth?

Sarael used the sitting room adjoining her bedroom as an office when she visited. Quin opened the door and gestured for them to precede her. The furnishings, once luxurious, had been sold down to the threadbare bones. The chamber still managed to be inviting, and the sounds of people laughing and celebrating in the fields below provided a cheer Quinthian didn't share.

Sarael chose her favorite chair by the darkened fireplace. She wouldn't meet Quin's eyes. Barrand guarded by the door.

Quin wanted to throw herself to the ground at the woman's feet, have her run her fingers through Quin's hair, and say everything would be fine. It worked when she was a girl seeking reassurance after falling from a tree. This was simply a matter of degree.

"Why didn't you tell me about Narnus?"

Sarael lowered her head.

"Why did you forbid me from seeking answers about Narnus and my mother's death? You knew Dalanar and Conthal weren't powerful enough to destroy the town. What else didn't you tell me?"

Tears rolled down Sarael's cheeks.

"Did Dalanar kill my mother?"

"I don't know," Sarael whispered.

Barrand sucked in his breath.

Quin deflated and sagged into a chair. Fifteen years wasted, hating the wrong person. "Why didn't you trust me, Sarael? You knew about the staff. That it created Astabar and destroyed the other gods. What did you suppose I would do with the knowledge? I've always been devoted to you."

Yhellania pushed Sarael aside and peered out with fiery intensity. Quin gasped and prepared to be crushed to the ground. She was not. Barrand fell, his weapons and armor clashing to the boards. Others in the rooms around them thumped to the floor.

"*I warned you, Quinthian. My patience is at an end.*" Yhellania arose and glared at her.

Quin stood and met her stare.

"*What? Astabar.*"

"Great Lady." Quin bowed her head. "I am your devoted servant. Why have you encouraged these lies? Did you think I would not serve you if I knew gods died or Astabar's birth killed my mother?"

"*No, Quinthian. You would have served, but you would not have suffered. I expect great things from you. You can plant pretty flowers on a thin layer of soil over bedrock. If you want a mighty tree to grow, you must break up the rock first. Breaking rock is a painful process.*"

Quin reflected on the meeting of the gods she witnessed at Dalanar's investment, and Yhellania's need to inflict suffering.

Everyone said she was the compassionate goddess. The one who cared about her avatar and her adherents. The opposite was true. She was the cruelest, set on making humanity more deserving through misery.

The destruction of the Tree made the Yhellani targets of vengeance. Did that serve her goals? No sorcerers of their own kept her people powerless and ignorant. Clearly, it wasn't a coincidence. Most Yhellani were healers and farmers, they weren't fighters, and they couldn't match the Throkari for intelligence and knowledge. They were the natural victims, plenty of torment for every devoted soul.

"I understand you now, Yhellania."

"*About time, Quinthian.*" The goddess retreated and Sarael slumped into her seat.

Quin watched, unmoved. She was too tired to care, although anger at Sarael was misplaced. She was as much of an innocent in this as Quin. Sarael was the only kindhearted person in the whole mess of avatars and gods.

Barrand rushed to Sarael's side and handed her a cup of water. "What happened to you, Quin?"

"Something went wrong when Astabar invested Dalanar. Because of his mark, he dragged me along. It appears I acquired some of an avatar's graces." Quin knew the commander was asking her a deeper question, one she couldn't answer. What hadn't happened to her?

Quin wiped a hand across her face. "I have to sleep. I have to get clean. Try to keep Morgir away from me."

Barrand looked at her as if she were a stranger.

CHAPTER FORTY-FIVE

THEY LET QUIN SLEEP until noon the morning of the festival. It was bad luck to wake the queen. The extra rest improved her outlook, and she felt refreshed and ready. Maybe things wouldn't be as ruinous as she feared. Guards and avatars were everywhere. What could Conthal and Dalanar do when everyone expected trouble?

No clouds marred the face of the sapphire sky. Beams of sunlight sparkled in the last dew drops, preparing to drench the celebrants in warmth. A roar of cheering came from the athletic fields. The events had already started. It lightened Quin's mood, and excitement stirred inside her. She devoured the plate of fruit and cheese that had been provided, but it scarcely took the edge off her hunger. She drew on a robe and left the room in search of more food.

As soon as she opened the door, chattering women swarmed around her, handing her hot tea and biscuits running with butter. They led her to the baths singing inappropriate songs about the Summer Queen. Quin wasn't too familiar with the festivals of other religions, but the Yhellani weren't terribly dignified. Everybody ended up in the water, splashing, laughing, and passing around flasks of burning liquor until Quin was dizzy.

After she washed with the ritual scents of lilac and honey,

they brushed out her hair. Someone set a cleverly woven crown of wheat, complete with jewels made of rose buds, on her head.

The women pinned two lengths of whisper fine fabric together at Quin's shoulders, and held them closed at her waist with a gold ribbon. The *stola* floated apart at the sides if she walked too quickly. The previous year had been windy, and nothing was left to the imagination of the attendees by the end of the day. No wind ruffled the leaves outside her window, thank the gods.

A cheer went up when she arrived at the contest grounds. Quin waved and joined the other notables in a covered platform overlooking the field. She held the place of honor in the center between Conthal and Sarael. Dalanar, and Morgir sat to her left beyond the Throkari, and Eulesis and an empty chair, set aside for Gardanath, were to her right. At first, she didn't see Rylir, but followed the god's attentive gaze and found her walking with some Yhellani girls her own age. A few Ravendi soldiers trailed at a discreet distance.

"That must be a new experience for you, Great Lord," Quin said with a smile.

"I admit I had no idea how much conversation a young girl was capable of." He regarded the child fondly.

Dalanar winced. "I had no idea how much talking a *god* was capable of. Aren't gods supposed to go off and pursue their own interests at some point?"

"Astabar enjoys being difficult." Morgir hadn't noticeably warmed toward Dalanar.

Conthal smirked at his former Seal. He turned to Quin. "Might I say how ravishing you are today? Your king shall be a lucky man."

"That remains to be seen." She waved to some passing children.

Gardanath, who had taken over announcing the events, called to the crowd. He glowed with the attention. "Now that our queen decided to get out of bed, I'm told it's time to find out who the best kisser is among our prospective consorts."

Several thousand people roared with approval.

"Oh," Quin said, glancing over at Dalanar.

"What is this?" The sorcerer sat up.

"I want you hopeful lads thinking you can woo the fair queen into the bower with your fancy lip work to step out on the field of battle."

"A silly game," Quin hastened to explain. "Most of these men won't even be at the selection ceremony tonight."

Laughter and applause rang out as a Yhellani youth entered the ring full of bluster and self-deprecating chagrin. He was quite drunk.

"Good man! What's your name? Daern? Is that it? Is this the only one brave enough to give one small woman a kiss? Are you men or mice?"

Dalanar looked on with distaste. "I'm expected to participate in this ... spectacle?"

"I won't care if you don't."

The Ravendi chanted and pounded their swords on shields as Kalin stepped out of the crowd. He wore his red sleeveless undershirt, and with the sun shining on his golden curls, he appeared to be as much of a god as his father. Several of the Yhellani women in front of the platform murmured in appreciation.

Eulesis watched Dalanar, her eyes strained.

"Ah, this fine lad is my own son, Kalin ... who should be on duty. He has his father's eye for a pretty girl. I can't blame him for shirking." Gardanath pounded Kalin on the back and pushed him into line next to Daern.

Dalanar glared at Kalin and rose from his chair. He offered Quin his arm, and she paused before taking it.

"Two? Is this an insult to our fair queen or a testament to the lack of backbone among the men gathered here?"

A grizzled man hobbled onto the field with his head held high. Quin recognized him as Mert, the Servant they met on the trip to Lyratrum.

The Yhellani cheered the old healer as he stepped into line.

"Don't become infected," Conthal said, as Dalanar escorted Quin out of the pavilion.

More applause and laugher as another person entered the line-up, but the press of people blocked Quin's view.

Dalanar led Quin to Gardanath and joined the end of the line.

Gardanath wore an expression of rapturous amusement as the sorcerer passed by, and then the big man pulled her into a rough hug. "Ah, Quinny, the look on his face may be the funniest thing I've seen in my never-ending existence. How did you get him out here?"

She lifted an eyebrow at Kalin. "I didn't do anything."

Gardanath turned to the crowd. "Now we have a decent showing for the queen!" He walked to the old healer. "Your name, brave sir?"

"I'm Mert." He wore a bright white robe and he shone like a beacon in the sun.

Quin grinned at him.

Next to him, a short man held a drooling infant of about a year old. The baby smiled at Gardanath and buried his head in his father's shoulder.

"Who is doing the kissing?"

"My boy, Lann. He thinks the more slobber when you kiss, the crazier it makes the girls. Seems to work on the women he's met so far. They swoon and pinch his cheeks."

Gardanath laughed. "Lann, the man with the slobber."

"Dalanar." The audience rustled and some of the Ravendi applauded. "Do you have any tips, or did Lann steal your technique?"

"I have a few ideas in reserve."

"Well, we'll discover who the queen chooses as the best kisser today."

Daern appeared to have sobered up enough to weigh his competition by the time Quin stood before him. He shifted nervously and placed one hand chastely on her shoulder.

"You're fine, Daern." She winked and pulled his other hand to her waist as she slid into his arms. She wasn't going to let him be embarrassed by a quick peck. He deserved it for being brave enough to stand up against Dalanar and Kalin.

A huge grin split his face when they parted, and Quin made a show of wiping her forehead. She nodded at him and turned to Kalin. No need to pretend here.

He smelled of an erotic blend of iron and clean sweat. He must have just removed his armor; his blond hair was damp from the heat. Kalin's brown eyes turned tawny in the bright sunlight. They held none of his usual merriment, only an intensity that called to something inside Quin. They kissed as if no one else was present. It was hard and desperate and her lips ached under his. She parted her mouth. She wanted nothing more than to be alone with him. To taste the salt on his skin and peel off his uniform.

"Ehm, children?" Gardanath's voice was rough with laughter. "Perhaps the rest of that should wait until tonight?"

Plenty of whistles and hoots came from the Ravendi, but the Yhellani were passionate about lovers, and their cheers of approval drowned out everything else.

Quin untangled her fingers from his curls with a laugh. Kalin smiled down at her and straightened the crown. He smirked at Dalanar over her shoulder. She narrowed her eyes at him. That kiss was part of their little rivalry? She stalked over to Mert.

"Careful, Quin. Careful," he said, eyeing the two men.

"We're well past careful, Mert ... I don't know how to find my way back to merely dangerous. Would you consider running away with the Summer Queen?"

"And miss the fun? Noria would be livid."

"Come over here and kiss me, anyway."

The old man laughed and gave her a noisy, bristly kiss.

Lann did his part and messily coated her with drool. Quin pinched his cheeks and rubbed her lips against his smooth forehead. Enjoying the sweet baby smell, and delaying having to face the sorcerer.

Finally, Quin stood in front of Dalanar. His teal irises were out of place under hawkish eyebrows. Unreal. She was too familiar with the black intensity of his gaze. He wore the long blue jacket Astabar stole for him in Lyratrum over a gray silk shirt. He was overdressed.

"Astabar asks me to convey his greetings."

Quin glanced up in surprise. She hadn't expected the god to be present. It made things even more awkward.

"Would you send him away?"

"He's quite excited. It's his first kiss."

"You're not serious?" Did Astabar intend to join them in the bower too? The situation was utterly ridiculous. She shook her head and turned to go. Dalanar placed one hand around her waist and kissed the side of her mouth. Heat surged through Quin's body and her heart raced. She stopped.

Dalanar stepped closer until he pressed against her down the length of their bodies. He twisted his fingers into the hair at the base of her neck. Quin slipped her arms around him, his body intertwining with hers. Dalanar nudged her lips apart, and opened the connection, flooding her with his need. Images of their lovemaking rushed into Quin, and she sighed with pleasure. Dalanar kissed her, almost too politely for the intimacy flowing between them. She pulled him closer, and bit his lip delicately. Dalanar crushed her into him and lowered his mouth to her throat.

"Avatar, that's outside the rules of this particular game. I'm certain a lot of people are eager to see who Quinny will choose tonight, eh?" Gardanath laid a hand on Dalanar's shoulder and the sorcerer released her. Titters and scandalized muttering came from the crowd.

"You cheated," Quin grumbled.

Dalanar's expression was infuriatingly satisfied.

"Your Majesty, you seemed to have a couple of favorites. Who is the winner?"

Quin took a shuddering breath and walked down the line pretending to consider. She whispered the answer in Gardanath's ear.

"The winner is Lann, the man with the technique of the ages when it comes to wooing women. Be a baby!"

The crowd cheered, which woke the winner up from his doze, and sent him into a fit of crying. Quin handed Lann's father a woven wheat wreath and pinched Lann's scrunched cheeks again. The contestants disbursed.

Kalin caught her eye as he headed across the field to the Ravendi encampment. "Find me," he mouthed.

Quin noticed Rylir standing with the other girls watching Kalin as he walked by. Her mouth hung open and she stared raptly after him. A first crush? Poor, sweet girl.

Dalanar retained his self-satisfied air as he returned to the pavilion. He radiated conceit through their connection. Quin hoped Astabar never allowed him any peace.

She wasn't going to sit on the platform with him now. She decided to find Kalin. Behind her, Gardanath announced challenge duels between the guardsworn and the Ravendi. Thera was fighting someone from the corps.

KALIN WAS RINSING OFF near the end of the valley. He pitched his tent on a low platform isolated from the nearby campsites by dense trees and flowering vines.

Quin paused to admire Kalin's body. The thick layer of muscle that bunched and flexed as he moved. The glistening water rolling over his fine skin. He raised an eyebrow at her, but didn't stop.

"I asked you not to come," she said.

"You needed someone on your side, Quin."

"I don't want you hurt."

"I don't need your protection." Kalin rubbed the water off his chest and head with a cloth, and tossed it aside. He took her hand and tugged her toward the platform. "I would like to discuss that kiss, though."

"I can't. Not before the selection tonight."

"God's blood, Quin. Why do you care about any of this? Any of them? They're forcing you to play a game with a monster. They *expect* you to choose him. They *expect* him to retaliate if you don't. And they're not going to lift a finger to help you."

"I love them. I have to protect them."

"They're supposed to love you, too. Isn't it time they proved it?" He slid onto the platform and pulled her between his knees. "I will not abandon you tonight."

"Even if I don't choose him, I can't pick you, either. It isn't worth the risk. This is three days. I don't want to go without you for the rest of my life."

"They're letting you be the sacrificial lamb to appease Dalanar. Even Gardanath is turning away. Instead of offering to help destroy him, they tell me I'll be killed. Maybe that's a lie, Quin. Maybe we can fight him, but they want him alive and pliable."

"It's not a lie. He and Conthal are powerful, more than Sarael, probably even Gardanath. No single man, however extraordinary, can beat them."

"Then why isn't anyone helping me?" he shouted at the sky.

He bowed his head. "I've failed you, Quin."

Quin held him tightly and smoothed his hair. "It wasn't your task to fail."

"When everyone else turned away, it became mine."

"Would it make you feel any better to know Yhellania wants it this way?"

"What?" Kalin looked at her as if she had gone mad.

"Conthal and Dalanar didn't destroy Narnus, and Sarael has no idea who killed my mother?"

"What?"

"Mmm." She pushed a curl back from his forehead. "Some religion I belong to."

"I don't understand what you're saying."

Quin laughed bitterly. "Neither do I."

Kalin was silent for a long time. He held her and stared out over the verdant trees and flowers enclosing the campsite. "I'll be at the selection. Choose me and I will fight for you. If you don't ... If he hurts you ... I will do everything in my power to destroy him."

"Maybe things won't come to that. They no longer need an excuse to be here. Dalanar can bow out, and they can still follow through on their plan."

Kalin's face was bleak. "You believe they're going to attack Sarael."

"More than ever. Their real goal is Yhellania, but they need to kill Sarael to get to her."

"If he does show up at the selection?"

"Well, Dalanar can't harm Sarael if he's with me. It's one less sorcerer to worry about. Watch Conthal."

"I'm going to be busy guarding the bower. I'll call in some favors."

Kalin took one of her hands in both of his and started rubbing the place on her palm she always found arousing.

"You made an admirer today," she teased half-heartedly.

Kalin eyed her. "Who?"

"Morgir's Avatar, Rylir."

"She's four years old." He rolled his eyes and kissed her wrist.

"She's thirteen and quite a beauty in the making. Little girls do grow up."

"I like older women." He pulled her down and nuzzled her neck. Kalin slid his hand along her side to cup her thigh.

"Only by a few years."

Kalin brushed his lips over Quin's collarbone. "When you're an eleven-year-old boy, those years are full of deeply fascinating developments in the girls around you. You made a lasting impression."

Quin shivered with pleasure at what his hands were doing.

"I want you to remember me tonight."

"I will, Kalin."

CHAPTER FORTY-SIX

Q UIN WASN'T SURE HOW she survived the rest of the day. It was a blur of judging events and socializing with the celebrants. Her helpers kept her flask filled with the raw mead and made her eat the things they placed in her hands. Sarael and Barrand also mingled with the revelers, but the other avatars preferred to stay in the pavilion, observing.

Thera won her bouts against the Ravendi, earning a nice amount of prize money from private wagers. Kalin and Barrand fought. The match outcome came down to a flaw in the visibility in Kalin's visor that allowed the guardsworn to blindside him with a weapon.

Before dinner, Quin returned to the Chapterhouse to lie down and rest with cool compresses over her face. She managed to sleep, but woke groggy and ill-tempered. The women responsible for helping her dress were merciless. They pushed her down into a tub of salted water and proceeded to primp and prepare her for the evening. They draped her in a pale rose gown with matching jewels and sandals, and brushed her hair until it resembled a sheet of dark glass pouring down her back. Once they wasted an absurd amount of time twisting it up into a cascade of curls, the attendants declared Quin ready. She had never felt more like an offering or a sacrifice.

Braziers and lanterns cast light on the marble terrace below Quin's window. Pristine white linens draped over long tables and pooled at their feet in snowy mounds. Cheerful voices rang out as the celebrants and guests gathered. After dinner came the selection. Then, the bower. Nerves prickled in her stomach, and she swallowed hard.

Quin took a deep breath and left the Chapterhouse.

A TICKLISH BREEZE WAFTED the perfume of the thousand flowers through the warm night air. Someone handed her a goblet of wine, and she nodded gratefully.

Gardanath and Eulesis talked with several counselors from the Agrarian Collective, the rulers of Tyrentanna. The avatar had on his formal Ravendi uniform, but Eulesis wore a red silk gown encrusted with gold embroidery. Probably worth half the grain in the country. She looked divine.

Conthal's Throkari robes had silver banding along the edges. Quin supposed she should be honored he selected something formal for the occasion.

He stared out over the fields where bonfires glowed and the happy sounds of feasting and celebration wafted back to them. Did he daydream about destroying the valley? Killing all the people? Quin shivered. Could he summon a god there?

Morgir and Rylir already sat in their places at the table, and others began drifting to their assigned seats. Quin stopped in front of the girl. "How are you doing, Rylir? Are you enjoying yourself?"

"I don't understand how you can be cruel to Kalin. He loves you, but you're going to choose Dalanar as the consort?"

Quin appealed to Morgir with her eyes. The god ignored her.

"Rylir...." She stumbled over the words, not sure how to explain. "Kalin is a good man. He understands."

"Those girls said Dalanar is wicked. That he hurts Yhellani, and is making you do this. He's always been nice to me. I told them they're liars."

"You should apologize. If anything, they understated things." Dalanar nodded to Quin and Morgir as he came up beside them.

Quin's stomach erupted in butterflies. Tonight. Time passed by too quickly.

Rylir set her jaw. "You're friends. Friends don't do that to each other."

"Are we friends, Quinthian?" His sea-green eyes appraised her.

She opened her mouth to deny it but stopped. "Of a kind. I didn't try to kill you after Rylir's investment."

"Astabar took your dagger."

"I had my sword." She regarded him speculatively. Did he have friends? He must have some among the Throkari. He was difficult to be sociable with, unbending and formal. Admittedly, she was the last person he would relax around, making it impossible for her to know. Being the Seal and the companion of the avatar could not have helped him. Jealous rivals, sycophants, and toadies, but not friends.

"*Are* we friends, Dalanar?" She was genuinely curious about his response.

Caught off-guard, he didn't appear to have an answer. The steward called them to dinner, and he turned and walked to his seat without another word.

Quin and Rylir shared a bemused glance, and Quin moved to her seat at Sarael's left, beside Gardanath and Eulesis. Conthal sat to Sarael's right. The seating arrangement would position the king next to the Throkari at every formal occasion, which worried Quin. Having Dalanar and Conthal so close to Sarael was a nightmare.

Sarael descended the steps accompanied by Thera and Barrand. They shone in new white garments.

The avatar stepped to her place at the head table and smiled in greeting. "Thank you for attending this year. As I'm sure you've noticed, the other avatars decided to renew the tradition of joining us to celebrate and ensure the prosperity of the year's harvest."

"Some more than others!" Someone called out from the celebrants gathering at the edge of the marble dais to listen. The crowd laughed.

Gardanath shifted next to Quin, and a Ravendi guard pushed his way through the throng.

She laid a restraining hand on her guardian's arm. "No, it's expected."

The big avatar grumbled.

Sarael tilted her head at the man. "Some have gotten into the spirit of things. We must also thank Gardanath and his Ravendi for providing security. The world is sadly a darker place than in the past, for us to need such precautions.

"Now we feast and forget our cares. The queen shall choose her king, and we will rely on them to provide us another year of bounty and hope. We, too, must do our part to help them through to the end."

The drunken revelers shouted their approval.

"As long as we're agreed, I hereby start the festivities." Sarael cast a bolt of light into a huge brazier at the center of the field. A flash like the dawning of the summer sun lit the faces of the watchers, and faded to a soothing sunset of red, magenta, and orange. The diners applauded and attendants brought the first course.

"What did she mean by 'do our part'?" Eulesis whispered to her.

Quin laughed. "It isn't only the queen and consort who are supposed to act like rabbits, the celebrants are expected to help. Their energy is transmitted to the royal couple to assist with stamina."

"This is your third year. Does it work?"

Kalin never experienced issues no matter where they were, but how to discuss that with his mother and father?

"Uh ... We don't talk about what happens in the bower. Bad luck."

Gardanath pulled Eulesis close. "Want to be Yhellani tonight? We can roar like mighty rabbits in the moonlight."

"You're going to need their healing if you keep that up."

Quin chuckled and turned to Sarael, who resumed her seat.

The woman watched her with sad eyes. "Will you forgive me, Quinthian?"

Quin snorted. "Would you be more specific?"

Sarael twisted her fingers together. "I don't know what to do about Dalanar. I'm sorry I put you in this position. I don't have any kind of power to destroy him and Yhellania won't. I pleaded with her. She said it was up to you to figure out."

"There's nothing to forgive. This is his fault, not yours."

"I'm sorry I let you believe he killed your mother when I didn't know."

"And you forbid me from finding out what happened."

"Yes."

Quin barely heard Sarael's soft reply. "I'm not ready to forgive you."

The avatar sighed miserably. Around the bonfires, the revelers called to each other and started singing a rousting work song about the wheat harvest.

Conthal leaned past Sarael. "Are you prepared to join the Throkari, Quinthian? Now you've seen the truth behind Yhellania. I need a Seal. Perhaps you would be interested in the position?"

Sarael snarled at him startling them both. "The Throkari are no better. What lies have you told Dalanar for his own good? To make him do what you wanted? To control him?"

"Why, none, of course." He sniffed. "That would be contrary to our principles."

Quin rolled her eyes at him. "Your active and ongoing prejudice against the Yhellani would cause too much strife between us."

"Having a devoted advocate might sway my opinion."

"Dalanar scarcely influenced you. I doubt I would have any greater success."

Conthal smiled thinly and resumed his dinner.

Dalanar stared at them. She picked up the feeling of puzzlement and resentment, but it was directed at Conthal. Did they have a falling out? Were their plans going awry?

Dalanar began a conversation with a Ravendi soldier, and the sensation faded. Quin wouldn't let herself grow too hopeful or relax her guard.

Yhellani minstrels performed a series of old songs about Sarael, the Summer Festival, and even one Quin now recognized as being in the language of the gods. Conthal and Dalanar listened, enthralled. The Throkari was clearly astonished to discover such a treasure hidden among his enemies. Conthal stared after the musician, a disquieting gleam in his eyes.

"Gardanath, how protective is Ravendis against kidnappings in Csiz Luan?" Quin asked.

The big man followed her gaze. "I'd say we'd welcome a Yhellani musician as fine and knowledgeable as that in our fair city, and find a situation for him that placed him above random street snatchings."

Sarael turned to Conthal. "What did the song mean? From your reaction it wasn't a love ballad."

The avatar's mouth pressed into a sour line. "Horribly mispronounced, of course, but it was a poem about how the gods engineered the mountains and the oceans. Isn't that right, Morgir? Seeing as you wrote it."

Morgir sighed. "Those days were quite something. I should teach that young man the correct words. Perhaps let him carry on believing it is a love song. In a sense, it is about the love between the gods and the world, not that you humans would understand."

"Sarael, do any more scraps of Old Knowledge linger among your people?" Conthal inquired casually.

"I don't think so. Our oral tradition is quite weak. Yhellania encourages living for the present, not preserving the past."

Quin went still. Would Conthal believe Sarael's lie? Or would he start another campaign of terror, geising Yhellani in search of any crumb they might possess?

"Pity," Conthal said.

When dinner concluded, Sarael rose to announce the beginning of the selection but Gardanath interrupted her. "Dear sister, there is another tradition we'd like to revive, if we may?"

The Yhellani waited in confusion as the avatars moved to the front of the tables. Gardanath offered Sarael his elbow and he led her to face the others.

"It was once customary for avatars to bring gifts to the hosts of the festivals they attended. We have each brought you our most ... thoughtful presents in appreciation for your gracious welcome."

Gardanath motioned to Rylir.

The girl tugged at her dress with one hand and walked up to Sarael with a shy smile. "Thank you for inviting us to the festival." She handed a velvet wrapped parcel to the avatar and waited expectantly.

Sarael pulled aside the cloth to reveal a delicate carving. *A white-clad Servant held a wounded soldier in her arms in the middle of a battlefield. He curled into her like a sick child, and she gazed down at him with compassion. Blood from a sword slice across his stomach soaked them both, and he was dying. The Servant prayed, her hand glowing with power.*

Sarael gasped in wonder and held the sculpture up to the light. "Rylir, this is marvelous!"

"Morgir says it's my best one. My drawings were good, and I didn't crack the marble."

Sarael hugged her. "Well, I imagine he'd be the one to judge. Are you sure? It's too precious for me to have."

"Oh yes. I made it for you!"

"Thank you."

Sarael placed it on the table in front of Quin. It was exquisite. The figures bore an uncanny resemblance to Sarael and Barrand, and Quin felt a sense of foreboding.

Dalanar held a small box out to the avatar. "Astabar insisted on this particular gift. Nevertheless, please accept my thanks for your hospitality."

Sarael gingerly opened the package and peeked inside. Her brow furrowed in confusion and she pulled out the small object. A pessary hung by the strings between her fingers. Quin choked on a laugh, while the Servants at the table gasped in shock.

Sarael glared up at Dalanar and shoved the box into the nearest brazier. He shrugged and returned to his place.

Eulesis convulsed with silent mirth beside Quin. "Astabar brought a fertility barrier to the Summer Festival? He has the guts of a warrior or a madman. If he hadn't been an avatar, what would have happened to Dalanar? Lynching?"

Quin nodded toward the outraged faces of the Servants. "They would tear him to pieces with their bare hands. We'll put up with a lot, but you don't interfere with pregnancy and birth around the Yhellani."

"You've never been pregnant." Eulesis watched her with a tiny smile.

Quin shook her head curtly. "Many of the faithful are quite concerned."

"Ah."

Gardanath placed a soft bundle in Sarael's hands with a wink. She sent him a questioning look. The wrapping fell away and a whisper of brilliant, white silk cascaded to the floor.

"Oh, Gardanath." She held the dress up to her shoulders and the beaded hem swirled around her feet.

"Since we're bringing back the old ways, I imagine you can find a use for it."

Sarael stopped admiring the gown and gave the avatar an injured expression. "Thank you." She sounded less than appreciative.

"And thank you for hosting us. You've granted me my fondest wish." He kissed her hand with noisy abandon. Sarael stiffened, scandalized.

At last, Conthal joined her in the center of the dais empty-handed.

"My gift is one of knowledge. A thing of immeasurable value. I will let her decide if she wishes to share it with anyone else."

The Throkari closed on Sarael, and Quin tensed. How long would it take to leap the table if he tried to attack? Sarael stood just out of arm's reach, could Quin be fast enough?

He whispered into Sarael's ear. Her face turned red then went pale. Sarael twisted the fabric of the dress she clutched forgotten in her hands.

When he finished, he stared soberly down at her. "Do you understand?"

Her eyes were wide and full of grateful tears. "I have no words. Your gift is beyond priceless. I must repay you—something."

Conthal half-turned to face her.

"A cough has plagued you since we met. Even with your great healing strengths as an avatar it has not subsided. I believe it will kill you."

The man glanced sharply at her.

"My thanks to you, is my healing." Sarael extended her arms, a globe of radiance held between her hands. He recoiled and almost blocked her, but he braced himself instead. His jaw tightened as she buried the sphere in his chest.

He gasped and coughed with a deep, congested sound. He brought a handkerchief up to his lips, and wiped blood from his mouth. After a minute, the hacking grew less, and higher in his lungs until it came out as a faint rasp in his throat. Sarael drew back, and the light flickered and died. She used up her healing powers on him. Damn it!

Conthal bent over, drawing deep breaths, but he didn't cough. He straightened up with a sardonic expression. "My thanks."

Sarael faced her guests as the avatars returned to their seats. She appeared lost in thought as she gazed around, focusing particularly on Quin and Dalanar.

"I am rendered speechless by your kindness and generosity. Thank you more than I can express. Now we retire to prepare for the selection and to allow the candidates to ready themselves. I have a gift to bestow on the handmaiden before the queen makes her decision."

Quin, unprepared for the sudden change in plans, knocked

her chair over in her haste to rise. What was Sarael doing? What gift? She followed the avatar and the guardsworn up the steps to the Chapterhouse doors.

Barrand muttered darkly to Thera.

SARAEL LED THEM UPSTAIRS to her bedchamber. "Help me prepare, Thera. Quin, change into your uniform. I'm the queen now."

The three of them stared at her stupidly.

With surprising iron, she snapped at them, "Go! Get ready." Sarael still held the silk dress Gardanath had given her, and she turned and walked into her bedroom, stripping off her fine robe before closing the door. Barrand hastily looked away.

"What's happening?" Quin asked him.

Barrand grinned. "Seems there's been a coup. Go change. That's an order!"

Quin slammed down the hall to her room, tearing the dress in her haste to remove it. She slid her clothes on, reveling in the familiar weight of chainmail and brigandine. A new, white tabard had been laid out for her. She slipped it over her head and belted on the sword and dagger, feeling complete. She tore out the curls and braided her hair tightly, pinning the ends in place. No time for the fighting style. It felt good to be a guardsworn again.

Sarael emerged from her bedroom as Quin returned. She wore the clingy, silk gown. The low-cut neckline and lace-up sides emphasized the lush figure she usually covered with demure clothing. Barrand turned purple when he saw her.

"Sarael, what are you doing? What's going on?" Quin asked.

"I'm taking my rightful place. The avatar was always supposed to be queen, as I have not-so-gently been reminded this evening."

"What?" Thera said, attempting to pin the woman's hair up.

"Let me do this for you, Quinthian. The handmaidens have always protected me, taking over this responsibility. It's time I repaid the favor I owe your family. I owe you, Quin."

"Not this, Sarael. It isn't worth the risk."

"What risk? What are you talking about?" Thera gave up, and brushed the hair straight.

"Conthal told me there is no hereditary risk of passing my illness on to my children. Centuries of watching others have babies. Families. Fearing the consequences." Sarael's face lit up with hope and excitement. She'd never sounded quite like this.

"What if he's lying to hurt you?"

"No, I can tell."

"My lady, you can't trust anything he says!" Quin closed her eyes. Conthal came to destroy Sarael; he didn't need the staff. Just a single, well-placed lie.

The avatar wanted to believe—it would save her handmaiden from Dalanar. Assuage some of the guilt she felt for lying to Quin about her mother's death. Free herself from many lifetimes of loneliness—at least until a baby was born afflicted as she had been.

Sarael drew herself up and swept out of the room. "The discussion is over, Quinthian. Are we ready?"

Her three conspirators followed her down to the entryway of the Chapterhouse. Quin was surprised Barrand didn't trip down the stairs. He focused on the avatar instead of where he placed his own feet.

BARRAND HELD OPEN THE door and they descended to the dais. Dalanar and Kalin waited in the center of the cleared space. In a semi-circle around them were the avatars and other dignitaries. On the outskirts stood the Yhellani revelers and Ravendi guards.

People didn't realize that Quin had changed her clothes and rejoined the guardsworn. They kept peering at the Chapterhouse expectantly. Kalin recognized her first and began laughing inaudibly, then louder as he sank to his knees, shoulders relaxing. Dalanar finally noticed Quin in her uniform. Instead of the anger Quin anticipated, she caught the brief impression of satisfaction. It disturbed her more than a furious tirade.

Sarael nodded to the witnesses. "Since we're returning to tradition in many ways this year, we've decided the same should apply to the Summer Queen. The role was intended for the avatar of Yhellania as her most sacred duty. I've neglected it for too long." The avatar addressed Dalanar and Kalin. "You came to be chosen as consort by a different queen, I offer you the opportunity to withdraw."

Kalin leapt to his feet with a triumphant grin and brushed past Dalanar. He bowed low before Sarael. "As lovely as you are, my lady, I'm bound to another. I intend no disrespect."

"None taken, Kalin." She grinned at him with equal delight.

The big Ravendi turned to face the celebrants as if about to speak.

Quin held her breath. *Kalin, don't say anything. Don't do anything to start a fight.* He flicked a final, contemptuous sneer at Dalanar, and pushed into the crowd.

To Quin's astonishment, Dalanar continued to focus his ire at Conthal.

Sarael favored him with a wicked smile. "You don't have to withdraw. You could try to intimidate *me*, Dalanar."

"I know enough to concede when outmaneuvered."

Quin still expected anger or irritation, but only picked up a sense of relief. He remained sufficiently distracted that he didn't recall their connection was open. He was not as calm as he acted.

"A wise man accepts defeat gracefully."

He bowed crisply and departed.

"Are any men brave enough to become the queen's consort?" Sarael asked. She walked a circuit of the dais, waiting.

No one moved, and Quin looked around. There must be a king! Now that no sorcerer loomed to chase off prospects, the platform should be flooded. Sarael was lovely, and sweet, and most of the supplicants were usually drunk anyway.

Barrand glared out at the crowd. Maybe his face was driving suitors away.

"Stop scaring people," she whispered to him.

He made an effort to soften his features. He wasn't terribly successful.

"Now quit pawing at your sword hilt."

Barrand grunted and dropped his hands from his weapons.

Sarael stopped beside them and smiled gently.

"What do we do?" Quin asked.

"I suppose I'll have to choose." She held her hand out to Barrand.

The big guardsworn looked down at it, and back up at her face, unmoving.

"Take my hand, Commander."

"You don't want me, Sarael."

"I'm the queen. I get to decide."

"Power has gone to your head," he chided.

"I intend to be demanding."

"I suppose I'm used to that already."

Sarael laughed. It was the joyful, carefree sound of a village girl on her wedding day.

He took her hand as if expecting her to change her mind. She clasped her fingers tightly around his.

The audience applauded and a procession led them toward

the bower. They whistled and sang bawdy songs as they dragged the royal couple along.

Quin remained on the dais alone, thankful to have a moment's silent respite. She closed her eyes and inhaled the rich, sweet air. Her part was over, at least for now. Sarael might not need a handmaiden any longer. But Quin was still guardsworn. She protected Sarael. There were no other distractions, and it felt right.

Her life would return to normal.

CHAPTER FORTY-SEVEN

THE PARADE OF CELEBRANTS deposited Barrand and Sarael in front of the sacred grotto, but lingered to provide advice and backslapping, until Gardanath interceded.

"Out! You have work of your own. Barrand is going to need every bit of help he can get over the next few days. He doesn't look like a man who is up for the challenge. Go on! Make like rabbits." He shooed the revelers out, and they staggered off singing.

A warm breeze ruffled the drapes of gauzy blue fabric enclosing the glade. The branches of the iron willow tree spread around them, leaving a room-sized bower at the base of the twisted metal trunk. Leafy shadows hid the stars. A huge bed, mounded with pristine white pillows, dominated the space. Cool water trickled down the mossy wall of the shallow cave behind the tree. Flowers were crammed in everywhere else. Barrand sneezed. He had never seen the bower decorated for a festival night.

Light from dozens of lanterns illuminated Gardanath's triumphant expression as he tucked Eulesis under his arm, and turned to leave. "Ha! We showed that sorcerous fuck not to mess with our Quinny. I'm glad you had the guts to step up and take over."

"You arranged this? Why didn't you tell me?" Barrand

glanced between Sarael and Gardanath, irritation flooding him. The guardsworn had been sick with worry. Knowing some intervention was planned would have given them peace.

"No, Barrand. Gardanath reminded me of my duty. I realized it could be a way out of the situation for Quin, too. I'm ashamed I didn't see it before."

He looked down at her and his anger faded. Her sweet face was flushed with pleasure. The candlelight flickered, picking up the highlights in her hair. It was in disarray after the vigorous march, and he hesitantly reached out and smoothed away a lock that fell across her forehead. She quirked her lips at him and her dimple showed.

Barrand turned back to Gardanath, embarrassed, but the avatar and his second had left unnoticed. Sarael and Barrand were alone.

"My Lady, you should choose someone else. Someone younger. Better. I have a mashed up old face and creaky joints. What good would I be to you?"

"We already discussed this."

"The sudden responsibility made you select the wrong man. Tell them that."

"I don't think so."

Barrand gazed at her hopelessly. She was so lovely.

"Unless ... you don't want me?" she whispered.

Barrand trained in the military his whole life, most of that in Sarael's service. He knew you always slept when you had the chance, you never surrendered a tactical advantage, and you never turned down the opportunity to make love to the woman of your dreams, no matter how much you didn't deserve the honor.

Barrand moved closer until he felt the heat of her body through the thin silk of her dress, and lowered his lips to hers. He kissed her lightly, not wanting to frighten or overwhelm her.

He wasn't ready to chance anything else; she might come to her senses at any time.

Sarael threw her arms around his neck and drew him to her with a sigh of contentment. She nuzzled his ear and kissed down his throat. His knees wouldn't hold him up much longer. She wasn't frightened; he'd have to risk her changing her mind.

He pulled Sarael closer, sliding his hands over her hips and up her back. The silk glided over her body, and he lifted the skirt to gain access to her hot skin. He wanted her out of the dress. Barrand untied the ribbons at the sides and started peeling the material over her head.

Sarael raised her arms and he swept it off. Her hair stood up like a halo and Barrand smoothed it down. Her body was perfection, more exquisite than he ever imagined. He groaned. He still wore his armor. It would take an entire lifetime before he could lie next to her.

Barrand yanked at his belt and stripped off weapons with shaking hands. He stopped to kiss her again.

Sarael stepped in and unfastened the buckles of his brigandine with quick, confident fingers.

"How can you undress me faster than I can undress myself?"

She flashed her dimple at him. "I've been watching you for a long time."

At last, Barrand tugged her down to lay beside him on the lilac-scented sheets. He reverently stroked the soft skin of her side. Golden light accentuated her curves. He felt scruffy and coarse.

Sarael traced a finger through his graying chest hair, across his stomach, following the line lower. She smiled as his breath caught.

"I've never been queen before." Sarael sounded shy.

He took her hand and raised it to his lips. "Not even when you first became an avatar?"

"Handmaidens have always taken my place."

Barrand frowned at the white dress. "I don't mean to pry, but have you ever...."

"More than anyone, I think you have the right to ask." Sarael's eyes twinkled. "Yes. Before my investment."

He whistled. "That's a long time for a Yhellani."

"Don't make me wait any longer."

He didn't.

CHAPTER FORTY-EIGHT

"THAT WAS UNPLEASANT," DALANAR growled at Conthal. "We agreed that you would carry out your plan before this evening."

Conthal paused in his stroll around the grounds to look at his former Seal. "It was much more dramatic this way." His lips curled into a pleased smile, and he resumed his pacing.

"You didn't think to inform me of the change? I could not have withdrawn once the selection began."

The Throkari Avatar laughed. "Didn't I? It must have slipped my mind." Conthal considered the rustling in a darkened alcove. He shook his head in disgust and moved on. When Dalanar didn't follow, he turned to face him. "You truly believed they'd let a Throkari ... *you* ... become the consort?

"I must admit you were unexpectedly brilliant as the libertine. You drove them into a corner they could not escape without forcing Sarael to resume her position as the queen. You even managed to compel Gardanath to intervene to protect the handmaiden. I only needed to nudge him along ... once or twice. Well done."

"You told me none of this." Dalanar clenched his fists in rage. He had been played as expertly as any of the others, and as callously. What else was Conthal forgetting to tell him?

Astabar, who had been gloating in Dalanar's mind since the selection, spoke up. :: *You should ask him who summoned me.*::

:: We don't know.::

:: You *don't know, Dalanar. Where was your master?*::

"Who created Astabar?"

Conthal tilted his head as if listening to some far-off music. "Ah. The inevitable question. I should have warned you against letting stray gods inside your head. *I* used the staff and called him."

"Why didn't you tell me?" Dalanar sagged onto a bench. "I trusted your story about our enemies creating him to use against us. I believed it was the Servants." He snorted at the idea now he had met them. "And the devastation of Narnus ... a city full of people?" The bodies of the ash-covered dead strewn across the hillside.

"A city full of *Yhellani*," Conthal said. "This is precisely why: your constant arguing. I know you far too well. You wouldn't have let me rest with your tedious dissension."

Astabar rumbled his agreement in Dalanar's head.

"You wanted my perspective. That's why you chose me as Seal."

"Yes, yes," Conthal snapped. "At times, things need to be accomplished without hours of debate. The staff provides us opportunities to achieve greater goals than we've considered in the past. It needed to be tested. You weren't going to convince me otherwise, and I didn't care to have the discussion."

"You controlled me with lies, just as Sarael manipulated Quin."

"Nothing like those witless fools."

"Your hypocrisy is staggering."

The Throkari Avatar huffed and stalked off.

Damn him! Conthal lied as casually as breathing, but Dalanar assumed he was the exception. They were supposed to be honest with each other; it was part of the oath between avatar and Seal. To do otherwise, negated the purpose of having the office of advisor. Dalanar now questioned his service, what he knew about the avatar, and the reasons behind everything he had done. Quin would laugh at *his* naiveté.

The Yhellani were not trying to destroy them. The torture, the anguish he inflicted tracking down conspirators, was based on a lie. Conthal used him as merely another tool in his campaign of reprisal, and Dalanar accepted it without question.

How did Quin travel with him and not murder him in his sleep?

:: *I don't like your master, even aside from his intending to kill me.*:: Astabar stretched out and tickled the memory of the attempt they made to imprison him.

:: He's not my master.::

:: *That is for the best. He's a bad influence on you. You should apologize to Quin. Do you suppose she'll ever speak to you again?*:: Astabar reviewed the memory of the kiss from the afternoon. Rewinding to his favorite part and replaying the images and sensations slowly.

:: Stop that.::

:: *Was that a good kiss? You liked it, but are there better ones?*::

Dalanar found no enjoyment in the recollection. He thought Quin knew of the Yhellani plot against the Throkari. It explained why her mind was so well defended. Now, he realized the idea was absurd. He had been persecuting an innocent woman.

His headache returned.

:: *Your brain is fine, Dalanar. It just got more crowded in your conscience.*:: Astabar chuckled and replayed the kiss.

:: Would you stop?::

He needed to talk to Quin.

:: *You're expected at the wine ceremony. I think the conversation with Quinthian will take a great deal longer than you have.*::

CHAPTER FORTY-NINE

QUIN CIRCLED THE DAIS waiting for Sarael and Barrand to make their appearance. She hoped they remembered to come out for the midnight ritual. If they didn't emerge from the bower soon, she would have to retrieve them, and Quin wanted to avoid that.

A candelabrum of pristine white candles sat on a small table and supplied the only source of illumination. Even the bonfires in the fields had faded to embers. Crickets droned softly in the darkness, and a few revelers moved around in the meadow, nothing like the boisterous celebration of prior festivals. Probably to be expected as the year's attendance was down to a third of normal. And Sarael's participation might have encouraged more people to offer their *personal* assistance to the Summer Court.

Quin smiled. Finally. Barrand's infatuation with Sarael had been a source of pity and exasperation among the guardsworn for years. He tried to disguise his feelings, but Yhellani were terrible liars ... for the most part. She hoped they were joyously bound.

She did another circuit. The avatars were otherwise present. Even a sleepy Rylir huddled next to her god. Conthal looked angry, but he usually did. Dalanar paced, occasionally glancing her way. Quin ignored him. She had nothing further to say to the man.

Quin grinned at Gardanath. "A little late for all the metal." She rapped on his chest with a knuckle. He wore his ritual armor of bronze breastplate and kilt.

"Ah girl, I want to appear at my best, even for these small observances. What are you doing here? Shouldn't you and Kalin be off making babies somewhere like good Yhellani? I need some grandchildren soon. I'm not getting any younger."

"You're not getting any older, either," she mocked. "Barrand and I have swapped duties. I get to patrol and order people around with a surly glare on my face. How am I doing?"

"We'll need to break your nose in a few places."

"Maybe it isn't too late to ask for my old job back."

"It is." He nodded to the stairs where Sarael and Barrand descended, fingers entwined. They were luminous in their delight.

The guests raised their wine glasses in a toast, and drained them as a sign of respect.

Gardanath frowned at Quin. "Where's your cup?"

"Barrand would break my nose himself if he caught me drinking on duty."

The servers came around to refill the goblets, and Gardanath grabbed an extra one for Quin.

"If you don't drink to their health and happiness, it's a poor repayment indeed for what she's done for you. Go on. I'll distract them." He winked at her and clapped her on the shoulder, sending her off to the edge of the platform.

"May the goddess ignore you both," she said, thinking of Yhellania and her suffering. Quin took a sip and grimaced. Rancid. She dumped the rest in a bush and set the cup down. She noticed Eulesis didn't drink her wine either. The woman had excellent taste.

Quin continued her patrol. She greeted the Ravendi Gardanath stationed outside the perimeter of the Chapterhouse and dais. Quin recognized her as the ex-elite guard who had been head of an orphanage for years. Telen? That didn't make sense. The other Ravendi on duty were old, too—white hair and battered faces. Still solid, though. Veterans. They needed to bring up retirees to have enough people for the festival?

The patrol route took her around the main house and the bower. She didn't want to leave it unattended for long. Kalin said he was posted there, but she hadn't seen him. Perhaps their routes just missed each other, although she varied her timing to avoid being predictable. She decided to wait a few minutes.

Where was Kalin? This wasn't like him. Quin would ask Eulesis on the next pass. Maybe he had been reassigned, or the schedule mixed up. Somebody needed to be on guard, nonetheless.

:: *Dalanar's drunk.*::

Quin fell to her knees in shock. :: Astabar?:: He shoved his way into her head and tucked himself in a corner. Her skull felt full and heavy, as if he was physically inside her. Quin's ears popped and the feeling of pressure faded.

:: *His brain is in shambles. I can't be there.*::

:: Dalanar won't get drunk. He's a sorcerer. What's going on?:: Her connection with the man was silent. :: How are you inside *me*?:: Foolish question. Doubtless, she completed enough of the investment the god could enter her mind as well as Dalanar's.

:: *Fuzzy. Pleasant. You're kinder than he is, but not as intelligent.*::

Astabar replayed the kisses from the afternoon's game, making Quin collapse limply to the ground. The complete tactile experience of being in another time and place overwhelmed her. Sunshine on her shoulders. Wind rustling her hair. The succulent aroma of meat grilling. She relived the entire event, even things she hadn't remembered noticing.

:: Please stop, Astabar.::

He found the memory of the meeting with Kalin.

:: *You have stimulating recollections, Quinthian. Dalanar is dull.*:: He played the one with his avatar again. :: *He did cheat.*::

:: What is happening with Dalanar? I need to check on everyone. Stop playing with my memories!::

The god gave the impression of his assent and the visions receded. She levered herself off the ground and worked her way around toward the front of the Chapterhouse. Just as she turned the corner, Gardanath brought the bottom of the staff down on the base of Morgir's neck, and guards grabbed Conthal and Dalanar.

Motion in the universe shuddered to a stop for the length of several heartbeats. No light, no heat, no power. Existence flickered on and off as a god died. The moment lasted a lifetime. In a tumult of sound that came from the stars, the earth, and the particles of their bodies, life resumed. A wash of energy like the waves of an incoming tide filled her with warmth. Each surge creating a new high water mark. The power of the god, once held contained, burst free.

Rylir screamed in horror and clawed at Gardanath's armor with manic ferocity, breaking her nails and leaving bloody trails down the polished surface. The giant avatar grimaced as he captured the girl's wrists. He waved and several of his Ravendi bound her.

Eulesis forced the girl to drink more of the wine by holding her nose, and at last, her screaming faded to sleep. Gardanath laid her gently on one of the steps and covered her with his red cloak.

The other avatars struggled, but the drugs prevented them from focusing their magic. Like Astabar, their gods had been driven away.

Gardanath? What was going on? Quin reeled from the death of Morgir and the influx of power his passing left behind. She couldn't move beyond the shock of seeing her guardian remorselessly destroy a god. The image replayed in her mind, but it wasn't Astabar who was responsible.

A step came from behind her. As Quin turned, a tremendous blow struck the back of her head.

CHAPTER FIFTY

W AKE UP, QUIN.:: ASTABAR poked at her brain. :: No.:: She groaned and touched her head where it felt as if another skull grew.:: Can you fix it?

:: *It's not broken. Stand up! They're going to kill Dalanar to get to me.*:: The god dragged at her mind.

:: Why didn't you take over and blow them to shreds?:: Quin pushed herself to her knees and looked around. They left her lying where she fell at the corner of the Chapterhouse. A handful of sleeping or drugged figures remained, but the avatars were gone. A few soldiers in Ravendi scarlet walked the edge of the meadow. No one else was visible. How long was she out?

Gardanath killed Morgir. Quin couldn't make sense of it. And now he intended to kill Dalanar to get to Astabar? And Sarael? All those sarcastic comments about gods. His anger and disagreements with Ravendis. His drinking. Yes, he hated the gods, but to kill them? Quin shook her head, attempting to clear it.

:: *You never agreed to become my avatar. I have no power when I'm inside you.*:: Astabar sounded sulky. :: *And, while I can't attack Gardanath, he can attack you. I didn't like those odds.*::

Quin climbed to her feet and staggered to the dais. Barrand lay still. Hands and ankles bound, unconscious. She cut away the restraints and tried to rouse him, but he couldn't open his eyes.

"Barrand, where did they take Sarael?" The man groaned and rolled his head to one side, trying to shake off the drugs. He reached for his sword, but lapsed into sleep before finding it. She patted his shoulder and left him. If the Ravendi intended to harm him, they would have already done it.

:: *Quin, COME ON!*:: Astabar begged. :: *You must find Dalanar.*::

The only place private enough to hide the imprisoned avatars would be the limestone ravines that formed the fingers of the valley. Quin needed help to search. She needed help to rescue them.

She headed toward the guardsworn encampment and found them crumpled around their meal. Quin didn't see any celebrants, either. Did Gardanath drug all the wine and food? The Ravendi patrolling now were the grizzled mercenaries, not the regular corps who had guarded during the day. They must have let the younger soldiers off duty for the evening, and put the ones loyal to Gardanath's plans in their place. She had no one else to turn to.

A Ravendi watched her on the way back to the dais. If she were the only celebrant awake she would attract attention. But they might decide that allowing a guardsworn to wander around was too risky. She ducked into a bathhouse. Several white robes hung from hooks, and Quin grabbed one, grateful it covered her uniform.

The path past the bower split into narrow tracks leading to the five fingers. The dry trails were well-traveled. There was no way to tell which had recently been used.

Quin centered herself and thought about the connection with Dalanar. It remained silent, but in the past, she picked up twinges of pull coming from his direction. She concentrated on his eyes, her mother's color, but still his deep, penetrating gaze. The stubble on his neck, and fondness for grapes. The astonishing beauty of his power.

She felt him. The furthest right of the narrow gorges. She stripped off her robe and new tabard. Her dark brigandine wouldn't show up against the dusky green foliage.

:: *Quin, I can help you.*::

:: How?::

:: *You have to agree to be my avatar.*::

:: No!::

:: *You can't slip past the guards.*::

:: Can you undo it?::

:: *I'm not certain.*::

Once located, Quin could follow the sensation of Dalanar's presence. Stalking down the ravine, she received a strong impression of him in a darkened cave with a narrow entrance to her right. Three Ravendi mercenaries, hidden behind mounds of vegetation, stood guard. She would have walked past without noticing.

:: *You can't get in there.*::

:: I know.::

:: *Say it.*::

:: I don't want to.::

:: *They'll kill Sarael, too.*::

Quin held her pounding head. Her suffering no doubt pleased Yhellania. If she found a way to destroy the goddess without harming Sarael, she might agree to it.

:: Can you clear Dalanar's mind of the drugs once we're in?::

:: *I think so, but it would mean taking you over, and I can't act against Gardanath.*::

Quin chewed on her lower lip. :: What if you took over

long enough to take care of the guards? We'd free Dalanar and clean him up. Then you go back where you belong.::

:: *We don't have time for another option. Hurry, Quin! Will you be my avatar?*::

Quin rebelled against the idea. To be an avatar was bad enough, to be tied to Dalanar through the god for an eternity was a fate too terrible to imagine.

Why had Gardanath done this to them? His betrayal formed a rot in the core of her life and it made her furious.

:: Yes, Astabar, I will be your avatar for the next full day.::

The god was silent. :: *Will that work?*::

:: I don't know!::

Power roared into Quin making her tremble from the impact. She drifted like a piece of foam in a waterfall of the god's essence. She couldn't contain him. He spilled on and through her until every molecule of his being sifted past the mesh of her body. She collapsed.

:: *No time for that.*:: Astabar shoved Quin aside and she dragged herself into a corner of her own mind with a whimper.

The god performed calculations Quin didn't understand. He pushed power into the equations, and light curved around their shared body. She was invisible. He pulled the dagger out of its sheath at their back and moved up behind the Ravendi guards.

He started another set of formulas, working with such speed each line became unreadable. When he finished, a group of revelers stumbled down the trail, laughing, and singing. They stopped near the guards, and one darted into the bushes to relieve himself. The Ravendi backed away from the entrance and deeper into the shadows. Astabar slipped around them and into the cave. The illusory revelers moved on along the path behind them.

:: Impressive.::

:: *I AM a god, Quin.*::

A TIGHT PASSAGEWAY OPENED into a large cavern. The imprisoned avatars lay in a crumpled heap against the wall by the entrance. Neither Sarael nor Dalanar moved, but Conthal thrashed groggily. Several of the guards attempted to secure his fingers to boards. Both of the sorcerers were lashed to wooden crosspieces that prevented them from moving their arms. Dalanar's fingers were also strapped down. He was blindfolded and gagged.

:: Does that work to control a sorcerer?::

:: *It appears to.*::

One of the guards broke Conthal's finger with a snap and the Throkari groaned.

Gardanath spoke with Eulesis on the other side of the chamber. He stroked her hair and wiped away tears. Two more mercenaries paced along the rough, limestone walls.

Any lingering hope Quin might have had that Eulesis would help to stop the slaughter was dashed. The woman was utterly loyal to her family. To Gardanath. If he wanted to kill the gods, then she'd be there at his side.

Bile burned in Quin's throat. :: Do something to clear Dalanar's mind.::

Astabar bent over the drugged man and started untying the hand hidden behind Sarael. The numbers flashed in her head, slower now, as if he wasn't certain. He erased and rewrote.

:: What are you doing?::

:: *I have to be sure.*::

Gardanath parted from Eulesis with a lingering kiss, and gestured to the guards. They started over to the avatars while he removed the staff from a thick, leather case.

:: Now, Astabar!::

He drew the numbers out and released them. Whom did the gods pray to?

:: Did it work?::

Silence. :: *His mind is still polluted, but it's ... better.*::

The guards grabbed Sarael and started dragging her to Gardanath. Mud crusted her white dress.

:: Get out.::

:: *It's nasty over there.*::

:: He's your avatar, and he needs you. Go!::

Astabar paused sullenly, and then the sensation of being in charge of her body again assaulted Quin. She was no longer invisible, although she hadn't been noticed.

Dalanar watched her though half-lidded eyes and flexed the fingers of his free hand.

The Ravendi mercenaries pushed Sarael to her knees in front of Gardanath.

Not bothering to draw her weapon, Quin bolted across the cavern and slammed into Gardanath's armored chest, knocking the staff from his grip. It skidded to Eulesis, who stopped it with a boot.

Quin slid her sword from its scabbard. Gardanath retreated and drew his own. He gestured for the mercenaries to withdraw.

"You weren't invited to our little party, Quinny."

"What are you doing, Gardanath? You killed Morgir. You're going to murder Sarael? They've done nothing to you!"

"They're gods. What haven't they done to us? I'm liberating the entire human race from their tyranny, Quin. Aren't you tired of being one of their pawns?"

"But you would need to die, too. How did you convince Ravendis to agree to this?"

"Agree?" He barked out a laugh. "The gods are damned fastidious about the brains they inhabit. It took me over a hundred years, but I trained her like a dog. She leaves whenever I take a drink of wine now. It was the only way to have any peace." The big man glanced over at his second. "I intend to die, and I want that red bitch to die beside me. Eulesis promised to do the honors when the last of this lot is gone."

Tears prickled at the corners of Quin's eyes. "But ... why?"

"No crying when metal is bared," he ordered gruffly. "Damned, soft-hearted Yhellani."

Quin dashed the water away with the palm of her hand. Gardanath started pacing toward her. She retreated.

"You can't win, and I don't want to kill you, girl. Surrender. Let Eulesis bind you. She'll release you when I'm dead."

"Why?"

"Because humans are capable of their own atrocities and redemptions without the gods' interference. We don't need them to poke and prod us and treat us like toys to teach us lessons. We deserve the dignity to experience the consequences of our actions. And I am sick to death of having Ravendis inside my head. She. Won't. Shut. Up."

"I may even agree with you in principle, but it's too much!" Quin tried to sound calm, although her throat constricted with sorrow and desperation. "With all four of you gone, the power vacuum would be enormous. People will panic. No god of Death? Who will deliver their souls into the afterlife? No goddess of Birth? Who will give souls to the babies?"

"Those things have worked without the gods' intervention since the world was created. Their existence is irrelevant. If it mattered, we would have been devastated each time a god was destroyed in the past. I want to complete the job started a millennia ago. Humans have endured the gods, they can withstand the chaos and rebuild. The church hierarchies will still be in place. The governments will continue to hold power and be damned happy we're gone."

"I can't let you kill Sarael," Quin said quietly.

"That is one point we cannot negotiate." He exhaled and raised his sword.

He swung at her gingerly, and she blocked. The sound echoed against the limestone. His heart wasn't in it. Gardanath retreated to a clear space away from Sarael's limp body. Just like any other practice session.

Quin never imagined fighting Gardanath in earnest. She didn't disagree with him. It was time to be rid of the gods. They caused her nothing but misery. However, to lose him and Sarael, the people who acted as father and mother to her ... He wanted too much.

"I'll crush you, Quin. Don't make me," he pleaded.

"Release Sarael."

He swung again and again, a series of blows, growing stronger. Quin defended herself easily. She tested his resolve with some of the techniques Magda showed her. She thrust at the bottom edge of his breastplate, parried and kicked him, and plunged in again. His eyes widened in surprise, but he managed to block her stabs. She caught him in the arm on a riposte sending a surge of crimson flowing over his bare skin.

Gardanath grunted in approval and pressed forward. The avatar was engaged now. He would kill her.

They clashed, their swords blurring, strike against strike. Gardanath lunged, forcing Quin to stumble back. He was so much bigger, long arms, and a longer sword. She had to use every fiber of agility she possessed to dodge out of his way. He was graceful, too. Far from lumbering in his heavy armor, he danced. Quin chanced a strike at the exposed area under his arm. If she injured his shoulder, he wouldn't be able to raise the sword against her. He shifted aside in time, and her blade screeched along the metal. It left a furrow in the bronze breastplate. Gardanath whipped around with a vicious backswing that would have severed her arm. She fell to a crouch and rolled behind him. He moved too quickly for her to take advantage of the position, but it earned her a fierce grin when he whirled to face her. He lunged forward again, hacking at her with short, vicious blows. Her arm tingled after every hit she couldn't evade until her fingers went numb. He was relentless.

Without Magda's unique fighting style, Quin wouldn't have been able to resist the onslaught. Attack left: parry. Overhead and to the side: dart away. Backswing and lunge: dodge right. She predicted where Gardanath's blows would fall and countered them. She lunged under his guard and stabbed him in the hip, under the breastplate. He grunted. Thick blood poured from the wound and drenched his leg. Quin retreated, horrified. So much blood. The life of a good man dripping onto the floor of a miserable cavern.

He limped as he moved after her. "Don't retreat, girl. Sword up. Finish what you start."

He had said those things to her a hundred times on the training ground. Quin wiped her eyes with her hand and gripped the hilt tighter.

Gardanath swung at her, but it was weaker than before. She parried easily and slashed his arm. Wounds stained his red shirt a darker crimson. Quin dove forward, trying again to disable him by injuring his shoulder. He stepped aside and slammed her in the cheek with the pommel of the sword. She staggered. The pain was a flash of brightness in the dimly lit cave. Her eye seared with agony. Something warm ran down her face. Blood? Tears?

A scream echoed through the cavern. Dalanar staggered

forward, his hands flaming. The two guards who had been strapping down Conthal glowed from within. They writhed in agony and fell to the ground. The air stank of human tallow and burned hair.

A cry of surprise came from further down the passage. Dalanar stumbled around and sent a blast of fire down the tunnel. The sound of the explosion deafened Quin. The side of the cave from floor to ceiling vanished; the rock crashed against the wall across the gorge and blew into the sky.

They paused, stunned for an instant.

Gardanath smashed into her, pinned her sword arm to her chest, and wrapped his own arm around her. He held her gaze, his green eyes staring into hers. Quin reached for her dagger. He closed his eyes, shifted his grip on his sword, and swung down at her back. Quin plunged her blade overhanded into his neck. It punctured an artery and hot blood sprayed them both.

"Stop." Dalanar commanded. He stood a few feet away, next to Eulesis, ready to touch her with radiant hands.

Gardanath managed to pull up on the blow that should have severed Quin's spine. Her ribs cracked and mail rings were buried in the wound that opened up. She cried out in pain.

Dalanar grabbed the staff from Eulesis' unresisting fingers and slammed Gardanath in the skull with the base.

The avatar slid out of Quin's arms and collapsed to the floor. He caught her hand and pulled her down with him.

"Kill Ravendis." He stared up at her and Eulesis, and then he was gone.

Eulesis fell to her knees beside him and wept silently.

CHAPTER FIFTY-ONE

QUIN DROPPED HER SWORD, and it clattered on the stone. Her insides were numb. Emotions deadened. She didn't want to think about how it felt to kill her own guardian. To feel the lifeblood of her beloved mentor spill through her fingers over a handful of worthless gods. To never hear his booming voice again, his teasing at dinner, his commands on the training field. The universe teetered off-balance.

Quin tried not to flex her injured back when she stood. She stumbled to Sarael and untied her bonds. The woman remained asleep. Dalanar worked near Quin, undoing Conthal's elaborate bindings. The Throkari stared around groggily as Dalanar helped him to his feet.

The sound of a patrol of armored Ravendi Elites echoed along the canyon. Quin let out a sigh. Kalin was with them.

"Nice of you to show up." Conthal glowered at the soldiers as he massaged his fingers.

"Where were you?" she asked, touching Kalin with her unbloodied hand.

He smiled briefly down at her before continuing his survey of the room. "'Nath assigned us topside. We didn't know anything was wrong until several hundred barrels of rock exploded up from this ravine...." His gaze fell on Gardanath, and he stopped.

"Kalin, I'm sorry."

He pulled away from her. Quin followed.

"Mother?"

Eulesis rose and wordlessly hugged her son.

"How did this happen?" Kalin noticed Dalanar holding the staff. "Is that *it*? Is that how you killed him, sorcerer?" He pushed his mother aside and stared down at Gardanath's body. Quin's weapons lay in the pooled blood. The woven wrap of the Kestrial blade Dalanar had given her, wicked up the dark liquid. "Quin? What is this?"

The expression of betrayal on his face cut her soul to splinters. "He was going to kill the gods. Sarael. We had to stop him."

"Has Dalanar done something to your mind?"

"Gardanath hated being an avatar. He wanted to die and take the gods with him. Eulesis, tell him!"

"Kalin, she's telling the truth." Eulesis took her son's hand, but he jerked free.

"You traveled with the sorcerer, too. He's corrupted both of you." Kalin drew his sword, face contorted with rage. "Now, Dalanar. It's time."

Dalanar shrugged and placed the staff on a ledge of limestone. "Eulesis, I am truly sorry. I don't know many non-lethal spells."

Eulesis stepped in front of her son. "As highest ranking officer of the Ravendi mercenary corps, I order you to sheath your weapon. If you do not, I will break you down to cadet and you won't even see a captain until you're fifty."

The blond man snarled at Eulesis. Quin wasn't sure he would obey. Finally, he slid the sword back into the sheath with a muttered curse. Quin let out a sob of relief. Kalin glared at Dalanar before turning to kneel beside Gardanath.

Ravendis manifested beside the body. "Who has murdered my avatar?"

The limestone rocks reverberated with her fury, and the ground shuddered beneath them. Her hair blazed with the color of arterial blood, and her armor showed the dents of a hundred killing blows. Her face held a terrible beauty that found mirth in the groans of the battlefield dying and delighted in backroom negotiations where everyone came out worse. Quin couldn't move away.

The Ravendi in the room collapsed with a cacophony of metal armor scraping against stone.

The goddess lifted Gardanath into her arms like a child. "Eulesis, who did this?" There was compulsion in her question.

The woman struggled, but couldn't resist. "Dalanar and Quinthian."

A surge of scarlet light swept over Quin. The spell dragged the air from her lungs and scalded her throat with fire, preventing her from crying out in terror. Dalanar reached for her, and she closed her eyes against the pain that was coming.

Nothing. Only silence punctuated by the occasional creak of metal. Quin drew her next breath and cracked open an eyelid. Everyone in the room looked at her.

Ravendis shrieked in outrage. "Astabar!"

Blue light flashed out of Dalanar's eyes and the god arose within him.

"How do you have two avatars? For what insidious plot or foul trickery did you set them to kill Gardanath?"

Astabar spoke gently, *"This is a terrible loss. I ache with sorrow at your pain. My ignorance of a magical bond between them caused them both to be invested. It was not my intent."* He regarded Gardanath. *"Your avatar had grown tired of his position and sought a way out. Unfortunately, he's never been one to retire peacefully."*

"It was a coincidence that you managed to invest two avatars who happened to both be involved in the murder, and are thus above my wrath and justice? How your heart does weep," she sneered.

"Great Lady," Kalin called to her. "The sorcerer convinced them Gardanath devised a plot to destroy you and the rest of the gods. Astabar is the god of trickery. He could have done so easily."

Ravendis laughed. "Gardanath plotted against me? Impossible! I owned his mind."

The goddess paced over to Kalin and reverently lowered Gardanath's corpse to the ground.

"You may rise, Kalin."

With a clatter of metal, the Ravendi heaved himself to his feet, and shifted the heavy armor into place with a shrug.

"You've grown." Ravendis drew a finger across his breastplate. Kalin watched her warily. She continued her circuit, inspecting him. "You hate the sorcerer, and there's nothing you can do about it, especially now he's an avatar."

He stared at Dalanar with an intensity that frightened Quin.

"Mmm rage, jealousy, revenge. Those are my emotions." Ravendis bit Kalin's earlobe. Blood ran down his neck. He jerked his head back in surprise. She kissed it and licked her lips clean.

Quin stared at them, appalled. The goddess wanted Kalin for her new avatar. Quin looked around desperately. She needed to find a way to stop this. Gardanath and Eulesis would be devastated.

"No, Kalin." Eulesis struggled to push herself off the floor.

"Your father was a good man in peace, but it's been a long time since I've tasted blood. You're not afraid of a fight, are you Kalin?" The goddess' voice was a harsh whisper.

"No, Great Lady."

"Don't make your father's death meaningless. Don't do this," Eulesis said.

"If you were my avatar, you would equal other avatars, even sorcerers. Gardanath didn't use the powers I gave him, but he possessed them. Did you know that, Kalin?"

"No, Great Lady."

"Mmm. And now you do?" Ravendis stopped in front of him, watching with burning eyes, Gardanath's corpse disregarded at her feet.

"Remember how unhappy your father was. Don't become her avatar." Quin stepped toward him, hands imploring.

Kalin turned to her. "I could protect you." He glanced down at her bloodstained fingers, and his face hardened. "Not that you need help. Was this the plan the entire time?"

"I didn't expect any of this! He attacked us at the wine ceremony—"

Ravendis stepped between them. "Enough of your lies, girl. An Avatar of the God of Trickery can't be trusted. Kalin knows this. He's not the fool you believe him to be."

Quin couldn't let Kalin make this mistake. She knew of only one way to stop the investment. Her soul recoiled at the idea, but she backed away until her shoulders brushed against the crumbling limestone of the cavern wall. Dalanar had placed the staff on one of the shelves.

Ravendis examined Kalin. "I want you to be my avatar."

Eulesis yelled at him, "Damn it, boy. No! Trust me, when I warn you. Revenge is not worth the suffering she—"

"Enough, Eulesis."

The Ravendi second's voice was cut off.

Kalin stiffly bent over his mother, and kissed her forehead. He turned to face the goddess. "I will be your avatar."

Quin scanned the wall. No staff. Her gaze flickered across the floor. Nothing. It was gone. A flash of darkness at the cave entrance caught her eye. Conthal withdrew into the gloom, scrambling over the rubble, clutching the staff to his chest.

"No!" Quin started after him, her back protesting at each jarring step. She didn't know what she could do to fight him. Conthal probably knew twelve different ways to kill her before she came close enough for him to use the staff against her. However, staying to witness Kalin become the Ravendi Avatar was the more agonizing option.

THE THROKARI WAS JUST ahead. The staff reflected the light from the stars, and she caught glimpses of its luminous form. Conthal didn't run. Debris from the explosion littered the trail. The uncertain footing made it easier for Quin to keep up, although she wasn't able to gain much ground.

Conthal turned on to the path leading to the bower and the festival. Quin clipped a rock hidden behind a leafy frond, and scraped her ankle. She stumbled, and the soft thud of her knee hitting the earth alerted him. The wound in her back began bleeding with renewed enthusiasm.

"Quinthian? I thought you were preoccupied," he murmured, the sound carrying in the predawn air. "Surely, you didn't come after me alone?"

She remained unmoving. The blood soaked into her shirt and cooled as it dripped down her sides.

"I don't have time for you. You may consider your life as thanks to your mistress for her healing. Don't expect my mercy in the future."

He whispered in a slow sonorous voice—the ancient words of the gods and of the world.

Power rushed up from the earth and swept down the con-

417

nection she shared with the universe, and met in her head. Abomination magic.

Quin fell to the ground in a patch of rotting flowers. She didn't hear Kalin's screams echoing down the ravine.

CHAPTER FIFTY-TWO

::QUIN?:: DALANAR CALLED TO her across their connection.

She opened her eyes and stared up into the trees. Their tips blazed with dawn sunlight. She rolled over and threw up. Damned Throkari sorcerers. Quin lay in a circle of dead vegetation stinking of rot and foulness. Conthal's spell. He killed everything but her. She pushed herself up, trying hard not to jostle her back and crawled away from the decay. The movement unsettled her stomach and she heaved again. The world tilted around her. How long had it been since Conthal escaped?

A footstep sounded nearby. Quin moaned and inched deeper into the underbrush. Mentally and physically, she had never felt more broken and demoralized. She wanted to be left alone to die.

"You're not going to die, Quin," Dalanar's voice soothed.

"Conthal took the staff."

"I'd assumed." He lowered himself down next to her, and carefully pushed the hair out of her face. "I brought water." He uncorked the skin and offered her a drink.

The cool liquid eased her parched throat. When she finished drinking, she lay limply beside him. "What are we going to do about Conthal?"

"I don't know," he admitted. "We'll figure that out later. Let's clear up this mess first. Are you ready to go? You need your back seen to."

"No. I never want to see any of them again."

"Ah." Dalanar hesitantly touched her hair. She didn't push him away, and he stroked it lightly. His fingers were hot.

"I'm sorry, Quin."

"For what?"

"What am I not guilty of?" He laughed cynically. "I thought I was defending my avatar and my religion ... But I acted to further my own goals, as well. You're not even the one I should be confessing to." Dalanar wouldn't meet her eyes. "Nevertheless, I am sorry for how I treated you. You didn't deserve what I put you through."

Quin gazed out at the shadowy ravine.

"Well?" he asked.

"All right."

"Does that mean I'm forgiven?"

Quin stared at him. "I don't know what to feel anymore."

He stiffened. "Of course."

"Thank you for the apology."

A Ravendi runner burst through the foliage and sped toward the encampment. Alarms sounded in the distance, and armored feet pounded down the trail the other way.

Events blurred for Quin after that. Dalanar called to a detachment of guardsworn searching frantically for Sarael. They carried Quin to the Chapterhouse where Jol tended her. He was mercifully silent, but regarded her with pursed lips. Gardanath's blow split her chainmail and drove some of the broken links into her flesh. Her accelerated healing lodged them under her skin and they needed to be cut out.

Except for bruising, most of the damage had already faded.

Jol bound her ribs to make her more comfortable. She doubted she would need it longer than a day.

Sarael and Barrand were brought in, groggy but awake, surrounded by anxious Servants. Once Quin assured herself they were being attended, she slept.

CHAPTER FIFTY-THREE

QUIN SHADED HER EYES from the morning sun as the last cartload of celebrants left the valley. The Ravendi were mounted and ready to follow. Gardanath's red-draped coffin led the procession in a humble farmer's cart.

She walked toward the dais where the remaining avatars huddled.

"Astabari scum." One of the scarlet-clad soldiers spat at Quin's feet.

"Hey now," another barked at the first, "leave 'er be. She's one of us."

Quin kept going. She needed to get used to it. The corps was divided. Those who knew her, or believed Eulesis' side of the story of Gardanath's betrayal, treated her well despite her involvement in his death. The other side, swayed by Kalin, sought ways to harass her. It would only worsen as time went on. Csiz Luan was denied to her now.

Kalin. He stood rigidly beside Sarael and Barrand, unsmiling. He barely acknowledged Eulesis, and ignored Dalanar. Quin's throat ached with unshed tears. No crying when metal is bared, she reminded herself.

"Safe journey, Kalin. You have our deepest sympathies," Sarael said.

Barrand patted him on the shoulder.

When Quin joined them, he at least glanced at her, however indifferently.

"You're taking Rylir with you?" Quin asked Eulesis.

The woman had shaved her hair down to stubble, as was the mourning custom of the Enng. "Sarael healed Rylir's body, but her mind is damaged. When Morgir died, it broke." She eyed her son. "I seem to have a great deal of time on my hands. I can care for the girl." Eulesis lowered her voice. "I'll inform Lyratrum, of course, but you know how the Morgiri are about imperfection. I won't let them treat her as an outcast. Sarael promised to send Servants with expertise in brain injury, and perhaps they can help."

More misery to add to your divine scales, Yhellania. Are we worthy yet? Have we earned some happiness?

Sunlight reflecting off Kalin's armor blinded Quin as he reached the lip of the ravine. Did he look back?

Dalanar nodded to Sarael. "A fascinating experience. I can't say it was anything like I expected."

Sarael smiled sadly.

The sorcerer turned to Quin.

She gripped her sword hilt and straightened. "Are you going to stop persecuting the Yhellani, or will you send your Astabari after us, as well?"

Dalanar opened his mouth to answer when Astabar took over. His presence flowed out from his avatar, but none of the Servants or guardsworn who remained were crushed to the ground around him.

"Well done, Astabar." Quin hadn't known it was possible. Rotting gods.

"*Forcing people to grovel is tedious.*" He grinned. "*The Astabari have no grudge against the Yhellani. Dalanar won't pursue his unfortunate preoccupation. I am hoping someone will wish to mate with him if he behaves. I intend to work on that."*

Perhaps some good had come from the anguish. Dalanar would stop torturing and killing Yhellani. One less sorcerer to worry about; one less monster in Conthal's service. Quin had wanted Dalanar dead, but now he might do something useful. Although, as the Avatar of Thieves, she wasn't sure what.

Astabar scanned the empty meadow and shuttered Chapterhouse. *"This is no place for you, Quin. Join me."*

"No. I'm done."

"Your trick worked. You're no longer my avatar. It is good Ravendis departed. I'm not certain how much protection that half-invested state provides."

"I intend to stay far away from the entire mess. I'd advise you to keep your people away from her, too." If Kalin didn't come to his senses, he'd start another religious war. She doubted either Astabar or Dalanar would take persecution as passively as the Yhellani.

"We'll see. You can always call on me. I'll send Dalanar for you." His eyes twinkled. *"Be at peace, Quin."* Astabar mounted and headed up the trail after the others.

Quin bowed before Sarael and held out the sun pendant of her office. "I'm leaving, Sarael."

"Sarael needs you," Barrand said.

The avatar laid a hand on his arm. "You still seek vengeance against Dalanar?" Sarael asked.

Quin shook her head in confusion. "No. My decision has nothing to do with him."

"Why are you going?" Barrand demanded.

"I'm done with the gods. I want to live a normal life with no magic, no avatars, no pawns."

"What will you do? The Ravendi are closed to you."

"Fighting has lost its appeal. I think I'll take up farming."

Barrand shuddered. "You have less of a temperament for farming than you did for being handmaiden."

Quin snorted a laugh, and sobered. "I'm tired."

"You'll get bored," he said.

"I'll find something."

Barrand tried to smile.

Sarael embraced her. "This is our gift to you for your families' service." She gestured to Jol. He handed Quin several wrapped bundles and a pouch. Judging from the weight, it contained a set of armor to replace what Gardanath destroyed. The pouch held a comfortable amount of gold.

Sarael had already known her decision. The woman's understanding made Quin's heart ache.

"I won't take charity."

"It's your salary as handmaiden."

"Handmaiden is an unpaid position."

"I changed that. Retroactively."

Quin shrugged. She had little money of her own. It would keep her from starving until she found work. She embraced Barrand and Thera, and gave Jol a genuine smile.

He regarded her with distrust.

"You've done a lot to help me over the years. I haven't properly appreciated it." Quin pulled him into a hug. "Thank you."

She grabbed her horse's reins and checked her gear again. She didn't know where she would go. Away from Csiz Luan, past Terrisca. See what Malesini offered. After that? She didn't care. For the first time, Quin experienced the giddiness of the unknown. Nothing held her to a set path. She wasn't beholden to a goddess, an avatar, or revenge. She might be the only one free to live the life Gardanath envisioned for humanity.

She paused. "Sarael, how did my mother die?"

"I don't know, Quin."

Perhaps she didn't need to know. Time to let those things in her past relinquish their control over her in the present. Knowing wouldn't change the fact her mother had died—was dead. It would never bring her back.

Quin needed to start living the life she had. She swung up on her horse and smiled down at the Yhellani. Barrand wiped a hand across his eyes, his face blotchy.

Sarael stepped forward with a frown. "Yhellania has a message for you."

Quin froze.

"You may be through with the gods, but it doesn't mean the gods are through with you."

EPILOGUE

WHAT WAS DALANAR DOING in a shit hole like this? Quin pulled her oilskin closer to keep the icy water from seeping down her collar. The mud from the wagon ruts nearly sucked off her boots as she squelched through the puddles trying to locate the Astabari. She felt his presence, but couldn't find the way to reach him. Quin had circled the block just up from the warehouses and wharves of Cathus three times. She was ready to set fire to the place to drive him out. Probably wouldn't stay lit in the downpour, though.

Rickety stairs led up to apartments on the upper stories, but she had the impression of the sorcerer ... avatar ... below street level. Perhaps she needed to go up, to descend. Did he trust his life to those stairs? Her first step made the entire structure squeal. The second started it shuddering in time with her heartbeat. Quin backed down hastily.

She traveled this far to find some answers and didn't intend to die in a building collapse or give up on locating Dalanar. She touched the stone foundation. He was right there! She found a loose rock and pounded it against the wall. The stonework couldn't be that thick. The construction in this part of town was atrocious. He would hear and come investigate.

"Aye! What are you doing?" A hand fell on her shoulder. Quin elbowed the owner in the side and drew her sword.

"No call for that!" The man stumbled away. "Just asking why you're pounding on my house."

"I need to talk to Dalanar."

"Who?"

"Tall, black hair, blue eyes."

"Sorry, girl. Don't know. Why don't you go back to your inn?"

"He's here." She started pounding with her pommel. The man moved closer and she held him at bay with the tip of her blade.

"Would you stop?" he pleaded.

"Bring him up!"

"I'm here." Fire blazed between Dalanar's fingertips, illuminating the street. He glimpsed her face and the light snuffed out. "Quinthian?"

THE MOST GENEROUS THING Quin could say about the basement was that it was warm and dry. The roughly finished room contained several beds, a cooking area, and a table for dining that doubled as an Evening room. Dalanar's influence was unmistakable. A desk, with precisely arranged books and writing paper, stood in one corner. A neatly folded shirt lay on one of the beds, freshly laundered. Everything was immaculate, even if the furnishings were bare.

Dalanar's face appeared less rigid, and his hair had grown longer. A curl or two now had the audacity to rest against his pale neck. Still too thin.

"I'm surprised you haven't gained three stone." She smirked. "Astabar has you casting so much?"

The sorcerer smiled briefly. "I've been given the opportunity to do some research I've wanted to do for entirely too long. He's indulging me." Dalanar studied her as if trying to memorize her. "You look ... relaxed. Is Sarael in town?"

Quin stiffened.

"I apologize. Poor question."

"I don't serve the Yhellani any longer. I don't serve anyone at the moment, although I just finished up a three-month contract as a caravan guard in Malesini."

"Agreeable?"

"Nothing happened. We played cards, poorly. Tended the animals. And drank ourselves senseless on our nights off."

"You're bored."

"Completely. I may head back after this."

Another slight smile. Dalanar was turning into a regular sunbeam.

"Why are you here?"

"How did my mother die?"

Dalanar's eyes widened and he searched her face. "Do you trust me not to lie?"

"Yes."

"THE SPIES REPORT NARNUS is the source of the threat, Dalanar." Conthal set the pen down. "We're going, but you are to *observe* from a safe distance. I will handle everything."

"How can I protect you? Isn't that my duty as your Seal?"

"I am responsible for my own safety. You are to do what you are told. When you become a full master, we'll speak of it again."

Dalanar grumbled his ascent, but the rebuke rankled. He was no longer a child to be set aside while sorcerers performed real magic. He had always been capable of controlling fire. His ability could be used to protect Conthal. At twenty-five, he was already nearing the completion of his mastery. Wasn't he becoming the terror of the Yhellani? They wet themselves when they heard his name. He would prove himself to Conthal. No one would doubt his loyalty or skill.

Narnus was a mountainside town at the border between Utur and Tyrentanna. Quaint, Dalanar supposed. Cobbled streets ran up the terraced hillsides from the shallow valley and picturesque window boxes frothed with red flowers on every house. The only thing to distinguish it from any of the other mountain towns in the region was that the residents were Yhellani faithful. White-robed Servants walked openly in the streets, and Yhellania's sun and wheat sigil decorated the buildings. It made him seethe.

Conthal set Dalanar to watch at a farmhouse on the edge of town, along the main road. The bodies of the farmers were stacked in the bedroom, drawing the attention of inquisitive flies. The day wore on and nothing happened. Perhaps the spies had been mistaken. Dalanar wasn't even sure what Conthal was attempting to stop. The avatar rarely shared his plans.

Dalanar paced from room to room, and finally settled at the table with a book. He couldn't focus on the words.

A knock sounded on the door. "Hey, farmer?"

Dalanar slid his feet off the table. "Yeah?"

"Can I bother you for a drink of water?"

Dalanar considered. He shouldn't let anyone report about a strange visitor at the farmhouse, and he needed to practice his spells. A perfect opportunity to accomplish two goals at once.

"No bother. Come in."

He started with some of the kinetic formulas Conthal requested he learn. They were fast and quiet. He managed to use several of them on the first Yhellani before the man died. Dalanar wanted to test the geis, a spell he developed himself. A

430

spell useful to the Throkari.

Over the next hours, he geised four travelers. They died, but he managed to keep one alive after three attempts. He refined his technique until he no longer left them mindless. A definite improvement.

Where was Conthal? The sun descended toward the mountains and shadows dominated the valley. How long should Dalanar wait before returning to Utur or trying to find him?

A small, wiry woman in her thirties came to the door. Her smile was genuine and full of happiness to be close to her destination. She possessed the most beautiful eyes he had ever seen. The dark blue-green of glacial ice. "Hello?"

"Uhm," Dalanar said.

"Are you well?" She tilted her head at him. "You look like you're running a fever. I'm a bit of a healer—but aren't we all?" She laughed a gentle, earthy sound.

"I'm fine. You want water?"

She smiled again, but her expression held uncertainty. "Are you new?"

"Yes, new. Water?" He opened the door wider.

"No, but Daniel has some herbs for me. Is he around?"

"In the kitchen."

The woman slipped past him, and Dalanar grabbed her in the geis embrace. She smelled of soap and horses, sunlight and now, burning skin.

He started the spell and memories poured from her. Sarael's smile. The woman's young daughter going away to train with Gardanath. Choosing a mate at the Summer Festival.

"You're the handmaiden! Is Sarael here? Is she in Narnus?"

The woman, Iyana, struggled weakly. "No! Sarael isn't with me. I'm alone. I'm here for herbs."

He saw the truth of it in her mind. Dalanar dropped the

woman to the floor. She tried to crawl away, but he pressed a booted foot down on her ankle. "What's happening today? Are you involved?"

The woman rolled over, supporting herself on her elbows. She winced as blisters popped on her neck. "What are you talking about?"

Dalanar lifted her back into his arms ready to begin the geis again, when a force wave ripped the roof off the farmhouse and shoved him into the wall beside her. The sky above them smoldered a bruised magenta and purple, roiling with clouds of dust and debris. Boulders and carved foundation stones the size of wagons rained down, and the noise thundered on. The sound echoed back and forth between the mountain ranges of Utur and Tyrentanna. Wailing poured down the hillside.

"Great Lord," Dalanar whispered.

The handmaiden gaped at the wreckage. "We must help!"

"I'm not letting you go."

"Then come with me! Help us!" She kicked him hard in the knee and scrambled for the door, which hung twisted off its hinges. She drew up with a gasp. Dalanar stared over her shoulder.

The hillside was devastated. Buildings blown apart, the contents and people scattered in pieces across the landscape. A few figures staggered from the shell of a building. At the center of the valley snaked a massive pillar of fire that drilled into the heavens. Another shockwave pulsed down its length and collided with the town.

Dalanar dragged Iyana back into the doorway as the wave blew a new crater of devastation into Narnus. Blocks of debris slammed against the house and toppled the front wall.

"You're burning me!" She jerked her arm out of his grasp.

"What did the Yhellani do?"

"Us? *We* don't have this kind of power," she said.

The handmaiden dashed up the hill. Dalanar followed, limping on his injured knee.

The next pulse wave sank through the clouds. Iyana pulled him behind a fragment of a wall, two rows of heavy granite blocks stacked against a natural rise in the land. They cowered and covered their ears. Pressure from the wave broke one of Dalanar's eardrums. They screamed, but he couldn't hear anything over the detonation.

"It's getting worse!" she said.

Dalanar grabbed Iyana's sleeve and helped her up. The terrain resembled an old lava field, a wasteland of powdered gray dust overlaying everything flattened outward from the center of the blast. He covered his mouth with his shirt. Nothing burned, but smoky particles made it difficult to see further than the next street. Every step wafted more into the air. The pillar of light touched down ahead.

Dalanar stumbled on a hand. The glassy eyes of the dead watched him. Bodies lay as if strewn by a petulant child. He had never seen so many. Blood mixed with wreckage. Bile churned in his stomach. He had killed. He didn't understand why this wanton death affected him. It did. These people were annihilated without warning. He might have been one of them. Whatever caused this needed to be stopped.

Within the pool of light, not even the grass fluttered around a plinth of creamy stone. A circular cavity pierced the flat top of the column, and the Tree of Knowledge symbol was etched into the base. The power flowed into the hollow. Nothing else moved. Was Conthal dead, or had he managed to escape the devastation?

"What if we cover the hole?" Dalanar asked. He tossed a scrap of wood into the light. It fell inside, and started burning.

He threw a rock. It bounced off the base and out of the circle.

"You have terrible aim." Iyana hefted a brick. Her throw was good, and it landed on the plinth, nearly covering the depression. The column of light flickered and surged, blowing them backward.

"Someone has to hold it on," Iyana said.

"Just leave it."

"The effect is spreading. Do you know where it will end ... *if* it will end?"

"What are you saying?"

"We don't have much time. The next wave will catch us without protection. It's getting stronger, we'd need to be further away."

"You can't know that. Let's go," Dalanar grabbed her arm. She had obviously been struck witless by the geis.

"I can't risk it."

"I won't die for this!" he protested.

"Promise me you'll figure out what did this and stop it from happening again. You have that ability. I don't. Go!"

"Do you even know who I am?"

She looked up at the sky and back at him. Another wave spun down. "Run, Dalanar." Iyana stepped into the circle of light and slammed a rock down across the mark.

QUIN LISTENED TO THE rain pour outside, her tea forgotten in one hand. "It was Conthal summoning Astabar?"

"Yes. I understand now that the surges would have stopped ... eventually. A god's power isn't limitless. She didn't need to die."

"I'm not sure she would have wanted to live as your prisoner, either. You were appalling."

Dalanar inclined his head in agreement.

They sat silently for a moment longer before Quin rose and wrapped her oilskin around her shoulders. "Thank you. I needed to know."

"Back to Malesini?"

Quin laughed. "I'm already tired of the rain."

She gazed up into his face. Iyana died so he could live, perhaps it was fitting he should have her eyes as a memorial. As a reminder. "Do you intend to keep that promise?"

"Yes."

Quin nodded, and with a last look into his eyes, turned and disappeared into the misty darkness.

Quin and Dalanar's story continues in *Astabar's Rogue*, Book Two of the Sundered Tree Trilogy.

Sign up for email announcements of new releases, find links to other works, and read bonus chapters at the author's website www.marniyjones.com

If you enjoyed this book and want to help other readers discover it, reviews are helpful and always appreciated!

ENCYCLOPEDIA

PEOPLE:

Aadavel   Merchant, Csiz Luan. Throkari zealot

Aerelan   Yhellani Servant, Csiz Luan

Actas   Major in the Ravendi elite guard

Alamandir   Professor of Alchemy, University of Dacten

Arnard   Morgiri Gallery Master, Sculptor

Barrand   Captain of the Yhellani Guardsworn

Cleary   Morgiri Gallery apprentice, Painter

Conthal   Avatar of Throkar. Founder of the University of Dacten, and the school of sorcery at the Golden Darkness

Dalanar   Conthal's Seal. Throkari priest. Sorcerer

Eccuro   Throkari Preceptor, Lyratrum

Ethalion   Ravendi mercenary corps engineer

Eulesis   Second-in-command of the Ravendi mercenary corps. Mother of Kalin by Gardanath

Gardanath   Avatar of Ravendis. Founder of Csiz Luan.
('Nath)   Head of the Ravendi mercenary corps. Father of Kalin by Eulesis. Former guardian to Quin

Gridarl	Head of the Department of Magical Studies, University of Dacten
Jairit	Yhellani Servant, Csiz Luan
Jol	Administrator to Sarael. Yhellani Servant
Josa	Ravendi Judge, Lyratrum
Kalin	Ravendi Elite guard. Quin's consort. Son of Gardanath and Eulesis
Laniof	Murdered Morgiri Avatar
Magda	Bandit, Dacten
Maloud	Yhellani Judge, Lyratrum
Markus	Yhellani guardsworn
Mert	Yhellani Servant
Mirindra	Sorceress, University of Dacten
Noria	Yhellani Servant
Onia	Throkari Teacher, Csiz Luan
Ordanna	Sorceress, University of Dacten
Quinthian (Quin)	Sarael's Handmaiden. Guardsworn to the Yhellani Avatar
Rylir	Morgiri Gallery apprentice, Sculptor
Sarael	Avatar of Yhellania
Telen	Orphanage administrator. Retired Ravendi
Thera	Lieutenant to Barrand. Guardsworn to the Yhellani Avatar
Torval	Deceased farmer, Fairwald
Varen	Throkari Priest, Csiz Luan
Welliver	Merchant, Csiz Luan

GODS

Yhellania	Goddess of Fertility and Healing
Throkar	God of Knowledge and Death
Ravendis	Goddess of War and Diplomacy
Morgir	God of Art and Color
Astabar	God of Trickery and Illusion

Glossary of Terms

Avatar
The human vessel of a god. Acts as a representative of the religion in the world. Shares their mind and powers with the god.

Adherent
Someone who has dedicated themselves to one god, to the exclusion of the others.

Chapterhouse
The mysterious valley in central Tyrentanna where the Yhellani gather to celebrate the seasonal festivals.

Csiz Luan
The fortress-city of Luan. Gardanath's base for the Ravendi mercenary corps and center of trade.

Faithful
Someone who has a cultural or personal bias toward one of the gods, although they may still worship the other gods at different times.

Fever
The rise in body temperature that afflicts sorcerers when they perform magic.

Geis
A spell that allows the caster to read the mind of the victim.

Golden Darkness
Conthal's fortress in Utur. Houses the school of sorcery.

Guardsworn

A solider who is a sworn adherent of a religion.

Investment

The process by which a god takes a new human Avatar.

Morgiri

The people devoted to the god Morgir.

Ravendi

The people devoted to the god Ravendis. Generally synonymous with the Mercenary corps.

Servant

A priest-healer of Yhellania.

Summer Festival

A Yhellani fertility festival to ensure a fruitful harvest.

Throkari

The people devoted to the god Throkar.

Tree Cultist

Member of The Tree of Knowledge Fellowship. Apocalyptic cult devoted to the regrowth of the Tree of Knowledge that Yhellania destroyed. Actively persecutes Yhellani.

Tree of Knowledge

The tree Throkar created that was to hold the world and provide knowledge to the newly created human race.

Yhellani

The people devoted to the goddess Yhellania.

I hope you enjoy this excerpt from the next book in
The Sundered Tree trilogy, due out Fall 2017.

ASTABAR'S ROGUE

THE SUNDERED TREE: BOOK TWO

CHAPTER ONE

TREE OF KNOWLEDGE CULTISTS surrounded three
bound and battered Servants in the glade. The
Yhellani priests knelt in the blood of their Ravendi
protectors, slain beside them. Their eyes shown with terrified
resignation as they watched the zealots wind ropes over the
lowest branches of a huge oak. If they were lucky, their lives
would end quickly with the snap of one of those lines.

Barrand crouched low in the thicket, his knees popping
under the strain from the weight of his chain mail. It was surprising the Throkari cultists in the clearing didn't hear his
joints protest. Barrand should turn the running of the
guardsworn over to his lieutenant. Retire to a life of caring for
his children, and keeping Sarael radiantly pregnant. He seemed
to have a knack for that. Not yet, though.

Barrand wasn't going to let these Servants die. The goddess herself interceded on their behalf, sending him here.
Eight guardsworn were more than a match for the zealots. He
turned to his companions, about to signal the charge, when a
man stepped into view.

The newcomer wore the severe black of a Throkari priest,

but wasn't like any priest Barrand had ever seen. A raw silk sash of deep purple circled his waist over dark brigandine, and a sword belt hung low on his hips. Even at a distance, the man's eyes were so pale as to be white. Skin nearly as colorless. A Rynd. The charcoal drawing of a tree marked his forehead like the others. His swagger, and the deference of the cultists, placed him in a position of authority.

"That one is mine," Barrand muttered. There was something sneering and superior about the man's demeanor that irritated him.

The priest regarded the prisoners, stopping in front of each of them with pursed lips and flared nostrils. "Kill them." He looked to be in his thirties, but he possessed the rough voice of a much older man.

Barrand growled.

The priest's order brought grins around the circle of cultists. They grabbed the youngest Servant, a Journiere by the look of him, and dragged him through the dirt toward the tree.

Barrand gave the signal. The guardsworn charged.

Sometimes, there's poetry to the flow of combat. Barrand found the surges and withdrawals, the pivots and lunges, to be a living meditation on the setbacks and triumphs of life. Not that he would ever tell anyone he saw it that way. Admitting that kind of thing got you retired, whether you were ready for it or not. This battle was no different. Life was always better lived when you had a goal. His goal was the man in the purple sash.

Barrand cut down the first zealot without pause. The guardsworns' lunge from the underbrush caught them off-guard. The cultists scrambled for weapons and order while Barrand and his soldiers took out three of them. They recovered and mounted a sketchy defense. The priest drew his sword and started towards the fight.

Barrand dodged a strike, and slammed his pommel down on his opponent's wrist. She slashed at him again, her face distorted with rage. He kicked her in the knee. The cultist screamed in pain and hunched over. Barrand cut her throat.

The scream caught the attention of the priest, and their eyes locked. Dark eyebrows drew down as the man changed course to intersect with him.

The fighting surged past the huddled figures of the Servants. Barrand whistled for his corporal. The boy knew his job. Disengage, cut free the prisoners, and get them away. Two cultists had him trapped.

Barrand stabbed one in the kidney with a dagger, sending the man howling to the ground. The other rushed him, but fumbled her great sword. The woman had the height for it, yet no skill or obvious training. Barrand swung his blade in a powerful arc that severed her weapon hand. He reversed his grip and plunged the sword into her chest before she had a chance to scream.

Who were these people? They were terrible fighters. How had they managed to overcome the Ravendi mercenaries to threaten the Servants at all? Nothing here made sense.

A flash of purple at the corner of his eye was the only warning Barrand got before the priest attacked. Barrand dropped and rolled heavily to one side, and regained his feet. He brought his sword up to block a tremendous blow that left wrist and arm numb. He shifted back, settling into his fighting crouch. *This* was a contest. Barrand smiled.

The Throkari's expression didn't change, but he lunged forward like a javelin. A perfect line of metal and man thrusting at full power, and recoiling when Barrand dodged away. Fabric tore where the blade hooked his shirt.

Barrand countered with a feint left, to test his opponent's

reaction. The priest's stillness was disconcerting. His frosted blue eyes narrowed in contempt. Barrand grinned. Humorless people were always annoyed by any hint of amusement in others.

Barrand sprang forward with a complex series of strikes most found impossible block. The priest met every blow with the perfect defense, as if they practiced for years. The man was skilled; Barrand could admit that.

Around them, the guardsworn fought the cultists. Either the ones Barrand killed had been the worst of the lot, or he needed to implement a more rigorous training program. The zealots were falling too slowly for Barrand's taste. The Servants were gone. Severed bindings from around their wrists littered the ground. Time to finish with the Throkari freak and get back to Sarael.

Barrand broke off his pattern of blows, and barreled into his opponent. The man hissed in surprise, and stumbled, trying to keep his feet. Barrand kicked his ankle out from under him, not allowing him to recover. The priest slashed up with his blade, and a gash opened in Barrand's forearm. Blood ran over his skin in a hot stream. His opponent scrambled away, moving out of the range of Barrand's sword, and finding his balance.

Behind them, another cultist fell with a scream. The guardsworn now outnumbered the Throkari. Barrand winked at the priest and flicked blood off his arm, spattering the man's pale face. The Rynd clenched his jaw, and made a fist with his free hand. Barrand snorted. Was the man threatening them?

The priest punched the air in front of him, and Barrand flew across the clearing as if an anvil slammed into his chest. Ribs cracked, and he gagged at the exploding pain. Tree trunks stopped his flight, knocking the wind out of him with a grunt. Barrand couldn't convince his lungs to draw breath through the agony. He fell to one side, holding his stomach. Spots dotted his vision. The others weren't doing much better.

Cultists and guardsworn were tumbled together in a pile of limbs and weapons. Swept aside like pawns from a chessboard. A few people staggered to their feet clutching injuries, willing to continue.

The priest began executing the guardsworn.

Barrand sucked in a breath, and the pounding in his head eased a little. "Fight *me*, you coward!" He groped around for his sword, only reaching it by crawling closer to the chaos and screams of the dying. Bone grated against bone in his sides. He hauled himself to one knee. It popped and protested. A last reminder of the old age Barrand would never see.

The remaining cultists, though injured, came to the realization that they won. They straightened, panted, and surveyed the human wreckage. The priest wrenched his weapon from the last guardsworn corpse, and turned to face Barrand with a thin smile.

One of the zealots stomped forward with ax raised. "Kill him!"

"No," the priest said. His sword shot out, and blocked the ax-wielder from moving closer to Barrand. The cultist stopped and bowed his head. The priest wiped his blade against the man's tunic in long, deliberate strokes then sheathed it. "If I am not mistaken, this is Sarael's dog. The father of her puppies. Barrag ... Barral ... Barrand? Conthal provided me with your description. Red hair, broken nose, loutish expression."

Barrand grunted and gripped his pommel tighter. His breath was returning. "You're the new Seal."

The man smirked. "And Conthal doubts your intelligence. He had several pointed things to say about you. Not many have made such a lasting impression on our deathless leader."

"He hates everyone." Barrand still couldn't move, but the pain ebbed to merely a sickening throb. If they wanted his sword, they'd have to kill him. He would not surrender.

"True, but he doesn't issue orders for their capture. You and Sarael share that honor."

Barrand's insides turned to water. Conthal wanted him ... *specifically*? Sweat broke out on his forehead. He could not be taken to the Avatar. They *must* be forced to kill him.

"Barrand." The man's voice sounded casual. "It's my reputation if you die. Don't fool yourself into believing I will allow any foolish heroics or noble sacrifices. If you give your word, you may save yourself *some* pain and indignity. No doubt, you will enjoy a great deal of each later."

"Fight me without your damned magic tricks. I'll cut you down like a filthy, pox-ridden sewer rat." Barrand tried again to stand, but his leg gave way.

The priest sighed. "This is tiresome. Drop the sword, and let my people bind you."

Barrand couldn't think of anything clever to say. He smiled, and spat at the man's feet.

The man frowned and gestured at him. Crushing force slammed Barrand into the hard-packed dirt. If ribs hadn't been broken before, they were now. He couldn't move his arms to raise the sword as the priest came to stand in front of him.

The Throkari leisurely ground his heel into Barrand's hand until he released his hold on the weapon. The man kicked it into the trees. Despair swelled inside Barrand. The pain was too great. He was too weak. He prayed that internal injuries killed him before they reached Utur.

Someone grabbed his arms and jerked them up behind his back, nearly dislocating his shoulders. The world spun away into darkness. *Sarael forgive me.*

ABOUT THE AUTHOR

Born to Hippie parents in San Francisco, Marniy turned out remarkably normal. Her mother attributes this to the reverse psychology experiments performed on her as a child.

Marniy turned away from a career in Archaeology when she suffered heat stroke doing field work. Although she completed the degree, and still feels stirrings of pride when watching Indiana Jones, she went on to study programming, illustration, and computer forensics.

Favorite authors and greatest influences include David Eddings, Sheri S. Tepper, Melissa Scott, and Joe Abercrombie.

Marniy lives in Portland, Oregon with a husband, and two dogs. She is currently working on the second book of the Sundered Tree trilogy and researching for a new fantasy series set in Cairo during the Ottoman Empire.

39299698R00280

Made in the USA
San Bernardino, CA
22 September 2016